"BENTLEY LITTLE KEEPS THE HIGH-TENSION JOLTS COMING."
—Stephen King

Praise for the Novels of Bentley Little

The Academy

"A tightly allegorical piece of horror."

—*Publishers Weekly*

The Vanishing

"A plethora of gore and perversion."

—*Publishers Weekly*

The Burning

"Stephen King–size epic horror." —*Publishers Weekly*

Dispatch

"Little has the unparalleled ability to evoke surreal, satiric terror . . . should not be missed."—Horror Reader

The Resort

"An explicitly repulsive yet surrealistically sad tale of everyday horror." —*Publishers Weekly*

The Policy

"A chilling tale." —*Publishers Weekly*

The Return

"A master of horror on par with Koontz and King . . . so powerful that readers will keep the lights on day and night." —*Midwest Book Review*

The Collection

"Snippets of everyday life given a creepy twist."

—*Booklist*

continued . . .

Also by Bentley Little

HIS FATHER'S SON

Bentley Little

A SIGNET BOOK

SIGNET
Published by New American Library, a division of
Penguin Group (USA) Inc., 375 Hudson Street,
New York, New York 10014, USA
Penguin Group (Canada), 90 Eglinton Avenue East, Suite 700, Toronto,
Ontario M4P 2Y3, Canada (a division of Pearson Penguin Canada Inc.)
Penguin Books Ltd., 80 Strand, London WC2R 0RL, England
Penguin Ireland, 25 St. Stephen's Green, Dublin 2,
Ireland (a division of Penguin Books Ltd.)
Penguin Group (Australia), 250 Camberwell Road, Camberwell, Victoria 3124,
Australia (a division of Pearson Australia Group Pty. Ltd.)
Penguin Books India Pvt. Ltd., 11 Community Centre, Panchsheel Park,
New Delhi - 110 017, India
Penguin Group (NZ), 67 Apollo Drive, Rosedale, North Shore 0632,
New Zealand (a division of Pearson New Zealand Ltd.)
Penguin Books (South Africa) (Pty.) Ltd., 24 Sturdee Avenue,
Rosebank, Johannesburg 2196, South Africa

Penguin Books Ltd., Registered Offices:
80 Strand, London WC2R 0RL, England

First published by Signet, an imprint of New American Library,
a division of Penguin Group (USA) Inc.

First Printing, September 2009
10 9 8 7 6 5 4 3 2 1

HIS
FATHER'S
SON

One

Steve Nye knew something was wrong when his mother called him at work.

His mother *never* called him at work. She seldom called him period, and the truth was he couldn't remember the last time they had spoken. Easter? Mother's Day? They didn't exactly have the world's closest family, and aside from birthdays and major holidays, he hardly ever saw his parents. So when Gina, the department secretary, told him that his mother was on line one, Steve braced himself, taking a long sip of coffee from the Starbucks cup next to his computer before pressing the lighted red button on his phone console. He took a deep breath, closed his eyes. "Hello? Mom?"

"There's something the matter with your father."

As usual, there was no greeting, no small talk, no introductory conversation, just the reason for her call, stated flatly, unadorned. He waited for more, not yet sure what to say.

"He tried to kill me."

That got his attention. Steve opened his eyes, sat up straighter in his chair. "What happened?" he asked. "Are you all right?"

His mother sighed. "Well, I have a broken wrist—"

"Jesus!"

A pause. "I think you should come over."

"Where are you? The hospital?"

"No. I'm home."

"Home? When did this happen?"

"Yesterday."

"Yesterday! Jesus, Mom, why didn't you call me?"

"There is no need for that type of language, Steven." Her voice was stern, hard, and his muscles tensed involuntarily at the familiar tone. "That is twice now that you have taken the Lord's name in vain."

He stood up to her. "I have a right to be upset, Mom. You should've called me when it happened." The next question seemed almost impossible for him to ask, but he asked it anyway. "Where's Dad? In jail?" His father was the most straight-and-narrow man he'd ever met, and just the thought of him sitting in a jail cell seemed not only incongruous but ridiculous. Steve tried to imagine the sight and couldn't.

"No. He's in the hospital. Under observation."

"He really tried to kill you?"

"Yes."

"*Kill* you," Steve repeated. He still couldn't believe it.

"Yes."

"What happened?"

"I'd rather not say over the phone. I think it would be better if you came over."

"Mom—"

"I don't want to talk about it over the phone."

"Okay, all right. I'll be there as soon as I can."

As always, they both hung up without saying goodbye, and Steve switched off his computer, trying to ignore a welling feeling of panic. He could not seem to wrap his mind around what his mother had told him. His father had attacked her—tried to *kill* her—and had broken her wrist, sending her to the hospital? It was inconceivable. His parents might not be the most loving couple he had ever met, but they were definitely the politest, and while he had never seen them kiss, hold hands or show any physical affection, he could not recall the two of them ever arguing or disagreeing. About anything. As far as he knew, they had always been completely in sync, especially in their constant criticism of him, and whenever they spoke to each other, their even-toned conversations were full of "pleases," "thank-yous" and other mannerly considerations. The idea that his father had attacked and injured his mother seemed utterly crazy, and Steve had no idea how on earth such a thing could have possibly occurred. That was what frightened him, the incomprehensibility of it all, and his hand was shaking as he picked up the notes on his desk, put them in his bottom file drawer and locked them in.

He told Gina he'd be gone for the rest of the day, asked her to transfer all incoming calls to his voice mail, then hurried past her desk and down the hall to Mark McColl's office. As usual, the department head was leaning back in the chair behind his oversize desk, reading the *Wall Street Journal*. Steve knocked on the doorjamb, and McColl looked up, an expression of mild annoyance registering on his face. "Yes?"

"I'm going to be out the rest of the day," Steve said. "Family emergency."

McColl looked not only unconcerned but uninterested. "Let Gina know," he said, returning to his paper.

Steve nodded and headed back down the hall, waving to Gina as he strode quickly out to the lobby and through the front door of the building. He was in Irvine and his parents lived in Anaheim, which meant that even if there was no traffic on the freeway—a highly unlikely scenario—it would be a half hour to forty-five minutes before he could reach their house. Why hadn't his mother called him yesterday, from the hospital, when it had happened? Why had she waited so long? There were a lot of possible reasons, not the least of which was the fact that they were not a close family, but what stuck in his mind was what his mother had said when he'd tried to ask for specifics: *I don't want to talk about it over the phone.* It made him think that there was something else involved here, and he sprinted through the parking lot to his car.

His GPS system was on, and his radio was tuned to a local news station that offered traffic updates every twelve minutes, but neither mentioned the slowdown that occurred between the San Diego and Santa Ana freeways, and it was close to an hour later that he passed Disneyland and pulled off the Euclid exit in Anaheim. He turned right at the old Taco Bell building, which had recently been converted into something called Moon's Teriyaki Burger, and drove past the series of auto repair shops and storage units that acted as a buffer zone for the residential area beyond. A streetlight, a stop sign, a left turn, a right turn and he was there.

His parents' house looked the same as it had when he'd lived in it, though the surrounding neighborhood had deteriorated badly. Next door, at what had once been the Swansons' place, a fierce-looking teenage girl with too many tattoos and front teeth that should have been fixed long ago stood defiantly in the middle of a dead lawn, arms folded, staring at him. The house on the other side of his parents' was empty, the yard overgrown with weeds, a red-lettered addendum to the freestanding For Sale sign reading, FORECLOSURE. Across the street, four young Latino men with shaved heads and identical white T-shirts were huddled together in front of a shocking pink house with a piece of plywood placed over its front window.

His parents' home, by contrast, was well maintained,

like something beamed down from the planet Brady: windows washed, house nicely painted, grass neatly trimmed, flower box full of blooming geraniums. He found himself wondering who mowed his parents' lawn, and realized that not only didn't he know, but he had never cared enough to ask. His father was obviously too old to do the work himself, but whether they hired a gardener or paid some neighborhood kid to do it, he had no idea. Although the lawn had been Steve's responsibility from the time they'd moved into the house when he was thirteen until he'd finally moved out after college, he had never been paid an allowance, not even as a teenager. His father had claimed that working around the house was part of his duty as a member of the family, an obligation that deserved no monetary reward, so he had had to find other work—including mowing *neighbors'* lawns—in order to earn spending money.

Not that he'd complained. At that age, he was grateful for anything that got him out of the house and away from his old man.

Steve tried the front door before ringing the bell, and the knob turned easily in his hand. He'd told his parents a thousand times that they needed to lock their doors even in the daytime, that times had changed, but the two of them were still stuck in some Ward Cleaver world that had never really existed, and refused to take even simple precautions to protect themselves. It was a wonder they hadn't been robbed blind—or murdered.

He walked into the living room. "Mom?" he called out. "Mom?"

"I'm in here!"

Steve went into the converted den his parents called the television room. His mother was watching *Oprah*. She looked small sitting in the oversize recliner. Small and old. Part of it, he supposed, was because that was usually his father's chair and he was used to seeing his dad in it, but part of it was the fact that she *was* old. In his mind, she remained perpetually in her mid-forties, and whenever he thought of her, she looked the way she had when he was in high school. Each time he saw her in person, though, he realized that those days were long gone, and looking at her right now, with her arm in a sling and the stress of everything that had occurred weighing on her face, he thought she seemed particularly frail and aged.

Steve sat down hard on the love seat next to her. "Are you okay?"

"Yes." She nodded.

It seemed strange to be talking to his mother alone. He could not remember the last time he had seen her without his father being present. "What happened exactly?"

"He attacked me."

"How? Where?"

"Out there. On the lawn. I'd just come home from Target and gotten out of the car, and he jumped me. Just ran off the porch and threw me on the grass."

"Jesus!"

She fixed him with a disapproving look.

"Sorry," he apologized. "But I just can't believe Dad could do something like that."

"A boy from across the street pulled him off me. If he hadn't, I probably wouldn't be here now. I was down on the lawn, and he was *hitting* me. There was a look in his eyes. . . ." She shook her head, remembering. "He wanted to kill me. I could tell he did. I *knew* he did. Then that teenager pulled him off me, and someone else called the police. By the time they got there, four young men were holding him down, and he was screaming for all he was worth. I'd fallen on my wrist when he knocked me to the ground, and I could tell that it was broken, but I'd gotten my breath back, and even though it hurt where he'd hit me, I didn't think there was any major damage."

"And you didn't think to call me? You waited a whole day?"

"Are you going to keep interrupting me or are you going to let me explain?"

He looked away from his mother, saying nothing. White motes of dust floated in and out of the shafts of sunlight slanting through the window, becoming visible then invisible then visible then invisible. He remembered seeing dust like that in his grandparents' house as a child, and he wondered when this had become an old person's home.

"They took me to emergency—Anaheim Memorial— and by the time they got my wrist all wrapped up, they already had your father in the psychiatric ward. I thought they might take him to jail, but I guess the police could tell that something was wrong with him— they probably deal with situations like this all the time—and they brought him to the hospital instead. I saw him for a few minutes and tried to talk to him, but he yelled at me. They asked if I wanted to stay with him, but I didn't, so they found someone to drive me home."

Again, he wondered why she hadn't called, why she'd gotten a pickup ride with some stranger rather than phone her son for help, but he knew she'd get mad at him if he dared ask. Besides, he wasn't sure he wanted to know the answer.

"They transferred him to the VA hospital last night sometime," she continued. "A doctor called to tell me. Your father's there right now, under observation."

"Do they know what happened? Why he did that? Did he have, like, a stroke or something? Some kind of . . . attack?" Steve had no idea what he was talking about and was struggling to find a reason for his father's behavior, something that could be labeled, quantified and eventually fixed.

His mother was nodding. "The doctors do think he suffered a stroke, and I'd better warn you right now: He doesn't make much sense when he talks. Something in his brain seems to have short-circuited. *He* thinks he's talking normally, but he's just saying nonsense." A pained expression passed over her face. "It's hard to listen to that. It's . . . it's hard."

"But that doesn't explain why he attacked you."

"No. The violence . . . that's something different. That's why he's under observation."

"And he's at the VA hospital?"

"Yes. In Long Beach. He's been there before—you remember, for his heart attack—but I'm not sure how good the care is there. I don't like that place. And after all of those VA scandals . . ."

"Have you heard from them today?" Steve asked. "Is there any news?"

She shook her head.

"Do you want me to call and find out his status?"

"I'm the one with the broken wrist. *He* attacked *me*. Called me . . . called me . . . things I can't even say." Her mouth was set in a straight line, what he thought of as her prude line, and he tried to imagine what sort of obscenities his father might have used on her. He was not sure he had ever heard his father swear.

"Sorry," Steve said. He should have known that he wasn't paying his mother's problems the proper attention. Of course, she'd already told him she was fine, and she was safely back at home with a bandage on her wrist while his father had been involuntarily committed to a psych ward, but his mother had always been a self-centered woman, and there was no way to convince her that in the long run a broken bone was probably not as important as a stroke.

They spent the next several minutes discussing her situation, although the conversation was weird and awkward because the two of them were not used to being alone together. Despite her plea for attention, she also kept insisting that she was all right, that he did not need to worry about her, so there really wasn't anyplace for the discussion to go. He ended up asking her lamely if she needed any prescriptions picked up, or groceries, or help with the laundry or her carpets vacuumed.

"I'm fine," she assured him.

Steve looked at his watch. It was two o'clock already. Getting late. He stood. "I should probably go see Dad. Do you want to come with me?"

His mother shook her head. "I can't right now." She looked scared, angry and embarrassed all at the same time.

Steve nodded. His father had tried to kill her; it was understandable that her emotions would be conflicted.

She didn't have the phone number of the hospital, so he called Information, got it and dialed. He asked the operator to connect him to his father's room, and the charge nurse, a man, answered and told him that his father was sleeping and still under observation. There were no new developments to report, but a doctor would be in later and Steve was welcome to come visit.

He hung up the phone, looked again at his watch. He and Sherry had plans to go out tonight, and he wondered whether he could make it all the way to Long Beach and back before he was supposed to pick her up at six. Probably not, since he'd be traveling the freeways at rush hour, and he tried to decide whether it would be better to cancel their plans for this evening while he went out to visit his dad, or whether it would be more convenient for him to see Sherry tonight and go to the hospital in the morning.

The mere fact that he had to think about it spoke volumes, and, shamed, he chose duty over pleasure, calling Sherry and telling her that he couldn't make it because his father was in the hospital. She was more than understanding, even offering to come with him, but he lied, said he was already on the way there, told her he'd call her later and hung up. The last thing he wanted on this trip was company. He said good-bye to his mother, promised to call to see how she was doing once he got back home, and took off.

The VA hospital in Long Beach was a multistoried rectangular building situated in the center of an enormous parking lot. It looked like one of those bureaucratic Soviet structures, all function, no form, and its drab coloration and dirty windows did not inspire confidence. Steve drove around the lot a few times before finding a place to park after a red Jeep unexpectedly backed out in front of him, providing an empty space. It was a long walk to the building, and he was almost run over by an asshole in a Hummer who sped through a narrow parking lot row at what had to be over fifty miles an hour, but he finally reached the entrance, and he stopped by the front desk to ask how to get to room 242, his father's room. The unsmiling man behind the counter directed him to the second floor, pointing out the elevator at the far end of the nearly bare lobby. Steve rode up alone, and after a suspiciously creaky ride the scuffed paneled doors parted slowly, opening onto a wide corridor that seemed to travel the entire width of the building and ended far away in what appeared to be a jumble of patients and hospital staff.

The air stank of vomit and medicine, cleaning fluids and feces. Steve gagged as he made his way down the corridor, but the nurses and orderlies he passed must have become immune to the stench, because they didn't seem to notice it. Cupping a hand over his nose, he tried to breathe only through his mouth. To his sides were darkened rooms filled with multiple beds that looked the way he imagined prison infirmaries did. A patient rolled toward him in a wheelchair, a man with no legs and a bandage over one eye. Steve looked straight ahead, not wanting to stare, then thought that the man might be offended because he was so obviously avoiding eye contact. He glanced down, ready to smile, but the man glared at him and sped by.

"*I need my meds!*" someone screamed from a room to the left. The terrible cry was filled with more pain than Steve could imagine, but none of the hospital workers made any attempt to address the man's needs or even placate him. "*I need my meds!*" he screamed again.

This was where they'd transferred his father?

Steve was not happy about that. He also felt a little bit nervous about seeing his dad. His father had had a stroke, and his mother had made it clear that the old man was not speaking coherently, but that was not the scenario he pictured in his mind. All Steve could think of was that *he* was going to get blamed for this situation, that by the time he arrived, his father would have snapped back to normal and would loudly berate him for allowing the transfer from Anaheim Memorial. In fact, Steve was already mentally composing a response to such criticism when he reached room 242.

He'd seen no sign indicating that he had entered the psych ward, and at first he thought there'd been a mistake, that his father had been placed in the wrong department. The men he'd seen here were all *physically* injured, and his dad was supposed to be under *psychiatric* observation. Then he realized that in a VA hospital, most of the patients with mental problems probably had physical injuries as well. This whole floor was probably the psych ward.

He stood for a moment outside the room, gathering his courage, then peeked inside. The room was semi-private, which meant that while there were two beds in there besides his father's, it was not one of those barracks-style spaces he'd passed on the way. His father's area was closest to the door, and though the lights within were so dim that they were nearly non-existent, enough illumination bled in from the corridor to show him that his dad was not just *in* a hospital bed but strapped to it. The old man's eyes were closed, he was breathing deeply, and the fact that he was asleep gave Steve the courage to go into the room. Walking to the opposite side of the bed, he drew the privacy curtain that separated his father's section from those of the other two patients.

The smell in here was even worse than in the corridor, so overpowering that Steve was forced to pinch his nostrils shut. One of the other two patients had to have some serious bowel problems.

"*I need my meds!*" the man down the hall continued to yell. Another patient, farther away, howled like a wolf.

His father's room was silent save for the bubbling of a machine on the other side of the pulled curtain. In repose, Steve noted objectively, his dad seemed so thin, drawn and impossibly pale that he appeared to be dead. He'd been strapped down, no doubt, to keep him from hurting or attacking someone else, but the presence of the straps only added to the impression that his prone, sheeted body was that of a corpse.

This is what he'll look like after he dies, Steve thought.

He knew he should feel sad or upset or . . . something. But he didn't. He didn't feel anything. He *wanted* to, but he didn't. He felt guilty about that. He tried to rationalize it, telling himself it was a case of reaping what you sowed, because even on his best days, his father had been a hard and unforgiving man, and it had always been obvious that he felt his only son had turned out to be a major disappointment. But that excuse didn't fly. Steve was an adult, not a child, and it was up to him to take responsibility for his feelings, his behavior and his actions.

Actually, he did feel something when he looked down at his dad. Relief. Relief that his father was not awake or coherent enough to lecture and harangue him.

He felt guilty for that, too.

Steve stared at the figure on the bed. His father had always been immaculately groomed, but now his thin hair was wild and uncombed and there was white stubble on his cheeks and chin. He looked like a derelict, and Steve found the sight disturbing. He didn't want his dad to look this way.

There was a chair against the wall next to the door, but he didn't feel like sitting down, so he stood there awkwardly, unsure of what to do. Was his father sedated? Was he going to remain asleep? If he did wake up, what would Steve say to him? What he really wanted was to talk to a person in charge and find out how his father was doing, but he could not find even a nurse, let alone a doctor, and he had to walk halfway down the hall to locate a distracted-looking man in scrubs who promised to send someone back to speak with him.

Steve returned to the room, holding his nose against the stench. It wasn't just the I-need-my-meds guy who was screaming, he noticed. There was a whole host of voices wailing and crying out, and he wasn't sure whether they had just started up or he hadn't noticed them before because he'd been too distracted. He heard them now, though, and thought that even if a patient wasn't crazy when he came in here, he soon would be after listening to *that* day after day.

He sat down in the chair, waiting. The physical appearance of the hospital had not given him confidence, and Steve expected to meet with a harried, overworked, elderly man long past the point of caring, but the white-coated doctor who introduced himself with a firm handshake and a smile seemed not only competent but kind.

"I'm glad you could come," Dr. Curtis said after the introductions had been made. "I understand that your mother does not wish to become involved at this time, but it's important to explain to a responsible family member exactly what your father's condition is. Decisions have to be made, and I want everyone involved to be as informed as possible." He consulted a chart that he'd taken from a hook above the bed. "We thought at first that your father was suffering from Alzheimer's disease, because that was the initial diagnosis we received from the admitting hospital. But his symptoms don't correspond with Alzheimer's, and we've had time to conduct some additional tests."

"I thought he had a stroke," Steve said.

"Oh, he has. Or rather, he's had a series of strokes, as a CAT scan showed us. But in addition to that, your father appears to be suffering from dementia."

It was as if a great weight had suddenly settled in Steve's stomach. *Dementia.* He was aware only of the common meaning of the word, not the specific medical definition, but even without that knowledge he could tell that it was serious, and any hopes he'd harbored that a quick cure or solution for his father's condition could be found faded quickly.

"Dementia's kind of a catchall phrase used to describe a host of brain disorders," the doctor continued. "What your father is suffering from, specifically, is frontotemporal dementia, what is sometimes referred to as Pick's Disease. This is characterized by frontal dysexecutive syndrome, in which the patient suffers behavioral abnormalities, most often apathy or aggression. Obviously, your father's symptoms involve the latter. Patients with the disease also suffer from semantic dementia, which means that the verbal memory is impaired. In your father's instance, he is unable to remember the meaning of words. He knows words, but does not associate them with their definitions. In effect, his brain chooses words at random in order to communicate, and more often than not, those words will have nothing at all to do with the thought he is attempting to express."

Steve was confused. "Has this been going on for a while? It seems like it just happened all of a sudden."

"I have no doubt that there have been symptoms for quite some time, although apparently they went unnoticed. Granted, the symptoms could have been mild. Perhaps he became irritated at things more quickly than normal, or found himself getting annoyed or angry at something that before he would have shrugged off."

His father had always been angry, Steve thought. He'd never shrugged *anything* off.

"He also may have had a difficult time finding the right word to express a thought while speaking, or perhaps he inadvertently called one object by the name of another. Your mother would probably have been in a position to notice these changes more than anyone else, although oftentimes the slide is so gradual and the symptoms exhibited so infrequently that they are overlooked."

"So was it the stroke . . . ?"

The doctor nodded. "The stroke undoubtedly accelerated the degeneration. But this would have happened with or without the stroke."

Steve took a deep breath. Time for the big question. "Is there any way to stop it, anything that can be done?"

"There are treatments," the doctor said, "but there is no cure. We will be putting your father on medication that will help us manage his symptoms, but I need to stress that there's no way to stop or reverse the effects of the disease. The steps we're taking will, at best, only slow its progression."

Steve knew that they should get a second opinion—and he was going to suggest to his mother that she do so—but he wasn't one of those guys who was going to go out, do his own research and become an expert on mental illness. For one thing, he had no doubt that his father was violent, a danger to himself and others. There was definitely something wrong with him, and he needed to be in a hospital environment. He also trusted Dr. Curtis, although for no reason other than gut instinct. The man seemed knowledgeable and competent, and Steve believed he knew what he was talking about.

With a jerk and a start, his father awoke. He strained against the straps holding him down, and his neck craned about, eyes bulging in his head. He tried kicking his feet, but the restraints offered little give, and the end result was an odd vibration at the foot of the metal hospital bed.

"Dad?" Steve said.

"No!" His father looked at him with undisguised anger—but also with confusion. It was clear that he was furious at Steve, but it was just as clear that he had no idea who his son was.

There was a sense of liberation in that. The fact that his father didn't recognize him and might not remem-

ber this encounter for more than a minute didn't free
him from responsibility, but it did protect him from re-
percussions, and the fear Steve had had of his father
lecturing him, blaming him for his being here, evapo-
rated. But as he looked into the blankness of the old
man's gaze, there was also a sense of regret, of opportunities lost and missed. Now even if he made something
of his life, became a great writer or discovered the cure
for cancer or, hell, just won the lottery, his father would
never know. His chance to change his father's perception of him, to redeem himself in his dad's eyes, was
gone, and Steve felt more than a little cheated by that.

"Pens!" the old man screamed. "Pencils!"

"You're seeing both primary symptoms at once
here," the doctor said softly. "The aggression and inappropriate emotion as well as the affected semantic
memory."

"Pencils!"

"Does he think he's saying something we can understand?" Steve asked.

The doctor nodded. "Yes. And that makes him frustrated, which triggers even more aggression."

Steve stepped closer. In a movie, this would be the
moment where he'd put his hand on his father's. But
their family wasn't like that. Instead, he tried to smile.
"It's me, Dad."

"Steve?" Clarity suddenly returned to his father's
gaze. Taking in his surroundings, his eyes met those
of his son, and he said beseechingly, "Why am I here?
What happened? Where's your mother?"

This was worse somehow than the anger. Anger
Steve could deal with; anger he was used to. But fear
and sadness were not emotions that were comfortable
for either of them, and he looked down helplessly at
his father's lost expression.

"What happened? Steve?"

Before he could come up with a response, the old man faded out, like the tuner on a broken radio wandering off station. His father frowned at him, then smiled and said clearly, "Lifestyle fax puppy."

"This is an example of what I was talking about," the doctor said. "And as time passes, those moments of coherence are going to become fewer and farther between. As I said, medication will not cure him or make him better, but it may be able to preserve for a little while longer such periods of lucidity. If you have a few minutes, I'd like you to come to my office so I can give you some literature on the subject and outline treatment options that you can discuss with your mother before we make any decisions on our next course of action."

Nodding, Steve followed the doctor out of the room and down the corridor.

He drove home after nightfall, and was grateful for the traffic jam. He didn't want to go back to his apartment yet, didn't want to call his mother or talk to Sherry, and he sat in the darkness, listening to the radio, hands on the steering wheel, staring out at the sea of red brake lights as his Toyota moved gradually north, carried along by the slow flow of bumper-to-bumper cars.

TWO

Leaving New Mexico

She awoke after Albuquerque, stirring to life on the seat next to him. The desert was dark, the sky moonless, and in the dim illumination of the dashboard her face seemed to be glowing, greenly luminescent. "Where are we?" she asked.

"Almost to Santa Fe."

"Are we going to stop?"

"Yeah. I'm tired. I need to crash."

"Wake me when we get there."

She was asleep again in a matter of minutes, sinking back into the blackness of the seat, and for that he was grateful. Two weeks ago, she'd seemed the ideal traveling companion, always light, always cheerful, up for anything, but that sort of shallow enthusiasm wore thin quickly, and she now seemed to him more irritating than pleasant. He liked to drive in silence, liked to look at the land and be alone with his thoughts, but she needed noise, and if the radio wasn't on, she filled the silence with her own chatter. The only time he seemed able to get any peace was when she was sleeping.

He glanced into the rearview mirror, saw the lights of Albuquerque even from this far away. There were too many people in the world, he thought. The open spaces were closing. As a child, he remembered seeing a factory in his neighborhood torn down, remembered seeing grass grow through the asphalt and eventually take over the property. There'd been something reassuring about the fact that nature could reclaim its territory, but he no longer had faith that that could occur. Nature had been beaten down too well and for too long. It no longer had the strength or will to fight back. It had lost the war and knew it and it had given up the game, deciding to shut itself down.

That depressed him, and he was glad Suzie was asleep so he could think in silence.

He pulled off at the first Santa Fe exit and drove down the overdeveloped street until he hit a motel with a Vacancy sign. Suzie still slept, and he left her in the car as he walked into the lobby, not waking her until he returned with a room key.

In the room, she took off her clothes, crawled into the bed and instantly fell asleep. He was disappointed. He'd been half hoping for sex, but she was obviously too tired, and he went into the bathroom and took a shower and masturbated.

He was awake after the shower, no longer sleepy, and he crawled in bed next to her and used the remote atop the nightstand to turn on the TV. She instinctively snuggled next to him, burying her face in his armpit, throwing a clutching arm around his midsection, making him wish he'd waited for sex. She wouldn't've minded being awakened that way, he thought, taken in her sleep. She probably would've liked it.

He flipped through the cable channels, stopping when he reached an old Jack Lemmon movie with an actress who looked remarkably like his ex-wife. He watched the movie for a while, losing himself in its featherweight plot, but then a commercial came on, breaking the spell, and he leaned back into the pillow, closing his eyes. He found himself wondering where Phoebe was now, whom she was with, what she was doing. She had to be happier than she'd been with him.

He was certainly happier.

They'd lived on a cul-de-sac on the edge of Phoenix in a subdivision with small, identical houses with small, identical yards. It was a low-rent neighborhood, and the houses hadn't come with lawns. Even after two years, most of their neighbors hadn't bothered to plant grass, and patches of unkillable weeds grew in the sun-hardened clay of the untended yards. The driveways of the houses surrounding theirs were permanently littered with the broken toys of dirty children. A cop lived next door, and he and his wife had screaming midnight arguments at least once a week, arguments that always ended with the cop hopping on his motorcycle and taking off in the middle of the night.

That had been their neighborhood, and the frightening thing was that they'd belonged there. So they'd gotten divorced one day, not so much because they hated each other but because they hated their life together. They'd sold the house and he had moved on to Denver and Missoula and Cheyenne, and she had gone . . . God knew where.

He thought about those days sometimes and he wondered what would have happened had they stayed together, had they stayed in that neighborhood. Would he have begun beating her? Would she have stabbed him to death while he slept one night? One of the two, he assumed. Things could not have gone on as they were without violence erupting somehow.

The movie came back on but he could not get into it again, and he drifted into sleep thinking about Phoebe and Phoenix and the cop next door.

Morning. A New Yorker in the stairwell, lugging down a genuine Santa Fe Indian ladder made in the Philippines. Tangible proof that he'd been out to the Wild West. Where was he going to put it? In his New York Ethan Allen living room?

He felt superior to the New Yorker, and part of him wanted to laugh at the sheer absurdity of the struggling man, but instead he held open the stairwell door and watched with a growing sense of depression as the man thanked him profusely and awkwardly carried the ladder to his car. Farther down the parking lot, a couple was loading a giant Indian pot into their trunk, and that depressed him even more. What would they tell their friends when they returned home? How

would they describe their trip? They were at a Motel 6. Across
the street from Denny's. Next door to McDonald's. Would they
embellish the location in their conversations? Rearrange the
landscape of the town to fit their conception of a perfect trip?
Gush about the wild beauty of Santa Fe?

He checked out, grabbing some free coffee from the pot
in the lobby, filling the Styrofoam cup only halfway so he
wouldn't spill it as he walked back up the stairs to the room.
Suzie was up and dressed, zipping up her suitcase on the
bed, wearing white shorts and a white top, her blond hair in
a ponytail.

"Tennis, anyone?" he said.

She laughed, took it as a compliment though it wasn't
meant as one, and he made one last check of the room to
make sure they'd gotten everything, before picking up the
suitcase and walking out with her to the car.

They stopped at a fast-food restaurant called Happy Posole
and bought breakfast burritos, which they ate on red plastic
chairs at a red plastic table under a red plastic umbrella.

It was nearly ten when they hit the highway, but they were
in no hurry, and they took their time, driving the back road
to Taos. The sky was as he remembered it: deep blue with
massive white clouds that stretched to infinity in all directions. The Sangre de Cristos were beautiful, the tips of the
mountains covered with snow, and they stopped by the side
of the road to take a picture. Suzie also wanted her picture
taken in front of a wind-carved pillar of sandstone where two
other couples were already posing for snapshots. They pulled
onto the shoulder, waited in the car until the other people had
taken their photos and left; then Suzie ran across the road,
twirled, arms extended, and he turned the camera on its side
and took the picture.

They got into an argument at El Santuario de Chimayo,
an old Spanish church that was home to "miracle dirt," which
was supposed to possess healing powers and cure illnesses.
The small dusty parking lot was full when they arrived and the

narrow unpaved road leading up to it was lined with cars, an uneasy mob of Hispanic believers and white tourists trudging toward the church in a single-file mass.

The church itself was small and crowded, and they went in together, but he started feeling claustrophobic and had to walk outside. She was angry when she emerged from the chapel, and though he wasn't sure why, he didn't care enough to ask. It would end up being something he'd done, or something he hadn't done, and he wasn't in the mood to apologize to her for things entirely unintentional.

They got into it anyway on their way back to the car, she claiming that he hadn't held her hand in the church when she'd offered it to him, he explaining that he hadn't seen her hold her hand out, she saying that that was the problem, he didn't pay enough attention. It was a stupid argument, but as always they fought as if their lives depended on it, neither of them backing down, the subjects they each brought up careening further and further afield until they were yelling at each other over the hood of the car about something he'd said in Wyoming four days ago that she'd been too polite to mention.

Neither won but neither would give in, and it was a stalemate as they both got into the car.

They did not speak until the road started down the mountainside toward Taos; then she put a hand on his leg, said, "Let's not fight," and snuggled next to him on the seat. He allowed his cheek to be kissed, and then everything was all right, and she started talking about the small villages and verdant valleys through which they'd passed, sharing with him the bottled-up thoughts and observations she'd been unable to express during their silent drive.

He tuned her out, ignored her, concentrated on driving.

Taos hadn't really grown, but it was much more crowded than the last time he'd been here. There was a permanent traffic jam on the highway that doubled as the town's main drag, and as they sat unmoving behind an olive Mercedes, a seemingly endless parade of middle-aged women wearing oversize sunglasses and clownishly exaggerated Southwest clothing walked past on the faux-Western sidewalk.

"I thought it would be bigger," she said.

He shook his head.

"It's a small town."

"Always has been."

"I thought it would be bigger."

Part of him wanted to continue the argument from the church, to get back at her, to hurt her, to point out how inane her observations were, how simple her conversations, but he decided against it, and he did not respond to her statement but waited silently in the traffic, inching the car slowly forward as the shopping pedestrians passed them by.

Suzie stared out the side window, looking away from him. "Pretty soon," she said, "everyone will do everything through their computers. Shop. Pay bills. Read books. Watch movies. Listen to music. They'll never have to leave the house."

He tried to imagine that but could only conjure up in his mind a nation of agoraphobes, paranoid shut-ins who left the road and open spaces to outlaws and psychotics who tooled around in souped-up *Road Warrior* vehicles. It might be better for the land that way, he reasoned. It would put a stop to the endless building, the parceling of America's finest locations into condo tracts and time-share resorts. People would remain cloistered in their little living spaces, staring at their computers, leaving the remaining land unspoiled.

Would he be one of the outlaws? One of the computer illiterates still riding the roads and using real money? He thought he would.

Traffic thinned out on the east end of town, and they took the right branch of the road that led to the pueblo. They went on the tour, Suzie paying an extra five dollars so she could take photographs, and a young Indian man led them into a church and around a small square and gave them a brief history of the pueblo and its people and then let them go and moved off to conduct another tour.

Suzie rhapsodized about the pueblo lifestyle and being close to nature and living off the land, but the pueblo to him looked like an unusually small and unusually dirty apartment complex, and the sections of sheets hung in the small windows as curtains and the raggedy-clothed children playing with dusty toys in front of their homes reminded him of Phoenix.

They ate lunch at a small restaurant on the edge of the reservation. The dining room was empty, but there were still uncleared dishes on most of the tables and they were led to a booth next to a window. There was a bug on the dirty glass, a furiously buzzing black-winged creature that looked like nothing he had ever seen, but both the waitress and Suzie pretended that it didn't exist and he figured that if two women could ignore the bug he could too.

They both ordered Indian tacos—deep-fried dough piled with beans and lettuce and cheese and tomatoes—and he stared past the bug and out the dusty window at the reservation as they ate. He wondered what it would be like to be a member of a conquered race. Did the Indians working at the restaurant resent having to make food for him? Or was it just a job to them? Maybe they'd been conquered so long ago that they didn't even think about it. He tried to remember if he'd ever seen an Indian man with a white woman or a white man with an Indian woman but couldn't. It seemed to him that Indians kept to themselves more than other races.

He'd be angry, he decided, if he were Indian. He'd resent having to live by the rules and strictures of the conquering culture.

On the way out, paying the check at the cash register by the door, he asked the waitress if she preferred the term "Indian" or "Native American."

"Neither," she said.

"Why?"

"They're both European terms. We were called 'Indians' because Columbus made a mistake and thought he was in India. The word 'American' comes from Amerigo Vespucci. Either way, we're named for Italian explorers. I prefer to think of myself as—" She said some word he'd never heard before and couldn't make out.

He liked that attitude—it cheered him up for some reason—and he felt good as he walked with Suzie out to the car.

"What was her problem?" Suzie said. "What's she so angry about?"

"She wasn't angry," he said in her defense.

Suzie did not respond, but a few minutes later, in the car, on the road, she said, "Did you think that girl was pretty?"

"Who?" he said.

"The waitress."

He hadn't really thought about it, but now that he looked back, she had been attractive. "No," he said.

They were silent for several minutes.

"It looks like a scene out of a movie here," she said. "The landscape. It looks fake. Not real."

He nodded.

"I bet they filmed a lot of movies in this area."

"Yeah."

"In the future," she said, "everyone will be forced to sell the movie rights to their life at birth and be given, like, fifty thousand dollars. Then movie studios or television networks will be able to make movies and TV shows about anything that happens anywhere to anyone and not have to worry about buying the rights to the story and being sued and all of that."

He glanced over at her. She spent entirely too much time thinking about the future, he decided.

She wanted to stop tomorrow at the Rio Grande gorge before they headed on up into Colorado, and he'd been toying with the half-assed idea of pushing her over the edge. He'd even rearranged their schedule around the idea, telling her that they needed to leave early if they were going to sightsee. In the back of his mind was the idea that there would probably not be any people around to see him push her if they stopped by the gorge early enough in the morning.

But of course he would not go through with it. Too much trouble. He'd have to drive back to Taos, report that she'd fallen off the bridge, answer questions. He'd probably be responsible for the body and the funeral arrangements too. It was easier to let her live.

The idea appealed to him, though, and he thought again of Phoebe.

Could he have pushed Phoebe over the edge?

Probably.

Would he have regretted it?

No.

They checked in at their motel. The room smelled of Lysol, and the single wrapped glass on the sink counter was speckled with dried white water stains. He turned on the TV, but the only station that came in was an NBC affiliate out of Albuquerque, and the only thing on was a soap opera. The rest of the channels showed static.

He lay on the bed, staring up at the spackled ceiling, while she went into the bathroom and peed with the door open. He saw in his peripheral vision, through the closed translucent outer drapes, the vague silhouettes of children running to the motel pool.

A few moments later she emerged from the bathroom bottomless, obviously in the mood for sex, but he didn't feel like it and he rolled over and off the bed. "Let's go swimming," he said.

She looked at him, puzzled, idly scratching her pubic hair. "What?"

"I want to swim."

He didn't wait for her but opened his suitcase, took out his trunks, and went into the bathroom to change, locking the door behind him.

She was completely naked and pulling on her one-piece when he came back out, and he waited for her, holding the towels, and they walked out of the room together.

"You have the keys?" she asked.

He looked back at the closed door. "No."

She smiled. "That's okay. I do." She held up the room key, the ring around her middle finger.

The pool was crowded with what appeared to be children from only two families: one white, one Hispanic. The parents were seated on lounge chairs on opposite sides of the pool, the white mother and father reading separate magazines, the Hispanic mother keeping a close eye on the kids while her overweight husband, who had obviously just come out of the water, dried off next to her.

The kids were all playing together. Two white boys, five or six Hispanic boys, one Hispanic girl. They were playing Marco Polo, and the girl was "it," swimming with her eyes closed, hands extended, as around her the other kids, screaming and splashing, scattered about the pool.

He and Suzie walked over to the adjacent Jacuzzi, dropping their towels on nearby chairs. She sat on the edge, dangling her feet in the hot water, while he went over to the wall behind the tub and turned on the timer that ran the whirlpool. He got into the water, walking down the short steps and sitting down across from where Suzie still dangled her legs. He caught the glance of the Hispanic mother as he sat down, and she smiled at him. He smiled back. He pretended to look slowly around the pool area, but used the opportunity to study the mother more carefully. She was in her mid- to late thirties, and though she was a little on the chubby side, she was still fairly attractive, and she definitely rated better than the fat old man who was her husband.

He wondered, if they'd both been here unattached, if they'd met at the pool and she hadn't had a husband or kids and he hadn't been here with Suzie, if they would've gotten together tonight.

He wondered what it would be like with her.

He hazarded another look. She was focused on her kids this time, yelling something at one of them, but when she glanced up she looked in his direction and she smiled again.

He smiled back.

The first woman he'd ever been with had been Mexican. He'd been sixteen and she'd been in her early thirties, and she hadn't shaved her legs or under her arms, and he'd been pretty sure that she hadn't bathed in a while, but it had been a wonderful experience anyway, one that had remained unmatched for him until Phoebe, years later. There'd been something sexy about it all, about the fact that she didn't shave like American women, that she smelled of sweat and musk rather than flowery perfume, and that made it seem nasty and forbidden. He remembered the way she'd bucked crazily underneath him and held his buttocks tightly to keep him in, and even now the memory stirred him. She'd kept him inside even after he'd finished, allowing him to grow soft within her, and it had seemed to him that that was the part she'd liked best.

She was a *puta*, a whore, he heard later from his friends, but she hadn't charged him anything, and he wondered whether what they said was true or if they were just jealous.

He glanced across the roiling water of the Jacuzzi to see Suzie staring at him. "What are you thinking about?" she asked.

"Nothing," he said.

After swimming, they returned to the room. She was still in the mood, and she pulled down his trunks. His penis was shrunken, water-shriveled, but she knelt before him and used her mouth, and though he still didn't feel like having sex, he allowed himself to be pushed onto the bed and even let her be on top.

Afterward, she showered and he lay there watching TV. She'd shown no interest in seeing Taos, in looking through the shops and galleries, and while he should have been grateful for that, somehow it didn't sit well with him. He didn't want to walk through shops and galleries, but he wanted *her* to want to. The thought that she was content to stay in the room, like him, and watch television was depressing.

She came out of the bathroom naked, her hair still wet, and jumped on the bed next to him, bouncing on the hard mattress as though it were a trampoline. She leaned over and kissed him, tried to get him to be affectionate, but he pushed her aside and said he wanted to watch the news. She pouted, tried to make him feel guilty, but he didn't care enough to feel guilty, and she eventually fell asleep while he watched a joking weatherman predict tomorrow's temperatures.

He woke her up an hour or so later, took her to dinner at an outdoor café that he said was supposed to have the best food in Taos but which in actuality he'd chosen at random as they'd walked down the street. There was a short, astoundingly ugly woman eating alone at the table next to them, and while Suzie chattered away about subjects in which he had no interest, he watched the woman eat. He found himself wondering whether she'd ever had sex, whether any man—or any woman—had ever wanted her. She might be good in bed, he reasoned. Someone like that would probably be extra giving, more attentive to a partner's needs than someone with less to overcome.

The woman caught him looking at her and she grimaced in distaste, forcing him to turn away.

When they returned to the room, Suzie hinted that she'd like some oral sex, and he started working on her, but it took so long that she fell asleep in the middle of it, and he quit and fell asleep next to her, his jaw hurting.

He awoke the next morning early, before dawn, before her, and he carefully pushed off the covers and got out of bed. She was curled up on the opposite side of the mattress, facing away from him, and when he walked around the foot of the bed he could see that she was smiling in her sleep, her expression one of unconcerned, unburdened happiness. He stood there for a moment, watching her, thinking, then quietly put on the clothes he'd been wearing yesterday and had dumped on the floor. He picked up his keys, put his wallet in his pocket.

He left everything, left his suitcase and other clothes, left the toiletries and ice chest. They were peripheral, extraneous, and would only tie him down. He opened and closed the door without waking her, sneaking out to the car. He started the vehicle, waited for a moment to see if she would hear and recognize the noise and come out after him, but the door to the room did not open, the curtains did not part, and he backed the car out of its space, swung around and peeled out of the parking lot.

He drove through Taos, north, past the reservation.

He thought of Phoebe, then thought of Suzie, still asleep in the motel room, and as he passed over the bridge that spanned the Rio Grande gorge he smiled. He was still smiling as he crossed the border into Colorado.

Three

"That is rough," Jason said sympathetically, clapping a hand on his back.

Steve winced. He didn't like other men touching him, something that Jason, one of those touchy-feely guys, never could seem to figure out. Steve did not understand why certain individuals felt the need to invade the space of others, but, hey, that was the way some people were, and Jason was one of them. Live and let live.

Dennis and Will merely shook their heads, staring into their glasses.

Despite everything that was going on, Steve had met his friends for their regular round of drinks after work on Friday, and while he'd debated whether to tell them about his father, he'd decided at the last minute to come clean and let them know what was going on. He was glad he had. He'd been a bundle of knotted nerves all week, his mind going over and over the increasingly bleak possibilities, and it felt good to unburden himself, to fill in Jason, Dennis and Will on the horrors of the VA hospital and frontotemporal dementia, and tell them the hellish half-life his father had to look forward to before he finally succumbed to his disease and died.

He hadn't told Sherry yet, although he wasn't sure why. She knew that his father was in the hospital, of course, and he'd told her about the stroke, but he hadn't gotten down to the nitty-gritty, hadn't come clean about the violence and the dementia. He felt a little guilty spilling his guts to his friends before his fiancée, but for some reason he found it easier to talk to them about it. Probably because Sherry would make him go deeper, would try to probe his feelings about his father and his family—and he really didn't want to delve into that right now. He had enough emotional burdens to deal with as it was.

Dennis looked over at him. "So have the meds made any difference?"

Steve shrugged.

"What do the doctors say?"

"It's downhill from here. It's only going to get worse."

"How bad is it now?" Jason asked.

"He only recognizes me sometimes. And he usually talks nonsense. Yesterday, he saw me and said, 'Crap the biscuit.' "

Will let out an involuntary laugh, then stifled himself. He immediately held up an apologetic hand. "Sorry, dude. Sorry."

Steve smiled. "That's all right. It *is* funny sometimes. Even my mother laughed yesterday when he told her to 'Purple the cat.' Sometimes it's all you can do."

Dennis nodded. "Laugh or else you'll cry, huh?"

Steve nodded. "Yeah." But the truth was that he'd never been in any danger of crying. His father's situation might be heartbreakingly tragic, but his realization of that was all intellectual. Emotionally, he felt completely disengaged. He told himself it was a coping mechanism, the way he protected himself from hurt, but he knew that wasn't true. He simply did not have the loving feelings toward his father that most sons had. What he did, he did out of obligation.

At least his mother had finally started coming with him to the hospital. It had taken two days and a lot of guilt-tripping, but he'd convinced her to accompany him so she could speak directly with the doctor. She moaned and complained all the way there, putting on an exaggerated show with her broken wrist to show that *she* was suffering too, but when she finally saw her husband, drugged and strapped to the bed, all of that went out the window, and she burst into tears. Obviously the two of them did have a deep emotional connection, something he'd always suspected but had never really known for sure.

"Does your dad know that he's talking gibberish?" Jason asked.

"*He* thinks he's making perfect sense."

"That must be frustrating."

"It is. But it still shouldn't make him so *angry*. That's the freakiest thing, the way he gets so mad. I mean, he's never been Mr. Sunshine, but when he's saying things that we don't understand, he gets furious. He starts screaming, his face gets red, his hands clench. That's why he's restrained. The medication seems to have helped, but the anger's still there, and if he weren't tied down, I know he'd try to attack us."

"So are you going to have to take a lot of time off work for this? These family emergencies really eat into your vacation and sick days, you know." Jason worked in the human resources department of Automated Interface, and he tended to see things from that personnel perspective.

Steve shrugged. "I don't know."

Will laughed. "It's not like you have a real job anyway."

Steve forced himself to smile. Will was always saying things like that, insinuating that because he'd gotten a job with AlumniMedia and spent his days putting together newsletters and yearbooks for various high school and college reunions, he didn't do as much work as the rest of them but just sat around staring into space and doodling on scratch paper. Usually after such a put-down he'd come back at Will with something like "That's not what your mama told me last night," but he was too tired today and didn't want to get into it.

"I interviewed a sex researcher this week," he said. "She's doing a study of pornography."

Will grinned. "Now you're talking!"

"You know, I never really understood before what people meant when they said pornography was anti-women—"

"Oh, come on," Dennis said. "Not that feminist crap!"

"No, really. She had a point. She said most of the acts depicted in porno movies and on hard-core Web sites and things were ones that didn't give pleasure to women: BJs, spanking, anal. . . ."

"Was she hot?"

"Kind of," he admitted.

Will grinned. "Hot babe? And her job is watching movies with anal action?" He shook his head appreciatively. "Mmm, mmm, mmm."

His friends laughed, and Steve decided to drop the subject. He wasn't sure why he'd brought it up in the first place other than to change the topic of conversation, but he should have known that they would find it titillating, and he sat there and nursed his beer while Jason, Dennis and Will riffed endlessly on the various acts the sex researcher had to chronicle and whether she used the information she gathered in her private life.

He left early.

Sherry was waiting for him when he got back to his

apartment. She'd used her key to let herself in and was cooking something in the kitchen. The TV was on and turned to *NBC Nightly News*.

Steve's first reaction was one of annoyance—*how dare she do that without calling and letting him know?*—but that was replaced by a weary gratitude. He hadn't thought to pick up junk food on the way home, and there was no way he was in the mood to cook something, so if she hadn't come over his dinner probably would have consisted of Doritos and Dr Pepper.

He walked into the kitchen, gave her a quick squeeze and looked over her shoulder at what was on the stove. "What are you making?"

"Fettuccine Alfredo," she told him. "I figured you could use a little home cooking. I know it's been a rough week. How's your dad doing?"

He wanted to tell her the truth, the *whole* truth, but he didn't know how.

He was just like his parents, he realized. The old Harry Chapin situation: He'd grown up just like them.

Steve didn't like that, didn't want that, and he forced himself to explain everything that had happened, from his mother's day-late phone call about the attack and her broken wrist, to yesterday's outburst after a nurse had neglected to administer one of his father's afternoon dosages. It was awkward at first, and the discomfort made him realize that one reason he hadn't been completely honest with her was because he was embarrassed. Embarrassed for his father and his family and himself. He didn't want Sherry to see his dad the way he was now and didn't want her associating that behavior with him.

He was also afraid, although of what he was not exactly sure. That she would see his family as something it wasn't? Or that she would see it for what it was? He didn't know. Something, though. He was afraid of something.

She kissed him when he was done talking, and she was crying. Her tears were warm on his cheek. His own eyes were dry, and he felt more tired than sad, but he was glad that she'd been so touched. She clung to him tightly, and he squeezed her back, grateful that she was still there.

He hadn't lost her.

Was that what he'd been afraid of?

Maybe.

She stayed over, and they spent Saturday at the beach: walking along the pier, eating lunch at the Crab Cooker, taking the ferry to Balboa Island and browsing the tourist shops. A tan blond teenager and his equally tan, equally blond friend were poking at a beached jellyfish with sticks on one of the sections of sand between boat docks on the island, and among the crowd of people that had gathered, Steve saw Gina from work. She was with a paunchy, balding older man, and they were both wearing bathing suits, she a string bikini. Steve didn't know whether the man was her father, husband or boyfriend, didn't know if her family lived on Balboa Island or if she was just visiting. All he knew was that he didn't want her to see him, and he ushered Sherry back into the strolling crowd on the sidewalk and made a quick getaway. It felt strange coming upon a woman he knew from work, whom he'd encountered only in that rigid, formal environment, on the beach and barely dressed. He thought it would be embarrassing to both of them if they met here, and he did not relax until they were once again on the ferry and heading back across the bay.

They stopped at Roger's Gardens afterward so Sherry could look at the flowers, and on the way home he realized that he hadn't thought about his parents all day. The reprieve had been nice—but he felt guilty. What kind of son was he? He should be able to think of nothing else, and the fact that he was so easily distracted, that ordinary weekend activities could make him forget that his mother was home alone and suffering with a broken wrist because his father had dementia and had tried to kill her, made him feel ashamed.

He started to turn left into the driveway of his apartment complex, but at the last minute remembered that Sherry's car was parked on the street. He drove around the block, then pulled behind her Prius. They got out of the car. She hadn't planned on staying over last night, so she was still wearing the same clothes as yesterday. She wanted to go home, take a shower and change.

"Do you want to come over tonight?" she asked him. "Stay?"

Steve shook his head tiredly. "I'm going to go see my dad before it gets too late."

She smiled, giving him a quick kiss. "You're a good son. That's one of the things I love about you."

He forced himself to smile back. *Was* he a good son? He didn't know. Was his dad a good father? That was an even harder call. But the fact that he still went out of his way to visit his old man despite the problems they'd had indicated that he'd probably come out on top in a head-to-head comparison. He doubted that his dad would do the same if their situations were reversed.

Why, though, was he keeping score? Why did he even care about how the scales balanced? He didn't believe in heaven, hell or an afterlife, didn't think he'd be called to account for his actions. And his father certainly wouldn't know whether he had stopped to visit. But Steve had always looked at his life as though disassociated from it, as though watching it from afar. It was as if he were in a movie, and the truth was that many of the thoughts he had, many of the actions he undertook, were for the benefit of that movie's unknown viewer. He was writer, director, star and critic of his own life.

He wasn't alone in this, he knew. What were all those plugged-in teenagers doing with headphones in their ears but playing a sound track to the everyday occurrences that made up their lives? In their heads, they too were pretending they were on a screen and someone was watching.

It was what everyone did, to one extent or another.

He kissed Sherry good-bye, promised to call her tonight when he got home, and watched her drive off, waving, before getting back into his own car.

Ultimately, Steve thought, he did the right thing because it made him feel better about himself. And maybe, just maybe, somewhere deep down, his father was aware of it and knew it too.

He stopped by a Del Taco on the way and had a quick, unsatisfying dinner sitting in a plastic bench in front of a plastic table. The sun was down when he got to the VA hospital, his father asleep. For that Steve was grateful. He settled into the chair with a sigh. It was easier, somehow, when the old man was out of it. He could sit by the bed like a dutiful son, but he didn't have to actually see the effects of the dementia. Trying to communicate with his dad was nearly impossible unless he was in one of his brief periodic bursts of lucidity, and Steve much preferred being here when his father was not awake. It was familial devotion without the mess.

There was a low, strangled cough, and Steve jumped, startled. He glanced over at the bed. The room was nearly dark, and even the lights in the hallway outside seemed subdued, toned down for the night. The privacy curtain was open because one of his father's roommates had been transferred elsewhere this morning and the other had been released two days ago.

He felt afraid all of a sudden, scared, like a child who thinks he's heard a ghost, and he realized that there were no other patients screaming or crying out. The entire floor was silent.

His father's eyes opened wide, the pupils too dark in the dimness, the whites too white.

"I killed her."

The old man's voice was dry and raspy, and in the rhythmic quiet of the hospital room, it sounded absurdly loud.

Steve felt chilled. But his first reaction was to quickly reach over and close the door so that no one passing by would be able to hear. That seemed important.

Behind him, his father said it again.

"I killed her."

The door swung shut, and Steve turned back toward the bed. His father's eyes were closed; he'd fallen asleep once more.

Steve breathed deeply, the hairs on the back of his neck still prickling as his gaze focused on the old man's lightly open mouth. He was tempted to wake his dad and ask him what he'd meant, but even if his father *knew* what he'd meant, he probably couldn't explain it. Very little of what he said made sense anymore, and most likely this was meaningless, a non sequitur dredged up from someplace deep in his brain that had nothing to do with anything. Still, there were occasional periods of clarity—just yesterday, his father had recognized him, asking about his job and his car before his mind drifted away and he confused Steve with his long-dead uncle Gene—and it was possible that, intentionally or unintentionally, he had revealed something true.

Besides, it *felt* real. There'd definitely been a confessional tone to his father's cryptic utterance, and try as he might, Steve could not dismiss it out of hand.

I killed her.

That dry, raspy voice haunted his dreams when he returned home and went to sleep, and the nightmare he remembered upon waking was a rerun of one he'd had in childhood. In it, he had been a kid again, sleeping in his old bed in his old room in Phoenix. There was noise from outside, a low rustling he could hear because the night was hot and the window was open. He stood on his knees at the head of the bed and pushed the curtains aside, peering out into the backyard. He could see nothing at first, but he could still hear the rustling—and what sounded like a hissing laugh as well. His eyes adjusted to the darkness, and suddenly, through the rusty screen, he saw movement. It was a man slithering along the ground like a snake, legs together, arms at his sides as he wound his way along the ground through the bushes. A shaft of light from the back porch lamp shone for a second on the figure's face, and Steve saw that it was a clown, a smiling clown with torn satin clothes and poorly applied makeup smeared with dirt. Then the dream took a right turn, changed from the original, and the clown slithered over to the body of a woman that was lying directly below the bedroom window. The clown looked up and spoke. His raspy voice was that of Steve's father. "I killed her," he said. "I killed her."

It was probably something to do with the war, he thought at breakfast. *If* it was anything at all. His dad was in the VA hospital because he was a veteran, and while his father had never been one of those guys who shared war stories with his son—did *any* Vietnam vets do that? wasn't that mostly a World War II thing?— Steve knew that his old man had seen combat. Admittedly, what he knew of the war he'd learned mostly from movies, but it wasn't that much of a stretch to think that if his dad had been over there, he had prob-

ably killed people, some of them no doubt civilians.
And it was quite possible that one or more of them had
been female.

So maybe that was what he'd been talking about;
maybe that was what he'd been remembering.

Strange, Steve thought. His father had killed people.
His dad was a killer. He'd never thought of that before,
never seen it that way. In his mind, his father was . . .
well, a father. And a husband. And an auto parts salesman. A regular, middle-class guy. But there *had* been a
time in his life when he'd spent three years in a foreign
country, shooting at people and trying to kill them.

It was an odd and disconcerting realization. But his
father was not alone. The fact was, Steve's generation
and the ones immediately surrounding it, those who
had come of age after the abolition of the draft, were
an anomaly. Up to that point, nearly all of the men in
the country had been trained by the government to kill
people—and many of them *had*. The uncomfortable
squeamishness people his age experienced was not
typical. It was probably why, when he was growing
up, no parents had ever had any problem with their
kids playing with guns and pretending to shoot and
kill one another. Moms and dads who would have a
shit fit if little Johnny pretended to be a pusher or little
Julie pretended to be a whore, gladly gave their kids
toy pistols and rifles so that they could act out killing
bad guys—even though, in the real world, murder was
considered a much greater crime than either drugs or
prostitution.

He'd heard it said that man was a naturally violent
species, and maybe that was true. Maybe that was
why the crime rate was so much higher now than it
had been fifty or sixty years ago. Back then, men got
to take out their aggression in wars. People these days,
unless they wanted to spend years of their lives work-

ing for peanuts in the armed forces, had to resort to violent confrontations here at home in order to satisfy the same jones.

What the fuck was he thinking? That was lunacy. The stress from all of this was muddling up his mind. His dad hadn't killed anyone.

So why was he already trying to come up with rationalizations?

At work, Steve could not seem to concentrate on the article he was supposed to be writing. Gina smiled at him when he came in, gave her usual cheery greeting, but though Steve said hello and smiled back, in his mind he saw her on the sand in her string bikini with that paunchy older man. Between Gina and his father, he remained distracted all morning, and by the time noon rolled around, he had completed exactly two sentences of his article—and neither of them was very good.

He met Sherry for lunch at Wahoo's Fish Taco, but even as he listened to her describe a hectic morning dealing with irate patrons furious that the library's computers were down, his father's words continued to echo in his brain.

I killed her.

Steve had given up all pretense of believing that his father had been out of it when he spoke. He hoped with every cell in his body to be proved wrong, but until that happened, he was going to assume that his dad had been telling the truth.

I killed her.

Who could *her* be? He wanted to cling to his war theory, but the personal connection implied by the word "her" made that seem increasingly unlikely. So who, then? A friend, an acquaintance, someone off the street? Had Steve had a deceased sister he'd never known about? Could it have been his paternal grandmother, whom he'd never known? His *father's* sister? An old girlfriend?

The questions remained with him throughout the rest of the day.

On impulse, he asked his mother, "Was Dad ever married before?"

It was after work, and they were sitting in the kitchen, his mother slicing coffee cake with her good hand. Her reaction was not what he'd expected. "Yes," she said, eyes downcast. "I was not his first choice." She handed Steve a plate.

He was stunned into silence for a moment. His mother gave him a fork for the coffee cake, and, numbly, he took it.

"Who was she?" he asked finally.

"His high school girlfriend. They married the summer after he graduated from high school, before he was drafted."

"What happened—"

"She died."

Died. Steve's pulse quickened. "How?"

"I don't want to talk about her."

"How?" he pressed.

"I don't know. It was before I ever met your father."

"You must know *something* about it."

"Everything I know I learned from Marion, your father's sister." Steve remembered his aunt Marion. He'd met her only a couple of times, when they'd gone back to New Mexico for a visit. He hadn't liked her. Several years ago, his parents had gotten a notice in the mail that she'd died. "She told me on the day we got engaged that your father had been married before and that his first wife was a much better match for him than I was."

"But didn't you ever ask Dad about it? Weren't you curious?"

She shook her head, lips tight. "No."

"That's why you never told me?"

"It's not something we talked about. And it was none of your business. It didn't concern you. It was not something you needed to know."

Steve continued to ask questions, but that was all the information he could get out of her. She felt that she had already revealed too much, and when he suggested that it was psychologically healthier to discuss this and get it out in the open rather than hide it and keep it a secret, she got angry and told him that if he did not stop talking about it, he would have to leave. She did not ask why he was so interested in this subject, however, did not wonder why he had asked about his father's first wife to begin with, and he found that more than a little odd.

It really was time to leave, and Steve made nice, thanking his mother for the coffee cake, promising to drive her to the VA hospital tomorrow for a visit, and they parted on good terms. But halfway home, instead of taking the Santa Ana Freeway back to Irvine, he turned west on the Garden Grove Freeway and headed toward Long Beach. He hadn't realized he was going to do that until he did, and though he considered getting off the freeway and turning around, he didn't.

He found a parking spot near the hospital's front entrance.

His father was awake. His mind might not be clear and rational, but his eyes were open, and they followed Steve as he walked into the hospital room, closed the door and sat down in the chair at the side of the bed. "Dad?"

The old man nodded.

He was here.

Steve scooted his chair closer to the bed. His father was undergoing therapy—anger management and memory training—as well as receiving medication for his condition, and Steve knew he should talk this over with the doctors first, make sure it was all right, confirm that he wasn't throwing a monkey wrench into their treatment plans. But he also knew that if he thought about it too long he wouldn't do it, so he leaned next to the old man's ear and asked, "Who did you kill, Dad?"

There was no answer for a moment, and he thought that his father hadn't heard or that he had slipped away or that maybe the question *had* triggered some unwelcome reaction within his dad's head.

Then came that whisper, the dry, raspy voice that had been echoing in his brain for the past twenty-four hours. "My wife."

These periods of lucidity were extremely short-lived. If he was going to find out anything, he'd have to do it fast. "What happened?"

The same words again, in the same voice. "I killed her."

"Where did you kill her?"

His father chuckled, and it was the creepiest thing Steve had ever heard. In this place, under these circumstances, the sound of his dad's dry chuckle sent goose bumps racing down his arms. "I took her to the top of the roof," he rasped. "The bank building." He coughed.

And then he described what happened.

Four

He lures her up to the roof of the bank building on the pretext of seeing the view. It is a gorgeous day, and the brown brick structure is the tallest in town. She is thrilled to be there. It is the lunch hour, so the bank and the offices within the building are closed. There are very few people inside, but he cannot afford for them to be seen with each other—one sharp-eyed witness could unravel the entire plan—so he walks ahead of her, pretending they are not together. It is not until they are in the stairwell, walking up the concrete steps, that he slows and takes her hand.

On the roof, they walk about, strolling along the bordered edge, admiring the view of the town from every angle. "I love you," she tells him.

"I love you too," he says.

He was planning on poisoning her at first, and he went to the library to do research on toxic substances, but she has steadfastly refused to take any of the "medicine" he provided for her chronically upset stomach. Is she suspicious? He doesn't think so, but still he has decided to take a different tack.

He got the idea yesterday when, standing up after sitting on a bench, she fell. For a brief, hopeful second, he thought she'd hit her head on the concrete hard enough to do damage, but then she struggled to her feet and he offered her a hand.

He would be the primary suspect, however, should any-

thing happen to her, so he needed an extra precaution, something to throw suspicion from himself. He remembered that
she'd done well in Spanish class in high school, and again he
went to the library. He found a Spanish–English dictionary
and wrote, in disguised handwriting, in Spanish, a vaguely
worded paragraph that could be interpreted as a suicide note.
At home, last night, he'd asked her to translate it for him—
he told her a guy at work had received it and wanted to know
what it said. She started to tell him, but he asked her to write
it out so he could give it to the guy.

This morning, on his break, he had placed the note in an
envelope and mailed it to her parents. He had typed their
address.

Now it is time.

She turns to him, puts her arms around his neck and
kisses him. "What a perfect day," she says.

They are close to the edge.

He looks into her eyes. "Yes, it is," he tells her.

Then he pushes her over the low wall, and she falls off the
building, screaming in terror until her head hits the sidewalk
below.

Five

Steve stayed at his desk for lunch. Usually he went out, sometimes by himself, sometimes with Jim Cristlieb, the production manager, or Pete Hughart, the art director, but today he'd brown-bagged it, and he waited until McColl was out of his office and Gina had left before using his computer to look up information about his father's first wife.

It was easy enough to do. After all, a good portion of his regular job was spent tracking down the whereabouts of high school and college graduates who had somehow fallen off the radar of their classmates or whose current address was unknown by their former schools. Although Will liked to make fun of what he did for a living, Steve found it both challenging and rewarding. He was almost like a detective, and if he did say so himself, he was pretty damn good at locating people, even women who had since married and moved.

He didn't actually have a name for his father's first wife, but if he searched public records in Copper City, New Mexico, under the last name Nye, he figured he'd be able to come up with one pretty quickly. Steve calculated back. He'd been born in 1982. His parents had been married for ten years before they had him. If his father had been married right after high school and sometime within the next year or so been drafted for a four-year tour of duty, that meant the first marriage would have occurred sometime in the early 1960s. If he focused his search on marriages recorded between 1960 and 1965, he should be able to come up with a name.

Steve took a bite of his brown-bagged turkey sandwich and Googled Copper City, New Mexico. He found a Web site for the city that was aimed at tourists, and while it offered no links to public records, he did find out the name of the local newspaper, the *Copper City Sentinel*, and learned that the community was located in San Miguel County. He accessed the county recorder's Web site for San Miguel and was able to locate a marriage certificate for Joseph Nye and Ruth Haster, dated August 21, 1961.

Ruth Haster.

Ruth *Nye*.

He tried to imagine what she'd looked like, what type of person she'd been. His father was no prize, so she couldn't have been a great beauty. He imagined that she was probably a perky, somewhat cute, typical small-town girl, less dour than his mother perhaps, maybe a little more outgoing. What if *she'd* been his mother? Of course, that was a biological impossibility, but even if it weren't, he would be a completely different person today just by virtue of being raised by someone else.

Maybe he'd be better off. Maybe he'd be happier.

She was a skeleton now, Steve realized. She was rotting in a cemetery somewhere because his father had pushed her off a roof and killed her.

Why, though? Why would his father have done such a thing? His dad wasn't a psycho, so it couldn't have come completely out of the blue. She had to have done something. Had she hurt him? Had she lied to him? Had she cheated on him?

Ruth Haster. He wrote down the name, then searched for a death certificate but could find none. There'd probably been an obituary, he reasoned. Calling up the Web site for the *Copper City Sentinel*, he found that the newspaper had no archives online, although he did print out a mailing address and telephone number for the paper. He then tried the local library, but it too had only a rudimentary Web page that offered no way of looking up any of its holdings.

Steve paused to finish his sandwich and pop open a can of Coke before accessing an online phone directory for Copper City.

Pay dirt.

There were no Nyes listed, but he found four Hasters, and he printed out their names, numbers and addresses. The first number he dialed, for a J. Haster, turned out to be Jessica Haster, Ruth's aunt. Steve flirted with the idea of lying, taking cover behind his job and pretending he needed information for a class reunion booklet, but at the last second he decided to come clean, and he identified himself as Joseph Nye's son and said that he was looking for information about his father's first marriage. He didn't tell the woman *why* he was so interested, but let her think that it was part of an effort to reconnect with his roots.

Jessica was eighty-two years old, as she told him proudly, but her memory was clear, and she described Ruth and Joseph as a typical young married couple. Her death, Jessica said, had been a complete shock to everyone, especially when it got around town that it might be suicide.

Suicide.

Steve felt cold, but he kept his voice even and detached as he asked if, after the fact, anyone had noticed any signs or clues . . . perhaps evidence of strain in the marriage?

"No," Jessica said firmly. "And don't think we all didn't go over everything she ever said to us with a fine-toothed comb. Besides, she had so much to look forward to. And she was so excited about it."

Steve felt his stomach drop. "Excited? About what?" he forced himself to ask.

"She was pregnant, poor thing. With a girl."

The news hit him hard. He closed his eyes, gripping the phone tightly. He would have had a sister. Or a half sister. He wasn't even sure that was something of which his mother was aware, and he wondered if that was the reason his father had done it. Such a crime was not unheard-of, and right now it was the only thing that seemed to make any sense. He'd been hoping to hear that Ruth was a shrew, a slut, a castrating bitch. He'd wanted to believe that his father was somehow justified in his actions, but any hope for such rationalization was slipping away.

"Would you mind if I came over so we could talk more about this?" Steve asked.

"That would be fine," Jessica said. She sounded pleased at the thought of having a visitor.

"I have the phone numbers and addresses of some other Hasters in town," he said. "I assume those are relatives. Would any of them have known Ruth or my father?"

"Greg would, yes. The rest are Trudy's children, so no. But Ruth's sister's still here, only her name isn't Haster anymore, so you wouldn't find her in the phone book. I know several people who could tell you what you need to know, though—people who knew Ruth and Joe. Friends and family. When are you planning to drop by?"

"This weekend," he said impulsively.

"I'll call everyone up. We'll have us a little get-together. It'll be fun."

He confirmed her address, gave her his name and home phone number, thanked her profusely for her kindness and her help and said good-bye. He sat there for a moment, staring at the telephone. It was stupid of him to make a trip to Copper City, a waste of both time and money.

But he wanted to go there.

Needed to go there.

The truth was that he could just as easily have questioned these people over the phone, but they were not missing alumni he was tracking down for a class reunion; these were people related to his father's first wife—

whom he'd killed

—and he wanted to see where they lived, what they were like, wanted to see the expressions on their faces as they told their stories to him. Some of them might even have photographs. Or they might be able to direct him to other family members or friends who had stories to tell.

He also wanted to see where it had happened.

That was the primary impetus. It made no rational sense, but he wanted to see the spot where his father had murdered his pregnant wife. Steve didn't know what he hoped to learn from the exposure or what he thought he'd exprience. All he knew was that there was an urge within him, an almost primal compulsion to stand where his father had stood and work out in his mind the details of what had occurred on that roof.

Gina came back from lunch with a large Burger King cup that she put on top of her desk, and moments later everyone else started arriving, walking out of the elevator and down the hall to their offices in twos and threes. Steve crumpled up his lunch sack, threw it away, and closed the notebook in which he'd been writing. He terminated his Internet connection, accessing one of the three articles he was writing for a UC Brea twenty-year class reunion. He went back to work.

He had promised to take his mother to the VA hospital this evening but didn't want to, and he made up an excuse when he called her from his cell phone in the car, telling her that he didn't feel well. He actually felt *very* well for the first few seconds after ending the call—an evening without seeing either parent felt like a well-earned reprieve at this point—but then he thought about his father's first wife and everything he'd learned today at lunch, and the weight that had been temporarily lifted from his shoulders came crashing down on his head with extra force.

When he arrived home, Sherry was there, only she wasn't cooking dinner this time; she was sorting through his mail. In her hand was the usual assortment of bills, but one of the envelopes, he saw immediately, was addressed to him in his own handwriting. It was one that he'd sent along with a short story he'd submitted to a small-press magazine. Another rejection.

"What are you doing?" he demanded.

Sherry looked up. "What's the matter?"

"That's my private stuff!" He grabbed the envelopes from her hand and practically threw them onto the dinner table.

She was taken aback by the vehemence of his reaction and instinctively leaned away from him. "I'm sorry," she said contritely. "They were on the floor when I came in, and I just picked them up to put them away."

They no doubt had been on the floor—Steve's mail slot was in the door, and whatever was pushed through it fell on the ground—but she hadn't merely been picking up his mail; she'd been sorting through it, and he felt an unwelcome surge of anger as he thought of her holding his rejection letter.

He was embarrassed. That was all it was. Not at the rejection, specifically, but at the writing. His previous girlfriend, Nadine, knew all about his literary aspirations—they'd met in a creative writing class in college—but when things hadn't panned out the way he'd hoped and he'd had to get a real job after graduation, writing fiction had become like masturbation: something furtive and private, something he both enjoyed and was ashamed of doing. He'd never shared it with Sherry because he didn't know any way to discuss his ambitions that didn't make them sound juvenile and pathetic.

What would happen if he actually sold something, though? How would he explain that? Wouldn't it seem like a betrayal to her that he'd kept such an important part of himself secret for so long? She might feel like she didn't know him at all. Such a revelation at such a late date had the potential to seriously harm their relationship. It might be better to come clean now and just deal with the embarrassment.

He looked at her wary expression.

But he couldn't.

Besides, his batting average was zero for twenty. He doubted that it was a problem he would have to deal with anytime soon.

Steve sat down next to her. "Sorry," he said. "I'm . . . I'm sorry."

She put her hand on his, nodding her understanding.

"It's been a long day."

Sherry started to say something, then changed her mind, then changed her mind again. "Do you not want me to come over?" she asked carefully. He was about to protest, but she continued quickly, "It seems like every time I try to surprise you, you don't like it."

"That's not true!" he said.

"I think it is. You gave me a key, so I assumed you wanted me to use it, but maybe I should give it back to you. I don't want to be here if you don't want me here."

"Of course I do!"

"I think you'd be more comfortable if we stepped back a little and things were the way they were before, with dates on Friday and Saturday, occasional sleepovers, a midweek meeting here and there." She looked sad as she said this, resigned, and he hated that he had made her feel this way.

Impulsively, he grabbed Sherry, hugged her, held her close. "It's been a long day," he repeated.

He felt her nod against him, and when he pulled back to look at her, he saw that although there were tears in her eyes, she was smiling. "I love you," he told her.

She reached up to kiss him. "I love you too."

They went out for dinner. There was a Mexican restaurant near the Orange County Performing Arts Center that they both liked, and after they finished eating, they wandered through the nearby sculpture garden, along with a handful of other couples. Ground-level floodlights shone on the rock installations and geometric artwork, casting shadows on the surrounding concrete walls. A teenage boy was crouching in front of one of the lights, making comical hand shadows to the inappropriately raucous delight of his ill-behaved girlfriend.

Steve stopped before a waterfall cascading over a series of cement steps. "I need to go on a business trip this weekend," he said.

Sherry frowned. "Business trip?"

"I need to interview a few people in New Mexico."

"Can't you just talk to them over the phone? Or e-mail them?"

He thought fast, glad he was standing in shadow and she couldn't see his face. "They live on kind of a commune. No electricity, no phone, the whole thing. Completely off the grid."

She paused, and the hesitation in her voice when she spoke made him realize that he'd better be careful. "Why don't I come with you?"

"It's not a vacation. It's just a quick trip. One day there, one day back. It's not going to be fun. Besides, I was kind of hoping you could look in on my mom for me. You know, make sure she's okay?"

That did it.

"Sure," Sherry said, putting a hand on his arm.

"Thanks. I really appreciate it. All you have to do is pop in, take a quick peek, see if she needs anything. I'll tell her you'll stop by."

"What about your dad?"

"He won't even notice I'm gone."

"Do I need to . . . ?"

Steve shook his head. "That place is rough. And it's all the way in Long Beach. It'd be better not to go there. I'll check in on him when I get back."

Sherry nodded. Her face looked strange in the angled lighting, her eyes shadowed, almost skull-like, but he drew her to him and kissed her passionately, grateful for the feeling of her body pressed against his. Over her shoulder, he saw the shadow of a rabbit on the wall as the teenage boy moved his fingers up and down in front of the light.

Steve took a red-eye flight Friday evening and landed in Albuquerque shortly after midnight. He'd booked a rental car as well as a room at a hotel near the airport, and he drove the car to the hotel and crashed on the queen-sized bed without bothering to open his suitcase, leaving his clothes in a pile on the floor as he crawled under the covers in his underwear and promptly fell asleep.

He awoke with the dawn. The curtains covering the east-facing windows had not been fully closed, a detail he had not noticed in the dark, and sunlight streamed into the room in a funnel-shaped beam that fell across the bed. He staggered into the bathroom, took a warm shower, then shaved and combed his hair. After eating a quick meal of orange juice and bagels from the self-serve breakfast bar in the lobby, he hit the road. Copper City was a good two hours away, and he wanted to be there in plenty of time to do some research at the library and see the bank building—

where his father had murdered his wife

—before meeting Jessica Haster and her relatives at noon.

The sun was up, the sky blue and filled with billowing clichéd clouds as he drove east from Albuquerque. He felt invigorated despite the shortness of sleep time, and soon after leaving the city he was in open desert, with flat sandy ground sloping down to his right and rocky mountains rising upward to his left. There was something oddly cheering about being in another state, and the unaccustomed freshness of the New Mexico morning made him feel exhilarated and excited despite the grimness of his mission. The rental car had satellite radio, and he found a channel specializing in nineties grunge, cranking up the volume as he sped through the austere and unfamiliar landscape.

He reached Copper City just after ten.

It was a community that seemed stuck in time. Approaching from the west, Steve encountered no fast-food chains or nationally known gas stations, only local businesses with names that seemed dully provincial. The houses he passed were all from another era: individual styles on large lots rather than the cream-colored cookie-cutter homes found in modern developments. There was a park with a bandstand, a town square with benches and a fountain. Everything probably looked much as it had when his father had lived there.

The tallest structure in Copper City was still the bank building.

Overdressed people were walking along the downtown sidewalks like extras in an old movie, and as Steve parked in a two-hour spot in front of a closed pharmacy, he saw a couple of them go into the bank. He got out of the car, locked it and dashed between moving cars across the street. Inside, the building lobby offered entrance to three different offices: the Copper City National Bank, Wilson-Adams Realtors and H & R Block. In the fourth wall, the back wall, was an elevator, and it was to this that Steve gravitated. He read the listings for each floor's businesses in the glassed directory to the right of the closed metal door, noting that the number of tenants decreased until, at the top floor, there were no listings whatsoever.

He pressed the call button and the elevator door slid open instantly, as though it had been waiting for him. Entering the small car, he pressed the number six on the control panel. The button lit up, the doors closed and the elevator began its slow, creaky trip to the building's top floor, where it opened onto an empty hallway. There was an exit sign above a closed door at the far end, behind which Steve assumed was a stairwell. He walked down the corridor, pushed the bar that opened the door. There were indeed stairs that led both down and up, and Steve climbed the steps that led upward, pushed open another door at the top and found himself on the building's roof.

It was clear that this location was not merely restricted to maintenance personnel. There was a picnic table in the center of the flat area, half-full ashtrays sitting atop both ends, and around the raised edge of the roof someone had placed potted geraniums. Spaced out here and there were individual deck chairs. It appeared to be a spot where employees took their breaks, and Steve walked slowly past the picnic table to the north edge of the roof. From here, he could see past the town to a series of small chaparral-covered hills that arose on the other side of a dry, winding riverbed. He looked down at the street below. Where had she fallen? Which sidewalk had she hit? He walked carefully around the perimeter. In the rear of the building was an alley. Had she landed there?

He'd expected to be more affected by this than he was. He knew, intellectually, the gruesomeness of such a death, could see in his mind's eye a shattered, twisted body, a cracked head with blood and brains spilling out, but that's all the knowledge was—intellectual. Emotionally, he was distanced from the event, and he wondered if that was a protective measure on his part, if his mind just didn't want him to feel the horror of what his father had done.

Steve stopped, leaning over, both hands on the side wall, and stared straight down, trying to imagine what it had been like for Ruth Nye as she'd plummeted screaming to her death, still feeling on her body the pressure of her husband's push.

What could have led him to do such a thing? He had never done it again. He had remarried, had a son, and lived a quiet, respectable life for the past thirty years. Maybe *she'd* done something. Maybe the killing had been done in self-defense or had been somehow justified. All killings weren't created equal. That was why the legal system recognized various categories and gradations of the crime. That was why juries were given such sentencing latitude. Sometimes there were extenuating circumstances.

His father had told him what he had done but not why, and Steve was hoping on this trip to sort out the truth behind the facts.

His next stop was the library, and it took him a couple of passes through town before he found out where it was. Located on a side street near the elementary school, the single-story building barely looked big enough to have a children's section, much less a collection designed to serve the entire community. His heart sank when he walked inside and saw no computers on any of the desks or tables. Nevertheless, he approached the lone librarian on duty and asked if the library had any back issues of the *Copper City Sentinel*.

"What month?" she asked.

"The early nineteen sixties," he said.

She was surprised by that. "We don't get much call for anything past the last few weeks usually," she said. "But we do have all previous years on microfiche. Although I have to say, you're the only person in my recollection who's ever asked to see it." She stood heavily and made her way between the stacks to a small alcove at the rear of the room. Here a single microfiche reader stood on a table next to a metal filing cabinet. The librarian slid open the top drawer of the cabinet and withdrew two packets, which she handed to Steve. "Here's 1960 through 1963, and 1964 through 1967."

"That's perfect," he said.

"Do you know how to use the reader?"

"Not exactly," he admitted, and watched as she showed him how to turn on the machine, place the flat sheet of microfilm into a tray in the center of the apparatus and scroll through individual issues of the newspaper.

"Thank you," he said, and started scanning obituaries.

He found what he was looking for in the April 10, 1966, edition of the paper. Even before he reached the obituaries, he saw a headline on the front page announcing, "Mom-to-be Dies in Fall," and he quickly read the accompanying story. But whether it was out of deference to survivors, respect for the dead or merely shoddy journalism, the article revealed very little. Disappointed, he scanned the next few months' worth of newspapers, hoping for a follow-up story, but could find no mention of either Ruth or his father. Glancing at his watch, he saw that it was almost eleven thirty. He was supposed to be at Jessica Haster's house by noon, and he wanted to get there a little bit early so he could have a chance to talk to her before everyone else arrived. Switching off the machine, he returned the microfiche sheets to their packets and handed them back to the librarian. "Thank you," he told her.

Since he wasn't familiar with the city and didn't have a map, Steve withdrew Jessica Haster's address from his shirt pocket and asked the librarian if she knew how to get there. As it turned out, Jessica lived only a few streets over, and the woman gave him absurdly simple directions that would lead him right to the front step.

The house was an unexpectedly dreary dwelling badly in need of paint. From the sound of Jessica's voice on the phone, he had imagined a cute cottage, one of those white-clapboard-with-green-shutters homes you saw in country decorating magazines and children's storybooks, a place with rose trellises and a blooming side garden. But, in truth, he had seen nothing like that in this town. Copper City was a poor community long past its prime, and the residences here all seemed to be singularly drab structures with nonexistent yards.

Most of the guests, it seemed, had already arrived. Although it was still early, the long driveway was full of old cars and dented pickup trucks. He was forced to park on the street, and he made his way along the narrow edge of the drive between the line of vehicles and the sunken patch of weedy ground beside it. Before he could gather his thoughts and plan out what he was going to say, the torn screen door flew open, smacking against the wall, and a host of women and men came hurrying out to greet him.

In the space of three minutes, he was introduced to nearly a dozen people, not counting the children who were now running around the house, playing. He was not good with names under the best of circumstances, and though he tried very hard to remember everyone he met and place a name with every face, the only two people he knew he could recognize with certainty were Jessica and Ruth's sister Hazel.

Jessica Haster was as chatty and vivacious as she'd seemed on the phone. A short woman with oversize Coke-bottle glasses, she was dressed in purple stretch pants and a bright Hawaiian-print blouse. She took him around to everyone, explaining over and over again that he was Ruth's husband's son and was here to learn what he could about his daddy's first wife.

There was a potluck. All of the guests save himself had apparently brought some sort of food dish, and they each grabbed paper plates from one end of the long dining room table and helped themselves to fried chicken, potato salad, coleslaw and rolls while Jessica, Hazel and another older lady reminisced about Ruth in the doorway of the kitchen. From what Steve could tell, his father's first wife had been a saint: smart, patient, kind, loving and all of the other positive attributes that could be applied to a young woman in the early 1960s. Even granting the exaggeration that inevitably accompanied an early death, Ruth seemed to have been extremely nice and universally well liked.

Lyman Fischer arrrived soon after. He'd gone to school with both Ruth and his dad, and his memories were different from everyone else's. For one thing, although Lyman and Steve's father had been friends since childhood, they had both competed for Ruth Haster's affections in high school, and Steve still sensed some residual bitterness there. Consequently, Lyman's recollections were a little less rosy, a little harsher and, Steve assumed, a little more realistic. Sensing a rare opportunity to learn the unvarnished truth about his father's early years, Steve cornered Lyman near the desserts and quizzed him in depth about what type of person his dad had been. The picture that emerged was of someone impetuous and outgoing, fun loving and friendly, not qualities that he would ever associate with Joseph Nye, but not ones that would lead him to believe that his father would be capable of killing someone either.

Not for the first time, he thought of Vietnam, and he asked Lyman if he thought his father had changed after he'd come back from the war, if he seemed different after he'd seen combat.

"Not really," Lyman replied after giving the matter some serious thought. "A lotta people, yeah. They come back hard or angry or paranoid. But not Joe."

Jessica and the others had gathered around as they'd been talking, and as Steve looked at the assembled faces, he thought it was probably time to ask about Ruth's death.

Murder.

He turned to Jessica. "When Ruth died," he said, "they thought it was suicide?" He felt awkward bringing it up this way, but the discussion had to start somewhere.

"Or an accident," Jessica said.

What about the note? he almost asked, but didn't dare. He wasn't sure how many of *them* knew about the note, and if *he* was somehow aware of it, questions would be generated, questions he was not prepared to answer. "Did anyone see it happen?"

"There were a lot of people there that day, if that's what you mean. But no, not really. It happened so fast. No one was looking right there, and in just one second, she was down."

"The only reason people thought it might be suicide is because she was up there in the first place, in her condition," Hazel said. "But she could've slipped." The line of her mouth grew straight and prim, and in that second she reminded Steve of his mother. "I *always* thought it was an accident."

"Did she say anything before she died?" someone wondered. He thought it was one of Ruth's sister's kids, but he wasn't sure.

"She hit her head on the cement when she fell," Jessica said. "She died instantly. But they did think at first that they might be able to save the baby, so they took her to the hospital and performed an emergency C-section. Probably now they *would've* been able to save her, but the girl was born dead."

"We lost Joe after that," Hazel said sadly.

Lyman nodded. "He cut everybody off, even his old friends. A couple of us tried to get him back into the swing of things, but he was hanging out with a new group of people, and all of a sudden we weren't part of his life."

"I remember he went to a prostitute," one old woman said disgustedly. It was one of Ruth's friends, but he couldn't remember her name. The woman lowered her voice. "A Mexican."

Steve was still having a hard time reconciling the

rigid, straitlaced father he'd known all his life with the picture painted by Lyman, and this newest revelation seemed impossible to connect with the uptight law-and-order Republican who railed against the influx of immigrants on an almost daily basis.

But not with the type of man who could murder his wife.

Jessica nodded. "It's true," she admitted. "I heard that he fell in love with her and was heartbroken when she was deported back to Mexico. I never knew what happened to him after that. I think he left town."

"He did," Lyman said. "Moved to Las Cruces, I think."

"What about his family?" Steve asked. "His parents were still alive then, weren't they? And what about his sister, Marion?"

"There was a . . . falling-out . . . with his family," Jessica said.

Hazel nodded. "Over Ruth."

Steve was surprised. "But my mother was under the impression that Aunt Marion preferred Ruth to her. She acted like my mother couldn't hold a candle to Ruth."

"Marion didn't like *anyone*," Lyman said, and most of the older guests laughed.

Steve thought for a moment. "I know my dad went to Vietnam," he said carefully, deciding to put the question to the room. "Did he seem . . . changed after that? Did he seem different when he came back?"

All eyes turned to Hazel. "Not that I noticed. And Ruth never said anything like that to me, which she would've if it were true. Do you have a reason for asking?"

"No," he said quickly. "I was just wondering. I'm just trying to find out what he was like when he was young."

"It was Ruth's death that changed him, not the war,"

Hazel said, and Jessica, standing next to her, nodded in agreement.

"All of our lives would have been different if Ruth had lived," Jessica said sadly.

They were good people, Ruth's family, and from all indications, she had been a good person too. His father was not. He was a murderer, and as much as Steve would have liked to believe that there'd been a legitimate and justifiable reason for him to do away with his wife, there was absolutely no evidence to support it.

The sun was low in the west when Steve finally took his leave, a chunk of angel food cake that Jessica had made him take wrapped in aluminum foil beside him, and the streetlights in Copper City were already on as he passed by the bank building on his way out of town. He had a long drive ahead of him, and he sped through the gathering darkness, back to his hotel in Albuquerque, troubled.

He called Sherry when he arrived home the next day. And his mother. Although both reported that everything had gone smoothly in his absence, that there'd been no trouble, his mother asked him to check on his father. She was worried because no one had gone to see him since Thursday. He didn't feel like driving all the way to Long Beach, though, and the truth was that he didn't really want to see the old man. His brain had still not had enough time to process all of the new information it had absorbed, and he compromised by calling the VA hospital for a status report. Dr. Curtis was not on duty, but he spoke to a charge nurse who told him that everything was status quo, no change. His father had slept most of the time and, when awake, had been only briefly coherent.

What had he said at that time? Steve wanted to ask, but didn't dare.

After sorting through the pile of bills and junk mail that lay on the floor by the front door, he checked his voice mail and his e-mail. Jason had left several messages on each, and Steve called his friend, who said that his mother and stepfather were visiting and he needed to get out of the house. "I'm going stir-crazy," he confided. "They're here for a week, and I'm expected to entertain them twenty-four hours a day. I was with Maria the last time they came over in April, and now my mom's giving me grief for screwing up such a wonderful relationship. One more bit of kindly advice about how good she was for me and I'm going to tell them that she was fucking some other guy and that's why she's not here anymore."

"Is that what happened?" Steve asked incredulously.

"Of course not. I told you, she didn't even like sex that much. That was part of the problem. Anyway, I don't want to get into it now. Just call me back in about a half hour and invite me out to play racquetball or something. It'll give me an excuse to get away from them for a while."

"Okay."

Steve did just that and met Jason at the gym. They were both members, had both joined at approximately the same time, but Steve seldom went there—he hardly ever had the time—and it was only when something like this came up that he took advantage of his membership. He didn't actually know how to play racquetball, so he and Jason just walked side by side on adjacent treadmills, talking. Jason asked about his dad, and Steve replied simply that he was doing as well as possible under the circumstances. He didn't bring up anything about his trip.

"Fathers and sons," Jason said in stentorian tones. He shook his head slowly, his voice at once utterly serious and completely insincere. "Fathers and sons."

"Hank Kingsley," Steve said, laughing, catching the reference.

His friend grinned, nodded. "Tell me the truth," he said, adjusting the speed of his treadmill. "Before all this happened with your dad, were you two close? Now you probably have to see him every day, but how often did you see him before the stroke?"

"Not much," Steve admitted. "Holidays mostly."

"I can't remember the last time I saw my dad. My *real* dad. I talk to him on the phone sometimes, but I have no idea where to reach him. He moves around a lot. And he only calls when he's in trouble, when he needs money or when there's some sort of health crisis. Not that he really *is* in trouble or really *does* need money or really *has* a health problem. It's just that he always calls about some catastrophe because he doesn't know how to talk to me otherwise. We can't just have an ordinary conversation, like normal people. He needs a reason to call me, an important reason, and he'll concoct some outlandish scenario for us to talk about—and then I won't hear from him for six months."

"Wow."

"Unlike my mom and stepdad, who are *too* much in my life." Jason sighed. "Deep down, I suppose my dad's a good guy, but the two of us just don't connect with each other. Never have."

Steve had no idea what sort of man his father was "deep down."

"The funny thing is," Jason said, "we still crave our dads' approval. No matter how big a jerk they are or how badly they've screwed us up, we still want them to be proud of us, don't we?"

Steve nodded slowly. "Yes," he said, and it was true. His father was a *murderer*, and deep down Steve still longed for his approbation, though he knew that, due to his old man's condition, that was never going to happen.

"Will says the only way to become an adult is to break off all contact with parents as soon as you turn eighteen."

"Will," Steve said, "is an asshole."

Jason laughed. "You're right," he agreed. "He is."

His legs were getting tired, so Steve stopped the treadmill and got off. He hadn't realized until now how badly out of shape he was. He limped over to the bench and grabbed a towel to wipe off his sweat. He really should work out more often, he decided.

"Want to swim a few laps?" Jason asked.

Steve shook his head. He told Jason he was tired, was going to take a quick shower and bail, and his friend clapped him on the back and said that he'd done his good deed for the day. "I guess I'll hang out here for a few hours, maybe get something to eat afterward, then go home after those two are asleep. Hopefully." He grinned. "Don't worry. Tomorrow it's Will's turn to bail me out. You've gone above and beyond, bud. Don't think I don't appreciate it."

Steve grabbed dinner for himself at McDonald's and took it home to eat in front of the television. He turned the channel to CNN, and winced when a commercial came on for senior health care. The screen showed a smiling, happy Alzheimer's patient. He looked away. Last night at this time, he had been getting back to Albuquerque after his sojourn to Copper City. The death of his father's first wife had been on his mind then just as it was on his mind now.

Jessica and Hazel had both shown him pictures from the wedding, photos of his father and Ruth looking young and happy and in love, and he kept trying to imagine what Ruth had looked like after his father had pushed her off the building. Where had she hit the ground? The top of the head? The back of the head? The face?

Everything he imagined was horrific.

Steve's thoughts went back to his father. What was he going to do about what he knew? This was an ethical question, one of those *Sophie's Choice* things, the kind so ably exploited by board game makers and reality-TV producers. Should he go to the police? There was no proof. He had nothing really, only a theory based on the ramblings of a stroke victim with dementia. And what purpose could it serve at this late date? His father wasn't competent to stand trial, and probably wouldn't understand whatever punishment was meted out.

Did he even want his father punished?

No.

If his old man had *not* had a stroke, did *not* suffer from dementia and was *not* in the hospital, Steve still didn't think he could turn him in.

Why, though?

He didn't know.

Steve dreamed that night of his father, looking not as he did now, not as he had in those wedding photos, but like some unholy merger of the two, half young, half old, with a deranged smile on his face, standing at the top of the Copper City bank building, gleefully pushing off women who were lining up next to him: Ruth, Jessica, Hazel, his mother, Sherry. . . .

His mother called him at work the next day—this was getting to be a habit—and asked if he could take her over to the hospital in the afternoon. She thought they should both see his father. Steve said okay, but on the way there, driving down the Garden Grove Freeway after picking her up, he had a change of heart. Well, not a change, really. He simply realized that he was still not ready to face his father.

Fifteen minutes later, they reached the VA hospital. Without saying anything, he pulled up in front of the entrance and left the car idling. His mother looked at him in surprise. "You're not coming in?"

He shook his head. "I don't feel well," he lied. "I think I caught something on the plane. All that recirculated air. I'm just going to wait in the parking lot for you. I don't want to contaminate Dad. His immune system's probably down. . . ."

"I don't want to go in there by myself," she said.

"My immune system's down too. And who knows what kind of germs are floating around? They say hospitals are the easiest place to get sick, all those diseases and everything."

She looked at him, lips tight. "I'm not going in there by myself."

He thought about Copper City, then about his father lying helpless and strapped down in the bed—

I killed her

—and realized that he couldn't do it. Not today. Not yet. He shook his head. "No, Mom."

"He tried to kill me. I can't face him alone."

"I don't feel well," Steve repeated. "And I can't afford to get sick."

"Take me home, then."

"Mom . . ."

"Take me home."

He put the car into gear. "Fine, then. We'll go home."

Six

Like his friend Will, Steve's parents had never thought much of his job. His father, in particular, had not been able to see any worth in writing for a living, and fiction was even farther removed from his dad's approved list of vocations and avocations than nonfiction. *Unlike* Will, his parents did not think he was slumming in his occupation or wasting his time. This, they thought, was the only thing he was good for, the only thing he could do.

So he didn't tell his mother that he'd sold a short story to a magazine. It was a small publication anyway—she'd never heard of it; *no one* had ever heard of it—and she wouldn't be impressed. His father, at this point, wouldn't even understand.

But Sherry was ecstatic that his fiction was going to be published. He had called her right after opening the mail and reading the acceptance letter, and though he'd cringed on the other end of the phone as he told her, embarrassed, she was hugely impressed. They'd gone out that night to celebrate, eating at an expensive restaurant in Newport Beach and having some mildly kinky sex in her apartment afterward, a tradition he hoped to continue when the magazine actually came out.

The story itself was nearly two years old, but he could

have written it yesterday. Rereading it, Steve wondered why he had written about New Mexico. That seemed odd in light of recent events. Yes, his parents had met and married there, but they'd moved away before he was born, and the few scant memories he had were from those two ill-conceived trips to see Aunt Marion when he was young. The Land of Enchantment was as foreign to him as the Garden State, and since most of his short stories took place in Southern California, it was strange that this one had been set there.

A Mexican prostitute was mentioned in the story as well, and while that had to be a coincidence, just thinking about it sent gooseflesh rippling down his arms.

He was proud of his story, but the circumstances surrounding it definitely made him uneasy.

Sunday dawned gloomy and cold. He'd spent all week avoiding the VA hospital, but he had finally decided that he should visit his father again. The gloom had turned to drizzle by the time he reached Long Beach, and he parked as close as he could, then ran through the parking lot to the entrance. He'd brought neither jacket nor umbrella, and his hair and shoulders were damp as he dashed between the slowly sliding doors into the lobby.

He stopped, shook out his hair, and looked toward the bank of elevators. The lobby was warm, but that didn't decrease the chill inside him. He was nervous about seeing his father again. No, not just nervous. *Scared*. Since the trip to Copper City, Steve had built up the old man in his mind as some kind of monster. He was, of course—although not in the horror-show way his imagination was conjuring up now. But emotion overruled reason every time, and he couldn't help dreading the upcoming meeting and wishing he'd brought along Sherry or his mother for moral support.

He went over to the elevators, took one up to the

second floor, and when the doors opened walked down the long corridor, past the darkened barracks with multiple beds, past the patients in wheelchairs, past the rooms of screaming men.

"I need my meds!"

He slowed his pace as he approached room 242.

Steve took a deep breath, licking his dry lips. He did not know the man in there. He thought he had, but the trip to New Mexico had shown him that he didn't.

Summoning his courage, he walked inside.

The first thing he noticed was that there was someone in the second bed now, another man who was strapped down and didn't appear to have any arms. He was young, probably Steve's age, and he lay there moaning, moving his head rhythmically back and forth, eyes shut tight. His television was on and loud—some sort of travel show—and for that Steve was grateful. It helped mask the moans.

He pulled the curtain between the two sections of room, wondering why no one had done so earlier. He was going to have to talk to the nurses or orderlies about that. He had no idea whether his father was even aware of the other patient, but he wanted that barrier in place.

The fear had left him the second he walked into the familiar hospital room and saw that his dad was not a terrifying fiend but merely a fading shell of the man he had been. Now his father stared at him blankly, and Steve wasn't quite sure what to do. Sometimes when he visited he just sat silently next to his dad. Other times he talked to him as a parent would an infant, holding one-sided conversations. Every once in a while, when he suspected the dementia had temporarily receded and thought he detected a glimmer of awareness, he attempted to engage his father in conversation. This time, though, the old man looked completely out of it,

and while Steve could sit down on the chair next to the
bed, he didn't feel entirely comfortable doing so.

His dad looked at him. "I suitcase the five and clown
you."

He nodded at the old man as though he understood.

"I *suitcase* the five!" his father said with more emphasis.

Steve decided to be honest. "I'm sorry, but I don't
know what you mean."

"*Suitcase!*" his dad yelled, frustrated. "*Suitcase!*"
There were tears in his eyes, and he screamed the word
again. "*Suitcase!*"

Steve stepped back. His father shouldn't be getting
this agitated. The medication was supposed to control
these sorts of outbursts. Moving next to the door, he
poked his head out, but saw no staff members anywhere near.

"*Suitcase!*" his father screamed.

"I'm going to get the doctor," Steve said. "I'll be
right back."

But he couldn't find Dr. Curtis, couldn't find *any*
doctor. He ran into an orderly at the nurses' station,
but the clearly overwhelmed young man told him in
a frazzled voice that the only doctor on duty this hour
was busy treating a newly arrived patient, and all of
the other nurses and orderlies were dealing with an
emergency involving two patients in another part of
the ward. He'd send someone over as soon as it was
feasible.

"My father needs someone *now*," Steve said.

"I'm sorry," the orderly told him. "There's no one
we can spare."

Steve walked back down the corridor toward his
father's room, angry—not at the orderly but at the system in general. They needed more staff at this hospi-

tal. Even after unending VA scandals, the politicians still hadn't allotted enough resources to care for all of the admitted patients. So much for that "support the troops" bullshit.

He slowed as he neared room 242. His father's nonsensical sentence kept repeating in his brain: *I suitcase the five and clown you. Clown you.* It made him think of the dream he'd had where the dirty clown had been crawling through the backyard toward the body of a woman he had murdered.

His dad was smiling as Steve walked into the hospital room, watching the door and grinning as though he'd been expecting his return and waiting for it. Chilled, Steve looked away, not wanting to see that face. The blankness was gone, replaced by what looked like not only comprehension but craftiness, and the collusion between those eyes and that smile sent shivers down his spine.

His father spoke, and it was in a voice Steve didn't want to hear, the dry, raspy voice that had been haunting him for well over a week.

"I killed them."

It was suddenly hard to breathe. *Them?* Steve forced himself to look at his father, who was still grinning.

"The first one in the room where she plied her trade."

Plied her trade?

Prostitutes, Steve thought instantly. His dad had killed prostitutes.

That whore in Copper City hadn't been deported back to Mexico.

His father had killed her.

He waited for the old man to continue, but as quickly as cognizance had come, it was gone. That was it. The show was over. The smile faded from his father's lips, and his eyes closed as he sank into sleep.

Them.

It couldn't be true.

No. That wasn't correct. He didn't *want* it to be true.

He thought back. They'd moved several times when he was a child, Steve recalled. He had never been quite sure why. His parents were not the type to confide in their son, to explain the family's financial situation, and he had no idea whether his parents had wanted to move because his father had gotten a better job offer or because he'd been fired from the job he had . . .

. . . or because he'd killed a prostitute and didn't want to hang around and get caught.

Them.

If he searched through old police records, would he discover that hookers had been killed in the same cities that they'd lived in at the same time that they'd lived there? How many could there be? Salt Lake City, Flagstaff, Tempe, Tucson, San Diego. Even allowing for only one per city, that meant five more deaths.

His father was not just a killer.

He was a serial killer.

No, Steve thought.

Yes.

He stared down at his father's sleeping form. What should he do? Telling the police was no longer an option. The killing of an ex-wife forty-some years ago could be understood as a crime of passion, but a series of murders was an entirely different story and would take down not only his father, but his mother and himself. These killings had occurred on their watch and, fair or not, the media and the public would convict them of complicity. Not outright, perhaps, not to their faces, but the two of them had been there when the murders happened and they weren't victims. The stain from his father's crimes would be on them.

He could not live a normal existence as the recognized son of a serial killer.

His dad stirred, muttering something unintelligible. Steve looked at that ravaged face, at once familiar and unfamiliar. Whatever had happened, his father had kept it to himself all these years and at the same time had managed to build up a respectable life. Steve needed to keep the secret now too. He couldn't tell anyone. Not even his mother. This was something he had to take to his grave. In fact, the best course of action would be to forget everything he had heard, learned or suspected, just put it out of his mind and pretend the previous week hadn't occurred.

But that was not going to happen.

His father stirred again, unable to turn over because of the straps. His muscles strained, then relaxed. What was he going to say when he awoke? "I suitcase the five" or "I killed them"? It was impossible to predict, and Steve thought that he needed to find some way to shut his dad up, to keep him from blurting out confessions to anyone else.

Of course, no one would believe anything the old man said, which was one of the advantages of being diagnosed with dementia. That might buy Steve some time, allow him to talk to the doctor about upping some of the medications or at least come up with some sort of plausible explanation should anyone start to believe his father's revelations.

He peeked out the door again to see if any doctors or nurses were on their way, but the corridor was empty. There was no one in sight, not even the usual wheelchair traffic, although from one of the nearby rooms came a high-pitched yelping that sounded like that of a dog in pain.

The death of a prostitute was not as bad as the death of a regular woman, he rationalized. A lot of them were thieves and junkies. Some of them were murderers. That woman Charlize Theron had played in *Monster* really had been a monster—and she was based on a real person. So perhaps he shouldn't be so quick to judge.

He knew that he was making excuses—but this was his father. Joseph Nye might have been a demanding, intolerant, insensitive asshole, but he was still Steve's dad, and as strained as that tie might be, it was still there.

What if they *hadn't* all been prostitutes?

Better not to go there, Steve told himself.

There were voices in the hall, and suddenly he saw nurses and orderlies, doctors and interns. Whatever emergencies there had been were apparently resolved, and moments later a young doctor Steve did not recognize knocked on the metal doorframe and stepped into the room. "What seems to be the problem here?"

Steve described the overreaction to his inability to understand the meaning of "suitcase," and said that the medications his father was being administered were supposed to prevent this sort of thing from happening.

The doctor looked at the chart at the head of the bed. "These are pretty high dosages, so I'm surprised such a thing occurred. Or *could* occur. He's pretty heavily sedated." Pulling a small penlight out of his pocket, the doctor opened his dad's eyelids and checked the pupils. "He's out now."

Steve suddenly felt defensive. "You think I'm lying?"

"No. Of course not. Mr. Nye, I'm only saying that the medication he was given this morning at"—he checked the chart again—"six seems to have kicked in. I'll mention this to Dr. Curtis, however, and the two of you can perhaps agree on some adjustments to the schedule." His eyes met Steve's. "I assume Dr. Curtis has discussed with you the severity of your father's condition?"

Steve nodded.

"And you realize that at this point we can only manage his condition, not cure it."

He sighed tiredly. "I know."

"Very well, then. Is there anything else you need? Because I have a lot of patients waiting to see me."

Steve waved him away and sat down heavily in the chair next to the bed.

I killed them.

He looked over at his father's face, placid in its medicated repose. What was he going to tell his mother when she asked how the visit went? Or Sherry?

He thought for a moment.

Nothing, he decided. Nothing at all.

Seven

He put the poison into the glass carefully, along with the milk: one drop, one pour, one drop, one pour. The milk had been heating on the stove and was warm but not hot, a condition the pharmacology book said would not affect the efficacy of the toxin. When the glass was full nearly to the brim, he placed it on a tray. He'd never known anyone other than babies and grandmothers who liked warm milk, but she did, and this had become sort of a ritual with them.

She was already upstairs, in bed. He had had her earlier, and afterward she'd claimed to be tired, but the sex had been quick, and he knew that it was not he who had tired her out. The thought of that enraged him, as it always did, but he'd never let on before, and he didn't this time either. The knowledge stayed with him, though, and he imagined her in different positions with different men, energetic and not tired, enjoying herself far more than she did with him. He'd known she was a whore when he met her—that was how he met her—but he hadn't expected to fall so hard for her and hadn't expected it to matter.

He heard her asking for him from the bedroom, calling out his name in her thick, sexy accent. He liked that accent. He was going to miss it. She called out to him again, but he did not respond, just kept walking slowly up the stairs, balancing the tray before him. He stared at the milk in the glass. He didn't have to go through with this. He could put a stop to it *right now. He could go back down, dump the contents of the glass in the sink and heat up some more milk for her, some fresh milk, undiluted.*

But he continued walking up the stairs.

At the top, he turned to the right and went into the bedroom. She was lying down, eyes nearly closed, and he was not sure she even wanted a drink anymore. But he made her sit up against the headboard and, smiling kindly, handed her the glass of warm milk. She pulled up the right strap of her flimsy nightgown and smiled back at him. "You're so good to me," she said.

"Drink it," he told her. "Drink it up. It's good for you. It's what you need."

Eight

There was a message on his answering machine when he got home from work on Friday, and, listening to it, Steve was thankful that Sherry hadn't invited herself over tonight to make dinner. Since Christmas, she'd been hinting around about moving in together, but his little freakout when she'd touched his mail seemed to have made her wary of coming over unannounced, despite his apologies, and lately she'd been much more cautious about overstepping boundaries. For that he was glad.

He'd met his friends at the bar after work, pretending all was normal, but it had been a tough week, and it was getting harder and harder for him to act as though nothing were wrong. Will had been an asshole as usual, making fun of everyone and everything, and somewhere around his second beer, Steve had realized that he didn't really like his friend very much. Looking around at his companions, he wasn't sure he liked Dennis any better, and he thought that if he'd met them now instead of back in college, he probably wouldn't hang out with either of them.

Although he'd still be friends with Jason.

He felt like a fraud, keeping the secret of his father from them, acting as though everything were the same as it had always been despite the fact that his entire universe had been turned inside out, and he wondered how the old man had done it all those years, pretending to coworkers, friends and family that he was just an ordinary middle-class guy—and not a cold-blooded murderer.

Steve was slightly buzzed when he arrived home, but he was dead sober by the time he finished listening to the phone message.

He didn't recognize the voice on the answering machine at first, but the caller identified himself almost immediately. "Hello? Is this Steve? Steve, uh . . . Nye? This is Lyman. Lyman Fischer? I met you at Jessica Haster's potluck?" There was a long pause. "I been thinkin' about what you said about your dad and, uh, Ruth. You might be onto somethin' there. About your dad bein' differnt after he came back, I mean. Maybe we should talk about it." There was another long pause. "Yeah. I think we should talk."

Steve's breath caught in his throat.

He knew.

No. How could he? It was impossible. Still, Steve was possessed by the uneasy feeling that the old man was suspicious, that he'd had time to mull things over and had realized how odd it was that Joseph Nye's son had flown all the way out from California just to attend a potluck and ask questions about his father's first wife's death.

Steve listened to the whole message, listened to it again, then got out a pen and a promotional notepad that some real estate agent had left on his doorstep, and wrote down Lyman's number. He stared at it for a few moments, thinking, but it was getting late—it was an hour later in New Mexico—and if he wanted to catch the old man tonight, he should probably call now.

He dialed the number, waited two rings, three, four, and then Lyman Fischer picked up with a croaking, "Hello?"

"Hello," Steve said. "This is—"

"I know who you are."

"Okay," Steve said carefully.

"Are you sure you want to do this over the phone?"

He *did* know.

"Why not?" Steve said, feigning casualness.

There was a pause. "I been thinkin' about what you said. At Jessica's."

"Yeah?"

"Yeah." He sighed. "Joe—your dad—was a good guy. A fun guy. What kids today would call a 'party animal,' I guess. You asked me if he was different when he come out of the service. I said no, but I thought about it a bit, and now I have to say yes. I mean, after he come back, we did the same things we always did, but the joy weren't there. He was more . . . serious. Underneath. And mean." There was another pause, and Steve could hear the rasp of Lyman's breathing. "He'd *killed* people over there."

This was the same train of thought Steve had taken, and it was not a road he wanted Lyman—or anyone else, for that matter—to go down.

"Okay," Steve said a little too heartily. "Thanks for calling and letting me know."

"Don't you want to hear—"

"No," he said, and hung up the phone. His hand was trembling. He stood there for a moment. Maybe he should have waited to hear what else the old man had to say, but what could it be? Blackmail was the first idea that came to him, and that sounded right. He hadn't seen where Lyman lived, but Copper City was a poor town, and he had no doubt that the man could use some extra money. The idea filled him with fear, and he imagined a series of endlessly escalating payments, imagined himself living in constant dread of another phone call from Lyman Fischer demanding more money. His hands were still trembling, and he grabbed his right hand with his left, trying to keep both from shaking, the way he had as a child when his muscles started quivering after trying to perform some physical feat that his body was not strong enough to handle.

Steve stared at the phone. What should he do? Pay? No. He doubted that anything could be proven, and he certainly didn't care about gossip that might spread around Copper City. On the other hand, he wouldn't put it past Lyman to look up his parents' phone number and call. And he didn't want his mother to know anything about this—even the *hint* of such a scandal would traumatize her.

What would his father say if he were well and back to normal? What would he want Steve to do? Beg? Bully? Cajole? Let the whole thing slide?

Kill him?

Steve's breath caught in his throat. That was crazy thinking. What he needed to do was talk to the old man, reason with him. They were both adults; they both knew the way of the world, and if Steve explained his father's condition, told Lyman that his old friend had had a stroke and was suffering from dementia and would probably be dead sometime in the not too distant future, a lot of ugliness could be avoided.

He picked up the phone, was about to call Lyman back, but suddenly thought that it would be a lot more effective if he talked to the old man in person. His head was still a little light from the beer, but he wasn't tired and was thinking clearly. He could do this. He glanced over at the clock on the DVD player atop the television. It was almost eight. If he took a red-eye tonight, he could be in Copper City by morning and back here by early afternoon. No one would even notice he was gone.

He went online, and sure enough there was a plane to Houston that stopped off at Albuquerque leaving from nearby John Wayne Airport at eleven. He could catch that flight and book a return trip that left New Mexico at noon tomorrow and arrived in Orange County just after one, Pacific time. The daytime flight cost nearly twice as much, but it was worth it not to have to sit around the Albuquerque airport for an extra eight hours.

He booked the flights, printed out the tickets, arranged for an after-hours car rental, and tried to think whether he needed to take anything on the trip with him. Clothes? No. Toiletries? No. He couldn't come up with anything, although he decided to bring his checkbook, just in case. If the old man wanted money and the attempts to dissuade him didn't work, maybe they could come to some sort of agreement—as long as everything was in writing.

He looked up Lyman Fischer in an online phonebook and wrote down the address. He wasn't going to make the same mistake as last time and wait until he arrived before trying to find the location, so he printed out a map of Copper City, New Mexico, with Lyman's house starred.

The airport was less than ten minutes away and he still had over two hours to kill, so Steve turned on the television and started flipping channels, looking for something to distract him. But there was nothing good on, and he ended up going back to the computer, using tool packages from work to try to find more background information about Lyman Fischer.

The man was a cipher. His current life intersected

with cyberspace not at all, and whatever high school records existed, they had not been recorded online.

On the plane, he fell asleep, though he did not know for how long. Ten minutes? Fifteen? A half hour? He dreamed of his father. It was an incident that had actually happened. Steve had been a freshman in high school, and his project had come in first place in the school science fair. He'd made a primitive solar oven out of a box and a pane of glass and some tinfoil, and while that might not have been as complicated or elaborate as some of the other creations, he'd done a tremendous amount of research, and his presentation more than made up for any possible shortcomings. Steve had never won anything before in his life, and he came home excited with the news. His project was going to be on display in the public library for a week, he told his parents, along with projects from all of the other schools in the district, and at the end of the week there was going to be an awards ceremony where ribbons would be given out. But his father had merely shrugged and turned away, and his mother's awkward attempts at praise had not been enough to counterbalance the hurt and disappointment he felt. In the dream, the ending was different. His father congratulated him and gave him a hug, told his son he was proud of him, and when Steve awoke there were tears leaking out from beneath his eyelids onto his cheeks. He wiped them off, embarrassed and confused, thankful that it was night outside and the lights in the cabin were low.

They landed in Albuquerque without incident less than twenty minutes later, and walking through the terminal he felt almost as though he were coming home. He had been here only once before, but that had been a mere two weeks ago, and everything around him seemed intimately familiar, from the closed McDonald's stand to the Hertz rental kiosk to the gray-uniformed black man buffing the floor near the restrooms. Strange, he thought, how an acquaintanceship with physical surroundings gave a person a sense of belonging. But there was something comforting in that, and it gave him confidence as he made his way to the front of the terminal.

The woman at the airplane's ticket desk had the key and rental agreement for his car, and Steve signed the paperwork and walked outside, where he found his vehicle—a blue Toyota Camry—at the far end of an open lot. The Camry was equipped with a GPS system, and though he had a vague idea of how to get to the eastbound highway that led to Copper City, he programmed the system to make sure and followed the on-screen instructions through the maze of streets near the airport.

There were only two hours until dawn, and he thought he could sense already a slight lightening of the sky in the east. It was probably just his imagination, or an effect caused by the overbrightness of the low full moon, but it caused him to speed up, and ten minutes later he was out of Albuquerque and into open country, the lights of the city nothing more than a faint glow from behind the series of low, rounded rises behind him.

He drove. Through the desert, through the dying night. Hands tight on the wheel, clenched as though they were holding on to a rope suspended over a bottomless pit. There was not a thought in his head. He was like a driving machine, intent only on reaching his destination, and he kept his attention focused only on the road.

It was nearly seven by the time he approached Copper City. Seeing a sign for a nearby lake, he suddenly remembered that he and Sherry were supposed to go to Laguna Beach today for an antiques flea market, and he stopped on the outskirts of town, pulling to the side of the road next to an abandoned diner and taking out his cell phone to call her. It was six rings before she finally picked up—she liked to sleep late on the weekends—and when she answered with a tired, "Hello," he summoned up a fake cough and made his voice sound as low and ragged as possible. "It's me," he said. "I'm sick."

"Oh, no!"

"I don't think I'll be able to make it today."

"What's wrong?" she asked, concerned.

"Food poisoning, I think. I had some of those happy-hour tacos last night with Jason, Dennis and Will. There might've been something wrong with them."

"Do you want me to come over and—"

"No!" he said quickly. He sounded too healthy, so he coughed again. "No," he said, lowering his voice. "I feel *really* bad. I'm just going to stay in bed and sleep it off."

"Why are you on your cell phone?" she asked.

Was she suspicious?

"The phone next to the bed doesn't have a dial tone," he lied, "and I didn't feel well enough to go out into the other room to see if that one works." He started making gagging sounds.

"Are you all right?"

"I think I'm going to throw up again. I'll call you tonight."

"Take care of yourself," she said worriedly.

"I will," he promised. "I gotta go."

He clicked off and took a deep breath, praying that she'd listen to him and wouldn't try to come over to visit, thinking he'd better come up with a good excuse in case she did. He waited a moment, then started the car, pulling back onto the highway.

Lyman's house was little more than a shack. If it ever *had* been painted, the color had long since been beaten off the decaying boards by years of harsh weather. There was a folded newspaper at the edge of the wild thigh-high grass that constituted the front yard, and he picked it up and carried it with him to the front stoop. He looked for a doorbell but couldn't find one, and ended up knocking on the metal frame of the rusted screen.

Lyman was at the door seconds later. He was dressed in Levi's and a work shirt, and had obviously been up for some time. "Yeah?" he said gruffly, then started when he saw who it was.

"You said you wanted to speak with me?" Steve said.

The old man seemed unsure at first how to react; then he opened the door, took the newspaper from Steve's hand and said, "Come in."

Life had not gone well for Lyman Fischer. He and Steve's father had set out from the same starting point, but their fortunes had forked early on, and now their lives had nothing at all in common. In contrast to his parents' immaculately maintained home with its tasteful if slightly outdated furnishings, Lyman's place was a charmless pigsty, with a recycling bag full of beer cans next to the door and piles of newspapers atop every available inch of furniture. Through the open doorway into the kitchen, Steve could see an old radio that had been taken apart on the breakfast table. He would not have expected such a level of squalor from the man he had met at Jessica Haster's potluck, and it went a long way toward explaining why he might be after money.

Steve stood just inside the door, determined not to be the one to break the ice. He wanted Lyman to spell out what he wanted without the help of any cues Steve might inadvertently give him.

The old man held on to the newspaper. "Why're you here?" he asked finally.

"You said you wanted to talk."

"Talk. Not visit. I dint invite you over."

"Well, I'm here now."

"You're just like your dad," Lyman said, and though the words were spoken derisively and meant as criticism, Steve didn't take them that way. No one had ever compared him to his father before—certainly not either of his parents—and he actually felt a little proud that this old fuck saw a resemblance.

"How am I like my dad?" he said. "Am I *mean*?"

He saw a flash of fear in the old man's eyes then, a recognition that he wasn't in control of the situation. Steve felt emboldened. He took a step forward. "I don't appreciate spending my night flying halfway across country and driving out to the middle of nowhere because you're trying to blackmail me."

"I don't know what you're talking about."

"Really? Is that why you called to tell me that you think my dad might have *killed* someone?"

"That's not what I meant," Lyman assured him.

In two steps, Steve was upon the old man. He whipped his right arm around that wrinkled neck and got him in a headlock, filled with a rage so deep and wild that his pulse was pounding in his ears, his vision blurred. He'd teach the greedy bastard to try to hold him up for money. Lyman let out a single-syllable squawk, and then he was gasping for air, his bony hands trying in vain to pry off Steve's arm.

Steve squeezed. Although he'd brought along the checkbook, this was what had been in the back of his mind all along. Deep down, he had known it would happen, had known he would do this. Why else had he arrived here so early in the morning if it wasn't to make sure that he would not be spotted, could not be identified?

Dry, wrinkly skin pressed against his arm and the crook of his elbow, and beneath the floppy wattles he felt ridges of cartilage. At that second, he literally held the old man's life in his hands. Or arms.

He didn't have to go through with this, he told himself. He could simply let go and walk away.

But it had already gone too far. If he quit now, Lyman would press charges, he would end up in jail, and his whole life would be ruined. Not to mention the fact that his father's deeds would be brought to light and the entire world would know what had happened all those years ago.

It came to him then—the reason his father had killed his first wife. She had been pregnant with another man's baby. Lyman's baby. While his father had been in the service, his friend had moved in on his wife and she had succumbed. The two of them had dated in high school. Maybe they'd never stopped seeing each other. Maybe even through the blissful early days of the marriage she had been fucking her old boyfriend behind his father's back.

Steve was doing this not just for himself but for his dad.

He squeezed.

Lyman kicked against him, lashed out wildly. A hand slapped his forehead, and Steve doubled the pressure, constricting the old man's airway. A foot connected with his shin, but the foot was shoeless and the pain was minimal. In the last few seconds, the dying man grew more desperate, throwing the weight of his body backward, forward, to the left, to the right, trying to break the hold, trying to pull Steve down to the ground. But nothing worked, and with one final spasmodic jerk, Lyman stopped struggling, his hands falling limply to the sides. Steve let go, and the body slumped to the floor. For it was a body now, not a man. Whatever it was that had made Lyman Fischer Lyman Fischer was gone, and all that was left was this inert form that would soon start to rot.

Steve was breathing heavily: a combination of panic, exertion and fear. Backing away from the body, he looked frantically around, trying to determine what in the room he had touched. *Nothing*, he thought. He had rapped on the edge of the screen with his knuckles, but Lyman had actually opened the door, and since he had done nothing but stand there and talk, the only prints of his fingers were on . . .

The newspaper.

Close call. He picked up the newspaper from where Lyman had dropped it on the floor, intending to take it with him and toss it in a trash can at the airport before getting on the plane.

Walking to the door, he peeked out, saw no one on the sidewalk, no one on the street. He pulled his hand inside his sleeve, opening the door that way, touching the handle with the cloth rather than his fingers.

Striding quickly to the car, he got in and drove away.

He threw up in the desert about twenty miles out of town, leaping out of the car just in time and puking into the gravel on the side of the road. He had seen scenes in movies in which this happened, and he had never really understood them. Why would someone vomit after killing a person? But he knew the answer now. It was the body reacting against doing something it had been taught never to do. He felt another onrush of nausea, leaned over and puked again.

There was no one around to see him, and Steve

wiped his mouth with his hand, wiped his hand on his pants, then got back in the car and drove west toward Albuquerque.

It was raining in California when he returned. A cold off-season storm had settled over the region, and, landing in Orange County, the plane descended through what seemed like miles of cloud before emerging in a downpour. Since the terminal connected directly with the enclosed parking structure, he was able to reach his car without venturing out in the weather, and by the time he pulled onto MacArthur Boulevard, the rain had subsided to a drizzle. Thank God for that. He turned onto the 405 freeway, heading toward Long Beach. Aside from that short snooze on the plane on the way over, he had not slept for over thirty hours, and he needed to go home and go to bed. It probably wasn't safe for him to be on the road. But he felt wide-awake and wired, and before he turned in, he wanted to visit his father.

A red Corvette with tinted windows sped by on the left, splashing water onto the driver's side of the windshield, and for those few seconds that it took the wiper to make its return arc across the glass, Steve was blind, seeing the freeway before him as a blurry world of dark shapes and crimson lights. If he'd been driving closer to the Explorer in front, he might have hit the vehicle and gotten into an accident. But the wiper swished over the window, the glass was cleared, he could see again, and he continued on.

Halfway through Fountain Valley, traffic started to slow, and while on a railroad overpass, he saw the bright red of braking taillights for miles ahead, winding through the commercial/industrial section of the city. The slow lane seemed to be moving the fastest, so when he could, he switched over until he was eventually all the way to the right. This start-and-stop traffic continued on for the better part of an hour, and the freeway narrowed to two lanes as they reached the source of the slowdown: an accident in the far left lane between a motorcycle, a car and a pickup truck. The car, Steve noted with some satisfaction, was the red Corvette that had sped past him earlier, and while it was difficult to tell the extent of the damage in the dark, in the rain, with the distorted reflections of police lights on puddles, it looked to him as though the Corvette had gotten the worst of it.

At that he smiled. Sherry invariably expressed worry, concern and sympathy as they drove past auto accidents, but Steve was generally pretty happy whenever he slowed down to look at the wreckage. More often than not, the vehicles involved were ones that had passed him earlier, driving recklessly, heedless of the conditions, and he felt no small degree of pleasure when he came upon the site of their downfall.

If anyone in that accident had been injured or killed, he hoped it was the driver of the red Corvette.

The freeway opened up after that. Steve continued on to Long Beach, exiting at the off-ramp that led to the VA hospital. He had no umbrella and was forced to park far away, so he was drenched by the time he dashed into the building's front entrance. He wasn't sure he would be allowed into the hospital like this, but no one stopped him and he took the elevator to the second floor.

His father looked worse than he had on Thursday, if that was possible. His skin was sallow, his face gaunt, and he had not been shaved. The rough white stubble on his chin made him look not only much older than he actually was but dumber and less successful, like some alternate-world version of himself. Underneath closed lids, his eyes moved spasmodically, his hands twitching like the paws of a dreaming dog. There was a time, not so long ago, when Steve would have been happy to see his dad like this. Standing over this broken version of his father would have been a dream come true, and he could admit now what he had never admitted before: He had hated the man. But something had happened. Maybe his true feelings had emerged or maybe he had evolved, but whatever the reason, he now felt sorry for his dad.

He wished his father were awake, alert and functioning on all cylinders, so he would know and understand what his son had done for him.

He sat down in the chair and waited by the bedside, hoping his father would awaken but not wanting to disturb him. The air in the room felt warm and stuffy, too stuffy, and after several moments had passed, Steve's eyes began to close. Though he tried with all his might to keep them open, his lids felt heavy as the lack of sleep finally caught up with him. He had to go home and get some rest, and he was about to reach over and shake his father's arm to wake him up when, with a sharp, startled yelp, the old man jerked, eyes flipping open, his body pushing against the straps constraining him.

"Dad?" Steve said.

His father settled down, eyes focusing. He said nothing, but even this level of contact could mean that he was in one of his lucid periods, and Steve checked to make sure the man in the next bed was out, looked around to make sure no one else was nearby, then quickly explained how he had gone to Copper City and met Jessica and Hazel and Lyman, how Lyman had figured things out and was going to try to blackmail him, and how the only way to put a stop to it was to put a stop to Lyman.

He paused, waited for a response, received none.

"So I did it, Dad," he said wearily. "I took care of it."

The old man smiled up at him with a complete lack of comprehension. "Futon," he said. "Gold bouillon beef."

Nine

The Hand of God

She fell in love with his hands.

He was a welder at the plant, and before she even saw his face, she saw his hands. They were strong and brown, the fingers blunt but graceful, and they manipulated the plates of metal in front of him like an artist molding clay. There was something sensual about the way they moved, the way they brought continual freshness to what should have been rote work. He was covered very nearly from head to toe, a welder's mask concealing his face, heavy boots on his feet, blue standard-issue coveralls hiding everything else, but for some reason there were no gloves on his hands, nothing protecting his fingers and palms at all, and she was grateful for that, because it was his hands that made her stop.

She was late for a meeting already, but she paused between the yellow safety lines of the walkway to watch him. Her gaze was so focused, she was paying such rapt attention to the movements of his fingers, that it was only when they stopped working for a moment that she noticed he was looking at her.

She reddened, feeling the flushed heat in her face, and he pressed a button on the panel next to his workstation and flipped up his mask. She saw only the small central portion of his face—eyes, nose, mouth, no forehead, cheeks or chin—and it looked kind, intelligent. It fit his hands.

"Can I help you?" he asked.

She shook her head, shifted the clipboard and reports in her hand, and continued on her way.

But, knowing his station on the floor, she looked up his name and position on the computer—Jim McMillan, senior welder—and cross-referenced his hours, arranging to "accidentally" meet him in the lunchroom at the beginning of his noon break.

He believed even to this day that their meeting had been accidental. She'd never told him how she'd seen him and stalked him and claimed him for her own before he was even aware of her existence. But by the end of his lunch hour, she had manipulated him into asking her out for dinner.

And she had given herself to him that night because she'd known he was the one.

She'd had other beaux before, of course. Rough, fumbling teenagers who attempted to feel her up in the backseats of their fathers' cars. And it was that stage of the relationship that she'd always enjoyed the most: when their hands would touch her breasts or unbutton her pants and try to slide between her legs. She struggled against it like she was supposed to, but they knew and she knew that it was only a pose, only perfunctory, and each time their fingers found their way inside her, her tight jeans making anything but rudimentary movement all but impossible, she closed her eyes and rode on the waves of sensation, blocking out all thought of her surroundings, her partners, their faces, concentrating on the hands that were working on her, imagining how their white palms looked against her black pubic hair, seeing in her mind a lap's-eye view of the proceedings. Tony Livesey was the best of the bunch, an otherwise unassuming kid with long, slender fingers and the gentle touch of a practiced masseuse, and he was the only one she had continued to see. He was not her true love, she knew that, but he was competent in a journeyman way, and he did not demand anything else from her. He was content to remain where they were, and she saw him each week and allowed him to engage in what was euphemistically referred to as heavy petting, and if she was feeling particularly good she would reciprocate and give him what was commonly called a hand job.

But Jim was totally unlike anyone else before. His hands, his glorious hands, were skilled and assured, manly yet tender. They felt as good as they looked, were as wonderful as she'd known they'd be, and she allowed them to do what she'd never allowed anyone else's to do before: take off her blouse, take off her bra, pull down her pants, pull off her underwear.

Even as he entered her from behind, as she braced herself on her hands and knees, he was cupping her breasts, his strong fingers pressing into her flesh in a way that did not hurt but aroused. His thumbs flicked her nipples, and she bucked against him, pulling him in deeper, bringing him to climax as he clutched her body for all he was worth.

Two months later they were married.

Ten years later they were still married.

His hands, if anything, had become more accomplished over the years, better able to satisfy her needs and urges, and it was because of this that their sex life had remained as vibrant as ever, that they made love as often now as they had those first few months.

People liked to talk about the head or the heart as if they were the most important parts of a man. But it was hands that translated thought into action, that set down the words composed in the poet's brain, that sculpted or painted the forms imagined in the artist's mind, that played the music born in the composer's soul. Hands were the intermediary between the ethereal and the material, the celestial and the base, and nowhere was this truer than in the realm of love. There was a maneuverability in hands that was not found in the penis, an ability to perform multiple movements at once. The penis could only grow soft or hard, could only move in its function as an appendage to the pelvis, but the possibilities of the hand were endless. Often, as she orally pleased her husband, he would insert thumb and forefinger in both of her holes—vagina and anus—and massage her that way. She could feel the two parts of his hand through the thin membrane of tissue separating them, and it never failed to bring her to climax.

The penis could only be what it was, but the hand was endlessly varying and multifaceted. It could be as small as a pinkie inside her, as big as a fist. It could do anything and everything she wanted: rub, penetrate, pinch, stroke, tickle. Even after all these years, hands had not lost their attraction for her, and it was her secret fantasy to be groped by a group of men, to be on her hands and knees in a box filled with holes through which the hands of many men felt her and squeezed her and slapped her and entered her. She wanted hands on her tits, hands in her hair, fingers in her mouth, fingers in her pussy, fingers up her ass. She wanted to be kneaded and prodded and poked, and it was this fantasy that brought her to orgasm each time she masturbated, as her own hands rubbed herself, and it made her climax in a way that had never happened with traditional intercourse.

Hands could hurt or heal, and there was something in that duality that appealed to her. The nature of humankind was expressed in those two appendages more eloquently than they could ever be by any other part of the body.

She remembered, as a child, seeing a horror movie: *The Hands of Orlac*. It was about a surgeon who grafted the hands of a killer onto the arms of a pianist who had lost his own hands in some kind of accident. Was that possible? she wondered. After Jim died, could she save his hands and have them sewn onto another man's arms? She knew she could have them bronzed or plaster cast, but it was their movement and flexibility that made them so special, that she loved, not their static shape or form. Maybe they wouldn't be the same even if they *were* grafted onto someone else's arms, because the movements would not be the same as the ones ordered by his brain, and any attempt to re-create them would be merely a copy of the original, a false reenactment of an actual event.

That was her biggest fear: losing his hands to death. And she prayed each night for them to both live a long and healthy life, but for God to take her first so she wouldn't be forced to live without Jim.

And his hands.

Even now, after all these years, he did not know her feelings, did not know her mind. Sex for him was focused on the genitals. Pussy and cock. Hands were for foreplay, a necessary evil, the mechanical preparation needed to make him hard and her wet so that true sex could begin.

But coitus for her was a form of cuddling, a relaxing breather after the orgasmic rigors of hand sex. She would lie there as he entered her, feeling the diminishing waves coursing through her body as he began pumping. It was a favor she did for him, though he did not know it, and she allowed him his mistaken belief, let him think that it was his cock that turned her on, that it was his manhood that drove her to heights of ecstasy.

Ironically, her own hands he found too rough. He liked to be stimulated orally, liked her to fellate him, to use her hands only to hold still the base of his penis. He did not like to be stroked, and when she attempted it, he invariably said, "If I wanted that, I'd do it myself." He'd then press a light hand against the back of her head and push her face into his lap. "Use your mouth," he'd say.

She'd take him into her mouth happily, accept his semen and swallow it, but her hands felt useless, ignored, and that was the only part of their lovemaking with which she was not completely satisfied.

It happened sooner than she'd hoped, sooner than she'd thought, even sooner than she'd feared.

She was at work, in her office, and she received a call from his supervisor that he had collapsed on the line and was being taken to St. Jude's Hospital. The supervisor was vague in his description of Jim's status, too vague, and she didn't press him because she was not yet ready to hear what she knew she would. Instead, with a feeling of panic, she sped to the hospital, where she learned that he'd been pronounced dead on arrival, the victim of a massive coronary.

The next week was a blur, and at the end of it, she was sitting alone by his newly bermed grave, crying, missing him. She looked down at the ground, and when she thought of him lying in the coffin, hands folded uselessly across his chest, she was filled with a sadness so deep and profound that it seemed only her own death could relieve it. She would never find another man like Jim, never find hands like his, and she knew that her life had nowhere to go from here.

She contemplated suicide many times over the next few months, always chickening out at the last minute, and she had finally decided to swallow a bottle of sleeping pills, when she saw a movie that changed her life.

A children's movie.

A Dr. Seuss movie.

The 5,000 Fingers of Dr. T.

In the surrealistic world of the film, a mad piano teacher imprisoned five hundred boys, all of whom were required to wear on their heads a beanie atop which sat a realistic rubber hand. It was the sight of all those hands sticking up proudly from the young boys' hats, waving around as they ran, that caused a tingling sensation between her legs, a feeling that spread outward to the rest of her body through electric nerves that hadn't been used since Jim's death.

She checked the cable guide to see if the movie was on again—it was—and she set the timer on her VCR as well as programming her TiVo. The film was recorded while she slept, and she awoke feeling not only refreshed but enthusiastic.

She watched the movie again.

And again.

And again.

Seeing the film, with its plethora of hands and tacit understanding of the importance of the five-fingered extremities, gave her courage and hope, and each viewing was like another tug on a lifeline pulling her back from the brink. Years ago, before meeting Jim, she remembered reading about a tribe, somewhere in New Guinea, she thought, that worshiped a god whose form was that of a hand. She'd cut out the article and saved it, and now she practically tore apart the house searching for the yellowed scrap of newsprint. She found it in the place she least expected—between the pages of a cookbook, next to a piece of lined paper containing a friend's recipe for lemonade pie—and immediately after rereading the article, she went to the library to look up more information about the tribe and its god.

The problem was that there *was* no more information. Aside from that one article, she could find no mention of the subject in any book or periodical, or on any Web site. The article did, however, have a dateline, and on impulse she went home, picked up the phone, and booked a complicated series of interconnecting and increasingly smaller plane flights that eventually led to Port Moresby, New Guinea. From there, she figured, she should be able to find someone who knew of this tribe and could take her to its village.

The reality was slightly more complicated, but three days later she was on a jeep in the jungles of Papua with a driver and a translator, heading for a remote canyon that was supposed to be the home of the Lingbacao people. The road turned into a trail, the trail into a path, and after they'd driven several slow hours along the increasingly narrow and erratic track, the underbrush grew too thick to continue, and they were forced to abandon the jeep and continue on foot.

The first sign that they were getting close was a detailed painting of a hand on the open face of a rock cliff. It was gigantic, and obviously only recently completed. Surrounding it were smaller, much older handprints, and the impression given by both together was of a parent with its children, or a king with his subjects.

Or a god with his followers.

She stared at the rock face, enraptured. Even if the god did not exist, here was a people who understood the divinity of the hand, who appreciated its significance and importance in all things, a realization that was reinforced when they finally came upon the village and were met by a man who said, "We are honored by your presence in our community. New hands are always welcome here."

She turned to the translator after he repeated the greeting in English and asked him to relay her own message: "I, too, worship the hand. It is why I am here."

The man nodded, smiling, and spoke rapidly after the translator had finished speaking.

"It is hands that till the field, hands that hunt the deer, hands that gather the fruit," the translator said in English. "It is our hands that hold us together. It is our hands that keep us alive."

The Lingbacao man said something else, then pointed across the length of the village.

"God," the translator said, "lives in that building."

It was a shack only slightly larger than a storage shed.

She did not know what she had been expecting. Something like the Judeo-Christian God, she supposed, a vague unseen presence to which the people gave fealty. She had not been expecting a physical being in a defined location, and she looked toward the shack, not sure if the emotion that filled her was excitement or fear.

This was why she'd come here, however, and she asked the translator to ask the man if she could go into the building and see God.

The man seemed to speak several rapid sentences, but the translator boiled it down to one simple word: "Certainly."

She walked forward slowly, her eyes focused on the shack's closed wooden door and the single glassless window covered by a black cloth that fluttered slowly in a nonexistent breeze. The village around her fell away, the conversations of the people she passed, even the words of her translator, fading into a muffled drone she could not understand. It was hot and humid, but her skin sported gooseflesh, and her heart was hammering hard enough to break her rib cage by the time she reached the small building and reached for the rusted doorknob.

"Wait here," she told the translator. She didn't know what she would see or what would happen, whether she would find herself alone in an empty room or facing a fierce deity that would destroy her on sight for daring to invade its sanctuary. But this was her destiny, and she was determined to face it alone.

She opened the door, stepped inside, and carefully closed the door behind her. As her eyes adjusted to the dimness of the shack's interior, she saw a man seated against the opposite wall. He looked familiar, and she squinted, peering closer.

"Tony?" she said, shocked.

It was indeed Tony Livesey, her onetime boyfriend, all grown up and much the worse for wear. He was dressed in a drab robe of rough cloth, and his face was lined far beyond its years. There was a scar down one cheek, and on that side of his face the corner of his mouth drooped as though there'd been nerve damage. His right hand was gone, the arm ending in a wrapped stump.

"Do you remember me?" she asked, stepping closer.

He nodded, meeting her eyes. "I never forgot you."

She glanced around the empty room. "Are you their . . . god?"

"No," he said tiredly. "Not exactly."

He told her his story. He had joined the marines after high school and had been stationed in Saudi Arabia, where he had deserted, fed up with the horrors of regimented life. He had survived on the streets as a musician, a busker. But times had gotten hard and he'd been forced to steal and he'd been caught. A judge of one of America's foremost allies in the Middle East ordered that his hand be chopped off as punishment for his crime.

It was his hand that was the god. For it had not died but continued to live, to grow. It had followed him, though he had tried at first to escape it, from the Middle East to South Africa to South America to the Pacific islands. It was now the size of a chair, and Tony slowly stood to reveal that he had been sitting atop it, that what she had taken for a throne was in reality the stump of wrist, palm and fingers of his enormous hand. Before her eyes, the fingers moved, reconfigured themselves, and now it was not a seat but something resembling a monster spider from an old science fiction movie.

He still felt its feelings, Tony said, was still connected to it, and when the local women polished and trimmed its nails, rode atop its oversize fingers to give themselves pleasure, he experienced those sensations as well.

"I can feel it, but I can't control it," he admitted. "It does what it wants."

She stared at the gigantic hand, overcome by a feeling of wonder, awed by the majesty of the sight. "Does it perform miracles?"

"It *is* a miracle," Tony said.

That was true. She looked at his empty sleeve, then at the hand on the other side of the room. Perhaps her husband's hands would have survived had they been amputated. Maybe they would now be autonomous and independent, and she could be enjoying them, taking them into her bed each night, letting them roam over her body and do what they would with her. The idea made her ache with longing.

"Is it really a god?" she asked.

He nodded. "They're all over the world," he said softly. "The followers. They are not just here in this village. There are even pockets of believers in the United States. Men and women who recognize the divinity of my hand.

"It's not *the* god but it's *a* god."

She reached out, touched the stump of his wrist, remem-

bered when he had a hand there and what it had done to her.
"It's *my* god," she said.

His voice was thick, raspy. "Go to it."

They said no more to each other. Slowly but with purpose,
she crossed the short space of the room. The hand had
shifted position yet again, was now stretched out in a way
that made it resemble a bed. She touched it, was surprised
by the softness of its skin. Its size, location and backstory had
led her to believe it would be rough, leathery, but despite the
prominence of the whorled ridges that made up its enlarged
fingerprints, the skin of the hand felt supple and silken. She
got goose bumps just rubbing it.

She received no messages from the hand; it did not speak
to her, but it didn't have to. She knew what she had to do, and
she sat down on the hard floor and pulled off her shoes, her
socks, her blouse, her bra. She stood, pulled down her pants
and panties, then climbed atop the palm. The hand seemed
to recognize her. She recognized it as well, remembered its
movements and unique individual attributes, and she leaned
back, settled into it, rubbed herself against it.

It was too big to be able to do what it wanted to do, what
she wanted it to do, and as the huge fingers, fingers as big
as her legs, attempted to push into her, penetrate her, but
managed only to press futilely against her, she saw the look
of frustration on Tony's face across the room.

She understood how the other women did it, sitting astride
a finger, riding it as though it were a mechanical bull, but that
was not what she wanted, not what Tony wanted, not what
God wanted. She grabbed the thumb, held it, hugged it, felt
the power surging beneath her, behind her, all around her.

"Get off!" Tony ordered. He sounded angry.

"It's okay," she said softly.

"No!"

She knew what he was thinking and understood all of a
sudden what had to be done. "It's okay," she said again.

She settled more fully onto the hand, and as it closed and tightened, squeezing the life out of her, as Tony screamed and the translator and tribesmen pushed open the door and rushed inside, she thought what a glorious way this was to die.

Ten

It had been easy.

That was what really got to him.

The first few days were torture. Every time the phone rang at work, Steve assumed it was the law, some Columbo-like cop who would hound him with casual questions until he inadvertently revealed the truth. Sitting at home, he kept waiting for a knock at the door, knowing that when he answered it, the police would be there to arrest him. He was afraid even to look up information about Lyman Fischer's death on the Internet for fear that any site he accessed would be red-flagged and all inquiries traced back to him.

But as the days passed, and then the weeks, he understood that he had gotten away with it. And he realized how easy it had been. He'd made a quick trip, done the deed, and while he may have left chaos in his wake, his day-to-day life went on as normal.

Maybe he should've silenced Jessica Haster at the same time.

He'd been telling himself his father would have been proud of him had he still been able to think clearly—wasn't this the way *he* would have handled the situation?—but Joe Nye had never been proud of anything his son had done. It was far likelier that he would have been angry. After all, his dad was an old hand at this. He'd been killing for years, decades. Steve could easily imagine his father criticizing his poor planning and the fact that he had not tied up all of the loose ends—and then telling him how he *should* have gone about it.

Because if Lyman had talked to Jessica . . .

If Lyman had talked to Jessica, she would have called the police with any suspicions she had, and Steve would have been questioned.

It stopped here. He was already far more deeply involved than he should be or wanted to be. Not a day went by that he didn't regret returning to Copper City, and when he was with Sherry or his friends, with normal people, he felt dirty, guilty, like a secret leper. At unwelcome moments, his mind returned to the scene inside that dark, filthy house, and he felt again the sickening sensation of hard cartilage under dry, wattled skin as his arm tightened around Lyman Fischer's neck.

He wished his father had just died from the stroke and he himself had never gotten sucked into this maelstrom.

And yet . . .

And yet he felt a strange sort of kinship with his father now, a sense of shared experience. In an odd way, he felt closer to his dad today than he ever had before. They had both killed people—how shocking it was to even think that!—and yet they both pretended as though they hadn't, maintaining lives of middle-class normalcy rather than succumbing to the lifestyle of the criminal. He understood now the emotions that had lain within his father for all these years. He remembered, several years back, hearing about "millionaires next door," average people who, unbeknownst to their neighbors, were rich. He and his father, Steve thought, were "murderers next door," and that made him wonder how many others like them there were.

It was horrifying what he'd done, and the sensory elements of those few terrible moments were always with him—the sight, the smell, the feel, the sound—but the truth was that in addition to horror and revulsion, Steve experienced a feeling of tremendous power when he thought about what had occurred. Because he had been almost godlike in that moment when he had squeezed the life out of Lyman Fischer. The problem he had faced was insurmountable: The blackmail could have gone on forever and not only ruined his life but the lives of his family. So he had gone outside the human paradigm, had eschewed society's acceptable half measures and compromised solutions, and had dealt with the situation in a more omnipotent manner by taking Lyman's life, solving everything with one bold, clean stroke.

And still all was as it had been. He went to work, watched TV, hung with his friends, went out with Sherry.

Sherry.

He wondered how she would react if she knew the truth. Not well, he thought. But then, who would? He was a murderer and the son of a murderer. He did not deserve someone like her.

She was spending the night one Saturday when he let her read his story about the hand. Emboldened by his first sale, he showed her the new piece before submitting it, confident that she would appreciate his work. But she remained silent after reading the story, and when pressed admitted that she found it disturbing.

"Is that how you see women?" she asked. "Are we creatures controlled by our crotches and defined solely by our sexual urges?"

"No," he said, confused. He was not sure how she had even come to that conclusion. "That's not what I meant at all."

"Then what did you mean? Her husband dies and all she misses is the way his hands gave her an orgasm?" She shook her head. "I'm sorry. I really don't mean to criticize. And I'm glad you're showing me your writing. But this is . . . I don't know. This is creepy."

He felt hurt but was determined not to show it. "It's supposed to be creepy," he said defensively.

"I don't think it's creepy in the same way you intended."

He dreamed that night of the clown again, only this time the clown was somewhere in Lyman Fischer's house and it was Steve's job to find him. Lyman's dead body was lying on the floor where he had left it, only now it was decomposed, the whiteness of skull showing through the putrefying flesh. Steve was standing inside the open front door, staring at the body, and the screen was banging in the wind against the backs of his shoes. From down the hall, from one of the bedrooms, perhaps, came a high-pitched laugh that sounded both crazy and feminine. The clown. He didn't *want* to find the clown, but he *had* to, and he stepped over Lyman's decaying corpse and crept through the darkened living room toward the hallway. The furniture to either side of him—the couch, the tables, the chairs—didn't look like furniture in the dimness but like people or creatures, the slumbering denizens of some carnival freak show. He kept his focus on the blackened rectangle of the hallway entrance, however, and saw when he reached it that swirling kaleidoscopic colors were seeping out from underneath the closed bathroom door. He tiptoed down the hall, trying not to make any sound, reached his right hand out to grab the bathroom doorknob, then quickly turned the knob and flung open the door. The small room was empty, no one in the tub, in the shower, on the toilet. There was only a round multicolored filter turning in front of a freestanding lamp atop the sink counter. He turned, intending to search the bedrooms—

—and the clown was right there behind him, his evil face lit by the swirling colors from the bathroom, laughing that horrible high-pitched laugh.

Steve awoke with a start, and for a second, Sherry's face on the pillow next to him looked white in the darkness, as though she were wearing clown makeup. He looked up at the ceiling, taking a deep breath. He realized that it had been exactly a month since Lyman's death. Now wide-awake, he carefully and stealthily got out of bed and made his way out to the hall and into the bathroom, where he closed and locked the door before leaning over and vomiting in the toilet.

At lunch on Monday, he decided to look up information about unsolved murders in the towns and cities his family had lived in over the years. It was high time that he started researching in more detail his father's crimes. The partial knowledge he possessed and the speculation he engaged in were only slightly better than willful ignorance, and while the whole truth might make him uncomfortable, it was something he needed to know.

As it happened, he was working on putting together a twenty-year reunion booklet for a religious college in Utah, so that gave him a head start, made it easier to research unsolved murders from the two years his family had lived in Salt Lake City. He'd been five when they'd pulled up stakes and moved to Flagstaff, so his memories of the city were nearly nonexistent. He recalled a blue house, a red tricycle, a picnic in the backyard where he and some friend had eaten peanut-butter-and-honey sandwiches, but that was about it. Their family had lived in Utah the same year the college students had graduated, so he used the database he'd been consulting for the reunion booklet to search for Salt Lake City residents who had disappeared or died mysteriously during that time, and whose whereabouts remained unknown or whose killings had never been solved.

There were three teenage girls and one teenage boy who'd been abducted and had never been found, a retired policeman who had been shot execution-style in his garage, a transient who had been stabbed outside a bar, a young woman who had been raped and strangled, and two brothers who had been the victims of an arson-caused apartment fire. His first impulse was to look carefully at the young woman who'd been strangled—although he didn't think his father was capable of raping anyone—but then he thought of something his dad had said the other day: *Both of them burned.* It was a non sequitur, not something mentioned in the context of a conversation, and he'd thought it meant nothing at the time, was just more nonsensical rambling, but now it seemed to him that his dad had been recalling the arson fire that had killed those two brothers.

If he'd thought it meant nothing at the time, then why had he remembered it?

Because part of him had known that it *had* meant something, and he tried to recall other isolated phrases or sentence fragments that had stuck with him, that might be clues to the past rather than merely indications of his father's mental condition. Nothing stood out, but maybe deeper research into some of these deaths would jog his memory.

He looked up what he could about the brothers who'd been burned. Alex and Anthony Jones. The real details were tied up in police case files not available to civilians, but there was enough public information for him to piece together what had happened. Salt Lake was also not Copper City, so the local newspapers—

there were two!—had not only covered the deaths in depth but had online archives that he could access. Steve wrote down names, dates and places, then used a directory to look up the addresses and phone numbers of surviving relatives and witnesses who'd remained in the area.

He paused, looked over the information he'd written down. Did he really think his father was involved here?

Yes.

If so, his theory was wrong. They hadn't all been prostitutes.

They hadn't all been women.

He stared at the names of the two brothers on top of his paper. *Why* would his father have killed those men? Had they cheated him? Threatened him? There had to be a reason. He refused to believe that his dad had just gone out and murdered people at random.

But that's what serial killers do.

He pushed the thought from his mind and moved on to Flagstaff, where they'd lived after Salt Lake City. Aside from a stabbing and a shooting in two unrelated bar fights, the only other murder on record for the year they were there was the brutal slaying of a college coed from Northern Arizona University. The bar killings both had plenty of witnesses, and the drunken perpetrators had been apprehended immediately, so the coed's murder was the only one that remained unsolved. Although he doubted that his father was behind it. The young woman had been stabbed repeatedly, assaulted on her way back to campus after attending a friend's birthday party at a nearby bar. Her face had been slashed across both cheeks, and there were so many crazily inflicted knife wounds in her chest and abdomen that segments of partially shredded organs ended up outside the rent skin. It was the insane ferocity of the killing that made Steve think it had not been his father. Arson he could see. Pushing someone off a building? Yes. But no matter how hard he tried, he could not imagine his dad getting in there and stabbing someone over and over again while blood gushed out and spurted in every direction.

The only other possibility was that his father had been responsible for the two unsolved child abductions that had occurred in Flagstaff that year—although that seemed just as unlikely to him and even more distasteful.

Maybe there'd been no killing in Flagstaff. Maybe they'd moved on to Tempe for legitimate reasons.

He chose to believe that.

The office started to fill up as everyone returned from lunch, and Steve logged off the missing-persons registry, hiding his scribbled notes in the top drawer of his desk. Gina stopped by, asking how his father was. She'd been coming by a lot lately, even acting a little flirty—had she seen him that day by the bay?—but he always managed to maintain his distance, and he gave her the generic nonanswer "Fine," rather obviously turning back to his computer screen in order to get rid of her. Surreptitiously, he watched her walk away. Not for the first time, he found himself wondering about the older man he'd seen her with, and was disgusted with himself because he didn't *want* to wonder about the secretary's personal life.

After work, he went to the VA hospital. His father was awake when he arrived, and though he looked dazed and blank, there seemed a shred of comprehension in his eyes when Steve said hello. Hoping to take advantage of that and glean some more information, Steve closed the door to the room, checked to make sure the patient on the other side of the curtain was asleep, then sat down, scooting the chair close to the head of the bed so he could speak into his father's ear.

"Do you remember when we lived in Salt Lake City?" he asked softly. He waited a moment, but there was no response. He repeated the question, adding his father's line, "Both of them burned," hoping it would trigger a reaction. Nothing. The old man wasn't smiling, though, wasn't spouting nonsense, and Steve chose to believe it meant that on some level he understood.

"I think you killed those two brothers, Dad. Alex and Anthony Jones. I think you set fire to their apartment. But did they die in the fire or did you set that fire to cover up how they really died? And why did you kill them in the first place? What did they do?"

His father's eyes closed even as they looked into his. Had he fallen asleep or was he just trying to avoid the questions? Steve remained where he was for several moments, waiting, but when it became clear from the deep, even breathing that his dad was honestly and truly out, Steve stood. Maybe his father had only fallen asleep after pretending to do so, or maybe he'd actually nodded off, but either way, it would be quite a while before he awoke again.

One of these times, Steve thought, he wouldn't wake up at all.

He wasn't sure how he felt about that.

He arrived home after dark. The apartment seemed emptier than usual, and listening to the hum of the refrigerator, the only noise in the silence, he wondered whether he should ask Sherry to move in with him. Or, better still, talk to her about finding a place that could be *theirs*, a condo or a house, maybe not in Irvine but in a less expensive part of Orange County. It would be nice to come home to noise, to light, to have someone he could talk with as he ate dinner and breakfast, someone he could sleep next to not just occasionally, but every night.

If that was the case, though, why did he feel as though his personal space was invaded each time she invited herself over unannounced?

His head hurt, and his neck. Stress. Buried somewhere in his bedroom closet was something called Twinkle Neck, a present given to him by his parents several Christmases ago that supposedly helped soothe tired neck muscles. But he was too lazy to look for it and instead sat down on the couch, using the remote to turn on the TV.

If Sherry were here she could give him a massage.

Was she even the type of woman who gave massages?

He wasn't sure. It had never come up.

He thought of calling her. Didn't. Whenever he thought about Sherry these days, he thought about Lyman Fischer. It was an almost Pavlovian reaction, one that he could not seem to shake, and each time, the juxtaposition in his mind of her pretty, kind, trusting face with the dead body of the old man made him realize anew that he did not deserve her.

He had killed a man.

There was no reason to feel guilty, he tried to tell himself. Lyman Fischer had been a horrible person, a blackmailer, a criminal. And Steve was certainly not like his father. He had done what he'd done only to *protect* his father, to protect their whole *family*.

But his father didn't deserve protection.

Steve closed his eyes. No matter which path of reasoning he took, guilt lay at the end of it.

He sat there for a while, but when neither his headache nor his neck pain lessened, he opened his eyes, stood and went into the kitchen, where he opened a box of Tylenol, popped three gel tabs into his mouth and washed them down with Coke. He threw a frozen Stouffer's dinner into the microwave, then stood next to the sink and ate it, staring out the kitchen window at the leafy, well-manicured courtyard of the apartment complex.

Sherry phoned soon after—Where had he been? Wasn't he supposed to have called her?—but he explained that he wasn't feeling well, and she was instantly solicitous, asking what was wrong, whether there was anything she could do. Ironically, his headache disappeared halfway through their conversation, and by the end of it even his neck didn't feel as stiff and sore. The Tylenol kicking in, he supposed. But he continued to maintain the illusion that he was ill and promised to call her in the morning before work, saying that he was tired and needed to sleep it off.

He wasn't tired, though. He was wide-awake. He tried to read, couldn't concentrate, tried to work on a new short story but wasn't inspired, and he ended up camped out in front of the television all night, rewatching shows that he'd already seen, before finally going to bed sometime after eleven.

He continued his research the next day. And the next. By Friday, he had a pretty good idea of his father's trail of carnage. There'd been a married middle-aged woman from Tempe tied to a rock in the desert and left to die, a pimp in Tucson strangled in a cheap hotel, a single mother drowned in the bay in San Diego. The MOs were different each time, and Steve assumed that that was not only intentional but was probably the reason his father had never been caught.

It seemed impossible that there could be legitimate reasons for all of those killings. The first wife, yes. Maybe even the Mexican prostitute. But murder after murder in city after city? Looking at the situation objectively, he could think of no circumstance in which such a string of killings could be justified. Perhaps his father *had* felt wronged or slighted by each of those individuals, but death was an extreme punishment for such transgressions, and the chances that his father had been in the right each and every time were not only remote but virtually nonexistent.

Still, as with Copper City, Steve had a desire—no, a *need*—to go to those places, see for himself. He wasn't going to make the same mistake as last time and talk too much or ask leading questions—he didn't want a repeat of *that* experience—but he wanted to poke around, find out what really happened. And if his dad did kill those people, he needed to understand *why*.

He was almost done with the reunion booklet for the religious college. A few more days and he'd be through. And since the deadline for his next project wasn't for another month, this was the perfect time to take a few days, a week even, and investigate these deaths more thoroughly. He had plenty of vacation time saved up. He could bring along his laptop and stay at hotels that offered wifi so he could continue to do research on the way. His father's situation was stable enough that he didn't have to check in every single day, and if he was ever going to find out what really happened, he needed to do it now.

Instead of meeting his friends after work, Steve decided to surprise Sherry and drop by her place. When he arrived at her apartment, however, no one answered the door. He walked down to her parking spot in the rear of the complex, but it was empty, so he dialed her cell number. After one ring, it went straight into voice mail. Rather than leave a message, he hung up and returned to her apartment, letting himself in with his key.

He closed the door carefully behind him, feeling like an intruder. She had given him his own key some time ago, but this was the first time he had used it, the first time he had been in here without her, and it seemed strange being in the apartment by himself. He turned on the lights. Glancing around, he saw the entertainment section of yesterday's *Los Angeles Times* on the coffee table next to a hairbrush and a pair of nail clippers. Lying open on the couch was a decades-old issue of *Time* with Jackie O on the cover. He frowned, wondering where she had gotten the magazine—and why.

Steve walked slowly from the sitting room to the kitchen. Looking through an apartment was like dropping in on a life. More intimate than mere spying, it allowed the intruder access from the inside, enabled him to almost *become* that person. Since Sherry had not known he was coming, she had not cleaned up or rearranged anything, had not prepared for his visit by putting on a false front. This was her life, raw, without any aspect of performance. He saw breakfast dishes in the sink: a spoon in a coffee cup, a trio of Cheerios floating in milk-tinged water at the bottom of a rinsed-out bowl. He not only knew *what* she'd eaten this morning, he knew *how* she'd eaten it.

It was this admittance to the personal and private, the exposure to details of everyday living, that had raised his hackles when Sherry had shown up at his place without his knowledge. Maybe she was right; maybe he was not ready for real intimacy, because he didn't feel comfortable allowing her unfettered access to his life. Which was probably why it felt so wrong for him to be snooping around her apartment like this.

But she had given him a key. She had given him permission.

Besides, turnabout was fair play.

He opened her refrigerator, looking for something to drink, but found only orange juice and bottled water. He settled for a water, twisting the lid and downing half the bottle in one swig. The clock on the wall above the breakfast table said six twenty-three, and again he wondered where Sherry could be. The library closed at five on Fridays, and she didn't really hang out with her coworkers, since all of the ones who weren't old and/or married were basically high schoolers working part-time. He hoped she hadn't been in an accident or had car problems. Just in case, he called her cell again. Once more, he was put directly into voice mail.

He decided to wait here until she returned.

What if she was out with some guy?

He pushed that thought from his mind, walking into her bedroom. The bed was unmade—she was sloppier than he'd thought she was—and yesterday's clothes were piled on a chair. *She's not bringing anyone home*, he thought. *Not to this.* The realization left him relieved. He didn't know he'd been worried, but he had been.

It didn't seem right snooping through her bedroom. It seemed a little pervy, and Steve turned and made his way out to the short, nearly nonexistent hallway. He took a quick peek in the small bathroom—

—and stopped.

There was a dead puppy in the trash can next to the toilet.

Sherry didn't have a puppy. He was not even sure pets were allowed in her apartment complex.

He took a step closer, staring at the animal. It was lying atop an empty toilet paper roll and a mound of white tissues, its head pressed against the far side of the rounded yellow plastic, one ear pointing upward. The small brown body was twisted in an odd way that made it appear as though the animal's neck had been snapped. There had to be a reason behind this, but at the moment he could not for the life of him think of what it could possibly be. If she'd found the dead puppy outside, why had she brought it into her apart-

ment? If she'd discovered the body *in* her apartment,
why hadn't she told him about it or called the apartment manager? Even if she'd found a live puppy and
for some bizarre, incomprehensible reason killed it herself, why hadn't she disposed of the body in the trash
bins near the parking area? Why had she dropped it
into her bathroom wastepaper basket?

None of this made any sense, and, frowning, he
went back out to the sitting room to see whether he
could find anything else amiss.

Moments later, there was a rattle of keys and doorknob as Sherry walked into the apartment. She found
him crouched on the floor, searching through the contents of a low end-table drawer. He looked up at her,
caught, but saw none of the hostility that he had exhibited toward her when she'd shown up unannounced
at his place. Instead, she seemed thrilled that he was
there, and she put down her purse, threw her arms
around him and kissed him, her happiness and excitement obvious in every movement, every breath. "What
a great surprise!" she said. "I'm so glad you're here!"
She obviously didn't care that he'd come over and let
himself in without giving her fair warning, and didn't
worry about him digging through her stuff while she
wasn't there.

Which probably meant that there was nothing weird
about the dead dog at all, and there was no doubt a
perfectly logical explanation behind its presence in the
trash can.

But he didn't ask her about it.

They went out to eat at an Italian restaurant in Newport Beach, and afterward she invited him to come back
to her apartment to spend the night. He was still curious about the puppy, and using her bathroom would
give him the perfect opportunity to find out why it was
there, but the thought of making love and sleeping in

an enclosed area with a dead animal sickened him, and they ended up going back to his place as usual.

Sherry had to work on Saturday, filling in for someone on vacation, and after she left in the morning, he stopped by to see his mother, something he had not done in nearly a week. He had called her a couple of days ago, but while they'd spent a lot of time together at the outset of his father's hospitalization, making joint decisions and having daily discussions, there now seemed to be a disconnect, and the two of them had reverted to type, both of them forging their own new relationships with his father, dealing with him separately, though Steve still drove her to the hospital when she asked.

He pulled into his parents' driveway, parking behind his dad's old Chrysler. There were spiderwebs visible between the tailpipe and the right rear tire, and he thought that it was probably time for him to take the car out for a drive, just to keep it in decent running condition. The lawn, he saw, was overgrown, though the plants had been watered and were in good shape, and he wondered whether his father had been the one to mow the grass. He needed to ask his mother about that and make arrangements with a gardener if necessary. He didn't want his parents' yard to sink to the level of their neighbors'.

One good thing that had come of all this was that his mother locked the doors of the house now. He tried the knob, then rang the doorbell and waited on the stoop. Several moments later, he heard movement from within. There was a rattling of the latch chain, a click as the dead bolt withdrew, and then his mother was opening the door and telling him to come in.

There was no hug, no kiss—even after all that had happened, they still didn't do that—but he followed her into the kitchen, where she motioned for him to sit down at the table. He turned down pound cake, accepted coffee, and waited for his mother to join him before telling her of his plans. She sat down in the chair opposite him, put down her own cup of coffee, and he cleared his throat nervously. He knew she wasn't going to like this.

"I'm going on a little trip," he said. "A business trip," he lied.

"Oh?" Her mouth tightened into a line.

"I'll be gone about a week, probably. To Utah and then Arizona."

"You're just going to abandon me?"

"I'm not abandoning you, Mom."

She looked at him.

"Mom . . ."

"All I know is, if *my* father were dying in the hospital and my mother were the victim of a crazed attack, I would not be gallivanting around the country on a holiday vacation."

"It's a business trip, Mom. I told you."

Her face was set. "I am very disappointed in you, Steven. Your father would be too, if he knew what was going on."

"Jesus, Mom—"

She reached over and slapped him. He heard the slap before he felt it, whip-crack loud in his head, followed by a stinging so severe it brought tears to his eyes. He raised his own hand in response, an automatic defensive measure, and she pushed her chair away, shrieking. He dropped his hand instantly—the reaction was involuntary, and he never would have gone through with it—but her eyes were wide and frightened. "Just like your father!" she screamed. "You're just like your father!"

"I'm sorry, Mom."

"Blasphemer!"

He had never seen her like this before, had never seen her worked up into such a state, and the sight frightened him. He wondered for the first time whether *she* had some sort of mental problems as well.

He held up his hands in apology. "I'm sorry, I'm sorry. But I have to go on this trip. It may be only a few days. A week at the most. I'll make sure you have enough groceries before I go. We can stop by and see Dad. . . ."

"I can drive! I'm not a cripple!"

"That's fine," he said placatingly. "But I know you don't like driving on the freeway—"

"You don't know anything about me. You or your father. Birds of a feather." She glared at him. "Just leave; just get out. I've had enough of you."

He should have been used to her anger. He'd had a lifetime of it already. As a child, he had had to deal with it on a daily basis, watching what he said, where he went, what he did, aware at all times that anything could set her off. Unlike most of his friends' mothers, she had never been able to put his needs in front of her own. If she was out of sorts, he knew it, felt it, and as a result he'd grown up a very serious boy, forced to provide his own emotional support. It was still difficult for him, even at this age, to cross her.

He stood. "I have to get things sorted out, so I won't be going for a week or so. Probably next Saturday. I'll call you tomorrow."

"You don't have to," she said. Already the anger was giving way to her poor-me routine.

He sighed. "Bye, Mom."

Once outside, he saw the Chrysler again, saw the grass, and realized he hadn't talked to her about any of the practical things that needed to be done around here. They had to figure out who was going to do what, work out some sort of schedule, but this was obviously not the time.

Getting in the car, he wondered how his father had put up with her for all those years. Then he remembered that for all those years the two of them had been almost competely in sync, "please"ing and "thankyou"ing through their days in a polite, formal bubble that had shown little resemblance to the real world. It was only since the stroke that the seams had started to unravel.

He backed out of the driveway, gave a quick cursory wave to the darkened front window, though he was not at all sure that his mother was even watching, and gratefully drove away, not relaxing his death grip on the steering wheel until he was on the freeway and headed south.

He'd been avoiding Sherry lately. It was hard to be romantic when his brain was weighed down with thoughts of his father's murders, when the contemplation of anything normal brought to his mind the feeling of Lyman Fischer's corded neck beneath his tightening arm, the sight of the old man lying dead on the floor. But last night had put some of that to rest, and he decided to surprise Sherry and drop in on her at the library. He wasn't sure exactly when she had her lunch hour, but it was only ten thirty right now, and he figured he could settle down with a book or a magazine and just hang around until she was off.

She was working behind the counter when he arrived, and was so engrossed in checking out books that she didn't notice him come in. Grinning to himself, he went over to the New Releases shelf, grabbed a book at random and stood in the checkout line behind an overweight woman toting a stack of romances in a Defenders of Wildlife bag. He waited his turn, then stepped up and handed Sherry his book. "May I see your card?" she asked, looking up. She smiled as she recognized him and hit his shoulder playfully. "What are you doing here?"

"I came to see you. I thought we could eat lunch together."

The old man behind him cleared his throat rudely, and Steve shot him a look that made him glance nervously away.

"I'm off at eleven thirty. But I only get a half hour."

"That'll work."

"I just brought yogurt and some nuts."

"That's okay. I'll go out and grab us something. We can eat at one of those tables in the park outside."

The old man behind him made another noise, and Steve glared at him, shutting him up.

"Tacos," she said. "I'd like two chicken tacos. And a Sprite."

"You got it," he told her. "I'll meet you at eleven thirty. I'll find us a table."

She held up his book. "Do you want to check this out?"

He noticed for the first time that it was a chick-lit novel with a bright pink cover featuring a miniskirted young woman talking on the phone. He laughed. "Actually, I seem to have forgotten my library card."

With a wave at Sherry and one last look of disgust at the man in line behind him, Steve headed out of the library and back to his car. He drove down the street to Chipotle, got tacos and a Sprite for Sherry, a burrito and a Coke for himself, then returned to stake out one of the picnic tables on the lawn adjacent to the library. There was a homeless guy sitting at one of the other tables talking to his overstuffed backpack, but Steve ignored him, and moments later Sherry came out of the front entrance. He waved her over, tore open the food bag and handed her the tacos as she sat down.

"Full service," she said. "I like that."

A half hour wasn't a lot of time, so they ate in haste, then threw away their trash in a nearby receptacle and took a walk around the park, nursing their drinks. Sherry started telling him about her day, but his mind wandered and he found himself looking at a well-dressed man striding down the sidewalk on the other side of the street. It made him think of those 1950s people populating downtown Copper City.

"Steve?"

Sherry had stopped walking, and he turned around, surprised. He realized from the expression on her face that this was probably not the first time she had said his name.

"Something's up with you," she said. "You're acting very strange lately."

He tried to smile. "No, I'm not."

"Yes, you are. I know the situation with your parents has put a lot of stress on you," she added quickly. "I'm not talking about that. It's . . ." She took a deep breath. "Did something happen when you went to New Mexico? You've been acting weird ever since you got back."

His face felt hot, and he prayed the redness didn't show. He made a concerted effort to keep his voice as neutral as possible. "No," he said.

"You didn't *meet* anyone there? You weren't going there to visit an old flame?"

He relaxed. "No," he said honestly. "Nothing like that. Why would you even think such a thing?"

She shrugged. A little embarrassedly, he thought.

Steve smiled at her. "I'm not seeing anyone else; I'm not thinking about anyone else; there is no one else."

"There's still *something*," she insisted.

He thought of his father, looking the way he had when Steve was young, and imagined him poisoning, burning, strangling, drowning people. "There's nothing," he promised her.

She eyed him suspiciously. "I know you," she said.

He saw in his mind Lyman Fischer on the floor of his dirty shack, saw the dead puppy in Sherry's yellow plastic trash can, one ear pressed up against the curved side.

No one knew anyone, he thought.

"I have to go on another trip," he told Sherry on impulse. "This time I want you with me."

Her expression softened.

"It's a business trip," he made clear. "So we won't be together the entire time. There are a few things I have to do, some people I have to look up. But in between . . ."

She gave him a quick, happy kiss. "That sounds great. I have some time saved up, and I'm earning extra hours today. I'll need to give a few days' warning. . . ."

"I'm thinking next weekend."

"For how long?"

"I don't know yet." He did some quick calculations. "Five days, maybe. A week at the outside."

"That sounds perfect. Where are we going?"

He described the religious college's reunion booklet, explained that he needed to talk to some of the people at the school in Salt Lake City, then said he needed to go to Tempe and Tucson, Arizona, for his next assignment, which he left unspecified. Thankfully, she didn't ask for details. "We'll stay someplace nice," he said. "Do some sightseeing."

"It sounds wonderful."

He still needed to go to San Diego as well, check out the bay and look up some people, but he could do that at any time. It was less than two hours from Irvine, and he could take a day off, speed down there, and be back before anyone knew he was gone.

Sherry's lunch was almost over, and they turned, heading back through the park toward the library. She was excited and said that she would look up some information about Utah and Arizona so they could make more specific plans. He gave her a kiss when they finally reached the library door, asking her to come over to his place when she got off work.

"I can check online and see if there are any airline deals," she offered. "Would we be leaving from Orange County or Ontario?"

"Neither," he said.

"LAX?"

"No," he said, and kissed her again. "I thought we'd drive."

Eleven

He wanted, for some reason, to visit the cities chronologically, thinking he might glean more insight if he followed the same trail in the same order as his father. So they went first to Salt Lake City, leaving Southern California shortly after five on a Sunday morning in order to avoid traffic, grabbing a quick McDonald's breakfast in Barstow, bypassing Las Vegas entirely, eating a Subway lunch at a truckstop between St. George and Cedar City, and arriving in Salt Lake City sometime near sunset.

It had been a long trip, but Sherry had found the landscape inspiring, and she'd filled the hours with happy chatter, looking through books and magazines that she'd borrowed from the library, sorting through pages she'd printed off the Internet that detailed some of Utah's more obscure sightseeing destinations. It was a far cry from the trips he remembered with his parents, where all three of them had sat in stony silence, and he was glad that he had asked Sherry along.

It kept him from thinking too much.

He'd booked them a room at the Royal Arms Lodge. The AAA guidebook had given it three stars, as had a hotel-rating Web site, but he would have considered one star overly generous. Not only was it adjacent to a boarded-up convenience store and across the street from a shabby storage facility, but the painted sign affixed to the front of the hotel was chipped, and there was a conspicuous white patch in the center of the tan stucco wall.

"This is where we're staying?" Sherry asked.

"Only for tonight," Steve said grimly.

He pulled into the parking lot two spaces over from the only other vehicle: a dusty black Buick with a cracked rear window. Looking at each other but saying nothing, they got out of the car. Walking past the room in front of the Buick, they saw standing in the open doorway a potbellied woman wearing what looked like men's pajama bottoms and a New Kids on the Block T-shirt so old that its words had faded into near illegibility.

"This is, like, a transient hotel," Sherry whispered.

"Three stars," Steve reminded her.

"Three stars, my ass. I don't know who's paying off whom, but there should be a minus sign in front of those stars."

"We'll get out of here tomorrow," he promised.

They walked into the small, dingy lobby. The room smelled of fried bacon and stale cigarettes.

"May I help you?" asked the tube-topped woman behind the counter. She was so skinny she looked scary, and she smiled at them, revealing a missing tooth on the upper right side of her mouth.

Steve handed her his printout. "We have reservations. Under Nye."

She typed something into her computer. "Two nights," she said, reading the screen.

"Actually, only one. Our plans have changed."

"We have a twenty-four-hour cancellation policy," she told him, an accusatory tone seeping into her voice.

"That's why I'm telling you now," he explained patiently.

"It's almost six o'clock. Check-in time's at four. That's *less* than twenty-four hours."

He leaned forward over the counter, the polite smile on his face hardening. "You don't want to *fuck* with me on this." She blanched. Next to him, he felt Sherry tense up. "We're staying one night, we're paying for one night. Is that understood?"

"You have to—"

"Is that under*stood*?"

She nodded, handing him a pen and an information card to fill out. "May I see your driver's license?" she said nervously.

"What was *that*?" Sherry asked a few minutes later as they walked back to the car to get their luggage.

He shrugged.

"Don't you think you were a little hard on her?"

"You want to stay in this hellhole for two nights?"

"No," she admitted. "But . . ."

"I got us out of it." He took a deep breath. "Come on. Let's unpack." He reached for her hand. "It's been a long day."

They'd traveled light, one suitcase apiece, although Sherry had brought along an extra book bag filled with reading material and a grocery sack filled with snacks. He opened his suitcase in the room, took out his laptop—and suddenly realized that he didn't want Sherry to see what he would be looking up online. He placed the laptop on top of the dresser and left it there as though that had been his plan all along.

"What are we going to do about dinner?" Sherry asked, opening her own suitcase.

"I'm too tired to go out," Steve told her. "Why don't we just grab some junk food and bring it back here to eat?"

"Sounds good to me," she said, pulling some clothes

out of the suitcase. "Let me take a quick shower and then we'll see what we can find."

"Shower?" he said, frowning.

"Yes. I want to be clean."

He understood. She was having her period.

There went his plans for the evening.

She went into the bathroom and closed the door. Seconds later, he heard the rush of water and the loud vibration of bad pipes as she turned on the shower. Walking over to his laptop on the dresser, he happened to look into her open suitcase as he passed by.

Lying atop a folded yellow blouse was a small red dog collar.

Steve stopped. The collar seemed about the right size for a puppy, and he reached down and picked it up. "Boo" was the only word engraved on the silver heart-shaped dog tag. He put the collar back exactly where he'd found it. Inside the bathroom, the water was still running, the pipes still making noise, but she wouldn't stay in there forever. As concerned as he was about Sherry and the puppy, he had his own business to attend to. He hurried over to the laptop, opened it and logged on.

The hotel was actually not too far from the spot where Alex and Anthony Jones had burned to death in their apartment, though that incident had happened twenty-some years ago, and he wasn't sure if an apartment building still stood at that location or if something else had been built there in the decades since. The hotel provided neither pen nor notepad, but he'd brought along both, and he scribbled down directions on how to get there before exiting the page and moving on.

The father of the brothers was still alive and living in Salt Lake City. Steve had the man's address and wanted to meet with him, although of course he needed to call first. He couldn't have Sherry tagging along, though. And he didn't want her accompanying him to the site either. Or anywhere else. So until they checked into their new hotel tomorrow, he wasn't going to be able to get started. They would have to spend their time together doing innocuous things. It would waste half a day, but he could see no way around it.

He quickly looked up directions to a few more addresses, writing them down on the top sheet of his notepad, then tearing off the paper, folding it and putting it in his wallet. The water had been turned off in the bathroom, though he was not sure exactly when that had happened, and he quickly closed his laptop and grabbed the remote control from its perch atop the television, lying back on the bed as he flipped on the TV.

Sherry emerged from the bathroom seconds later, hair washed, wearing clean clothes and smiling. "Let's get something to eat," she said. "I'm starving."

Morning dawned cool and beautiful, though the local newscast the previous night had said it would heat up to ninety degrees by the afternoon. The sky was bluer than it ever was in Southern California, and the mountains towering over the city, unobscured by smog, were capped with pure white snow.

They were packed and checked out by eight, and they ate breakfast at Denny's before following Sherry's sightseeing itinerary. They toured the Mormon temple, or the part that was open to the public, took a walking tour through the historic downtown, and checked out an art museum. It was fun, relaxing, and felt almost as though they were on a real vacation—though not for one moment did Steve forget the reason he was here.

After lunch, they found a new hotel in a nicer section of the city, and while the official check-in time was three o'clock, Steve explained that they'd come all the way from California, and were really tired. The accomodating desk clerk said there was a room ready on the second floor that they could have if they didn't mind a view of the parking lot.

Grateful, he took the room, and they quickly unpacked.

Now, finally, he was ready to go.

"My meeting starts at one fifteen," he lied. "So I'd better get going. I'm not sure how long it's going to last, but it could be all afternoon. So I'll probably see you tonight." He leaned forward for a kiss.

"Wait a minute."

He stopped, looked at her.

"You're just going to take off and leave me here?"

"You knew ahead of time this was a business trip. I told you I'd be on my own a lot, and you said that was okay."

"I didn't come all this way just to sit in a hotel room and watch TV."

"There's a pool."

She looked at him. "No."

"Then why don't I drop you off somewhere? Someplace historic. You can go sightseeing. Or a mall. You can go shopping. I'll pick you up after I'm done."

"Why don't I drop *you* off?" Sherry said. "Then I'm not stuck in one place. You give me a call when *you're* through, and I'll come and get *you*."

He had to think fast. "The meeting is at the college, but they may need me to go to wherever the reunion will actually be held."

"Then they can give you a ride."

He had no answer for that, at least nothing that didn't sound suspicious, so he let her drop him off at the college. He'd brought his laptop and his cell phone with him, and the moment she was out of sight, he trudged over to a nearby café, where a banner out front promised, FREE WIFI. He ordered coffee, then set up his laptop on the small square table before him and accessed the information he had for Frank Jones. Taking out his cell phone, he called the displayed number.

As he listened to the phone ring, Steve wondered how his father was doing. Since he'd been put on medication, there wasn't much day-to-day change in his condition aside from those occasional bursts of lucidity, but according to Dr. Curtis it was possible, if not probable, that his dad could suffer an episode that would further debilitate him.

Someone answered. "Hello?"

The voice on the other end of the line sounded not only old but angry, and Steve chastised himself for not coming up with a good rap ahead of time, some sort of cover story that would have enabled him to easily invite himself over. "Hello," he said. "Am I speaking to Frank Jones?"

"Who wants to know?"

"I'm . . . a reporter," he said, winging it. I—"

"What's your name?" the old man demanded.

Shit! "Jason Greene," he said quickly, wincing as he gave out his friend's name. "I'm writing an article about—"

"Who do you work for?"

Steve ignored the question. "—about unsolved murders, and I wondered if I could talk to you about Alex and Anthony."

There was silence on the other end of the line, and Steve wondered what was going through the man's mind. Was he remembering his sons? Thinking about how they died? Recalling what they'd been like as children?

It was a weirdly real moment, and Steve found

himself, for the first time, fervently hoping that his father had not killed this man's sons. What had been, moments before, a puzzle to piece together, an intellectual exercise, had suddenly become much more personal. And the truth was that he was not at all sure that his father was behind these murders. After going to Copper City, he'd been able to more easily picture his dad pushing his first wife off the bank building to her death, but the bustling impersonality of Utah's capital somehow made it more difficult for him to imagine his father taking the lives of two young men in such a cold and brutal fashion. And the fact that Steve had spent his early childhood years here made it seem even less likely to him that his father would drive to a different part of the city in order to execute the brothers.

Frank Jones had still not spoken, and Steve cleared his throat. "I have some questions about your sons' deaths. . . ."

"Go to hell!" the old man said, and broke the connection.

He'd probably slammed his phone down, Steve thought, and though he had no idea what Frank Jones looked like, he imagined a chubbier Harvey Keitel stomping angrily around a small, shabby house not unlike Lyman Fischer's.

It was clear that this was not a subject Frank Jones wanted to discuss. Steve needed to talk to the man, though, and wasn't about to let a little setback like this deter him, so he called a taxi and gave the driver Jones's address. He was from California and had never taken a taxi in his life, but the service was a lot cheaper and a lot more convenient than he'd thought it would be. The driver—not Indian or Middle Eastern, as the cinematic stereotypes would have it, but a sulky white guy about his own age—took him directly to the Jones residence, a modest house in an older but well-kept neighborhood. He asked the cabbie to wait, telling him that this wouldn't take long, and the driver shrugged. "Meter's still running. Take your time."

Walking up the short cement path to the porch steps, Steve wondered whether he was supposed to tip the driver. He was bad at figuring out that sort of thing and never seemed to know what was expected or what was appropriate.

He blamed his father for not teaching that to him.

Steve walked up the steps, knocked on the door. No answer. He tried the bell, heard not even a muffled ring from inside the house, and knocked again, louder this time. After a few minutes of this, it soon became clear that if Frank Jones was home he had no intention of answering the door. Steve was about to give up and go away, take the taxi to the site of the fire and then to the house of Issac Donovan, the man who had noticed the blaze and called it in, when he noticed an old woman in a bright housedress watering flowers on the porch of the house next door. Frank Jones and his wife had raised their kids in this house, and there was probably a good chance that the woman next door had been living here way back then.

"Excuse me!" he called, walking over.

The woman glanced up from her watering can. "Yes?" she said cautiously.

He stopped at the edge of her well-manicured yard. "I'm sorry to bother you, but would it be all right if I came up and asked you a few questions?"

"Depends," she said. "If you're trying to sell me something . . ."

"No," he assured her. "I just have a few questions about your neighbor."

She'd seen where he'd come from, and she looked over at the Jones house next door.

"I'm a reporter," he said, the lie coming more easily this time.

Nodding, she motioned him over.

He walked between two low hedges. "I'm doing a story on unsolved murders, and I was hoping to speak with Mr. Jones about his sons, Alex and Anthony. He doesn't seem to want to talk to me, though." Steve stood at the bottom of her porch steps, looking up.

"I'm not surprised," the woman told him.

"Why's that?"

"Frank went through a lot with those boys, and after they died . . . Well, he never really got over it. Lost his job. Drove away his daughter. Took it out on his wife, though she stayed with him until the cancer took her, poor thing."

She glanced around as if afraid of being overheard. "Those Jones kids were monsters," she confided. "No one was surprised when they died badly." She lowered her voice. "Personally? I always thought they'd be shot by the police while they were robbing a bank or something."

It was wrong to take pleasure in the misfortune of others, but the news lifted his spirits. Maybe the killings were justified; maybe his father *had* had a legitimate reason for doing what he'd done. It could have been self-defense. Or payback for a crime committed against him. Whatever the circumstances, Steve felt better about his father's involvement—*if* his father had been involved—and, for the first time, he could imagine his dad doing away with the two losers.

"Can you think of anyone else who might be able to tell me more about Alex or Anthony or the fire?" Steve asked.

The old woman shook her head. "That was a long

time ago. Most of the people who knew them are probably long gone."

"Do you remember the names of any of their friends? Or enemies?"

"Oh, no," she said. "I'm not sure I ever did know."

"What about after the fire? Did the police ever question you or any of the other neighbors about the family and your opinion of the boys?"

"They did, but the officer who talked to me was no spring chicken. I'm sure he's long since retired. I don't recall his name anyway."

Steve continued to ask questions, but the woman— Lurlene Langford, she said her name was—had nothing to reveal, so he finally thanked her, walked back to the taxi, and gave the driver the address of the apartment building where the Jones brothers had perished. It was a Target shopping center now, he discovered, so there was no point in even stopping, and Steve told the cabbie to continue on to the next address on his list: the home of Issac Donovan, the man who had first reported the fire. On the way, he thought about how Alex and Anthony had died. The coroner's report stated that they had burned to death, but that seemed vague to him and unsatisfying. Even if they had not been shot, stabbed or strangled, with the fire set to cover up the true cause of death, there had to be a reason why they had not run out of the apartment at the first sign of trouble. An apartment was not large. Why had they both remained inside rather than dashing out the door or jumping out a window? It had been ten o'clock in the morning. Even if they'd still been asleep at that late hour, the smoke or the heat should have awakened and alerted them. Perhaps they'd been out of it. Drunk. Or stoned.

Or they'd been drugged insensate by someone else.

Or restrained so they would be unable to flee.

And they'd experienced every torturous second of their death, gasping for breath as smoke overpowered the oxygen in the air and filled their lungs, screaming in agony as their skin burned and peeled like cheap lead paint.

He called Sherry on his cell, told her that the meeting was going to run longer than anticipated and he would get a ride back to the hotel; she didn't need to pick him up. He ended the call quickly, before she could ask any questions. He had a lot of ground to cover today, and he could get more done if he didn't waste time trying to get back to the college and pretend to be coming out of a conference room.

"Can you wait for me again?" Steve asked the taxi driver as he pulled up to an assisted-living center.

The cabbie tapped the meter, grinning. "You're my best fare in three weeks. Stay as long as you want."

Steve looked at the displayed amount. The miles and minutes were starting to add up. It was now up to the amount he'd thought his original ride to Frank Jones's would cost. If he stayed here for any length of time, it would probably be cheaper to call for a new cab when he was finished. On the other hand, this was an old-folks' home. And if his meeting with Donovan went anything like the previous stops on today's itinerary, he'd be in and out in a matter of minutes.

"Wait here," he said.

"No prob, Bob."

He stayed longer than expected, and definitely longer than was necessary. Issac Donovan remembered the fire clearly and gave a coherent, detailed account of what had happened and what he'd done. But he had no real information to impart—nothing new, at least—and the only reason Steve remained in the depressingly bare room was because he felt sorry for the ex-custodian, who was obviously starved for company.

Something about Donovan's situation reminded Steve of his father's, and guilt also conspired to keep him there.

After finally getting away, he tried some of the other names on his list—a witness named in one of the articles and the two reporters who had covered the story—but only one of the reporters was home and he barely remembered the case. The day was getting long, and Steve needed to get back, so he gave the cabbie the address of his hotel.

He thought ahead to Tempe and Tucson. Why had he invited Sherry along? He'd be able to talk to a lot more people if she weren't there. He wouldn't have to cram everything into such a short period of time, and he could keep on going from nine o'clock in the morning until nine o'clock at night, instead of having to pretend that this was a real vacation.

Why *had* he brought her? Guilt. Because he hadn't been spending much time with her lately and she deserved to be treated better. And because she tethered him, because he needed the connection with her to keep him grounded, keep him focused, keep him from drifting too far into himself.

And because he knew he couldn't do anything rash with her along.

He remembered how it had felt to squeeze the life out of Lyman Fischer and promptly pushed the memory away.

That was not something that would ever happen again.

The cabbie dropped him off—last minute instructions—at an Italian restaurant two doors down from the hotel. Steve paid him, threw in a ten-percent tip, though he didn't know whether that was necessary, and thanked the driver before walking up the street to the hotel.

A scene greeted him there when he arrived. On the short red carpet in front of the lobby, a little boy stood sobbing uncontrollably while his mother hugged him tightly. A middle-aged man who must have been the boy's father and a uniformed hotel employee were bending down in the center of the parking lot before them, looking at something on the ground. The hotel employee was holding a shovel.

Steve's curiosity must have shone in his face, because the mother said without prompting as he approached, "My son's puppy was killed."

Steve nodded his sympathy, assuming it had accidentally been run over by a car, but the woman offered, "Strangled." She'd lowered her voice as though the boy wouldn't be able to hear if she spoke quietly, but of course he did, and his wailing intensified. She held him more tightly. "It's okay," she said softly. "It's okay."

Steve felt cold. A dead puppy? He thought of Sherry's apartment and automatically looked up at the window of their room. As he'd feared, as he'd somehow known, she was there, staring through the glass between the parted drapes, her attention riveted on the scene in the parking lot. She hadn't noticed that he'd returned, and he quickly walked into the lobby and took the steps two at a time as he headed to the second floor and their room.

Sherry was turning away from the window as he entered.

He walked over to the window, looked out. The hotel guy was carrying the puppy's body across the parking lot on the shovel. "Someone killed a little boy's dog. Strangled it."

"Oh," she said, uninterested. "That's what's going on down there."

He watched her walk into the bathroom, debated

whether to ask about the dead puppy in her apartment, and finally decided to let the matter drop.

By the time she came back out, he was on the bed with his shoes off, watching CNN.

"Where do you want to eat?" she asked brightly.

Twelve

They had only six days total for this vacation, and two of them were gone already, but he decided to spend an extra day in Salt Lake City.

Bad idea.

He had no real leads to follow up on, but gut instinct told him that if he dug a little deeper something might turn up, and he was a firm believer in gut instinct.

Who was he kidding?

As Will never tired of pointing out, he was probably the least spontaneous person on the planet. He planned his weekends a week ahead of time. He didn't need a BlackBerry or any sort of day planner because he *always* kept a schedule in his head. But he *had* been getting better lately. This trip was pretty spontaneous, even if he had had a week to prepare for it. He'd shown up at Sherry's apartment—

and seen the dead puppy

—on a whim. Yesterday, cruising around the city in the taxi, he'd flown entirely by the seat of his pants.

And Lyman Fischer's murder certainly hadn't been planned out.

Or had it?

Because not only had he told no one about his trip to New Mexico, he had made that trip in the middle of the night, had lied to Sherry about being sick during that time, and had taken a plane headed for Houston that happened to stop off at Albuquerque, so that anyone trying to trace his itinerary by computer would assume that he had gone to Texas.

He didn't want to think about that, *wouldn't* think about that, and he told Sherry that he had one more meeting today and then he was through. "I have to do this," he lied. "This is a very important account. That's why they sent me."

"How long's it going to be?" she wanted to know.

"Quicker," he promised.

He took the car this time. Sherry had seen everything she wanted to see in Salt Lake City, and she hadn't had much fun by herself anyway, so she was just going to lounge around the pool and read until he returned. He left shortly after nine, while she was still getting into her bathing suit, and he gave her a quick kiss on the lips and an even quicker one on her exposed left breast before taking off. She laughed, pushing him. "Get out of here."

There were a couple of people who hadn't been home yesterday, and he pulled the car into the empty parking lot of a shopping center that hadn't opened yet and made a few quick calls. One of the men, Gil Patrick, identified in an article as a friend of Alex Jones's, was home and willing to talk, though only on the phone. That was good enough for Steve, who asked a few generic questions to gauge the man's mood before querying, "Did the brothers have any enemies who might have had it in for them? Do *you* have any ideas about who set the fire?"

What he wanted to know was whether his father's name would be one of those mentioned, whether Patrick knew about any beef his father might have had with the Jones boys. Once again, he had one of those weird moments as he thought about his red tricycle and their blue house and realized that if his dad *had* set the fire, he had come home afterward and both Steve and his mother had seen him, had been there, had talked to him as though nothing out of the ordinary had happened.

Patrick considered the question. "Not really," he admitted. "I thought it might be this guy named Elijah at first, but he was real squirrelly and would've bailed once the heat was on, and he didn't. Tony and Alex did have a lot of enemies, though. They were selling coke at that time, and they used to cut it, which pissed off a lot of their customers. But . . . I don't know. It could've been a lot of people. Tony's girlfriend might know more about it than I do."

"What's her name?"

"Anna something. I don't remember. It was twenty fuckin' years ago."

"Do you have any idea where she is?"

"No." There was some sort of commotion in the background, what sounded like a shouting woman, followed by a series of knocks and static. "Sorry," Patrick said, his voice suddenly louder. "Gotta go."

Anna, Steve thought as he listened to the click and then the dial tone. He turned off his phone. There'd been no Anna mentioned in any of the articles or reports he'd read, and while it was possible that the police file contained such a reference, he did not have access to that information. On impulse, he dialed Frank Jones's number. The old man answered on the first ring, and Steve said, "I'm looking for Anna, Tony's old girlfriend."

"Anna French?"

He'd been hoping for such a response, figuring that if he asked quickly, without introducing himself, he might find something out before Jones hung up. "Yes," he said.

The old man must have recognized his voice. "Go to hell!" he yelled before terminating the call.

Anna French. He had a name now, and Steve drove to the café by the college, the only place he knew for sure that he could get Internet access, and he used one of the programs from work to call up information about her. Either she hadn't married or she'd kept her maiden name, because he found an entry for "Anna French" almost immediately. A photo even came up, and to his surprise he recognized the woman. He'd seen her before, though he had to read her stats in order to figure out where: She was one of the students whose reunion booklet he was assembling.

This was where people usually expressed their what-a-small-world platitudes. But it wasn't a small world, and he was starting not to believe in coincidences.

According to the information on his screen, she was now an instructor at the school. He didn't understand why a student at a religious college who went on to become a teacher would hang around with an apparent lowlife like Anthony Jones, but stranger things had been known to happen. He took out his cell and was about to call, thinking that, with the booklet, he even had a legitimate reason to contact her.

Then he flipped off the phone.

He couldn't let her know who he was. He couldn't even give her any clues, any way to track down his identity. He needed to remain completely anonymous.

Untraceable.

Why?

He refused to think about that.

Steve stood, gathering his phone and laptop, thinking he might drive by Anna's house and see if she was home. He had often described his job to his friends as a cross between being a journalist and a detective, and he wondered if this wasn't the right time to start acting on the detective part. He could find her and follow her, learn what he could by—

"Watch it, dillweed."

A smirking, bearded young man, obviously a student, bumped into him intentionally, almost causing him to drop his laptop. "Poseur," the student said derisively.

Without thinking, without pause, Steve hit the other man hard in the face, and was gratified to feel the collapse of cartilage beneath his knuckles as he sucker punched the man in the nose. Warm blood spurted over his clenched fist, and the student screamed like a rabbit being disemboweled, a harsh, high shriek that sounded barely human. The student doubled over, covering his nose with his hand, blood seeping from between his fingers and dripping off the bristles of his beard. Everyone in the café had suddenly stopped what they were doing and were staring at him with almost identical expressions of shock and horror on their faces. A few moved toward him threateningly, and someone in back of the counter yelled, "Call the police!"

Steve ran.

Clutching his laptop and shoving his cell phone in his pocket, he took off. He'd parked down the street at a public lot because there'd been no spots available on the street in front of the café, but he was afraid to head directly there in case a police car came speeding down the street and a cop saw him. So he headed in the opposite direction, intending to go around the block until he reached the parking lot. When he got to the corner and saw that no one was chasing after him, he slowed to a normal walk, trying to look inconspicuous.

He was breathing hard. He had never actually been in a fistfight before, and he felt proud of himself for not backing down, for standing up to that asshole. He remembered the one and only time he'd gotten beaten up at school, when he was in fifth grade. Joe LoPrenzi had called him out on the playground, ostensibly for some imagined transgression but really just because he wanted to fight and Steve had been close by. Joe had taunted him, punching his arm, shoving his shoulder, pushing his chest, ordering him to stop acting like a pussy and fight. Steve hadn't even tried, because he didn't know how, and he had stood there dumbly, taking the punches and trying not to cry, while the other kids on the playground gathered in a circle around him and laughed. Joe LoPrenzi had eventually given up and walked away in disgust.

When he told his parents about it that evening, his mother had ignored him, leaving the dinner table and going into the kitchen for some unspecified reason, while his father had lectured and berated him for acting like a girl instead of a boy.

If his father could only see him now, bruised knuckles covered with blood, the other man down . . .

Steve reached the back of the parking lot at the end of the block. He'd heard no sirens, seen no patrol cars, and taking a chance, he ran across the lot to his car, fumbling with his keys until he unlocked and opened the door. He and Sherry had to leave; they had to get out of here. He didn't want to be arrested on an assault charge way out in Utah and end up in jail.

Driving extra carefully, he headed back toward the hotel. His hands on the steering wheel were red, dripping. He couldn't let Sherry see that, so he stopped on the way and washed off his knuckles in a gas station bathroom, happy to see that they weren't really bruised, that all of the blood was the other man's. He splashed water in the porcelain sink until all the red was gone, then looked up at the mirror. He was still breathing heavily, and he remained unmoving, watching his face, which no longer looked to him like his own. Those were his ears, his hair, eyes, his nose, his mouth, his chin, but their sum added up to something different now, and he could not see himself there.

Gradually, he calmed down, his breathing returning to normal, his skin losing its flushed hue, his features coalescing into a more recognizable countenance. The bathroom was out of paper towels, so, rolling a bunch of toilet paper into a ball, he wet it in the sink and used it to wipe blood off the door handle of the car and his steering wheel. He went back in for another roll to dry with.

Steve looked at himself in the mirror one last time. He would leave here, remaining calm, and return to the hotel, where he would tell Sherry that the meeting was over, his work done, and that he wanted to leave Salt Lake City now in order to get a head start on what would be a busy day in Arizona.

Of course, he wouldn't have to leave at all if that snide jerk hadn't bumped into him, and though Steve was glad that he'd punched the asshole in the face, he wished he'd done more.

He wished he'd killed him.

They spent the night in Flagstaff, a quick stopover before heading down to Tempe, and Steve told Sherry that he'd lived in Flagstaff for a year when he was six. He was curious to drive by their old house, but he'd been so little at the time that he had no idea where they'd lived, could remember only that there'd been a pine tree in their backyard. He thought of calling his mother and asking her, but she was angry with him already, and if she thought that he was driving around sightseeing instead of working she would probably snap. He had to keep up the "business trip" ruse for Sherry as well, which was why he decided not to tell her that he'd also lived in Salt Lake City, Tempe and Tucson.

He still didn't think his father had brutally stabbed that coed—the only unsolved murder for the year that they'd lived there—and he'd decided to believe that there'd been no killing in Flagstaff.

He'd hoped to learn more in Tempe, but the city had undergone a complete makeover since the 1980s, including the addition of a huge fake lake, and though he was able to drop Sherry off in Scottsdale for almost an entire day, every lead came up empty.

This trip was turning out to be a complete waste of time and money.

He'd been older when they'd lived in Tucson and remembered a lot more, and many of the locations connected to the killing were familiar to him. Not only did that give him an advantage in his search, but it cemented in his mind the connection between the murder and his father.

The dead man's name was Salvatore Garza, and he'd been a well-known figure to Tucson's vice squad in the 1990s. Arrested sixteen times on charges ranging from pandering to possession, he'd been convicted twice and was actually out on bail when he'd been murdered.

For the umpteenth time, Steve read over the account of the pimp's death, and even without his father here to explain or describe the scene, he knew exactly how it had gone down. He could see it perfectly in his mind.

He walks in, closes the door behind him. A neon sign is blinking outside, its blue-and-red light providing the only illumination, the light coming in at odd angles, leaving swaths of permanent darkness in shadowed segments of the shabby but once-elegant hotel room. From somewhere outside,

*somewhere close, comes the relentlessly repetitive pounding
of conga drums accompanying a shrill flimsy melody that's
been smothered and beaten down by the rhythm.*

*A half-naked woman on the bed is drugged, unconscious,
and it's clear that she's been fucked hard and left behind.*

*There's a man in the room too, a small, pudgy, oily man
with a used-car dealer's mustache who's not nervous, not
panicking, but calm and smiling, self-satisfied. It's clear that
the pudgy man is the one responsible for this scene.*

*He steps forward into the room, toward the pudgy man.
"Give me the key!" he orders, and the man complies. There's
no fear yet, but the smile beneath the mustache is gone and
there's a wary look in the darting eyes.*

*The hotel is old, the room doors requiring the use of keys
both inside and out, and he uses the key to lock the door before slipping it into his pocket.*

*He turns, advancing on the smaller man, who only now
seems to have realized that he is trapped in here and cannot
escape. The man stumbles backward, darts in and out of the
shadows and the strobing red-and-blue light. The music is
maddening, the conga drums coming through the window
sounding louder. The man scurries around him and tries the
door, as though expecting it not to be locked, but of course
it is, and the man jumps up, tears at a curtain covering the
window above the door, rips it down, breaks the window, but
he grabs the man, pulls him back, throws him to the floor.*

*The man crawls, cowering in a corner, the infuriating
sameness of the Latin drums and the incessant blinking of
the neon signs in sharp counterpoint to the man's frightened
movements. Approaching the whimpering man, he grabs a
stocking from one of the bars on the brass bed where it had
been thrown by the woman or her assailants, and he stretches
it taut between his hands, then whips it around the pudgy
man's neck, wrapping it once and pulling tight. The man
struggles, his flailing arms in the shadow, in the light, red,
blue, red, blue, red, blue, his kicking feet, in some bizarre man-*

ner, matching the beat of the endless music, making it look as though he is dancing.

And then the man is still.

He lets go of the stocking, and the dead man flops forward, his blue-red face hanging over the railing of the bed, his bulging eyes staring down at the unmoving form of the still-unconscious woman.

Salvatore Garza had been a monster, and his father had done society a favor in putting an end to his life. His father was a hero, not a villain—he'd done the job the police *should* have done—and Steve could not find it in his heart to criticize his dad. Even if there'd been no personal connection, no specific reason for him to have killed the pimp, it was a good thing that he had.

How could anybody fault him for that? He had taken it upon himself to solve a problem that until then had been unsolvable, though he had been forced to go outside the law, outside the normal rules and boundaries, and do what had to be done.

Some people needed killing.

That was the punch line to a joke he'd heard some comedian tell, but it was also the truth. Steve was not really a judgmental person—how could he be, after the way he'd always been judged?—but he recognized that certain individuals did not really deserve to live. His father had opened up his eyes to that, and the more Steve learned, the more he saw, the more he experienced, the more he realized that the old man was right.

He remembered watching the movie *Shane* when he was young. In one scene, Shane had said that a gun was just a tool, with no moral value of its own—it was only as good or bad as the man using it.

Killing was much the same, Steve thought. If someone had killed Mother Teresa before her time, that would have been a horrendously evil act. But killing Hitler or Charles Manson would have been an act of righteousness. Killing a killer was never wrong. His father had realized that, and while such a notion might not sit well with civilized society, it was still true.

Steve thought about Lyman Fischer, about that jerk he'd punched in the café in Salt Lake City.

He too had a chance to make a difference in this world, and it was up to him to make the most of it.

"What are you looking at?" Sherry asked.

She had come up behind him, and Steve quickly closed his laptop. "Nothing."

"Something."

He stood, stretched. "Just work."

"I thought we were going to have more time together here in Tucson."

"Oh, we are," he promised.

She suddenly paused, frowned. "What was that?"

"What was what?"

"I thought I heard a dog barking." She was still frowning. "Are pets allowed at this hotel?"

He shook his head, smiled. "Not to my knowledge."

"I hope not," she said. "I don't like dogs."

His smile had grown wider. He didn't know why, but all of a sudden, he felt incredibly happy. "I had a feeling you didn't," he said.

Thirteen

After the Date

She wants me to do her in her bedroom. I say her parents are home, but she says they don't care; she does this all the time. I don't like it, though. It doesn't feel right to me. She's pretty, has a good body even with just the one tit, and I probably would have done it in the car or in the theater, but I just keep thinking about my own parents, and I know I can't do it in her apartment. She calls me a pussy and a fag and she grabs my crotch and says I don't have enough there to do her anyway. Her father opens the window of their apartment and looks out. He's a big man, brown, and naked except for a dark green jacket. I can see his tattoos even from the sidewalk. "Give it to her!" he bellows. "Give my daughter what she wants!"

"He doesn't have anything there!" she screams, and there is anger and also hurt in her voice. "He's not big enough to handle me!"

I get in the car, and I guess I'm angrier than I thought. "Get a tit!" I yell, and I take off, rolling over the bodies of the rats and the cats and the dogs and the discarded gerbils as I speed down the street.

My window is down, and for once I can't smell the air. I take a deep breath. I can still feel the burning, but there is no smell. No rubber. No sulfur. This is what it's like in the country, I think. This is what it's like in the north.

I drive.

The sidewalks are teeming even at this hour, filled with hordes of hairy people pushing, shoving, jostling, maneuvering through the mass in different directions, toward different destinations. It is night, after the Time, and the crowds are silent, the familiar deafening babble of disparate, desperate voices replaced by muffled oceanic swells of sneakered feet on sidewalk. The absence of voices frightens me, and I realize that I can hear the hum of the machinery, the workings of the machines. There are no gunshots.

Clean air and quiet.

I feel chilled, and I look down an alley as I drive by. It is empty save for a short, ugly man in a dark green suit.

He points at me, beckons.

I accelerate, focus my attention on the littered road ahead, quickly turn onto another street. I have seen the man before, although I don't know where. In a picture? In a movie? In a dream? The memory is vague, thirdhand, more like the echo of a recollection than the remembrance of an actuality, but it is powerful and brings with it fear. The streets suddenly seem darker than they did, and I turn left, then turn right, trying to get away from the areas I recognize, knowing that if I keep heading east I am bound to hit the freeway.

I keep thinking that seeing the man was a warning, that I need to stay off the usual streets and that if I do I will be safe, but I am really scared and I wish my car had a radio. I sing to myself—songs my mom taught me—but it doesn't help.

On the corner, on a wagon, a still center in the moving crowd, is a Mexican woman with no legs. She is clutching what looks like a baby. It is unmoving. I hope it is a doll.

What went wrong with the date? I wonder. Why didn't I want to take her down? Last year, last month even, I would have done anything, endured any obstacle, for a chance to get in the pants of any female between fourteen and forty. But something has changed, and the clean air and the silence and the man in the suit are all on my mind and all contribute to the fear I cannot seem to shake.

If I'd just stayed another ten minutes, if I'd just done it the way she wanted, I probably wouldn't've seen the man. Or his suit.

It is the suit that scares me the most.

I pass by the blank gray front of one of the Homes, and I think of my grandpa and his friends in their pink shirts and powder blue pants. I wonder if my grandpa owns or has ever owned a dark green suit. The idea scares me, and I suddenly see the old man in a different light, not as a funny, slightly doddering ex-teacher, but as someone darker, more secretive, more sinister, a man who does not like me but pretends to.

I turn again. The sidewalks are empty, but the street here is filled with boxes and sleeping bodies, debris fallen off trucks and not picked up. I should slow down, but I don't. I swerve around the objects as though I am running an obstacle course. I look only at the road. I wish I could close my eyes and not look at anything. I am afraid of what I might see.

Gang members, as always, are crouched by the on-ramp of the freeway, but it is late and even they must be tired, because they don't come out of their hiding places, and I speed over their deliberate ruts and potholes and onto the freeway itself without being stopped.

I try to remember what Mom told me about my horoscope this morning. I hope I am allowed to go on the freeway.

Traffic is moving, but in the truck lane I see a bundled lump that might be a body and I think of my brother. I look up, but I see no ropes hanging from the overpass.

Now the air is beginning to smell, but the night is still clear and I can see the vague outline of the moon through the smog. I can even make out the diffused lights of office buildings and apartments on the sunken streets to either side of the raised freeway.

I start to feel better. Even though it was my fault the date went as badly as it did, even though I know I won't see her again, I don't really care. I think of her father, bellowing down at me to do his daughter; I think of her one tit and her missing finger and the story she told me about the *puta,* and I know that it wouldn't've worked anyway.

But why didn't I want to do her?

There are five cars stalled on the side of the freeway next to the skunk factory, smog lights blinking. One of the cars is covered with spit, and from inside peers the frightened face of an albino man. I reach over to the seat next to me and pick up my notebook: *5,* I write.

Yesterday it was *10.*

Halved.

A bad omen.

Past the cars, walking toward the off-ramp, is a tall man wearing a dark green suit.

I am so scared it's hard to breathe. I don't look at the man as I speed by, but I have the feeling that he is watching me, that he knows who I am, and that he is probably smiling.

My mind is blank for the last six miles. I think of nothing; I just drive. I get off on the Balcolm exit, still speeding, and leap the trench. A car honks at me as I dart into traffic on the street, and I am so rattled that I flip it off without first looking. I cringe and wait for the bullet, but it is just an old man and his wife, and they flash their brights a few times and then leave me alone.

I turn onto Bradley. A car pulls next to me at the stoplight. A gray Ford that I know I should recognize but do not. I glance over and look in the front window of the car, and the man at the wheel is my father. He is usually at home asleep right now, and I am not sure whether to honk my horn or hide. He is laughing happily, and I cannot remember the last time I saw him even smile.

A woman's hand snakes around my father's shoulder, and as he shifts position I see the woman's face. It is old, horribly wrinkled and caved in on itself, painted with overbright makeup that highlights instead of covers up, and it is the hard face of a seventy-year-old hooker.

My father laughs and kisses the woman, and the lipstick that comes off is dripping and looks like blood on his lips. Then his car moves forward, and I realize that the light has changed, and I press down on the gas pedal and speed by him, and out of the corner of my eye I see for the first time that he is wearing a dark green jacket.

I just want to get home. I wish I had never left the apartment today. I think of Mom. I know I won't tell her about my father, but I wonder what she will say when I tell her that I couldn't smell the air and I could hear the machines.

I pull into the alley. The open garages on both sides of ours are lit, but our bulb is either broken or burned out, and the double space within the garage is dark. I back in, and in my rearview mirror I see the piles of newspapers and cans, bathed in red brake light. Then I stop the car, take my foot off the brake and everything is black again.

I open the car door and my overhead light dimly illuminates the center of the garage. In the corner, I see a shape. A dark shape, more solid than the blackness of surrounding shadows. The goose bumps pop up on my arms as a chill passes through me, and I am shaking as I close the car door. I try to hurry out of the garage as quickly as I can. I see the shape out of the corner of my eye, and it seems to be suspended there. It does not seem to be touching the ground. It does not seem to have feet.

It appears to have shoulders the shape of a wire hanger.

I close my eyes. *Please let it be a prowler*, I pray. *Please let it be a rapist. Please let it be a murderer.*

Please let it be a person.

Anything but a dark green suit.

Fourteen

His father died alone.

No one was in the room Tuesday when he passed away at approximately ten a.m. Steve was at work, his mother was at home, and the hospital staff was busy elsewhere. It wasn't until a nurse came in to deliver his medication at eleven that it was discovered he was gone.

Steve cried when he received the news. He hadn't thought he would, and the tears surprised him. He held them in until he reached the restroom, passing by the office work cubicles, past Gina's desk, down the corridor to the recessed swinging door of the men's room. He stood before the mirror above the sink, looking at his face, and the tears began to flow. It wasn't his father's death, exactly, that made him so sad. That had been expected and was, in all honesty, something of a relief. It was the fact that he had died alone, that in his last moments there'd been no one there to keep him company, to care, to mark the end of his long and complicated life. Steve was crying for himself as much as for his father, at the thought that this might be how he too would end up. For while he saw himself marrying Sherry sometime in the near future; he could also see them apart, broken up, divorced, and he could easily imagine himself dying alone in a room with no one else in attendance.

He examined his face in the mirror. Someone—a visitor, certainly, not someone who worked here—had scratched the word "dipshit" into the glass, and it sat there beneath his chin like a caption. He was not sure what he hoped to see as he watched the quivering of his mouth, followed the shiny trail of a tear down his cheek, gazed into his red blurry eyes. Was he looking for similarities to his father? If so, there was very little resemblance. Physically, at least.

He stared at himself until his features became unrecognizable. It was a trick he used to do as a child, a type of self-hypnosis. For he'd found early on that if he stood before a mirror and concentrated hard, unblinking, his perception of himself would change. His face would become clearer, sharper, the background fading into blurriness behind that ever-expanding face until at last it no longer looked like his own but was distinct, separate and entirely unfamiliar. In the final stage, just before he had to blink, his head would appear three-dimensional, pushing outward from the flatness of the mirror. He had always liked that feeling of disassociation, the sense that he was outside of himself and seeing his face as others did, but he hadn't done that in years, probably not since early high school, and he realized now that the times when he used to do it were usually the times that he'd had problems with his father.

Someone else walked into the men's room—Jay Botiggi, from sales—and Steve pretended he'd just been washing his hands, reaching for a paper towel and crumpling it in his palms before tossing it into the wastepaper basket and heading out the door.

Back at his desk, he called his mother and told her he was coming by to pick her up, before informing Gina and McColl that he would be gone the rest of the day and possibly the rest of the week. Gina was solicitous, overly so, uncomfortably so, and Steve found himself almost grateful for the department head's aloof disinterest. He got out of the office as quickly as he could and drove straight to his parents' house.

His *mother's* house.

He had only one parent now, and he suddenly realized how much extra work and responsibility that was going to be. He'd been shouldering a huge burden ever since his father's stroke, but for some reason, in the back of his mind, the situation had always seemed temporary. He'd been under no illusion that his father was going to recover, but still, everything had been in flux, and emotionally that had enabled him to handle the situation by acting as though he would be doing it only for a while. Now, he realized, he was responsible for his mother, for the house, for the finances, for . . . everything. He felt overwhelmed thinking about all he would have to do, and if he were a less reliable son, he would have just stayed on the freeway and kept driving, losing himself in a new city, creating for himself a new life.

But he wasn't that kind of person, and he pulled into the driveway behind the Chrysler. He looked over at the lawn. He should probably take an hour or so this week and mow the grass, he thought, walking up to the door.

His mother had obviously been waiting for him, because she opened the door the second he stepped onto the porch, holding the screen for him. He'd expected to find her crying, or at least red faced and teary eyed, but she looked the same as she always did, perhaps a little more annoyed than usual. She had not bothered to change but was wearing one of the faded flowered housedresses she usually wore when at home.

"Do you want some coffee?" she asked.

He looked at her. "No, Mom. I think we should go. They're waiting for us."

"I've been cleaning," she said, and led him through the living room to the bedroom, where a pile of his father's clothes lay on the bed. She had to have been more broken up than she let on, had to have felt *something* for him after all those years together, despite the problems they'd had at the end. But her set face revealed nothing, and she told him flatly, "Go through his things and take what you want. I'm donating the rest to the Goodwill."

"We need to go see him first," Steve said. His mother nodded her acknowledgment, and he motioned toward her ratty housedress. "Do you need to change?"

She stared at him. "Why?"

"I thought—"

"I'm fine."

"All right." He sighed. "Let's go."

They were silent on the way over. He did not trust himself to talk, and his mother seemed to have no desire to speak to him. He was angry at her, and he told himself that if she mentioned anything negative about his father or brought up unrelated subjects as though what had happened had not happened, he would go off on her. She was a selfish and self-centered woman, and it was long past time that someone called her on it.

But she didn't speak, neither of them spoke, and they arrived at the VA hospital shortly after one. It was the busiest time of day, and the parking lot was full. He dropped his mother off at the entrance, then looked for a spot. He would have parked on the street, but the entire block was ringed with No Parking signs, and he ended up parking at a Wendy's two blocks away. The signs in the Wendy's lot said that parking was for customers only, so he bought a Coke, saved the receipt to prove that he was a customer, then ran back down the street to the hospital.

He was drenched with sweat when he arrived. His

mother had not moved, had not even gone into the air-conditioned lobby to wait, but stood outside, clutching her purse and staring primly out at the parking lot as a hairy wheelchair-bound man smoked a cigarette on the sidewalk next to her.

"Come on, Mom," Steve said, and led her inside. Out of habit, he almost walked over to the elevators to head up to the second floor, but then he remembered and went over to the front counter to ask where they'd taken his father's body. While the man behind the counter called someone to find out, Steve looked around, realizing that this was probably the last time he would have to come to the hospital. For that he was grateful.

"Sir?" the man said. Steve turned back toward him. "Mr. Nye has been taken downstairs to the morgue. Just take that elevator"—he pointed—"and press the button for B-one. Turn right when you get off, and you can't miss it. Dr. Curtis will meet you there."

"Thank you," Steve said.

"Sorry for your loss."

His father's naked body was not in a drawer or under a sheet; it was lying atop a metal table in the center of the room, and when the technician let them in, the sight was a shock. Dr. Curtis was standing to the side, reading what was doubtlessly his father's chart, but Steve could not help staring at the old man's embarrassingly exposed form. His dad's body was pale and looked both smaller and pudgier than he would have thought. Though his eyes and mouth were closed, the expression on his face was not peaceful, not one of rest or repose. Rather, the cheek and jaw muscles were frozen grimly in what appeared to have been an attempt to stoically deny tremendous pain.

He glanced over at his mother to see her reaction, but there was none. Her features were emotionless, unreadable, and her attention was squarely on the doctor, who looked up at their entrance and proceeded to give them a more comprehensive explanation of Joseph Nye's death and the events surrounding it, emphasizing that both a nurse and an intern had checked on him twice—before and after an orderly had fed him breakfast—and that this was the same routine that had been followed each day since his admittance. It sounded to Steve a lot like an attempt to shield the hospital from blame, but he didn't think it was negligence that had led to his dad's death and doubted that his mother did either.

Dr. Curtis said that while the exact cause of death could not be pinpointed until an autopsy was performed, his best guess at this juncture was another stroke, with an outside chance of heart attack.

There were forms to be filled out, claims and releases, and Steve and his mother spent the next half hour reading and signing what seemed like volumes of paperwork. Most families, he assumed, were grateful for the numbing distraction this offered, but his family was not normal and needed no such diversion to blunt their emotions. Neither he nor his mother were the type to break down or go into hysterics. Indeed, after completing all of the paperwork and discussing a few more details with Dr. Curtis and a morgue attendant, they rather formally said their good-byes and left.

The autopsy was performed later that day, and it was determined that, despite all of the medication and treatments, he had had another stroke, this one fatal. It was Dr. Curtis who called with the news, and he assured Steve that death had come quickly, that there'd been no pain or suffering. He had already called Steve's mother to give her the autopsy results, and out of curiosity, Steve asked if his mother had had any questions.

"No, none," the doctor said. "I suspect she's still in shock."

She doesn't care, Steve felt like saying, but he merely agreed.

Did *he* care?

On one level he did, but deep down, he suspected, he did not. His interest seemed more clinical than emotional, but by the time he hung up the phone, after promising to arrange for retrieval of "the body," he found that he was crying again.

He forced himself to stop, and the waterworks ended abruptly.

After pouring himself a stiff drink—an old-school drink, the kind his dad liked—he called his mother to talk about making arrangements. He would have preferred to speak with her in person, but she had been unbearable on the ride home, and when he had suggested that he should stay with her, she had told him angrily that she didn't require a babysitter. It was not that she needed to be alone; she just didn't want him around. That was fine. He wasn't thrilled with her either, and secretly he was relieved that he wouldn't have to watch her. He had offered only out of obligation, anyway.

She sounded irritated when he called, and she seemed to have no interest in talking about the disposition of his father's body, offhandedly letting him know that he could call the hospital and whatever funeral home he chose and do what he wanted. He tried to engage her, but she seemed on the verge of hanging up, so he asked about his father's belongings. "You were going through his clothes when I picked you up. If you need any help—"

"I don't need *help*," she said in a voice at once defensive and angry. "I've already sorted through everything. Look at it and take what you want. I'm donating the rest."

He didn't quite understand this *immediate* need to erase all trace of his father from the house, but Steve promised that he would come over the next day and look through his dad's stuff.

After that, he called funeral homes. He had no idea how to pick one, so he did what he did when searching for any consumer item: He opened the yellow pages, went down the list alphabetically and called them all, intending to choose the one that was cheapest and closest. He settled on Reichman and Sons in Santa Ana, and the Reichman to whom he spoke assured him that his father's body would be picked up tonight and taken to the mortuary. Since Steve had no preference in regard to cemeteries and had not had a chance to look at caskets or headstones (or even decide whether burial was preferable to cremation), a "consultation" was set up for ten o'clock the next morning.

Steve hung up the phone and wondered if, even now, Reichman was ordering some flunky to head out to Long Beach and retrieve his father's body. What kind of vehicle did they use? Was it something like an ambulance or a variation on a hearse? And how was the body transported? In a bag? In a box? In a temporary coffin?

Recalling his father's pale, lifeless form, an image that had not left the forefront of his consciousness all afternoon, Steve found himself thinking about the autopsy. He had never really considered exactly what an autopsy entailed, since, prior to this, that word had come up only in the context of television shows or news stories. There'd never been any sort of personal involvement. But he realized now that the doctor performing the autopsy had had to cut his father open and physically examine the heart, the lungs and other vital organs. He could envision the scene in detail, and he wondered what it would be like to slice someone

open himself, to use a knife or scalpel and actually saw
through skin to reach muscle and fat and vein. It would
be one thing to cut someone who was dead; quite another to do it to someone alive. The carving of living
flesh, the severing of a vein or artery through which
blood still pumped, would be much more interesting
and exciting. Gross, yes, but gratifying.

He looked out the window at the apartment complex across the street, which was a mirror image of his
own. Most of the windows in the three-story structure
were dark, and even the ones with lights on were visible only as a squarish outline around the edges of
closed blinds and shades. The sidewalks, as always,
were empty—no one walked in Irvine—though occasional cars passed quickly by on the street in between.

Night in the city.

Weren't those the lyrics of an old ELO song? One of
those that had been recycled into a commercial jingle?
He was pretty sure his father had had that album when
Steve had been a kid. What had happened to it?

He continued to stare out the window, and in a sky
ordinarily too bright to see such things, he caught in
his peripheral vision the split-second streak of a falling
star. He thought of Flagstaff, and it occurred to him
that maybe his father *had* been behind the stabbing of
that coed. He'd been seeing the killing through the victim's eyes, through the filter of the media and the police, but looking at it now through the other end of the
lens, Steve realized that he knew next to nothing about
the young woman. Just because she'd been attending
college didn't mean she was some virginal saint. She
could have been an evil, scheming slut or a vicious
physical abuser. It had been the ferocity of the killing
that had originally convinced him his father had not
been behind it, but he wondered now if the violence

had been justified—in which case, his dad *could* have been behind it.

He needed to go back and look at the case more carefully.

As odd as it might seem, he found it comforting to think that there was still more to learn about his father.

He was still staring out the window ten minutes later, thinking, when Sherry called, asking if he wanted her to come over, wondering if there was anything she could do. There was, actually. She could come over, suck his penis, then go home. But of course he couldn't tell her that, was embarrassed he'd even thought of it, and he told her wearily that he was exhausted and just wanted to sleep. He would call her in the morning.

Steve *was* exhausted, but he *couldn't* sleep, and after a night of fitful tossing and turning, he got out of bed shortly before dawn to make some coffee and toast. He left a message on Gina's voice mail that he still wouldn't be coming in to work, then phoned Sherry, waking her up to tell her that he would be busy this morning and would call her at the library around lunchtime. Afraid that in a fit of pique his mother might throw out his father's belongings before he had a chance to look at them, Steve decided to drive over to his parents'—

his mother's

—house and sort through what he could before his ten-o'clock meeting at the mortuary.

Like him, his mother had not slept much. She was in the kitchen when he arrived, drinking coffee and listening to talk radio. They spoke briefly, politely, distantly; then she told him that his father's clothes were in the bedroom and everything else was in the television room. He needed to go through it all now because she was going to donate it today.

Steve was taller than his father, so none of the clothes would fit, but he took a look at the pile of shirts and pants anyway to see whether he might want to keep something for sentimental reasons. He did not. As he dug through the boxes of belongings that his mother had assembled, however, his gaze alighted on a brown hardcover copy of Cervantes's *Don Quixote*. He had read that book in high school, and even then had wondered how it had come into his father's possession. Joseph Nye had not been a reader, and the other books in his possession all seemed to be biographies of sports figures and famous businessmen. So why *Don Quixote*? Steve didn't know, was not even sure that his father had bothered to read the book, but Steve had been intrigued by the cover art—a faded old-timey picture of a skinny knight with a long white beard riding on a bony horse next to a fat man on a donkey—and he'd picked up the book for that reason. Despite the density of the prose, he'd found himself engrossed in the story of the dreamy, deluded old man and his earthy, practical squire. Something about Cervantes's novel spoke to him, and over the next several years Steve had read it more than once, even writing a term paper in college on the work's layered narrative voice.

It was *Don Quixote* that had first made him want to be a writer.

Feeling a touch of nostalgia, he picked the book out of the box and opened it, looking closely at the flyleaf, searching for some indication that it had been a present given to his father at some point.

By his first wife?

There was no inscription, however, no dedication, no marks on any of the opening or closing pages. Perhaps, Steve thought, it had belonged to one of his father's victims, and he had taken it as a souvenir after dispatching the man. Or woman.

He liked that idea.

He put the book aside and read the spines of the other books in the box, finding nothing of interest. Discovering in the next box over an old notebook listing competitors' auto parts and their prices, written in his father's tight, cramped hand, he wondered whether the old man had kept a personal journal or a diary, if his dad had jotted down notes about his . . . kills. Steve doubted it. Doing so would not have made much sense, and if there was one thing his father had always been, it was sensible. The odds that he would create and leave around incriminating evidence defied all logic. Yet Steve wished he had, and he spent several hours searching not just through the boxes but in every nook and cranny he could think of, trying to come up with something that would explain or describe exactly what his father had done in all those cities.

A road map he could follow, part of his brain told him, but he pushed that thought aside.

"What are you doing?" his mother asked finally, annoyed, and Steve stopped his search. It was getting late, and he had to drive to Santa Ana and meet with the funeral director.

Not for the first time, he wondered if his mother knew more than she let on. Was that why she'd been so afraid of her husband at the end? Not just because of the stroke-fueled attack but because she was aware of the violence of which he was capable? Steve didn't know, and he could think of no way to hint around about the subject to test her out. He looked at her face, trying to determine whether he believed his mom knew of his father's hidden avocation. Would she keep that sort of secret for him? Would she carry it to her grave?

There was no way to tell.

"Are you done here?" she asked him.

"Yes," he said, picking up *Don Quixote*. "Do you want to come with me to—"

"No," she said flatly.

He looked at her for a moment, saw the hardness in her mouth. "Okay."

He went directly from there to the mortuary.

Fifteen

The funeral was short and simple. Neither Steve nor his father had ever been religious, and though his mother was—to a wacky degree—she did not belong to any church, so there were no required rituals for them to go through, no specific traditions that had to be honored or observed. He had instructed the funeral director officiating at the ceremony to keep everything as brief and generic as possible, the bare minimum required for decorum's sake, and the man was as good as his word. There was no wake, no memorial service, no viewing of the body at the mortuary, only a nonspecific Joseph Nye–was-a-good-man-and-we'll-all-miss-him speech by the graveside as the coffin was lowered into the ground.

If it were up to Steve, there would not have been even that much of a concession to convention. He would have been alone with his mother right now, watching silently as his father was buried without fanfare. But there were other people to think about—not family but friends, acquaintances—and this was the compromise.

After the coffin had been lowered, his mother took out her well-worn Bible and began reading, in fiery, angry cadences, a series of long judgmental verses that had nothing to do with his father and did not seem apropos of anything.

The cemetery was surprisingly crowded. Jason came, and Dennis and Will, though he could not remember inviting any of them. He had been in charge of the arrangements, but he realized that he did not recall inviting *most* of those who showed up. Standing next to Sherry, Steve looked around. There were a lot of people from the past. Men and women he hadn't known he'd known but whom he recognized immediately upon seeing again. Smiling politely, he greeted them as, one by one, they filed past, offering condolences. His mother, too, had on her public face, and though she was the grieving widow, she made sure to tell everyone that it was the *second* stroke that had killed Joseph; the first stroke had almost killed *her* because it had made him attack her like a crazy man.

Behind them, the grave lay open, the coffin unburied. He had never been to a funeral before, and had always gotten the impression from movies and TV that all of the mourners waited and watched while all of the dirt was filled in. But people were leaving, and though there was some sort of digging machine off to the side, there was no one around to operate it, and the pile of dirt that had been taken from the grave lay untouched. He had no idea what his mother's plans were, but he was going to wait here until his father had been buried and the grave was filled. And since she had ridden to the cemetery with him, she was going to have to wait, too, if she expected a ride home.

Will came over. He felt Sherry's hand stiffen in his. She didn't like Will, and had never tried to disguise the fact, although she made an effort to be polite.

"Sorry, man," Will said. And that was it. He was moving off with a nod, ignoring Sherry completely, not stopping by to see his mother.

Dennis awkwardly stuck out his hand, and Steve awkwardly shook it. "If there's anything you need . . ." he mumbled, and then he was following Will.

Jason came up and offered real sympathy, hugging first Sherry, then Steve, and while Steve wasn't a big fan of hugging and stood there stiffly, not reciprocating, at least he understood and appreciated the effort. "I'll call you in a few days," Jason said. "Once everything's settled down. We'll talk."

Sherry had arrived in her own car, but she remained after everyone else had gone, coming with him into the adjacent mortuary as he asked when the actual burial would take place and requested rather forcefully that they do it now so he could watch. The three of them watched together—he, Sherry and his mother—and after the dirt was replaced, the tarp protecting the nearby grass removed and the cemetery workers gone, his mother stood in front of the grave, eyes closed, and began reciting a prayer.

"When do they put up the headstone?" Sherry asked.

"Next week sometime."

She lowered her voice. "Do you want me to meet you back at your place? I could stay over tonight if you want."

He looked over at his mother and sighed. "Yeah," he said. "That'd be good."

Sherry was in the kitchen cutting chicken when he returned to his apartment after taking his mother home. She'd stopped off and bought groceries on her way over, and he saw a variety of foodstuffs spread over his counter.

The second he walked in, she quickly washed her hands and rushed over to give him a big hug. It wasn't sexual; she didn't even kiss him. She just threw her arms around him and held him close, pressing her cheek against his, silently offering her love and support. Improbably, he got an erection anyway. Embarrassed to have such a thing happen at such an inappropriate time, he shifted slightly, pressing his chest into her while pulling the lower half of his body away. She caught his move, though, and pushed herself into him, and then they were waddling over to the couch, still entwined, frantically pulling down pants and underwear. They did it fast and rough, coming at the same time, she with an escalating series of high-pitched screams, he with a single animalistic grunt, and afterward they pulled on their clothes without speaking.

"Are you all right?" Sherry asked, concerned, before heading back into the kitchen.

He nodded silently, still breathing hard, and turned on the television. He wasn't sure how he felt or what he felt or if he even felt anything, but he didn't want to dwell on it and knew that TV would keep his mind distracted enough that he wouldn't think about himself or his father or anything difficult.

After dinner, he told Sherry she could go home if she wanted—

I don't need you here I'm through with you

—but she insisted on staying, and she did the dishes for him, took a quick shower and met him in bed. They were both naked but neither of them seemed to be in the mood, and they were strangely tentative with each other as they kissed chastely and said good night.

"At least today's over," Sherry told him. "At least the worst of it's past."

"Yeah," Steve said, rolling over and away from her.

He closed his eyes.

He fell asleep instantly.

He dreamed.

In his dream, there was a clown lying in his father's uncovered casket, oversize shoes sticking up higher than the coffin sides. The clown's eyes were closed, but open eyes had been painted on his eyelids and the effect was disconcerting. As was the fact that a downturned mouth lay hidden beneath the red-painted smile that shone so brightly against the white pancake makeup. A wake was in progress, and it was attended not by clowns or other circus performers but by children from his elementary school, all grown up. No one looked sad; everyone looked bored, and Steve alone stood in front of the casket. He felt afraid and wanted to leave, but he understood that he was the host of this event, and it was his responsibility to make sure the clown stayed dead and did not attack anyone. He glanced down again at the open casket, but something was wrong; something was different. It was the clown's eyes, he saw. They weren't just painted open now; they were really open, and they were staring at him with a hatred so fierce he could feel it. The clown sat up, and Steve screamed, jumping back. The room was empty now, all of his former classmates were gone, and he started running, hearing the slap of leather on linoleum as those big floppy shoes came chasing after him.

He awoke with the slapping sound still in his ears, and for a brief, confusing second thought that the clown was here with him in his room. Then reality reasserted itself, the nightmare faded away, and he was in bed, next to Sherry, on the night of his father's funeral. He glanced at the clock. They'd gone to bed early after the stress of the day, but he was still surprised to see that it was only ten fifty-five. One or both of them had kicked off the sheet that had been covering their bodies, and Steve noticed that despite all of his thrashing around, Sherry was still dead asleep. She was on her side, next to him, but facing away. He watched her for a moment. He had an erection again and wondered what she would do if he just scooted a little bit closer and slid it up her ass. The thought made him smile, but he wasn't brave enough to do it, and instead he reached for the sheet, pulling it over them. He picked up the remote control from the nightstand next to the bed. Turning on the television to help him fall asleep, he closed his eyes and dozed off sometime in the middle of the weather forecast on the late local news.

He awoke again several hours later, instantly alert, and sensed immediately that he and Sherry were not alone in the room. Skin prickling, he looked to the right and saw his father sitting in the chair by the closed curtains. The television was still on, the host of a late-late-night talk show babbling in the background, and light from the TV illuminated his dad's motionless form. There was no smile on the frozen face, and the unblinking eyes appeared black and shiny in the flickering bluish glow, but there wasn't the expression of blank confusion that had been the fixed cast of his features since the stroke. He seemed . . . normal.

Steve didn't know whether it was a ghost or a figment of his imagination—the latter, he assumed—but the apparition seemed so real that he squinted into the dimness, trying to see it more clearly. The old man, he noticed, was wearing not the suit in which he'd been buried, but the type of dark pants and white shirt that had often served as his workday attire. Dark splotches were visible on the left sleeve and side of the shirt, irregular stains of various sizes, and though Steve couldn't be positive, he was pretty sure they were blood.

That should have made him afraid, but instead he found it calming. The instinctual fear he'd experienced upon waking was gone, replaced by a general feeling of sadness. There were so many things he wished he could have said to his father while he was alive. Not that he would have. Even simple communication had been beyond them since his early teenage years, and the complexity of the subjects he wanted to discuss was well past their comfort level. Still, if he *could* have talked to his dad, if they could have talked to *each other*, he knew they would have had a lot in common, a lot to discuss.

Life was a series of missed connections.

What was it that Jason had said about fathers and their grown sons?

We still crave our dads' approval. We still want them to be proud of us.

It was true, and Steve would have given anything to hear the ghost of his dad say something positive, something reassuring, something nice. But the figure remained silent, and when Steve looked away for a moment to see if his father's reflection was visible in the dresser mirror, the form vanished.

He was left with a sense of loss so profound that tears came to his eyes and there was a sick, hollow feeling in his gut. Then Sherry rolled over on the bed beside him, and he quickly wiped his eyes so she wouldn't see. By the time he realized she wasn't waking up, was only stirring in her sleep, the feeling was gone, and he settled back into his pillow, closed his eyes and within moments was sound asleep himself.

This time, he did not dream.

Sixteen

He was rereading *Don Quixote* for the first time since college, poring through his father's book each night after work, and it was turning out to be quite a slog. He was forcing himself to get through it, but the going was slow, and seemingly everything distracted him. He would finish a paragraph, then decide he needed a drink of water; read a page, then feel uncomfortable and need to change his seat or take off his shoes; get through part of a chapter, then tell himself that the nightly news was on and he should watch it to find out what was going on in the world. . . .

Sherry admired his ambition, and it was partly for her that he continued on and did not give up. But it was not only for her. There was something else involved as well. An attempt to recapture the past? An effort to relive old glories? Steve didn't know. Whatever it was, he couldn't quite put his finger on it.

He realized, however, that he was not the reader he used to be—he was not the *person* he used to be—and if he had picked up Cervantes's novel for the first time today, he doubted that he would have gotten past the first few pages. Something about that seemed sad, and though he wasn't sure why, he felt as though he had lost a part of himself.

In many ways, he and Sherry had grown closer after their trip. And his father's death had only drawn them together even more. They'd been engaged now for over six months—he'd proposed on her birthday in a breezy, lighthearted manner—but it was a casual, open-ended commitment to be married sometime in the indefinite future that he wasn't sure she took any more seriously than he did. Recently, though, they'd begun discussing their lives together in a less frivolous fashion, and rather than avoiding thinking about the subject, as he had in the past, Steve found that he liked imagining what they planned to do in the months and years ahead.

With his friends, on the other hand, he'd grown more distant and detatched. He'd given up the Friday get-togethers, and though Jason had called twice and they'd made tentative plans to meet next Wednesday evening at the gym, he hadn't heard from Will or Dennis at all. Not that he felt sorry about it. Things would be much easier, in fact, if they just drifted out of his life forever and he never had to see or hear from them again.

He and his mother had fallen back into their old habits. For that, he felt guilty. She was alone now and needed him more than ever, if not emotionally then at least to perform manual labor around the house. There was the car, the lawn, and God knew what else: lightbulbs to be changed, trees to be trimmed, rock salt to be put in the water softener, leaky faucets to be fixed. But she didn't ask, he didn't volunteer and the last time they had spoken, to discuss the funeral bills, the call had lasted barely over a minute.

At work, though, things were going great. Both the trip and his father's death had freed him somehow, made him stronger. It wasn't that he didn't care about his job, or no longer tried to do the best he could. It was that he had put his work into perspective. Tracking down and interviewing alumni, putting out newsletters and yearbooks, was important but not *that* important. Well, it had *never* been that important. But he had always done his best to impress his supervisors, had placed a lot of emphasis on the opinions of those above him in the company. He'd been behaving as though he were still in school, trying to impress the teacher and get all As. He realized now, though, that he didn't really care about gaining the approval of AlumniMedia's supervisors, managers and department heads. He would continue to do his best, but if they didn't like it, too bad. This position wasn't the be-all and end-all. There were always other jobs he could take, other companies he could work for.

The realization had unchained his mind, improved his focus, and it showed in the quality and quantity of his output.

Often, when he was sitting at his desk, he thought about how it had felt to punch that smirking, bearded man at the café in Salt Lake City. Even as he relived the moment, his mind made subtle changes to the scenario. Inevitably, the other man became more evil and actively aggressive, while he himself turned out to be more heroic. Sometimes the fight lasted longer and there was a cheering crowd egging them on. In the most satisfying version of events, he ended up beating the man senseless, pummeling his face until it was a raw, bloody pulp with virtually no trace of human features left.

He liked to think about Lyman Fischer too.

He had more confidence now, and that was reflected not only in his work but in his standing at the office. He was consulted quite often by the photo editors, and even the videographer had been asking his advice lately. Unfortunately, this also meant that Gina was trying to insert herself into his life even more than she had before—walking over to his desk rather than calling him on the phone, writing notes on her personal stationery rather than the company's memo forms, engaging him in conversation at every opportunity—and it was becoming increasingly difficult to avoid her. She seemed genuinely interested in him, though he was not sure why. She knew he was involved—Sherry's framed photo was right there on his desk next to his computer—and her relationship with that older man on the beach certainly didn't strike him as familial. Yet she was flirtatious and insinuating, clearly vying for his attention, and as much as he tried to evade her and put her off, he could not seem to discourage the woman. He'd taken to going out at lunch instead of eating at his desk just to avoid her.

One day after work, he was in his car in the parking lot, sorting through the stack of CDs on the seat next to him and trying to figure out what music to put on for the ride home, when he saw Gina come out of the building and walk over to a silver Saturn parked near the street. Steve watched her, curious. The two of them had never before left at the same time, or, if they had, he had never noticed. But he found himself wondering now about where she lived and whom she lived with, what her life was like away from work. Still pretending to sort through the CDs, he watched out of the corner of his eye as she removed the keys from her purse, unlocked her car and got in. She backed up, swung the Saturn around and headed for the exit.

On impulse, he started his engine and pulled out into the street, following her. She drove quickly, recklessly, like a teenager, but he maintained a steady pace, remaining one car behind at all times, and stayed with her. It seemed strange to be trailing someone like this, strange but good, and he felt happy and exhilarated as he sped down Culver Street, keeping the Saturn in his sight.

Surprisingly, she lived in a condo not too far from his own apartment. He'd assumed she lived by the beach, because that was where he'd seen her, but either she'd been visiting someone on Balboa or had just gone there for the day, as he and Sherry had, because she lived in Irvine.

Gina had her own driveway, and he parked across the street and watched as she pulled in and got out, ducking down in his seat when she happened to glance in his direction. Peeking out a moment later, he saw her step into the condo and close the door behind her. Seconds afterward, the closed blinds over the front window were opened, although the interior was too dark for him to make out anything.

It occurred to Steve that if she looked out the window and saw him out here, she might think he was a stalker. Or interested. He wasn't sure which would be worse. He thought about driving around the block and finding a new place to park farther down the street, where he couldn't be seen, but it didn't feel right. Not today.

Putting the car into gear, he drove down the street and reluctantly headed toward home.

Where Sherry was waiting.

The next day, at work, Gina delivered his mail, then decided to remain by his desk, casually picking up his stapler, his Batman paperweight, anything she could get her hands on, while she tried to engage him in conversation.

I know where you live, he thought. *I could show up at your doorstep and . . .*

The thought allowed him to endure her mindless chatter.

After work, he left early and drove to her neighborhood, parking down the street behind a blue Prius, making sure that he had an unobstructed view of her condo. Gina arrived at five twenty-four, about the same time as yesterday, but the second she closed the door of her car, she started frantically pulling on the handle, trying desperately to open it, though the door was obviously locked. She cupped her hands together, peered into the driver's-side window, and Steve understood that she had locked her keys in the car. He sat back, smiling. This was going to be fun.

He expected her to take out a cell phone and call AAA, but instead she looked furtively around, making sure no one was watching, then lifted a flowerpot on the porch and took something out from underneath it. A key. She unlocked the front door, replaced the key beneath the flowerpot, then went inside, returning a moment later with what was obviously an extra car key that she used to open the door of the Saturn.

Steve waited until she went back inside, then drove away, smiling.

He knew where she kept her spare house key.

He wasn't going to use that knowledge, Steve told himself. He wasn't going to do anything about it.

But he knew that wasn't true.

It was not until the next week that Gina left her condo unattended. It was possible that she'd gone somewhere over the weekend, but he was with Sherry from Friday night until late in the day Sunday and hadn't been able to drive by and check. On Tuesday, however, she told everyone at work who would listen that she had a big date that night, and she told it to Steve several times in an annoying, flirtatious way that made him think she was trying to make him jealous.

So what if she was going to be gone for several hours, and he knew where the key to her front door was hidden? That didn't mean anything. He didn't have to do anything with that information. There was no reason for him to break into her place. He didn't like her; he didn't care about her; he had no interest in her or her life. What could he possibly gain by spying on her home? Besides that, it was illegal. Breaking and entering. He could go to jail.

He was going to go straight home to his own apartment after work. He was going to call Sherry and ask her to come over, and the two of them would have a nice dinner, watch a movie or something and spend the night together.

He called Sherry.

And told her that he would be working late and would call her tomorrow.

At exactly seven fifteen, Gina turned on the porch light of her condo, stepped outside, locked the door, got into her car and left. Steve knew this because he was watching her from within his own car, parked across the street and two houses away. He had assumed that someone would come by to pick her up—possibly the guy from Balboa Island—and he was surprised to see her leave on her own. It made him wary, as well, and he waited five minutes, ten minutes, fifteen, before he finally got out and walked casually down the sidewalk to her microscopic yard. Pausing for a moment, pretending to check whether his shoelace was untied, he looked up and down the street, seeing no one on the sidewalks, no one watching him from any windows. Two quick steps and he was on her porch, lifting the flowerpot, taking the key.

He opened the door and waited for a moment, bracing himself, ready to run, but she didn't appear to have an alarm, and he slipped the key back under the flowerpot, hurried inside and closed the front door. He found the light switch and flipped it on.

This was where Gina lived.

It was sparsely furnished. There was a single couch against one wall, a coffee table in front of it, a flat-screen TV hanging on the opposite wall. A dying ficus tree stood next to the couch in a white pot.

Against the far wall, between two doors, was a bookcase. Although, he saw as he drew closer, it was not filled with books. Not real books, at least. For the volumes that packed the top four shelves were the yearbooks put out by AlumniMedia. The bottom shelf contained a series of white binders, and he pulled one out, opening it up. Inside, arranged sequentially, were copies of the newsletters they published.

This wasn't work related. The company had a massive archive of all of its publications stored in a fireproof, climate-controlled vault.

These were here for her personal use.

Exploring the condo more carefully, he left the living room and walked into the bedroom. Only it wasn't a bedroom. Instead, there was a draftsman's table and chair in the center of the otherwise cleared space, and on top of the table were a pile of photographs next to a pair of scissors and an X-Acto knife. He glanced around. The walls were hung with collages of faces, bodies, arms and legs that had been cut up seemingly at random and joined together in any way that the shapes fit, like some lunatic jigsaw puzzle.

Steve moved closer to the wall, staring at the intricately cut photos. There were literally hundreds of them, all men. The effort that had gone into these collages was impressive, but the fact that all of it added up to nothing was absolutely stupefying. He could discern no themes or motifs in the chopped-up photos, no attempt at an overarching composition in their arrangement. Maybe she considered herself an artist, he thought. Maybe this was her work. He didn't get that impression, though. This seemed more like the misplaced fantasies of an obsessed schoolgirl.

He walked slowly around the room, examining everything, marveling at the number of hours Gina had put into this . . . hobby. Counting, he found that there were thirty-three collages on the walls.

He wondered where she slept. As far as he could tell, this was a small condo: living room, single bedroom, bathroom, kitchen. Did the couch pull out? Did she sleep on the floor? No matter what the answer, the fact that she'd given up her bedroom for this madness sent up red flags. If before he had felt uncomfortable with the secretary's occasional flirty attention, he now recoiled at the thought of having even a casual conversation with her.

Steve decided to check out the bathroom. He went over to the open doorway, flipped on the light.

And stood frozen in his tracks.

The entire ceiling was covered by a massive collage. Corner to corner, from above the doorway to above the shower, the ceiling was hidden by a multitude of multicolored pictures clipped from various sources.

And this collage had a theme.

Every picture pasted onto the collage was the face of a clown.

Steve's blood ran cold. No matter what she did in here, whether Gina was bathing, showering, brushing her teeth or going to the bathroom, she would be spied upon and stared at by scores upon scores of unmoving clown eyes. Just the thought of it gave him the heebie-jeebies.

He flipped off the light, moving away, going back into the living room and then to the kitchen. His hand was shaking as he turned on the kitchen light, and he wanted nothing more than to get out of here and go home. But he had to finish this, had to see it through. He glanced quickly around the room, taking it all in: refrigerator, stove, sink, counter, microwave, breakfast table. Those were the normal elements, the ones Gina's kitchen had in common with an ordinary kitchen.

The abnormal elements . . .

On the counter next to the microwave oven, in a diorama constructed in a converted shoe box, was a scene of a man sitting in front of a campfire in a forest. Steve recognized the man as the paunchy older guy from the beach, and wondered whether Gina had sought him out, stalked him. He couldn't recall AlumniMedia putting together anything for a Newport Beach or Balboa reunion, but it was conceivable that he had graduated from somewhere else, and Gina had come across his name, photo and current address and had made an effort to meet him. Such an approach was slightly unethical, but it wasn't out of the realm of normalcy. A lot of people met online these days or through dating services, and this wasn't a whole lot different from that.

But the diorama, the collages . . .

His gaze alighted on a framed collage above the stove. In it were men, nearly all of them shirtless, many of them with their genitals accidentally or intentionally exposed, some with no pants on at all. Steve came across this type of thing at work periodically—people sending inappropriate pictures for their reunion photos. He usually deleted them if they'd been e-mailed or threw them away if they'd been sent in, but Gina had obviously been collecting them over a period of many years, and she'd made a special effort to piece them together in a sexualized way that made her intentions very clear. It was sick and disturbing, made more so by the fact that it was not near her bed or bathtub or someplace intimate but above her stove, where she cooked food.

She was the type of woman, Steve realized, whom his father would probably consider a slut.

His father had had no use for such people, and neither did he, and he found himself thinking that if something happened to her, she would not really be missed. At AlumniMedia, she was only a secretary, an annoying one at that, and could easily be replaced. She obviously had no real significant other, and judging from the state of her condo and the lack of personal pictures, she had no close family, at least not here in Southern California.

That was the moment he knew he was going to kill her.

No. That wasn't really true. He'd known earlier than that. He'd known it when he first found the drafting table and the photos.

When he first walked through her door.

When he first decided to break into her place.

When he first followed her home.

Yes. He'd known it all along, and it felt good to admit that now.

Steve glanced at his watch. It felt like only a few minutes had passed, but he'd been here for over half an hour already. Gina could come back anytime—the date could have gone bad, the guy could have stood her up, there could have been no date at all—and he did not want to be caught unawares, did not want to be forced into doing something hasty and rash. This time, he wanted to be able to plan it out, to take his time and arrange the best kill he could.

Something his father would be proud of.

He made sure everything was as he had found it, turned off all the lights, locked the front door, then hurried down the street to where he'd parked his car. He waited a moment after he got in, watching the houses and sidewalk through his windshield and rearview mirror to make sure he had not been spotted. When he was sure everything was clear, he started the car and pulled carefully out into the street.

He passed by a hitchhiker on his way out of her neighborhood. He would have thought nothing of it, would probably not have even noticed the man except for the fact that he was dressed like a hillbilly and dancing, doing a strange little in-place jog on the street corner where he stood, his arm windmilling up at irregular intervals to expose his outstretched thumb. The man stared at him as he passed by, paying entirely too much attention to Steve for his comfort. Dressed in bib overalls and a straw hat, he looked like someone going to a costume party, but it was a weeknight, as well as being an odd time of year for such festivities, and Steve had the distinct impression that this was not a costume but the hitchhiker's daily attire.

Keeping his eyes on the road, ignoring the man, his hands remaining at ten and two on the wheel, Steve drove by, heart pounding, thinking that maybe he should take this as an omen and call everything off, not go through with it.

But he knew that wasn't going to happen.

On the way home, he got dinner from the drive-through of a Jack in the Box and ate it in front of the TV while he watched a CNN broadcaster bash Mexican immigrants. He wanted more than anything to plan Gina's death, to decide how he was going to do away with her, but he enjoyed the anticipation so much that he decided to wait on that, to prolong the gratification and think about it tomorrow.

So he opened his mail, worked on a new short story until he was so tired that his eyes hurt, and finally went to bed.

He dreamed this time about a hillbilly clown, an overalls-clad yokel with a big red nose and bright green hair, who was hitchhiking by the side of the road, dancing with his thumb out. Steve himself was driving a clown car, a little miniature Volkswagen, and he pulled over to give the hitchhiker a lift. "Where are you going?" he asked.

The clown poked his big face into the tiny window and grinned evilly.

"You know," he said.

And Steve did.

Seventeen

The Promise

They stopped at a McDonald's in Blythe, pulling off the highway onto a cross street where the familiar red and yellow sign sat like a beacon amidst the darker billboards and buildings of the still-sleeping town. The McDonald's had just opened for the day, and only the vehicles of employees were parked in the lot. Dave pulled into a marked space near the entrance and, without even glancing at his sister, got out of the car, stretching loudly.

Dawn was still an hour or so away, but the sky was pink in the east with a faint white penumbra around the edges of the silhouetted desert mountains. To the west, where they were headed, the world remained night.

They had hardly spoken since he'd picked her up from her apartment in Tucson, aside from a few short sentences involving practical matters such as where to pack her luggage in the car. Dave felt guilty about that. He was the elder, and while it was awkward and uncomfortable, he should be the one to break the ice.

"Are you hungry?" he asked. He didn't wait for an answer. "Let's have breakfast."

The interior of the restaurant was bright, harshly so, filled with white light that illuminated every square inch of public space and seemed specifically designed to discourage intimacy. They were the restaurant's first customers, and he was about to tell her to go ahead and order anything she wanted, it was on him, when she strode to the front counter and asked for a Big Breakfast with hot tea, taking a ten-dollar bill out of her pocketbook and handing it to the girl behind the first register.

She'd received her change and her food and was walking over to a table in the corner by the time Dave decided to get a McMuffin, two hash browns and a coffee.

He had the feeling she wanted to eat alone, and he was tempted to give her her space, but at the last second he placed his tray on the corner table where she'd sat and took a chair opposite hers. He looked over at the food on her fork. "Sausage," he said. "Are you preparing yourself?"

She smiled. Or tried to. It was not much of a smile, more like a grimace, a pained expression of obligation to the social norms of the situation.

He was instantly sorry that he'd spoken, and, embarrassed, he looked down at his tray, took one of the hash browns from its greasy wrapper, and bit into it. The processed potato patty was so hot it brought tears to his eyes, but he pretended not to notice and took another bite. He glanced up surreptitiously and saw that she was staring down at her food as well.

He could not remember what she'd looked like as a child. That was the strange thing. In his mind, she'd always looked as she did now. He could recall playing with her, fighting with her inside the house, outside in the yard, at school, at church, but he could not picture the features of her face. His memory of her past seemed almost secondhand; he knew the factual details of former events, but the person to whom they had happened was unknown to him, and a generic girl-child had been supplied by his mind to fill the role.

She was still not looking up, and for the first time, Dave took the opportunity to study her carefully. He could see the beginnings of lines around her eyes, a coarsening and tightening of the skin around her mouth. She looked familiar yet different, and it was almost as though he could see through her to the elderly woman she would eventually be, as though the young woman before him had become transparent, a ghost, and was gradually fading into the hardened and more corporeal old lady beneath.

He wondered if he looked as old to her at that moment as she did to him.

A Hispanic family had walked into the McDonald's and was standing next to the wood-paneled trash receptacles, reading the menu from this awkward angle, trying to avoid the area directly in front of the cash registers where the teenaged girls in their unflattering uniforms stood waiting with demanding smiles. The parents spoke in Spanish, their children answering in unaccented English. The father wore a dirty blue windbreaker, the mother a ragged shawl, the two kids' faded T-shirts featuring characters from movies that had been popular several years before.

Dave felt sad all of a sudden. He didn't want to be here, didn't want to be doing this, but he had given his father his word, and of course that could never be broken.

"It's because I never gave him grandkids," his sister said suddenly. He glanced over at her. She still wouldn't look up. "Father didn't approve of that, didn't like that I never married."

Dave couldn't disagree, so he remained silent. He stared across the small table at her hands, clutching the undersized paper teacup. She had hair on her fingers, he saw. He had never noticed that before. Small clumps of fine black hairs grew on the flat segments of skin between each knuckle.

Their father had had hair on his fingers.

He watched his sister's hand as she lifted the cup of tea to her lips, and suddenly her hands looked like miniature versions of their father's. The thought repulsed him, and at that moment he wanted to back out. Promise or no promise, he didn't want to go through with it.

But he forced himself to look away, glancing out the window at the McDonald's Playland outside, plastic slides and crawl tubes sitting empty and idle and only-half-visible in the early morning dimness.

He had not wanted to see his father again. He had heard from the doctors and from Jocasta that the old man had been getting worse, that he was so thin his skull was visible, that he was often incoherent when he spoke. Dave's plan had been to arrive after his father's death and not to view the body, to convince Jocasta to have a closed-casket funeral. But in a weeklong burst of lucidity, his father had called, via speakerphone, that horrible speakerphone, and had specifically asked him to come. The old man wanted to extract a promise from him before he died, and, as always, he wanted to hear the promise made in person, to be able to look into Dave's eyes while he agreed.

There was no way he could refuse, and Dave had flown out to Los Angeles the next morning, renting a car at the airport and driving to Brentwood, to the house—the mansion—his father had bought for his fourth wife. His dad was lying on a hospital bed in the enormous living room, hooked up to oxygen, monitors and IVs, while an overweight woman in a nurse's uniform sat in a nearby chair reading *Us* magazine.

The cancer had taken its toll; his father appeared more corpse than man. Blue veins could be seen beneath the nearly transluscent skin covering his bald head, and his wizened face was so emaciated that his teeth protruded in a decidedly skull-like manner. Still, for all of that, he retained the aura of power that had always been his, and while the nurse had all of the disinterested attributes typical of a babysitter for the terminally ill, there was something in the stiffness of her posture that told Dave she would snap to at the slightest word from his father.

He had been afraid of that—it was why he hadn't wanted to return until the old man was dead—and he felt all of the familiar fear and intimidation as he stepped forward into his dad's sight line. "Hello," he said. "How are you?"

His father looked him over, saying nothing.

"I came as fast as I could," Dave said, a trifle nervously.

His father spoke slowly and with great difficulty. "Are . . . you . . . still . . . with . . . that . . . bitch?"

"No," Dave said. "Pam and I broke up, remember?"

Even with the weakened voice, his father's tone grew steely at the hint of condescension. "Of . . . course . . . I . . . remember. I . . . was . . . just . . . wondering . . . if . . . you . . . were . . . spineless . . . enough . . . to . . . go . . . back . . . to . . . her."

Dave tried to smile, though his heart was pounding.

"How . . . is . . . your . . . sister . . . doing?"

He shrugged. "I don't know. I haven't talked to her in a while." *Years*, he thought.

"I . . . know . . . how . . . she's . . . doing. Not . . . well."

"Oh." He didn't know what else to say.

His father beckoned him closer. "I . . . need . . . you . . . to . . . do . . . me . . . a . . . favor."

Dave's muscles tensed. This was why he was here. This was why he had been summoned. He knew he wasn't going to like it, whatever *it* was, but he was powerless to object. If he'd had any balls at all, he would have walked away right at that second and not looked back. But instead he leaned even closer and said, "What do you want, Daddy?"

What his father asked him to do went against every instinct that he had, everything he knew to be right and good. It was a sick and twisted request, exactly the sort of thing he should have expected, and what he wanted to do was kick over his father's bed, yank the IVs out of his arm and yell, *Die, you evil old fuck!* But he was still a cowed little boy in his father's presence, and he nodded his acquiescence, and when that wasn't enough, promised aloud that he would do his father's bidding.

"Do you want me to call—"

"Jocasta . . . will . . . call . . . your . . . sister . . . and . . . explain. . . ."

"What if she won't—"

"She . . . will," his father said, and laughed, a dry, coughing cackle that sent chills down Dave's spine.

He had not wanted to remain after that, had not wanted to catch up on old times or say good-bye or spend another second in that house. He'd walked out, driven back to the airport, and exchanged his ticket for one on an earlier flight.

By the time he arrived home several hours later, his father was dead.

Dave merely nodded when he heard the news. "Good," he said.

He thought now about reneging on his promise, not going through with it, but that sort of strength was not in him, and he knew he could not back out now. *Maybe* she *will,* he thought hopefully, but one look at his sister told him that she was as locked into this as he was.

He dropped the last bit of hash brown on his tray and picked up his coffee cup, drinking the final bitter dregs. His sister, he saw, was almost done too. Pretty soon it would be time for them to go. A bright sliver of white light from the rising sun cut through the smoked glass and shone into his eye, causing it to tear up. He shifted in his seat, turned his body away.

He reached across the table, took his sister's hands in his. She started, but did not pull back. There was a look of resignation on her face.

"It's the last thing he can ever make us do," Dave told her. "This is it. He can never push us around again."

She smiled, really smiled, for the first time since he'd picked her up, and for a moment she looked happy.

He remembered now what she'd looked like as a child. He could see in his mind her long blond hair, her little pinafore dress, her miniature black purse and small plastic pearl necklace. She'd been almost pretty, he realized.

He smiled back at her.

She'd been almost pretty.

Eighteen

"Do you have something to tell me?" Gina asked, leaning against his desk. She was facing him, her rear end pressed against the top edge above the drawers, her crotch purposely pushed outward. Her pants were thin and tight, exposing more than they should have.

He looked away.

"I know you broke into my home."

Steve's heart felt as though it had been slammed against the inside of his rib cage. His mouth, suddenly devoid of saliva, was so dry he did not trust himself to speak. How could she know?

She answered the question without his even asking it. "I have nanny cams in every room. Just in case. There are a lot of things I need to protect, and I don't want anyone snooping through my stuff." She leaned closer, lowered her voice. "I even have one in the bathroom."

Steve was concentrating hard on breathing regularly and not having an expression, but he still wasn't ready to respond.

"It's okay," she said, putting a hand on his shoulder and pushing lightly, playfully. "I know you didn't mean any harm. To tell you the truth, I was kind of flattered. I knew you were interested, and I was wondering when you were going to make your move." She laughed. "You sure made it last night."

"I . . ." he began, but didn't know where to go from there.

"You liked my collages, didn't you? I could tell you did." She lowered her voice again. "You could be in one, if you wanted."

"I don't know what you're talking about," he managed to say.

"I have four high-def tapes that say otherwise. But if you want to play it that way . . ."

He decided to try a different tack. "It's illegal to appropriate AlumniMedia property. That's theft. And punishable by jail time."

Gina looked impressed. "Touché!"

Rod Zindel, one of the PR guys, stopped by Steve's desk. "Can I have a minute of your time? I need a little help."

Steve's heart was pounding crazily in his chest and his mind was racing a mile a minute, but outwardly he remained calm, and he turned coolly to Gina. "Excuse us, will you?" Swiveling his chair dismissively away from her, he smiled at Rod. "Anything you need."

The secretary walked away, and he didn't look at her, so he had no idea what expression was on her face. He listened as Rod asked about integrating an alumni newsletter into an online promotion, but his brain was multitasking, and even as he offered advice on which newsletter to feature, he was thinking that Gina could not be allowed to live much longer. If she was not taken care of quickly, his window of opportunity would be lost and he would not be able to kill her without becoming a suspect.

For he had no doubt that if he murdered her now, no one would even consider the possibility of his involvement. It had to be done smartly, though. It had to be done well. He was going to follow his father's example and plan this one out, know ahead of time what he was going to do rather than improvise on the spot. As he saw it, the problem with most killings was that the people committing them panicked. As with a political scandal, it was the cover-up that caused most of the difficulties: trying to hide or dispose of the body, trying to come up with an alibi. He hadn't done that with Lyman Fischer, and he was going to make sure that he did not do it with Gina. The best way to guard against that, in fact, would be to work out in advance the specific details of the secretary's death.

Steve successfully avoided her for the rest of the day, and after work headed straight to Sherry's place, making sure he was not followed. Even if Gina didn't know where he lived, she had access to that information, and he didn't want her showing up on his doorstep uninvited, establishing for the outside world more of a connection to each other than the casual coworker status they shared right now.

The best thing would be to do it tonight, but that was not feasible. He needed time to think things through, to figure out the best way to get rid of her.

He could probably hold her off at work for a few more days, maybe even a week, stringing her along with a little false hope and some empty promises. But such a ruse wouldn't work indefinitely and would be tricky to pull off, since he had to make her believe he was interested in her while not allowing anyone else to get that impression. The challenge appealed to him, though, and he was smiling to himself, happy, as he pulled into Sherry's driveway.

She was not home from work yet, and he took the opportunity to snoop around the apartment. She wasn't expecting him today, so this was one of those rare chances to catch her unawares. A quick survey showed no dead animals in any wastepaper baskets; no blood in the tub, toilet or sinks; no recently washed knives, hatchets or sharp tools.

He'd decided he liked the fact that Sherry hated dogs.

He liked the fact that she killed them.

It made them almost a team, in a weird way, although she did not know that. It also made him feel as though they were kindred spirits, two of a kind, and that if she eventually found out about him or he one day told her about himself, she would be able to deal with it.

On impulse, he opened her hamper, sorted through her dirty clothes. He was looking for bloodstains or fur, ripped sleeves or torn cuffs, anything that would indicate she'd had an . . . encounter with a pet this week. He found nothing, though, and quickly piled the clothes back in the hamper in the order in which he'd taken them out. Seeing a pair of her panties, he tried sniffing them—he'd always heard jokes about that, though he'd never done it himself—but the silk smelled like cloth rather than sex, and he tossed them back into the white plastic basket along with everything else.

Sherry arrived home soon after, happy to see him, and they went out for dinner at one of their favorite Mexican restaurants. He kept an eye out for Gina, just in case they'd been followed, but saw no sign of her, and on the way home they stopped by a Borders so Sherry could buy *Northanger Abbey*, the only Jane Austen novel she had not yet read. In the store, Steve went over to the DVD section while Sherry looked for her book. He spotted on the New Releases shelf a recent suspense film. The cover of the DVD showed the shadow of a man behind a closed window shade placing a noose around the neck of a seated woman.

That was how he would kill Gina.

It came to him just like that.

Steve made no effort to pick up the DVD, and even as he was studying the artwork pretended to be looking at a movie on the shelf above it. He knew he was being paranoid, but it never hurt to be too careful. He couldn't afford to have anyone connect him in any way with anything remotely similar to what would soon happen.

The DVD's artwork was not a still from the film but a stylized depiction of something that illustrated the tone and subject matter of the movie. It was impossible to tell from the silhouettes whether the woman in the chair was restrained, but Steve thought it would be best to tie Gina up before hanging her. He liked the idea that she would *know* who was doing it, and he imagined the look on her face as she sat there, unable to move, and watched him slip the noose around her neck.

If he tied her up, he would have to gag her as well, so she wouldn't scream for help, and Steve started thinking about the supplies he would need for this operation: rope, duct tape—

"I'm done."

Sherry tapped him on the shoulder, and he jumped, startled. Recovering quickly, he smiled at her and turned away from the DVDs. "All right," he said. "Let's go."

The next day, he nodded at Gina as he passed by her desk, and she gave him a cutesy finger-wiggling wave. He imagined those fingers clutching desperately at a noose tightening around her neck and smiled. She smiled back.

Later in the morning, while he was busy compiling a list of reuniongoers' favorite bands and musicians from twenty-five years ago (Duran Duran! Michael Jackson! Def Leppard!), Gina sent him an e-mail containing two photos: one of a nude middle-aged man, shown from the neck down, pointing his erect penis at the camera; the other featuring a woman wearing a party hat, her eyes and mouth opened wide in surprise. When the two photos were placed next to each other, the way Gina had arranged them, it appeared that the man was preparing to ejaculate into the woman's mouth.

Steve deleted the e-mail.

The secretary had to die soon.

After work, he drove inland instead of heading home, stopping off at a Lowe's in Tustin, then a Home Depot in Santa Ana, picking up thin twine, heavy rope, duct tape and, just in case, paint thinner. He divided his purchases between the two stores so that no single person could see him picking up all of the supplies, and afterward tore up the receipts, letting the pieces flutter across the respective parking lots. Driving back to Irvine on the packed Costa Mesa Freeway, Steve felt calm and in control. He now had everything he needed to take care of the Gina problem. He could go in anytime.

The only thing that worried him was her security system, her "nanny cams." She said she had four high-def tapes of him breaking into her house and snooping through each room. He had to find those tapes and destroy them before he did anything. If the police found the tapes along with her body in the condominium, it was as good as a confession. He'd promised himself that Gina's death was going to be perfectly planned down to the smallest detail, and though his impulse was to kill her first, then search around for her cameras and tapes, Steve knew that he had to dispose of the evidence first—then dispose of her.

He started staking out her condo again. She knew his car—or he assumed she did—so he rented one for the week, a red Honda Accord, and kept it parked on the street down the block from his apartment building. Each day, after work, he shuffled through papers or worked on the computer or made an extra phone call to ensure that Gina would leave work before he did. Then he would go home, park in his garage, walk down the block to the rental car, then head over to the secretary's street, where he would find an inconspicuous spot from which he could keep an eye on her front door.

The first time, she tried to stay late as well, making her own after-hours phone calls and puttering around her desk before walking over to his workstation and doing elaborate and obvious stretching exercises that pushed out first her breasts, then her crotch. He smiled at her in a manner that he hoped she found encouraging, and told her in disappointed tones that he *really* needed to finish this project on schedule and after next week he would have a lot more free time. She took that the way he intended, and after flirtatiously bidding him good-bye, she left.

Two hours later, he was watching from across the street as she used a short hose to water the twin rose-bushes that took up almost the entirety of her postage stamp–sized yard.

She wasn't one for going out much, he learned. Once she arrived home from work, she generally stayed there. Steve understood. He was the same way. But he wished she would go out on a date or go shopping with a friend or do something that would take her away for a significant period of time, because he wanted to have an opportunity to search for the new location in which she'd hidden her extra key. She certainly wouldn't have left it beneath the flowerpot after learning that *he* knew where it was.

As luck would have it, on Thursday, the third day, she emerged shortly after he'd taken up his post and went out to her car to retrieve something she wanted to bring inside. There was a slight wind, more of a breeze, really, but it was enough to close the front door on her. Evidently, she'd left her keys in the house, so she put down her package, picked up the same flowerpot as before and used the key underneath to open the door. He couldn't believe it, and he watched as she returned the key to exactly the same spot. She *hadn't* moved it.

Maybe she wanted him to use it.

Steve smiled to himself as the secretary's front door closed. Well, he would.

He would.

Monday was the night.

He wanted to do it as quickly as possible, but on Friday evening and over the weekend he was occupied with Sherry. Besides, there were too many people out and about in Gina's neighborhood for him to remain unseen and unnoticed: kids playing, teenagers hanging with their friends, families going to movies. Weeknights were much more conducive to such an operation.

So he decided to do it Monday.

He thought about it a lot over Saturday and Sunday. His original plan had been to set up a fake meeting with her at a restaurant that was fifteen or twenty minutes away, wait for her to leave on the date, then ransack the condo to find the cameras and tapes. He would kill her when she returned. But it occurred to him that he might not find all of the tapes, that she might have made some copies and hidden them, so he decided to break into her house while she was there, torture her to get the information, destroy the cameras and tapes, and then take care of her.

But what if she screamed while he loosened her gag to get the information out of her, and alerted the neighbors? What if she lied and didn't tell him where all of the tapes were? What if she'd added some type of dead bolt or chain lock, and after using the key to open the door he still couldn't get in?

Maybe the first idea was better. Or maybe he should just kill her and *then* search the condo.

He went back and forth on the subject, and it wasn't until midday Monday, when Gina stopped by his desk and told him in low tones that not *all* of the photos of nude men had come from AlumniMedia, *some* she had taken herself, that he decided the torture option was the best.

He waited until it was dark, going home after work, eating a Pasta Roni dinner, watching the news, and calling Sherry just to chat and tell her that he loved her. He would call her afterward, too, and talk about *The Desk Set*, a Katharine Hepburn/Spencer Tracy movie that he'd seen before and that happened to be on TCM tonight. The calls would give him something of an alibi in case he needed one—although he did not anticipate that he would.

The supplies he needed were already in a plastic grocery sack in the backseat of the Accord, ready to go, and he shoved a pair of latex gloves in his pocket before walking casually down the block to the rental car. He drove for a mile or so in the opposite direction of Gina's condo, then swung around and took a circuitous route to his destination.

The street was devoid of pedestrians, as it usually was on weeknights, and he parked close this time, right in front of her condo, so he would not have to walk down the sidewalk and risk extra exposure. This way, his presence would not be so conspicuous, and he picked up his grocery sack, put on his latex gloves, locked the car door, and walked briskly but not too briskly up the short walk to the front porch. Every instinct he had was telling him to stop and look around the neighborhood to make sure he wasn't being watched, but that would be the action of a guilty man and would serve to draw attention if anyone *was* watching, so he forced himself to remain facing forward, take the key from beneath the flowerpot and open the door.

He had no idea where she was. The porch light was on, the car was here, and he assumed she was home, but she could have been in the kitchen cooking dinner, could be sitting right next to the door watching television, could be in that weird workroom, cutting and pasting photographs. He needed to get in quickly, subdue her, silence her, then get her to tell him where the tapes and cameras were.

He opened the door, closed it, and—

She was not there.

The television *was* on, as were seemingly all of the condo's lights, but at first glance he saw no sign of Gina. Then he heard a noise from the open doorway to the right of the bookcase, a click or a tap, and froze for a moment. No one came out, although he saw the trace of a shadow, and Steve locked the front door behind him and moved swiftly and silently through the living room.

The secretary was in the bathroom, naked, getting ready for a shower, and though she cried out when she saw him, startled, fear turned almost instantly to anticipation when she recognized who it was, and she smiled, moving toward him with an obviously practiced walk that made her hips sway and her breasts bounce. "I knew you'd come . . ." she began, but then she noticed the sack in his hand, saw the gloves.

He was on her before she could react, punching her in the stomach and grabbing the roll of duct tape from the plastic bag as he let it fall to the floor. She was gasping for air as he taped her mouth shut, and an expression of panic crossed her features, her eyes widening, her arms flailing as she desperately tried to breathe through her nose. He kicked her legs out from under her, and as she fell to the ground, her shoulder glancing off the side of the toilet, he stepped on her back, reaching down to grab the ball of twine that had spilled out of his sack. She might have been able to fight him at this point, but her first priority was to breathe, to recapture the wind that had been knocked out of her, and it was all she could do to suck enough air through her nose to remain conscious. She was thrashing around beneath his foot, her body heaving, making strange noises from deep within her chest, and he pulled out a length of twine with his right hand, grabbed one of her wildly flapping arms with his left, and started wrapping her wrist. He reached down for her other arm and bound the two together. He used a knife to cut the twine and did the same thing to her ankles before hauling her up and sitting her atop the toilet.

Her eyes were wild, her face bright red, and the noise made by the too-deep inhalation and exhalation of air through her nostrils did not sound human. There seemed a distinct possibility that she might pass out, so he partially pulled the tape from the right side of her mouth and allowed her to breathe for a moment. She *couldn't* scream at first, and he waited a few moments, until she was breathing more normally and he was sure that she *wouldn't*, before taking his fingers off the end of the duct tape and stepping back.

They stared at each other for a moment. Gina seemed confused. "Is this what you thought I liked?"

"Where are those tapes?" he demanded. "The ones with me on them?"

Understanding dawned in her eyes. "Oh."

"I want them."

"You didn't have to do this," she whined. "I would have told you."

"Where are they? And where are your cameras?"

"The tapes are in my desk drawer. They're labeled. The cameras are in the Buddhas."

He wasn't sure what type of reaction he had expected, but it had not been this. Screaming, maybe. Fighting. Defiance. But not this docile compliance.

There was indeed a Buddha in the bathroom, sitting atop the counter next to an array of lotions and a porcelain jar in the shape of a woman's head that held combs, brushes and other hair items. Picking up the small statue, he saw on its back a black switch. He threw the statue to the ground as hard as he could, smashing it, and amidst the shards of plaster saw wires and minuscule mechanisms along with a tiny cassette.

"We're even," Gina told him. "Now we're even."

"Yeah," Steve said. "We're even." He pulled the tape back over her mouth, picked up the cassette, then went through the other rooms of the condo, finding the other Buddhas and breaking them open, taking the tapes inside. In a drawer of her drafting table desk, he did find a neatly arranged collection of tapes, all of them carefully labeled with the names of people and, presumably, the dates on which those people had been filmed. The four tapes at the front of the final row contained his name, but unless he watched them, there was no way to know for certain whether they were the ones actually showing him going through the rooms, so he decided to take all of the tapes and dispose of them later.

He returned to the bathroom. Gina had not moved, had made no effort to untie herself or escape. He supposed that was because she wanted to show him that she was cooperating or not afraid or something.

She should have been afraid.

He said nothing as he took the length of rope from his sack and started to make a noose. She was talking behind the gag, not begging for her life but trying to say something, only he could not hear what it was and did not care. He continued with his efforts, tying off the end of the noose and pulling out the loop, which he shoved down over her head.

She was wiggling now, and the voice behind the duct tape sounded louder, more frantic, as though the seriousness of her situation had finally sunk in.

Good, Steve thought. He recalled how she had tortured him at work with her intrusiveness, her flirting and, most recently, her slutty blackmail attempts. He pulled the noose tighter, walking slowly around the other side of the toilet, looking closely at her neck. The coarse rope appeared especially rough against the smoothness of her throat, its stray bristles pressing like needles into the softness of her skin in a way that he could tell was painful.

He tugged on the noose, and she was pulled forward, falling off the toilet and hitting her head on the ground.

Now she was screaming behind the duct tape, and Steve jerked on the rope until those screams were cut off. The secretary thrashed around like a beached grunion, and he let out more rope as he stepped back, away from her, tightening the noose the entire time. Her head was bleeding where it had hit the floor, as was her neck where the rope was digging into flesh. Thin cuts bisected her breasts where the twine binding her arms had rubbed the skin raw.

He could see himself in the bathroom mirror, and his face was strangely placid. There was physical effort involved in pulling the noose so tight, and that was reflected in the set of his mouth, but he might as well have been picking up a heavy box or moving a piece of furniture. There was no indication on his features that he was killing a woman.

Her face was now purple, her eyes bulging grotesquely in their sockets, her twisted, tortured mouth wriggling under the tape. Blood was flowing in rivulets from where the rope was now embedded in her neck, and the surrounding skin was a deep red, on its way to turning the same shade of purple as her face.

And then she died.

It happened all at once, a sudden cessation of the force pulling against him as the secretary's body went limp. She rolled sideways, her head flopping onto the floor with an audible crack. Her bladder let go, and Steve dropped his end of the rope, backing away. He picked up the plastic sack containing the nanny-cam tapes and retreated to the living room. What would this look like when the police discovered it? Some sort of sex thing? A home invasion? Nothing had been stolen aside from the tapes, so it would be obvious that it wasn't merely a burglary. What would they make of Gina's collages and diorama?

Whatever motive and scenario they decided upon, it couldn't possibly involve him.

Steve glanced at his watch. The entire thing had taken less than twenty minutes. Peeking out from between the front shades, not opening the slats but placing his eye against one of the small holes through which the drawstring was threaded, he saw that the street appeared to be empty. He quickly opened the front door, closed it, then walked directly to his car, looking neither this way nor that. He got into the car, started the engine, and drove sedately down the street so as not to draw attention to himself.

As soon as he got home, he destroyed the videos, smashing the plastic cartridges and painstakingly cutting up the narrow lengths of tape, dumping the cut-up tape into the toilet and flushing it all away. He lost count at twenty-two flushes, but he continued the process for nearly an hour. The broken pieces of plastic from the cartridges he placed back in the plastic sack along with the leftover twine and duct tape. Heading out to the rear of the apartment complex, he tossed the entire thing in the Dumpster for the next building over. Returning to his apartment, he cut up the latex gloves he'd been wearing and flushed those pieces down the toilet as well.

And then he was done.

It was over.

The Desk Set was still on TCM, and he watched it for a few moments to get his bearings, trying to remember the story, then gave Sherry a call. Casually, he asked her if she'd ever seen the movie. She hadn't, and he told her that she'd like it; he'd been watching it for the past hour or so and thought it was really good. They talked for a while longer; then Sherry said it was getting late, and she needed to finish reading a book for a library discussion group she was leading, before taking a shower and going to bed.

"Wish I was there," he told her. "At least for the shower part."

"Do you want to come over tomorrow?" she asked him.

"Yeah," he said, and he did.

"I'll be taking a shower then too."

"I'll be there."

They said their good-byes, hung up, and Steve decided to take his own shower. First, though, he took off his clothes and threw them into the small washing machine in the alcove off his kitchen. He dumped in a bunch of laundry detergent and set it for full cycle. There was no blood on his clothes and no one would even be *looking* for blood, but a person could never be too careful. After the shower, he would toss the clothes in the dryer stacked above the washing machine and leave it on while he went to bed.

But he was too keyed up to go to bed, and he ended up writing a little, reading a little, then watching the last half of another Tracy-Hepburn movie before finally going to sleep.

He awoke after midnight.

And there was his father.

As before, the figure of the old man was silent and unmoving, sitting on the chair by the curtains, unblinking black eyes staring into nothingness. His white shirt was still bloodstained, but the splotches looked bigger, more saturated, and it was impossible to tell whether the blood was his own or someone else's.

Steve was alone in the bed this time—Sherry was not with him—and while he wasn't afraid exactly, he didn't feel the same peace and calmness he had before. This go-round, the sight of his father seemed creepy and disturbing.

What did it mean?

He was also not quite as convinced that it was a figment of his imagination. There seemed an objective reality to the figure, and from the corner of his eye he could see a reflection of his father in the mirror. Was this a ghost? It seemed so, but even if that were the case, it did not necessarily follow that the ghost had shown up for some specific purpose. It could simply be a natural phenomenon, like lightning striking randomly for no particular reason.

The room seemed cold. He had not noticed that until now, but he was chilly and there were goose bumps on his arms. Wasn't cold a traditional indicator that spirits were present?

He remained transfixed, and slowly, almost imperceptibly, his father's head began to swivel toward him.

The white face had been partially visible thanks to light from a streetlamp and moonlight leaking in from a crack in the curtains, and as the head turned in his direction, it entered an area of shadow before emerging once again into moonlight.

Now Steve saw that his father's nose was red and bulbous.

Clownlike.

I suitcase the five and clown you!

Steve recalled his father's nonsensical outburst, and suddenly there seemed something malevolent about it. The words no longer sounded like gibberish but like communication of some sort, a secret message, something he should understand but didn't.

The head stopped its slow pivot, shiny black eyes staring into his, and in the second before the figure of his father disappeared, Steve saw the mouth open wide in what looked like a scream but in what he somehow knew was a laugh.

He could not fall back asleep for the rest of the night.

At work the next morning, Gina was absent. She did not call in sick, was not answering her phone, and sometime around ten, McColl called a temp agency for a secretary.

Nineteen

It was a full week before everyone learned that Gina was dead.

Steve was not sure who had discovered the body or how—he was afraid to ask—but Monday morning McColl called a meeting of the entire department and announced that Gina had been found in her condo and that the coroner estimated that she had been dead for at least a week. He did not say that she had been murdered, and Steve wondered whether that information had been released yet by the police or the coroner or whoever had contacted AlumniMedia with the news. Maybe they were trying to keep it a secret in order to flush out the killer, hoping that whoever had done it would give himself away by accidentally revealing something no one else could possibly know.

Or maybe McColl was keeping the information to himself.

But why? Steve wondered. What would be the point? What could he hope to gain by doing such a thing?

Had the department head been involved with Gina?

The thought stopped him short. Steve had never even considered the idea before, but it did make a strange kind of sense. McColl had always been uncharacteristically nice to the secretary, much nicer than he was to anyone else, and had not found her anywhere near as annoying as the rest of them did. Morever, he had not had as much contact with her in the office as a person in his position would be expected to—almost as though he were deliberately avoiding her in an effort to make others think there was no connection between them. If Steve had looked more carefully through Gina's nanny-cam tapes before destroying them, would he have found ones featuring McColl? He suspected he might.

The meeting was dismissed after the department head read a policy statement from AlumniMedia's human resources director saying that grief counseling was not available through the HR department but was partially covered by the company's health insurance plan should any employee need to avail himself or herself of it. They all went back to their workstations sad and subdued, and Steve followed suit.

"I can't believe it," Rod Zindel said as they walked together past the temporary secretary manning Gina's desk.

"Me either," Steve said.

Luckily, the work today was mindless: compiling names for a ten-year high school reunion. He was in no mental condition to concentrate on anything difficult or challenging, and throughout the morning, he found himself wondering how Gina's body had been discovered. Had it been a neighbor who had noticed a bad smell coming from the condo? Or McColl or one of the supervisors who'd called the police and reported her missing? Or a friend or relative who had not heard from her and was suspicious? Any or all of those possibilities were viable.

He was still concerned about the fact that her death was not being talked about as a murder. It had to be a trap, and he wondered if the police had any suspicions about who the killer might be. Being out of the loop and not privy to the process made him nervous, and he realized that no matter how careful he thought he had been, he might have slipped up somewhere along the line. He had to be extremely cautious and on his best behavior.

After lunch, McColl called Steve into his office. "Close the door, please," the department head told him.

Frowning, Steve sat down in the proffered chair across from McColl's desk. He had no idea what this meeting was about, but he didn't like the fact that the two of them were alone and the door was closed.

"I just wanted to get your take on Gina's death. I know you and she were close."

Steve's heart was pounding crazily, but he managed to maintain a calm exterior. "Close?" he said, sounding legitimately confused.

"Yes. I noticed that she liked to talk to you, and . . ."

Steve did not hear any more. McColl had *noticed* that Gina liked to talk to him? That was a flat-out lie. It was not physically possible for him to have *noticed* any such thing. Even if the department head's nose weren't buried in a newspaper for most of each day—which it always was—he could not see Gina's desk or Steve's workstation from his office. And he had never been nearby when Gina had stopped off for one of her annoying flirty chats. So either McColl had been spying on the secretary—skulking around unseen, using hidden security devices, asking questions of coworkers— or Gina had confided in him. Which meant that the department head was far more interested in and involved with her than he was letting on.

Which meant that he probably had suspicions.

". . . so I thought maybe you would have some insight into what happened."

"What *did* happen?" Steve asked. "You told us that she died, but you didn't say how."

"They think she was murdered."

They think? he wanted to say sarcastically. *What gave it away? The fact that she was nude, bound and gagged? The fact that there was a noose around her neck? The fact that all of her Buddha statue spy cameras had been smashed?*

"I was wondering if she'd confided in you about anyone she might have been worried about or afraid of."

Steve didn't respond at first, just sat there trying to look stunned. "Murdered," he repeated.

"I guess I assumed that you'd already been informed."

Here was his chance. "No. Of course not. Why would I be?"

"I thought, since you were friends—"

"I don't know where you got this idea that we were friends. We weren't. We both worked here. That's it. To be honest—and I hate to say this under the circumstances— we didn't even particularly like each other."

"Oh." McColl smiled stiffly. "Then I guess I was mistaken."

But he didn't think he'd been mistaken, and Steve walked out of the office troubled. He still wasn't sure where McColl had gotten his information, but it was clear now that even if the police didn't suspect something, the department head did.

Which was why he had to die.

It was getting easier and easier to make that leap, Steve realized, and as much as he hated to admit it, killing had almost become his solution of first resort rather than last when it came to dealing with problems. Was this the way it had been with his father? Had the idea of killing become as seductive to him as it was becoming to Steve? Had murder grown addictive? His father had been a serial killer. Had he eventually weaned himself away from that?

Steve was a serial killer himself.

No. He had murdered two people, true, but those killings had been necessary. There'd been legitimate reasons for both. Serial killers murdered randomly, for the thrill of it. There was no logic or thought behind their actions.

What if he killed McColl? What would that make him?

Nothing. The man was a danger to him, a threat, and needed to be stopped. Even an objective observer could see that. What were his other options? None.

He smiled politely at the temporary secretary as he passed by and returned to his desk, getting back to work.

Sometimes the direct approach was the best, and he considered just walking into McColl's office during his lunch hour, stabbing the man in the face, and returning to his desk. But he had liked the orderliness of Gina's killing, the planning that had gone into it. It had felt right following her, learning about her, studying her before he did the deed. Such a tactic seemed professional, and he was sure that that was how his father would have gone about it.

His father, the serial killer.

Although perhaps the most professional strategy would be to observe the man first, make sure that he really *was* a threat, and do away with him only if there really was no other choice.

He thought about it over the next few days. A real coup, he decided, would be pulling off a kill that looked like a complete accident, one that would arouse absolutely no suspicion whatsoever. That was his goal with McColl, if push came to shove, and though he wrote nothing down, so there would be no incriminating evidence, he made mental lists of various fatal accidents that could befall a man both at his office and at his home, everything from slipping on a wet floor and cracking his head open to choking on a chicken bone.

Articles in the local newspapers spelled out the details of Gina's murder, and her death remained a hot topic of conversation in the office for the next week. Steve took part in discussions so as not to draw attention to himself, from all outward appearances as horrified and fascinated as everyone else. He had no further interaction with the department head and was grateful for that, but he had not forgotten their encounter and neither, he knew, had McColl.

As he had with Gina, Steve followed the man home in order to find out where he lived. It was a three-day process. McColl was smarter and no doubt more suspicious than the secretary had been, so Steve took extra precautions, remaining three cars behind and tailing him only part of the way the first evening, picking up from that point the second evening, and finally learning the last leg of the trip on the third.

He was planning to just observe the man, keep tabs on him, but he needed to keep the other option open, just in case. So on the nights he didn't see Sherry, he parked across the street from McColl's house, a baseball bat on the floor next to him, a hatchet beneath a towel on the seat. It was a nice house on the edge of Newport Beach, on the inland side of the hills, facing Irvine. Two stories, with side bushes tall enough to afford privacy from the neighbors, it was a typical Mediterranean-style dwelling with a two-car garage and trendy drought-resistant landscaping.

McColl had a family, which made things inconvenient. A wife and two daughters. Twins, from what

Steve could tell. Fortunately for him, the McColls were part of that new breed of upper-middle-class suburbanites who didn't believe in shades or curtains. Every first-floor window was uncovered, the lit rooms beyond exposed for the world to see, and from his shifting vantage points along the street, Steve saw a lot during his first few stakeouts, intimate scenes of family life that in previous generations had remained unseen even by the nosiest neighbors. He had never understood this compulsion of people to expose their day-to-day living to others as though it were some type of stage show, but he was grateful for it now.

The daughters, he learned quickly, spent very little time with their parents. They appeared to be around thirteen or fourteen and spent most of their hours at home upstairs in the bedrooms—which *did* have shades. As the girls ate dinner at the dining room table, their body language bespoke hostility, and they sat as far away from their mother and father as possible. Steve witnessed two big blowups in the living room, one on Thursday, one on Saturday, and though he couldn't hear what was being said, he could see the shouting faces, the gesturing hands, the stomping feet. So could the rest of the neighborhood.

Those unshaded windows might cause him problems in the future.

McColl, for his part, spent a lot of time in the living room watching television and in his exposed office working on his computer, while his wife ordinarily remained unseen from the street, probably in the kitchen or a room of her own at the back of the house.

Bedtime for the family was reliably consistent, and Steve would watch as first the wife went upstairs, after turning off lights in the rear rooms of the first floor, and then McColl followed, his progression visible as lights went off in the downstairs living room and on in the upstairs bathroom and bedroom. Steve would wait at his post—for that was how he thought of it—from eight or eight fifteen until sometime around midnight. McColl generally went to bed around eleven or so, but Steve was never sure when he actually fell asleep, and he would remain parked across the street until he himself grew sleepy and finally headed home.

Over the next few weeks, Steve grew to enjoy those vigils. There was comfort in the routine, and he liked learning about the family through watching their little habits, behavioral patterns and interactions with one another. It gave him a feeling of power as well, knowing that he could walk into the house at any time and put an end to McColl's life, and at work he actually began to feel a little resentful for the thoughtless, offhand way the department head treated him. It was no different from the way he treated anyone else, no different from the way he had treated Steve before, but knowing that it was his own compassion and largesse that allowed the man to stay alive each day made Steve feel insulted and annoyed. If he wanted to, he could show up one evening and lop off one of the daughters' heads—or both of the daughters' heads. He could chop up the wife's breasts and vagina or bash in her skull. He could cut McColl himself in half. But he did none of those things. He was magnanimous.

And the man didn't even appreciate it.

Often, when Steve arrived home, he was still wide-awake and energized, and he would turn on his computer and write for an hour or so before his eyelids grew heavy and he finally headed off to bed. As it turned out, those pages were some of the best he'd ever written, and as soon as he finished a story, he would get out his copy of *Writer's Digest*, find what looked like an appropriate publication and send it off.

He felt more creative and inspired than he had in

a long, long time—since college, really—and he wondered at the workings of the human mind.

Had the prospect of killing fired up his father as well?

He wanted to think so.

During his sixth stakeout, Steve waited in his car for an hour or so after all lights save the porch light were turned off in the McColl home, absently stroking the handle of the hatchet, as he'd often found himself doing. Feeling tired, he started the car, checked in both directions to make sure no other vehicles were coming, then pulled onto the street, heading north. There was movement up ahead and off to the right. A pedestrian, it looked like. Steve wasn't sure whether to slow down, speed up or maintain an even pace, but he opted for the latter, hoping not to draw attention to himself.

As he drew closer, however, the vague display of movement that he'd seen in his peripheral vision became more concrete, and he did slow down. Through glimpses caught between the spaces of the parked cars, he could tell that that there was something familiar about the figure.

Then came a no-parking zone, and he could see the man in full.

A hillbilly dressed in bib overalls.

Steve recognized the figure instantly. It was the same hitchhiker he'd seen on Gina's street the week before he killed her. Standing alone on the corner of the intersection, and illuminated by a streetlamp, the hayseed was moving very, very strangely.

Steve's heart was pounding like a taiko drum in his chest. Was there meaning in that? Was it an omen? Or was it one of those freakish coincidences, like the Lincoln/Kennedy thing, or *The Wizard of Oz* and *Dark Side of the Moon*? He didn't know, wasn't sure, couldn't tell, but the sight of the man frightened him. There was something about the odd in-place dance, and that weird windmilling thing he did with his arm before sticking out his thumb, that made Steve not just uneasy but scared. Now he did speed up. Once again, the man stared intently at him as he approached, and Steve had the distinct impression that the hitchhiker not only saw him through the darkened window and recognized him, but that he knew why Steve was here on this street and what he had been thinking about.

Despite his fear, or perhaps because of it, he was tempted to give the man a ride, drive him wherever he wanted to go.

And kill him.

Steve sped past, not slowing for the stop sign but barreling through the intersection. That would be taking too much of a chance.

Wasn't it taking more of a chance, though, to leave the hitchhiker alive?

He stared straight ahead, afraid to look back.

He traveled well over the speed limit all the way home and fortunately was not stopped, as it would have been very difficult to explain the hatchet and the baseball bat. He was using a rental car and parked on the street instead of in his garage, but it was after midnight, and walking alone on the sidewalk back to his apartment building he began to feel jittery. He knew it was irrational and impossible, but he kept expecting to look over and see the hitchhiker across the street, shadowing him, doing that odd little dance. Steve quickened his step, and by the time he reached the entrance to his apartment, he was practically running.

He wasn't in the mood to write, didn't want to stay up, wanted only to fall asleep and put this night behind him. Not even bothering to brush his teeth, he took off his clothes and climbed into bed. He tried to think about something else, anything else, but he couldn't get the image out of his head. He kept seeing the hillbilly staring at him as he drove by, feet dancing in place, arm going up and over and out as his thumb pointed up the street.

What did it mean? he wondered as he tried to fall asleep. What did it mean?

Twenty

On Saturday morning, Steve went to his mother's house to mow her lawn and pour some Drano down the bathroom sink to clear a clog. Strange how *quickly* his parents' house had become his mother's house. He'd thought the transition would take longer, but the human mind was endlessly adaptable, and though he thought of his father often, the old man's hold on the material world had ceased with his life.

He *did* think of his dad often, and seeing a commercial for Sea World on television the other night, Steve realized that he had never finished his pilgrimage, had never gone to San Diego to see the location where his father had killed what might very well have been his last victim. He wondered now if perhaps he should do so. He'd learned nothing, really, from that other trip, but it had cleared his mind and helped settle him. It had also made him feel closer to his father, and now that his dad was no longer alive, he had a longing to revisit that feeling, to reconnect with the old man in any way he could.

On a more practical level, he was still curious about what his father had done. And how.

And why.

San Diego seemed to have been his swan song. For after that, the family had settled in Anaheim and had stopped moving. Although, now that Steve thought of it, that didn't mean anything. His father could have changed his MO and kept killing but from a stationary home base. Perhaps, if he looked it up, Steve would find dozens of murders in and around the Orange County area that his father had committed.

But he didn't think so.

He wasn't sure why, but he was filled with the certainty that his father had gone cold turkey after drowning that single mother in the bay, and he wondered what had caused him to stop. Had he had a sudden epiphany? Had it been the result of a gradual buildup of regret? Or had he merely completed the job he'd set out to do and killed all the people who he thought needed killing?

Steve still had the information he'd printed out about the San Diego case, and he did a little more research over the next several days, using all of the skills and tools at his disposal to construct a likely narrative. It was all theoretical, however, and he wouldn't feel any of it was real until he actually talked to some people who had known the victim and seen the site where it had happened.

He didn't want Sherry along this time. He needed to do this alone, and he told her on Wednesday that he wouldn't be able to see her this coming weekend yet again, that he needed to take his mother to visit her sister in San Diego. *Friend!* he thought, immediately after saying the word "sister." He should have said "friend." But the damage was done. Now he would have to remember forever that he was supposed to have an aunt living in San Diego, and if Sherry ever asked about her, he would have to come up with a name and believable background details that he would *also* have to remember forever.

Lies had ripple effects, and he couldn't afford to get

caught in the crosscurrents. Not in his situation. He had to remember to keep things simple.

He had a few hours saved up, and his plan was to take off early from work on Friday, drive down to San Diego—it was only an hour-and-a-half trip, assuming there was no traffic—and come back on Sunday afternoon. That would give him part of the afternoon Friday, all day Saturday and Sunday morning to do his investigating.

So he skipped lunch on Friday, made sure his work was up-to-date, informed McColl that he was taking some personal time and set off shortly after one. There was a temporary tie-up by San Onofre, an illegal-immigrant checkpoint set up just south of the nuclear power plant, but other than that, the sailing was smooth.

His family had not been back to San Diego since they'd moved to Anaheim—they had never gone back to any of the places in which they'd previously lived, something Steve should have realized was suspicious—and he found that he didn't remember the city as well as he thought he did.

On the outskirts, on a hill above the freeway, taller than a building, was a towering white cross, like a giant's gravestone, and that odd and oversize landmark set the tone for his trip into the city proper. He had his laptop with him, and printouts concerning the single mother's life and death, but he wanted to set up a base camp and check into a hotel before doing anything else. He'd made no advance reservations, was trusting to luck, and when he saw a green traffic sign announcing, HOTEL CIRCLE NEXT RIGHT, he took the off-ramp. On both sides of a narrow highway that ran through what had once been a canyon were hotels, motels, inns and lodges, all located right next to one another, with no room for anything else in between. Lit No Vacancy signs protruded from nearly every lobby roof or hung from nearly every chain logo. In the parking lot and on the sidewalk in front of one hotel, he saw identically attired men who looked as though they'd been extras in *The Sound of Music*. They were here for a convention of some sort, although he could not imagine what kind, and farther down the street he saw a line of Asian men, all wearing business suits and carrying briefcases, emerging from a parked bus into the lobby of a Holiday Inn.

On the opposite side of the loop, between two new luxury hotels, was a tan- and rust-colored rectangular building whose worn sign read, HEARTHSTONE LODGE. The "No" was not lit in the No Vacancy display panel, and Steve pulled into the narrow parking lot to see whether he could get a room for the next two nights.

Although its decor looked straight out of the 1970s, the small lobby was clean, and the older woman behind the counter gave him a friendly smile as he walked in. "Good afternoon, sir. May I help you?"

"I sure hope so," he told her. "I'm looking for a room."

"For tonight?"

"Tonight and tomorrow night. Do you have any vacancies? I noticed your sign out there. . . ."

She'd been consulting something on the desk behind the counter. "We do have a room available, but I'm afraid it hasn't been cleaned yet. If you come back in an hour, though, we'll have it all ready for you."

"Can I check in now?"

The woman smiled. "Certainly. And I'll be happy to store your belongings behind the counter for you."

"That's okay," he told her. "I only have one suitcase. I'll just leave it in the car." He gave her a credit card, showed her his driver's license and wrote down the make, model and license plate number of his car on a form.

She handed him a receipt. "Here you go. Check back in an hour. I should have the key for you by then. Are you here for Sea World or the zoo?"

He shook his head.

"Convention?"

"No. Just a weekend getaway."

"You know, just around the other side of this hill a mile or two is Old Town. You might want to check it out. There are a lot of interesting sights and historic places. A state park, good food. We have one of the most haunted buildings in America there: the Whaley House."

"Maybe tomorrow," Steve told her. He looked around the small lobby. "Do you have a public restroom I could use?"

The clerk nodded, pointing out the window. "Over there to the left of that ice machine. We don't actually have a men's room or a women's room—just the one, for family use. So make sure you lock the door. Here's the key to open it."

He took from her a gold key chained to a piece of wood on which was painted a pink flower. "Thanks," he said, and headed outside.

The restroom, like the lobby, was small but clean: sink, toilet, wastepaper basket, paper-towel dispenser. He switched on the light, locked the door behind him, balanced the piece of wood on the edge of the sink and lifted the lid of the toilet seat. There was a doll's head in the bowl, staring up at him with glassy eyes topped by too-long lashes. The mouth was partially open in what could be interpreted as a mocking smile. Its neck was a gaping black hole. He stared for a moment. There was something oddly disquieting about the sight—

Why is it here? Who left it? Why?

—and he didn't feel right urinating on the object, so he flushed the toilet ahead of time, watching as the plastic head bobbed about, went under, was sucked down into the drain.

And popped up again.

It stared up at him, rocked back and forth by residual ripples. He flushed the toilet again, trying to get it to go down, but the tank hadn't filled up enough with water, and the doll's head just spun in lazy circles, long-lashed eyes looking upward, red-lipped mouth partially open and showing too-white teeth.

He no longer had to pee, and Steve left the bathroom, turning off the light behind him, not looking back at the toilet as he left. Returning the key and its attached piece of wood, he thanked the desk clerk and headed out to the parking lot and his car.

The first thing he wanted to see was where it had happened, and he sat for a few moments in the car, looking through his materials and reading over the new information he'd obtained this week. The woman, Karen Somers, actually hadn't been drowned in the bay, he'd learned. Those initial reports had been wrong. Further investigation had shown that she'd been stabbed first and then dumped in the water. Few details of the killing itself had been printed in the newspapers, and even the portions of the police report that were part of the public record did not illuminate the events leading up to the murder—probably because the killing remained unsolved and those facts remained unknown. But Steve knew his father, and, reading between the lines, he knew what had happened.

He followed the course charted on his GPS and headed out to the bay, to a spot that had been open land fifteen years ago but was now home to a minimall containing a Subway, a Baskin-Robbins ice-cream parlor, a women's swimsuit store and a surf shop. He parked in the lot behind the buildings and got out of his car to look out over the water, standing at the edge of a chest-high cinder-block wall and peering into the distance. Off to the right, on what looked like an island, was Sea World, with its tall landmark spire towering over everything in sight. To the left, on the far opposite shore, were some recently built condos or apartments, white buildings with red roofs that were almost mirror images of his own complex in Irvine. Straight ahead on the other side of the bay was a section of undeveloped land: a weedy, bushy, swampy area that had probably been protected for environmental reasons.

Down below . . .

Down below was where it had happened.

He leaned his arms on the wall, staring into the gently lapping greenish brown water.

And he knew how it had gone down.

She is in her bed, not asleep but simply lying there, staring up at the ceiling. Talking. To him, to herself, to no one. They are in her bedroom at her house, a rural dwelling from an earlier era. He is listening to her speak as he walks over to the chair on which he has hung his jacket. She continues talking and he continues listening as he opens the jacket pocket and pulls out a switchblade knife. He leans over her as though he is going to kiss her, but he raises his right arm and stabs her instead, and though she should have known it was coming, she does not, and her eyes widen in surprise as she dies.

Afterward, with her children asleep in their bedrooms, he takes her body outside and puts it in the old jalopy that is parked on the side of the house, strapping it into the passenger seat. She sits stiffly, but if no one looks closely, it will appear as though she is drunk or, at most, asleep. He drives through the night to the bay, to a spot where he knows the

*water is deep, where there is not a gentle slope to the bottom
but a sudden drop. There is no one to watch as he releases the
brake and pushes the vehicle in.*

He walks back, down side roads, unseen.

*It is not the police who find her body a day or two later,
but a fisherman whose line gets caught on the car's windshield. He's in a rowboat, and, looking down to see what has
snagged his line, he spots her in the water, ghost white in the
passenger seat, eyes open and staring at nothing, her hair
waving in the flowing current like the seaweed that floats
nearby.*

Steve remained by the wall until the belligerent manager of the surf shop, obviously thinking he was a transient, came out the rear door of his store and shouted
at Steve to get out of there or he'd call the police. He
pointed to a white sign with red lettering affixed to the
wall some twenty feet to the left. "Can't you read? No
loitering!"

Steve smiled, waved his acquiescence, and walked
back to his car. It had probably been close to an hour,
and hopefully his room was ready.

Feeling hungry, he stopped off at a Carl's Jr. on his
way back to the hotel. It was an off-hour, and although
there were three junior high school–aged kids leaning
their bikes against one of the outside tables, the inside
of the fast-food restaurant was devoid of customers.
Steve ordered an extralarge Coke and a Double Western Bacon Cheeseburger, then sat down at a table to
wait for his order. The three kids came in a moment
later, laughing to themselves at something they'd seen
or heard outside. One of the boys looked at him,
pointed and said something to his friends. The laugh-
ter intensified.

The overweight clerk behind the counter called his
number, and Steve walked over to pick up the food. The

same kid pointed again, mumbled a single word Steve could not make out, and all three burst out laughing. A few minutes later their order arrived, and the boys carried their trays to one of the outside tables.

Steve ate slowly, refilled his Coke, threw away his trash, then walked out the restaurant door. The boys were only about halfway through their meal, talking profanely about some girl they all knew, and he walked purposefully up to the punk who had pointed at him and punched the kid in the face. Hard. Blood sprayed out in all directions, not like the spurt that had coated his knuckles when he'd sucker punched that asshole in the Salt Lake City café, but a wild, uncontrolled eruption that not only drenched his fist but flew onto the table and the boys' food. This was a kid, after all, and his face was neither as big nor as strong as the young man's in Utah had been. It crumpled beneath his fist like a paper mask.

The other two boys immediately jumped back, out of Steve's way, and scrambled around another table, putting distance between them and him. "I'm calling the police!" the taller kid shouted. "That's assault!"

Calmly, Steve grabbed the hair of the boy he had hit and yanked his bleeding head up so they were staring eye-to-eye. His voice when he spoke was purposely low and calm. "You *can* call the police," he said. "And they *will* arrest me. But I will learn your address from the complaint. And do you know what I will do with that information? After I am released, I will go to your house, kill your parents and any brothers and sisters you might have, and then kill you. I will gut your mom and make her eat her own stomach. Then I will cut off your dad's balls and shove them in *your* mouth before I stab you in the eyes, in the chest and in the abdomen. You will die slowly and painfully." Steve looked up. "And then I will go after your friends."

He let go of the kid's hair and smiled, wiping his bloody hand on the boy's T-shirt. "Or you can forget this ever happened. The choice is yours."

He walked slowly across the parking lot to his car and was gratified to hear no noise behind him. No whispering, no yelling, certainly no laughing.

He smiled to himself as he got into the car. He took a napkin from the glove compartment, which he used to more thoroughly wipe the blood from his hand, and tossed the crumpled red and white paper on the asphalt of the parking lot.

He took off.

There was a traffic jam on the freeway, so Steve used his GPS to find an alternative route back to the hotel. He ended up taking a street that cut through a residential neighborhood before intersecting the eastern end of the hotel loop. Halfway through the neighborhood, he saw, up ahead and to the right, a dog dash out from between two houses. The dog sprinted across a lawn and in front of a parked car, heading directly for the street.

He could have slowed down, but he didn't. He sped up. There was a *bump-thump-crunch* as the car ran over the animal, and when he glanced in the rearview mirror, Steve saw an unmoving brown lump in the center of his lane.

He smiled to himself.

Dead dog in the middle of the road.

He wished at that moment that Sherry had come along on the trip.

She would have liked this.

That night, Steve went to Old Town, looking for that haunted house the desk clerk had told him about. The Whaley House. He followed the directions on a pamphlet he grabbed from the hotel lobby, and followed a throng of tourists walking down what looked like a dusty street out of the Old West.

The Whaley House itself was a not particularly imposing brick structure that would have blended in with almost any old neighborhood in the country. It was closed for the evening, but Steve stood in front of the dwelling, looking at the darkened windows. According to the brochure, it was supposed to be haunted by the ghosts of men condemned to death by the judge who lived there, as well as by the judge himself and members of his family. A portion of the home had apparently been built over the town's original gallows.

Did Steve believe in ghosts? Not really. He had seen the figure of his father in his bedroom, but now that he'd had time to think about it, he was pretty sure that had just been a figment of his imagination. A hallucination caused by stress. Besides, if all ghosts were as vengeful as the ones supposedly haunting the Whaley House, he would have some angry ones on his tail. And he didn't want that.

He walked slowly down the street, along with a smattering of tourists. There was a clown in front of a well-lit gift shop, making balloon animals and either selling them or handing them out to the families that passed by. Steve gave the clown a wide berth. In his book, that makeup-wearing man blowing up and twisting balloons was far creepier than the supposedly haunted house, although he could not say why.

Reaching a Mexican restaurant at the end of the street, he stopped, looking back. Had his family ever come here when they'd lived in San Diego? He didn't remember it, but then he didn't remember much about their time here. He could recall his school, his friends, their house, but for some reason almost everything else was a blur. What did that say about him? About his family? When you couldn't remember the facts of your own life, something was definitely wrong. Steve wondered now if he had sensed some irregularity in his father's behavior, in the old man's words or deeds, that had seemed suspicious. Perhaps, on a subliminal level, he had known what was going on in the *other* part of his father's life and his brain had chosen to block all of that out.

Whatever the reason, San Diego was like an unknown city to him, and whereas an hour ago that had made this nighttime sojurn seem fun, a tourist's exploration of a vacation destination, now it just seemed weird and uncomfortable, an amnesiac's exploration of what should have been familiar territory. He felt restless and uneasy, and he walked back the way he'd come, zigzagging between the strolling tourists, staying on the other side of the street from the balloon-tying clown, passing by the Whaley House and heading out to the parking lot.

Back at the hotel, he turned on the television, stared at the screen for a while without knowing what he was watching, called Sherry and talked for about an hour, then masturbated joylessly and went to bed.

On Saturday, he did nothing. He'd been planning to look up some of the people who knew Karen Somers or who'd been involved in the investigation of her death, but the truth was that he already knew what he needed to know and he didn't feel like doing any additional research.

It was after ten when he awoke, and outside the early morning clouds had burned off and the sky was swimming-pool blue. He'd brought a bathing suit, though at the time he wasn't sure why, and now he thought he might spend the day on the sand. He asked the desk clerk for the location of a good beach where he could lie out undisturbed, and she pulled out a map, showing him a spot that was not scenic enough for tourists and where the waves weren't good enough for locals. "It's my favorite spot," she told him. "There's hardly anyone there."

Steve stopped by a place off the freeway called Happy Taco, picked up a breakfast burrito and a forty-four-ounce Coke, and drove through the city to the beach. Lying out on a white hotel towel, he fell asleep, waking up sometime in midafternoon with the realization that he'd gotten burned. He sat up, shielding his eyes against the sun. Off to the right, the sky was bisected by a gigantic bridge that led across the water to Coronado Island. It was higher than the Golden Gate, high enough that the tallest ship could pass beneath it with more than a hundred feet to spare, and Steve couldn't help thinking that it would be the perfect spot from which to drop a body. Dead *or* alive. Because nothing could survive that fall.

There had to be railings on it, though. Fences. Probably security cameras. The bridge was the biggest suicide magnet he had ever seen.

He smiled to himself as he thought of what it would be like to throw McColl, screaming, over the side. He stood, shaking off the towel, his burned skin feeling tight, and wondered if his father had ever had a similar thought about the bridge.

He probably had.

He almost certainly had.

On Sunday morning, Steve slept until noon.

Then he checked out of the hotel and drove home.

Twenty-one

He killed Mark McColl on the day after he got back
from San Diego.

It wasn't planned exactly, at least not in the way
Gina's death had been planned, but Steve was so intimately familiar with the day-to-day routines of the department head's life that it was simple for him to step
in without thinking and do what needed to be done. He
knew McColl's habits so well by this point that even a
spontaneous killing might as well have been outlined
weeks ahead of time, and while this wasn't completely
impulsive and unpremeditated, it definitely wasn't
something he had intended to do at this time.

It just happened.

McColl had called Steve into his office first thing
that morning, ostensibly to talk about a new client, a
junior high school in Reseda, but really to hint around
about Gina's murder.

"What do you think of the new secretary?" the department head asked after they'd discussed the new
client.

"She seems fine," Steve replied warily.

McColl nodded. "I think she'll work out. It'll take a
while to get her up to speed, but she should do well. I
miss Gina, though." He shook his head. "I still can't be-

lieve she was murdered. In her own house. What kind of *lunatic* could do such a thing?"

There was an emphasis on the word "lunatic" that Steve found insulting. It was obviously aimed directly at him, and he stood firm under the department head's gaze, saying nothing.

That was when he knew it was time for McColl to die.

He didn't make it look like an accident, as he'd originally intended, but he did make it appear to be a suicide; which, to a suspicious mind, might tie the death to Gina's. It wasn't exactly a frame and wasn't even particularly well thought-out, but Steve trusted that the unstated haphazardness of the connection might lead observers, particularly the police, to think that McColl and Gina had been involved with each other, that he had killed her for some reason, and that guilt had led him to take his own life. Such a scenario was not implausible, and Steve wondered himself if the two of them really had been involved. The department head had certainly taken a personal interest in Gina's death. And in her life. It was conceivable that he had been . . . intimate with her.

Hell, his picture might even be in one of her collages.

It was McColl's good fortune that his wife and daughters were out, because Steve intended to kill the man no matter what. And if his family had been there, he might have been forced to dispatch them as well. He had no idea where they were or when they would be back, but if they were lucky they would remain at the gym or the basketball game or the band practice or whatever the fuck they were at, and not return until he was done. Because if they returned early . . .

Trash pickup in McColl's neighborhood was Tuesday morning, so each Monday evening, at eight or thereabouts, the department head took his two covered plastic garbage cans—one for household trash, one for yard waste—from the side yard out to the curb. He was vulnerable then, but too publicly visible. Steve *could* have taken him out in a drive-by at that moment, but guns weren't his style. He was hands-on. McColl did leave his side door open when he carried out the trash cans, however, to enable him to get back into the house, and Steve took advantage of that: arriving early, hiding in the high bushes on the side of the house, and sneaking through the open gate into the side yard and then through the open door into the laundry room while the other man was out by the street.

He moved quickly through the house—laundry room to kitchen to game room—staying at the back of the structure so he wouldn't be seen from the street through those curtainless windows. There was nothing he could do about the exposed stairway, though, and, waiting until he heard the sound of movement at the side of the house, he dashed up the steps as quickly as he could, hoping no neighbors or passersby had been looking in at that moment. Hurriedly, he checked each room—master bedroom, the two girls' bedrooms, guest room—before deciding to stake out the bathroom off the hall. Not only was it small, which was an advantage while lying in wait, but it echoed the location of Gina's death, which would hopefully trigger comparisons in the minds of the police.

From downstairs, Steve heard the closing of the side door, and then assorted knocks and scrapes and taps that indicated McColl was doing something in the kitchen. He remained standing just inside the doorway of the bathroom, wondering what his next move should be. Ordinarily, McColl would not go upstairs until bedtime—and by then his family would have returned. If Steve wanted to get this over with and get out—which he did—he would have to lure the other man up here. And soon. But he would have to do so in a way that did not arouse undue suspicion.

Waiting until there was silence downstairs, until he was sure that McColl was either reading the newspaper or at his computer, Steve walked over to the toilet, lifted up the seat and then dropped it down hard. The noise seemed loud in the stillness, though he was not sure it was loud enough to be heard from downstairs. He waited a moment, and when he heard no corresponding noise, no indication that McColl was coming upstairs to investigate, he walked over to the bathroom sink, picked up a glass bowl filled with potpourri, lifted it high and let it crash and shatter on the floor.

Now there was commotion downstairs.

It was go time.

He stepped into the shower stall, took the weapon from his pocket. He was wearing latex gloves and a raincoat. He expected this to get messy. And he was prepared.

He stood still.

Waited.

He didn't have to wait long. Footsteps sounded on the carpeted stairs, and a moment later, McColl was striding up the hall to the bathroom. Steve could see him through the narrow space between the hinges on the door. The department head didn't seem particularly worried—just curious. Maybe the family had a cat or some other pet that was given free rein in the house and that was what he thought had made the noise. Whatever the reason, he approached unawares.

And when he walked into the bathroom, Steve was waiting for him.

With scissors.

He wanted the advantage of surprise, but he also

wanted McColl to know who he was, to be aware of who was taking him out. Steve was fortunate enough to see, for the split second after he emerged from the shower, recognition, and then, before the other man could react or respond, the scissors were slicing through the air and stabbing him in the throat, blood gushing like water from a burst pipe. Steve stepped quickly aside, not only to protect himself from the spray but to prevent an outline from forming on the floor and wall, a clear, bloodless spot that might indicate to investigators that someone else had been there.

McColl fell forward, clutching his neck, trying to stem the flow, but he was too weakened already, and in a moment he was still, the only movement in the bathroom the feeble pumping of blood from the wound as his dying heart slowed, then stopped. The wall next to the shower looked like a red Jackson Pollock, and the white floor was covered with a growing pool of crimson. If he waited any longer, he would be trapped and have to step in the blood to get out, leaving incriminating footprints, so Steve took a mighty step over the expanding puddle and out into the hallway. Turning back around, he crouched down and gently took McColl's right hand, placing it on the scissors protruding from his neck, making it look as though he'd stabbed himself.

Both Steve's raincoat and gloves had blood on them, and he smeared the blood around so it was evenly distributed. It made him look like a ghoul, but it also made it less likely that any of the blood would drip onto the floor as he went through the house on his way out. *Strange*, he thought. Moments before, that blood had been contained within McColl's body, circulating through it, keeping him alive. Now it was on Steve. It felt wrong walking around with the vital fluid of a dead man smeared on his clothing, but it couldn't be helped. He'd had no choice. He'd had to kill the department head. He hadn't *wanted* to do it—McColl had forced it on him. It was the man's own fault.

Careful not to drip, careful not to touch, Steve made his way out to the landing, then hurried quickly down the stairs, once again hoping he would not be spotted through the window by someone on the sidewalk or in the street. He followed a reverse path back through the rear of the house to the laundry room. And stopped.

The door.

It was closed. Probably locked.

How was he going to open the door and get out of the house without getting blood all over the handle or leaving fingerprints behind? Door handles would be the first things police would check in an investigation. He hesitated only a moment before using his left hand to pull off his right glove. Tugging down from the wrist, he turned the latex inside out and quickly put it back on. Cool, wet blood stuck to his skin, feeling slimy and revolting. But the outside was clear and clean, and he opened the door and went out into the side yard. It briefly occurred to him that he'd been sweating inside the glove and that some of his DNA had probably been left on the handle, but he pushed that thought away. Real life wasn't a *CSI* show, and even if the police did suspect murder, his DNA wasn't on file anywhere. He couldn't be caught.

What to do about the gloves, though? And the raincoat? If he brought them into his car, there'd be blood on the seats, on the floor, in the trunk. If he dumped them in McColl's garbage cans, the police would find them. Where was he going to put this stuff? He hadn't thought any of this through, and his mind was racing now, trying to come up with some way to dispose of the evidence.

Next to the fence, adjacent to an old dented metal

garbage can that obviously hadn't been used in ages, was a black plastic sack filled with cans and bottles. It lay with its bottom flat on the ground, the top spread open to make it easier for the family to toss in their recyclables. The sack was nowhere near full, and, grateful, Steve took off his raincoat, then took off his gloves, and tossed everything in. Pulling up on the edges of the bag, he twisted them and tied a loose slipknot to seal everything inside. The only disadvantage was that the shifting cans and bottles made a loud clattering sound when he picked up the trash bag, but that was a problem that couldn't be helped. Treading as lightly and carefully as he could, he made his way out to the car, opened the driver's-side door, pushed the sack onto the passenger seat beside him, and took off.

The raincoat had been a long one, going down to his ankles, but the cuffs of his pants had still been exposed, and though he couldn't see anything now, there were probably flecks of blood on those cuffs and on the tops of his tennis shoes. Later—tomorrow or the next day or next weekend—he would wash both and then donate them to a Goodwill or Salvation Army in another city far away from Irvine. The plastic trash bag he would toss in a Dumpster tonight, maybe driving to Garden Grove or Westminster or one of the poorer cities in hopes that, even if it *were* discovered before being taken to a landfill, its presence would be attributed to a person living there.

Steve understood now the pressures his father had faced, and it amazed him to realize that the man had been able to simultaneously hold a job, head a family *and* kill the people who needed to be killed. He had not been close to his father, growing up. The two of them had never really gotten along, and after Steve left home, after college, they had drifted even farther apart. Theirs was a dysfunctional family, although that had never really bothered him. When he was living in the middle of it, the situation had seemed perfectly normal to him.

But something had happened after his father's stroke. Against all odds, the two of them had grown closer, and Steve had come to learn that he and his dad were more alike than not. He regretted all those years of emotional estrangement but at the same time was grateful that he had finally come to know his dad.

His father might be dead, but Steve still felt closer to him than he ever had.

He wondered if the old man had ever second-guessed himself or had ever felt remorseful about any of his kills. Steve didn't. At least, not yet. Everything he'd done had *had* to be done, although he could foresee a time in the future when it all might not be so black-and-white, when there might be shades of gray or room for interpretation. In fact, if McColl's family had returned and he'd had to take care of them, he would have felt bad about that.

But they hadn't.

The wife and kids were okay.

Things were good right now. All was right.

Feeling better, Steve headed down MacArthur Boulevard before pulling onto the Costa Mesa Freeway and heading north toward Garden Grove.

Twenty-two

Friends

"Sometimes it's better when people die. Because then you can love them unconditionally, with all of their faults. Then their faults don't matter."

Lydia had told her that when she was sixteen—and Zelda had never forgotten it. Yet it was not until now, after her own father had died, that Zelda finally realized the wisdom of those words. She'd always loved her father, of course, but he had often been thoughtless and unintentionally cruel. Most of the time he had thought only of himself, not caring how his words and actions might affect others. He had also sometimes been hard to get along with, even downright mean, and more than once she had wished that he was dead.

Now that he was dead, Zelda realized how superficial her complaints were, how ultimately inconsequential her objections to his behavior had been. Even his worst attributes, even his most obnoxious traits, were things that she could have lived with. She had been focusing on small negatives when she should have been looking at the big picture, and she regretted it now.

"Sometimes it's better when people die."

Well, maybe it wasn't *better*. But it definitely put things into perspective. And perhaps the survivors learned something about themselves.

It was to Lydia that Zelda poured out her heart after her father's death. Lydia was not only her oldest friend, she was her best friend. They had been through a lot together. They had shared the good times, the bad times, the boring times. They had entrusted each other with their hopes, their fears, their successes, their failures. They shared knowledge they shared with no one else. Lydia knew of Zelda's first sexual encounter. Zelda knew of Lydia's brief flirtation with drugs.

And Lydia had lost her father too. Her dad had died when she was fourteen, the victim of a freak accident at the foundry where he worked. So she knew what Zelda was going through.

Her friendship with Lydia sometimes made her wonder whether events were predestined, planned by fate, or whether they were the random result of chance. Could it be chance that made her, in fourth grade, answer the pen pal ad in the back of a magazine that her teacher, Mrs. Levin, had given her to help with a report, and just happen to choose Lydia's name from the list of two dozen the pen pal organization sent her?

She did not think so.

Something must have guided her.

Although she and Lydia had never met face-to-face, they had written weekly letters for the past twelve years, and they had called each other on special occasions. They had also kept up with each other's physical maturation through a series of exchanged photographs. It was amazing how alike both of them were physically, emotionally, intellectually. Zelda had once wondered, jokingly, whether the two of them were twins who had been separated at birth; they had so much in common.

Now Zelda wrote of her father, his minor faults as well as his major attributes. Before, she'd told her friend only his bad points, dwelling on his shortcomings. Now she told Lydia of his great love of animals, of his infatuation with photographs and artifacts of the Old West, of his unconditional love for her. It was a catharsis, writing about her father this way, and she felt emotionally drained as she sealed the ten-page letter in a manila envelope.

That night, alone in the empty house, she thought she heard her father's footsteps on the kitchen floor.

But she knew it had to be her imagination.

After my father died, we became the best of friends. It sounds like such a strange thing to say, but we became much closer after his death. No longer did I seek hidden motives for his actions or place my own interpretations on his words. I finally, unequivocally understood him, and for the first time in my life I not only loved him, I liked him.

Zelda read through Lydia's letter one more time, again focusing her attention on the paragraph concerning her friendship with her father. It was true, she realized. What Lydia said was absolutely true. Zelda still thought she heard her father's footsteps on the tile every so often. She still sometimes smelled his manly odor in the bathroom in the morning. The house still contained unexplainable traces of his existence, though he had been dead for nearly a month.

She wondered if she was going crazy.

But no. Lydia understood what she meant. Lydia knew exactly how she felt.

Maybe they were both crazy.

Now, *there* was a possibility. Zelda smiled to herself and folded up Lydia's letter, placing it back in the opened envelope. From downstairs, she thought she heard the sound of the refrigerator door opening and closing, the way it had each night at this time as her father poured himself some orange juice in order to wash down his battery of pills and vitamins.

Zelda listened, unmoving, but the sound did not repeat and there were no other noises from downstairs. She put the letter into her desk drawer. She knew she should have been frightened by the noise. She was alone in the house with a ghost. Her father's ghost. But, strangely, she felt comforted by the sound. It was nice to know that, alive or dead, her father was looking after her.

Crazy.

She began to write Lydia a response. On the TV, the local news ended and an old horror movie came on.

Zelda changed the channel.

She did not like horror movies. They scared her.

Three letters and one disastrous first date later, Zelda received her annual two weeks' vacation. The prospect frightened her. Father had always planned trips for them to take, and with him gone she really had no place to go. She could stay with her cousin Carrie for a few days, but Carrie had only recently had a baby and wasn't exactly in the best position to be entertaining guests. She could stay at home, fix up the house, clean the place up, but that was even less appealing. She had not only been hearing, smelling and obliquely sensing the presence of her father lately—she had thought several times that she had *seen* him out of the corner of her eye.

And she was afraid that, left alone in the house for two weeks straight, she might meet him face-to-face.

Zelda knew that her feelings and thoughts had long ago passed the problem point. Something inside her, for some reason or another, simply could not accept the fact that her father was dead. Her mind constantly registered stimuli that were not there in order to maintain the illusion that he was still with her, still in the house.

And anyone who could not accept the reality of a loved one's death had something seriously wrong with her.

Crazy.

So Zelda called Lydia. There were other friends, geographically closer, whom she could have gone to visit, but she wanted to see Lydia.

The arrangements were made simply and unbelievably quickly. Lydia was just as excited by the prospect of Zelda coming to visit as Zelda was herself. She gave precisely detailed instructions on how to get to her house from the airport, and she promised Zelda that she could stay as long as she liked.

Zelda packed her bags, arranged with Mrs. DeCamp next door for the care and feeding of her cat, and took a taxi to the airport. She was tempted, before heading out, to leave her father a note, explaining where she was going and what she was doing, but she knew that was not rational.

The taxi dropped her off right in front of the terminal, and Zelda had her bags checked at the counter. Going through the X-ray machine, her small valise caused it to beep, setting off some type of security alarm, and a burly guard asked her to please step aside. Her belongings were searched, and she was horrified to see that she had unwittingly packed several of her father's shirts and pants in the valise.

She did not remember putting any of that in there.

She had even packed some of his underwear.

Beneath the underwear was a kitchen knife.

Sweating, her voice halting and inarticulate as she lied, she told the security personnel that she was bringing the knife and clothes to her father in New York. The burly guard informed her that she would not be allowed to take the knife on the plane and that, unless she wanted it confiscated, it would have to be stored with other potentially lethal items in the cargo section of the plane.

Zelda had no objections.

New York was even darker and dirtier than she had been led to expect from the gritty detective shows she'd seen on television. After retrieving her luggage from the baggage claim area, she called Lydia. Her friend had said that she would not be able to pick her up at the airport, since she couldn't drive, but she had given Zelda precisely detailed directions.

Which Zelda had lost.

Now, writing the directions on the crumpled back of her flight ticket envelope, Zelda thanked her friend and said she'd arrive as soon as a taxi could take her there. Lydia giggled excitedly and said she couldn't wait to finally meet in person.

Zelda thought of her father's clothes and the knife in her valise.

Crazy.

The trip took much less time than Zelda had expected, given the slow flow of heavy traffic on the road. In a little over an hour, the taxi was pulling in front of a green-and-white wood house in a calm residential neighborhood. She paid the cabdriver and took out her bags. Her palms were sweaty, her heart pounding, and her mouth was dry. Walking up the short cement path and up the porch steps, she hesitantly rang the doorbell.

From inside the house came the sound of chimes.

An elderly woman, iron gray hair tied back in a bun, answered the door wearing a brightly colored muumuu. She peered out at Zelda through thick spectacles. "Yes?" she said.

Zelda smiled. "I'm here to see Lydia."

"Lydia? There must be some mistake."

"No. I'm her pen pal, Zelda."

The old woman's voice grew hard. "If this is a joke, it isn't a very funny one."

Zelda was puzzled. "She knows I'm coming. I called her. We talked about it."

"Lydia's dead," the old woman said.

Zelda felt her grip starting to slip. She'd just called Lydia, hadn't she? From the airport. She'd talked to her not more than an hour ago.

Zelda swallowed hard. She recognized the old woman now. It was Lydia's mother. Lydia had sent her a picture last year of the two of them together in Atlantic City.

"But I just called her," she found herself saying.

"Lydia died at birth," the old woman said. "I don't know where you dug her name up from, but if you don't get out of here, I'm going to call the police."

Zelda felt like screaming. She thought she *was* screaming, but she realized, as she bent down to zip open the valise and take out what lay beneath the underwear, that she was not making a sound, that suddenly, for some reason, she was very, very calm.

Twenty-three

The new secretary was not at her desk, and there were huddled bands of employees, three or four to a group, talking together in low tones throughout the floor. Steve knew what they were discussing the second he stepped off the elevator, and he braced himself, wiping all trace of expression off his face as he walked up to Ron Zindel and Bob Mattacks. The two PR reps were talking to one of the accountants.

"I heard it on the news," Steve said. "I wasn't sure if we were supposed to come in today."

"It's freaky," the accountant said nervously. "Who knows? Maybe there's someone stalking people from our company. Maybe one of us is next."

"This isn't a slasher film," Ron said. "There's no deranged alumnus on a killing spree."

Mattacks was nodding. "They think it was some sort of murder-suicide pact. Everyone knows Mark and Gina were having a thing."

"They were?" Steve said.

"Oh, yeah. You didn't know?"

"No one knew," Ron said. "Because I think you made it up."

Mattacks raised his hands. "I'm just telling you what I heard."

"There *could* be someone stalking us," the accountant said defensively. "Maybe it's someone who used to work here." He wandered off to talk to someone else.

Things were on the right track, Steve thought. Everyone was thinking along the lines he'd hoped they would, and as the employees began drifting back to their cubicles and workstations, he excused himself and went to his own desk, where he busied himself with work.

By midmorning, the subject had worn itself out, and it was almost possible to pretend that nothing had happened.

Steve's mother called in the afternoon.

The last time she'd called him at work it had been to tell him about his father's stroke and the unprovoked attack upon her. This time, she announced that she was selling the house. She sprang it on him just like that: "I'm selling the house."

He didn't know how to respond, wasn't sure his mother expected him to respond. It was obvious from her tone of voice that this was a decision she had made, a decision that had nothing to do with him, and that she was informing him only out of courtesy. On a superficial level, it occurred to him that this would relieve him of all those house-maintenance duties he had reluctantly inherited. But he also thought that, financially, it would be a mistake for her to pull up stakes, considering the fact that the place was paid off.

Strangely, he had no emotional reaction to the news. Despite spending his teenage years within those walls, he had no attachment to the house. It was not a home to him. It was merely the place where his mother lived.

"Where are you going to go?" he asked.

"I don't know. But I want someplace smaller. An apartment maybe. The neighborhood's not what it was, but even in this market I'll still get out of it more than we put into it. I was thinking of going to one of those senior communities."

"Have you thought this through?" he started to say.

"I won't have you telling me what to do!" she shouted. "You're just like your father!"

She hung up the phone.

Steve sat there, listening to a dial tone. Slowly, he put down the receiver. He hoped she'd move far away so he wouldn't have to deal with that shit anymore. Northern California. Another state. Someplace where he wouldn't be obligated to see her.

He recalled how she'd waited to phone him until the day after she'd been treated for her injuries and his father had been taken by the police to Anaheim Memorial and then transferred to the VA hospital. How far along was she on this selling-the-house-and-moving plan? Was she already packed and ready to go? Had she talked to a real estate agent? Did she already have a new place picked out? He wouldn't put anything past her, and part of him thought that the best thing that could happen would be for her to just disappear, to take off one day and not tell him where she was going and never come back.

But what if there were something of his father's still in the house? Something in the crawl space beneath the floors, or in the low storage attic between the ceiling and roof? What if there was incriminating evidence?

Or worse?

There would have to be an inspection if the house was sold. And his mother would pack up everything first, no doubt finding a lot of small, forgotten or never-seen items that she had missed while purging the house of his father's belongings. Which meant there was a good chance that some type of damning article could turn up.

He would not allow that to happen.

After work, Steve drove to his mother's house. He didn't call ahead of time, didn't tell her that he was coming. He just showed up. She seemed annoyed by that, and he wondered how many other mothers would be put out by a surprise visit from their only son. Not too many, probably.

He didn't know what to say to her, didn't know what to do, so he told her that if she really was going to move, he would help her pack. She neither accepted nor declined his offer but said that she was thinking of moving to Leisure World.

"I don't think it's called Leisure World anymore, Mom. It's Laguna Hills or Laguna Niguel or something."

"Do you always have to contradict me?" she demanded.

"That's not what I was doing."

"Don't you talk back to me!"

Steve sighed and walked away, out of the kitchen. He headed over to the room that had once been his. He looked around but felt no nostalgia, felt nothing really, only noted objectively where his bed and desk had been, where his movie and rock posters had hung. He'd spent a lot of time in this room—too much time, probably—but when he'd been a teenager the neighborhood had consisted mostly of older couples and there hadn't been any other kids his own age. Untold hours had been occupied reading and writing, and if it had not been for that, who knew what might have become of him; who knew how he might have turned out?

He definitely would have been a different person, although whether that would have been better or worse he couldn't say.

Last night, he'd finally finished *Don Quixote*. The

first half, at least. If he recalled correctly, the second half had been written some years later and for money. Cervantes had not wanted to go back to the knight's story, but had been broke and in desperate need of cash. So Steve felt no guilt at all for stopping where he did. The first portion of the work was the real story. The second was *Godfather III*.

He was not a sentimental guy, he had learned. He felt no emotional attachment to any object or place from the past, and he was willing to bet that his father hadn't either. It was how he'd been able to move around so much, to drag his wife and son from New Mexico to Utah to Arizona to California.

Steve was starting to wonder if maybe it was time for *him* to move on. The idea appealed to him, and he imagined how his father must have felt, lighting out for new territories, each city or town a blank canvas on which he could do his work. But that was a pipe dream. The economy was in the toilet, and it would be very difficult for him to find a new job if he moved somewhere else. Besides, as his parents had never tired of pointing out, he wasn't really qualified for anything; he should be happy to have the job he did.

Not to mention the fact that Sherry was here.

And she had a stable job too.

He walked out to the garage behind the house. The sun was going down, and the shadows in the backyard were long. He saw movement in one of the bushes near the fence, a dark, low shape that faded back into the branches. He hoped it was a cat and not an opossum. Opossums creeped him out.

After opening the big garage door, he pulled the string that turned on the light. After a hesitant flicker, the fluorescent bar his father had installed winked into existence, illuminating the right half of the room but leaving the left in semidarkness. As he'd remembered, the garage was a mess, filled with a jumble of yard tools, paint cans, boxes and old furniture. Through the grime-covered window above a workbench piled high with mason jars and magazines, orange sunlight cut a slanting swath through the center of the space, highlighting areas usually not exposed.

Steve stepped forward, noticing something he hadn't before: a piece of frayed rope tied to the garage's middle beam. Frowning, he reached up, tried to touch it. Even with him standing on tiptoe, his fingers couldn't quite stretch that far, and he sank back down. He had no idea why it was there, and as he sifted through memories of the last decade and a half he could think of no reason that a rope would ever have been needed at that spot.

It looked to him like part of a noose.

He hadn't wanted his mind to go there, but the thought was unavoidable. Steve stood beneath the frazzled rope end, looking up. The portion that remained was wrapped around the beam and tied tightly, as though it had been meant to hold a lot of weight.

But whom had the noose been for? Had his father planned to kill his mother? Or had he intended to hang himself?

Or kill his only son?

Or use it on other kids from the neighborhood, or their parents?

Or strangers?

The possibilities were endless, and the frustrating thing was that Steve would probably never know. Still glancing upward, he saw that a large square of plywood had been placed across the beams at the back of the garage. From this angle, he could see that there were boxes piled atop the wood, sealed boxes that for some reason had been segregated from those that lay stacked on the floor.

He pulled the stepladder from its spot against the side wall and set it up just in front of the plywood shelf. Climbing up, he grabbed the closest box and carefully brought it down, placing it on the cement floor and crouching to open the duct-taped top. Inside were dozens of small blue boxes containing hundreds and hundreds of toothpicks, more toothpicks than any family could use in a lifetime.

Weird.

Intrigued, he went back up the ladder and brought down another box. This one contained reams of carbon paper, the kind used to make copies on typewriters in the days before computers and word processors.

The next box was filled with framed photos of old airplanes and what appeared to be a collection of salt and pepper shakers. In a leather satchel within the box were several old knives.

Steve was sitting on the cement, taking out the knives and examining them, when he heard the back door of the house open. He turned around and noticed with surprise that the sun had gone down. It was night.

His mother walked into the garage. Because of the poor lighting, the left half of her face remained shadowed while the right half looked flat and pasty in the glare of the fluorescent bulb. She stared down at Steve. If he hadn't known who she was already, he would not have recognized her. "What are you doing?" she asked.

"Just checking out these boxes."

"Are you looking for something?"

He looked at the cartons of toothpicks, at the packs of carbon paper, at the knives in the satchel in front of him.

"I don't know," he said.

Twenty-four

"Come on," Jason said. "You haven't been out with us for . . . for I don't know how long."

He had not just called this time but had shown up at Steve's work at four thirty on a Friday, and there was no polite way to avoid this conversation. Jason had been trying to get ahold of him for weeks now, but Steve had successfully evaded him: monitoring incoming calls, not returning calls when messages were left, claiming to be busy on those few occasions when his screening process failed and he actually answered the phone.

At least he hadn't brought along Dennis or Will.

Jason did that touchy-feely thing and clapped a hand on Steve's shoulder. "What is it, man? You can tell me."

"It's my dad and all," he mumbled. "It's been a rough time."

"I understand," Jason said. "I get it. But we're your friends, dude. You gotta have friends." He grinned. "I think that's a song cue."

Steve looked down at his feet. He did sort of miss hanging out, but things were complicated right now, and he needed to keep his life as simple as possible. For how long he didn't know, but for the moment, at least, he wanted to maintain a discreet distance from any possible distractions.

"I promise we won't hold you there. If you want, one drink and you're out. We won't even ask you any personal questions. We won't ask you *any* questions.

But Dennis has been dating a model he met at a software convention. An actual model! She was in a print ad for a new PC. And I got a new job. I have an office and ten thousand more a year. Interesting stuff going on."

He was too tired to fight, and at that moment the retro normalcy of it all did seem awfully appealing. Slowly, Steve nodded.

"All right, my man! Pack up and let's get out of here."

"I'm driving myself," Steve said.

"Understood, understood. In case you want to bail early. I understand completely. But we've been going to a new place with a much better happy hour, and I thought you could follow me there so you can find it more easily."

Steve smiled weakly. "And so I won't skip out on you."

"That too." Jason laughed, put an arm around him. "Gotta stick by your bros."

Feeling uncomfortable, Steve pulled away. "Let me finish up here. I'll meet you downstairs in the lobby. Fifteen minutes."

Jason fixed him with a look of mock suspicion. "There's no back door to this building, is there?"

He smiled. "There is, but I won't use it. Promise. I'll meet you in the lobby in fifteen."

"I'll be guarding the front door."

The "new place" turned out to be an El Torito Grille located in an area of high-rise office buildings not far from the airport. The Mexican restaurant, a low Spanish-style structure, looked incongruous amidst the tall rectangles of mirrored glass, but welcoming. Steve could smell the delicious aroma of food as he and Jason walked inside, and it made him realize that he was hungry.

The two of them walked into the bar, but the room was so crowded that it took them a moment to locate the table where Will and Dennis were waiting. They maneuvered through the happy-hour throng. Will was sitting smugly, tipping back a Heineken, and Steve knew as soon as he got close enough to see his friend's face that this had been a mistake.

Friend?

No. Will wasn't really a friend, and Steve wondered if he ever had been. The other man was not only ego-centric and self-important but genuinely malicious in his disdain for others. Even in college he'd been petty and vicious, and while his attitude had seemed funny back then, it had become increasingly less so over the years, to the point that Steve now dreaded any contact with him.

"Look what the cat dragged in." Will smiled in a way that aspired to be mocking and gently sardonic, but, as always, there was an edge of real cruelty behind it.

"I'm the cat?" Jason said.

"Well, you're a pussy."

The four of them laughed, the way they always did, but the joke wasn't really that funny, and as usual it was at the expense of someone else. Steve wondered for the first time if Will was really a friend to any of them. Dennis had always been closest to him and often acted like an asshole himself, but on his own, Dennis really wasn't such a bad guy, when you came down to it. It was Will's influence that made him behave that way. It was Will who was dragging him down. And Jason had admitted that he thought Will was a jerk.

Would any of them miss Will if he died?

Steve tried to concentrate on the plate of taquitos

on the table. He shouldn't be thinking those kinds of thoughts.

"So where have you been?" Will asked, and it wasn't just a casual conversation starter. It was a pointed question.

"I've been busy," he said vaguely.

"Too busy for your buds?"

"Yeah," Dennis chimed in. "Where've you been hiding?"

"I've been helping my mom a lot. Ever since my dad died, she's been pretty rocky." That ought to shut them up.

It did.

Steve relented. "Jason said you're dating a model," he said to Dennis.

"Ohhh, yeahhh." The other man grinned. "Wanna see a picture?" He took out his wallet. "I keep one with me at all times because otherwise no one would believe me."

"I still don't believe you," Will said.

"Wow," Steve commented after seeing the photo. He had to admit, the woman was pretty impressive. She wasn't exactly his type—too plastic—but she had the finely sculpted cheekbones, piercing blue eyes, perfect teeth, small nose and big breasts that epitomized the advertising industry's concept of the ideal woman. She *looked* like a model.

"But how's the sex?" Will asked. "That's the real test."

"Better than you're getting."

"Does she do anal?"

Dennis grinned. "That's for me to know and you to find out."

Jason fixed him with a mock frown. "For him to find out? You want him to investigate your sex life?"

"It's an expression, a figure of speech. You never heard that before?" He put the photo back in his wallet as the rest of them started laughing. "Aw, fuck you guys. You're just a bunch of jealous pricks."

"You're right," Jason said.

The conversation flowed naturally from there, and Steve had to admit that it was nice to be hanging with his friends again. He hadn't realized until now how isolated he had become. Yes, he went to work each day and interacted with people, particularly on the phone, but there was really no one in his personal life other than Sherry, and he'd been spending a lot more time by himself than with her lately.

This was cool; this was fun.

Except for Will.

Steve kept glancing over at the other man, and each time he did he discovered something new that irritated him. Even Will's *teeth* were annoying. He'd obviously gotten them bleached, and every time he smiled he reminded Steve of Wink Martindale or Bob Goen or one of those old game-show hosts.

It would be so much better if Will were not here. . . .

Steve pushed the thought away and went over to the buffet cart, where he scooped an enchilada onto his plate and grabbed a handful of tortilla chips. He looked back at their table. Will sat in the center, smiling and self-satisfied, while Jason and Dennis flanked him on either side, like lackeys competing for His Royal Majesty's attention. He could tell that they would be happier if Will was gone. They might not condone his murder but neither would they mourn his death.

Steve would be doing them all a favor if he arranged for Will's killing.

This one would need to look like an accident, though. He had gotten away with Gina and McColl because they appeared to be linked; there was no real reason for anyone to look too closely at the people around them. But if one of his friends was murdered, it would be the equivalent of shining a spotlight on himself. He might as well stand in front of the police station with a megaphone and shout, *I'm the guy!*

No, Will's death had to be unidentifiable as a killing. It had to be bad luck, misadventure, wrong place, wrong time, something that appeared to have happened naturally.

He walked back to the table, thinking.

"Whatever happened to toxic shock syndrome?" Dennis was asking. "I remember when I was a kid and just learning about sex, there were all these reports about how tampons were dangerous and had these little threads that stabbed the wall of the vagina and killed people. Did they find a cure for that? Are tampons different now? What happened?"

Will smirked. "Ask your model."

"I will," Dennis said.

"What I want to know," added Jason, "is what happened to maxipads. Does anyone use *those* anymore?"

"Your mama," Will offered.

"You're probably right."

The three of them started laughing, but Steve watched only Will, unable to stop staring at the too-white teeth and the too-perfect hair, at the too-hip clothes that were worn with a studied nonchalance that was a little too casual to be real.

An accident.

At work or home or somewhere in between.

He was excited. This was a challenge, and already he was mentally sorting through the ideas he'd originally had in mind for McColl. None of them were any good, and he couldn't seem to come up with any new ones, but he wasn't worried. He had plenty of time.

He'd think of something.

*   *   *

"Ow!" Sherry cried out. "Stop!"

Instead of stopping, he began thrusting harder.

"The angle's wrong! It hurts!"

They were trying a new position, and though it was uncomfortable for him as well and he'd been about to pull out and go back to doing it their usual way, he liked the fact that it hurt, liked that she was begging him to stop. Despite the discomfort, he could feel himself growing harder within her.

"*Ow!*" she screamed.

And he came.

He held her in place until he was finished, then let her pull away.

"What the hell were you doing?" she demanded. "I told you to stop!"

"Sorry."

"It hurt, damn it!" She touched herself, wincing. "It still hurts."

He rolled over, sitting up, his back against the headboard. He should feel guilty, he knew. But he didn't. He felt good. "Why don't you like dogs?" he asked.

She frowned, confused. "What?"

"I was just wondering why you don't like dogs."

"I don't know. No reason. I just don't."

"You weren't attacked as a child or chased or something?"

"Not really. There was a mean dog down the street when I was little, but I never had any contact with it. Why? What made you even think of that?" She scowled at him. "You're just trying to change the subject."

"No, I'm—"

"It *hurt.*"

"Sorry," he said again.

"No," she told him pointedly. "You're not."

*   *   *

In the dream, he was seated on the floor of a dark-ened room. He could see nothing, hear nothing, but the air was warm with body heat, and humid, and he knew he was not alone. He remained perfectly still, unmoving, certain that he was in the midst of enemies and that if he made any sound or gave any indication that he was there, they would immediately turn upon him.

There was a loud click, and suddenly a light shone at the front of the room, a spotlight from the ceiling that illuminated a tableau of bloody carnage. The scene was arranged on a small stage, a rickety construct of moldy wood barely higher than the level of the floor, and consisted of a bloody man staring through a glass-less mirror frame at the mutilated body of a woman. The woman was seated in a chair, and her partially severed head drooped down over her chest, a wash of blood covering the butchered stretch of mangled skin that should have been her breasts. The man him-self was naked and hideously deformed, arranged in a similar position on an identical chair, and while it was not clear whether the blood that covered him was his own, the fact that he remained completely unmoving and unblinking, with wide, staring eyes, indicated that he too was probably dead.

The spotlight was focused on this grotesque spec-tacle, but its fading edges touched the area in front of the stage, and in the dispersed gloom he could see, a dozen feet in front of him, the first row of onlookers.

They were clowns.

His heart lurched in his chest, and it was all he could do not to cry out. He froze, not daring to move, hardly daring to breathe.

There was a click.

The light went off, and once again they were in darkness.

He felt hot breath on his cheek, smelled candy cane and popcorn.

"Hello," a voice said lovingly.

Twenty-five

"Will! Dude!"

"Steve?" Will sounded surprised.

I'll bet he is, Steve thought.

"What time is it?"

"Ten or so. Too late for you?"

"No. I just got in."

Steve kept the tone light. "Thought I'd give you a call and see what's up."

"Uh, not much." Pause. "What's up with you?"

"Sherry and I were going to go hiking in Modjeska Canyon tomorrow morning, but she has to bail on me. Someone called in sick at the library." This was a lie. "I thought maybe you'd like to come with me. I know you're always up for a good workout."

"Did you try Jason?"

"You don't want to come?" Steve made himself sound surprised.

"I just thought—"

"No, I didn't call Jason. It's been a while since you and I did anything together, and I thought a long hike on a nice day might give us some time to reconnect."

"Oh. Okay." There was suspicion in his voice.

Steve smiled to himself. Will had no idea how much cause he *had* to be suspicious.

"Isn't the library closed on Sunday?"

"To the public. But the librarians and everyone still have to work. Behind-the-scenes stuff." Another lie.

"Oh."

Steve was using a disposable phone so he could not be traced. He had bought it with cash. Tomorrow, after the deed was done, he would smash the phone and dispose of the various pieces in different trash cans throughout south Orange County. He was taking no chances. "I thought we could meet at the trailhead tomorrow morning around eight or eight thirty. Before it gets too hot. There are some pretty steep paths in those mountains. It's best to get an early start."

"Remind me where it is."

Steve gave him directions from Irvine to Modjeska Canyon. "The trailhead's across the street from the Tucker Wildlife Sanctuary. Next to the parking lot."

"I'll be there."

They said good-bye and hung up. Steve smiled to himself, looking at a ghostly reflection of his face in the window above the kitchen sink. He was dirty and sweaty and looked like he'd just gone three rounds with a pit bull. The truth was that he'd spent the day scouting around, hiking trail after trail, maintaining a detailed map in his mind as he searched for a spot where Will could have an "accident." He knew that the Santa Ana Mountains were home to numerous abandoned mines, many of them uncovered, unmarked shafts that dotted the landscape and lay hidden in the high-growing weeds. He'd read an article about it in the *Register* last year when a girl hiking with her high school class fell down one of the shafts and was killed, cracking her head on a boulder at the bottom.

He'd found what he was looking for shortly before noon. On the flat top of one of the mountains' foothills was a field of dried grass. The unofficial trail he'd taken to get to this point stopped at the edge of the field and appeared to resume at its far end, leaving hikers to navigate the terrain in between on their own.

That terrain was dotted with mine shafts.

Someone had obviously been here recently, and Steve followed the rough path of broken grass as it wound toward the opposite end of the field. Off to the right, he saw what was probably the area's most recent mining excavation: a raised well-like frame surrounding a hole over which a simple structure equipped with cable pulleys had been constructed. To the left were three mines in a considerably worse state of disrepair: one whose aboveground framework had rotted and collapsed into a jumbled heap over the opening, and two whose shafts had been sealed up with boards and posted with warning signs.

It took him a while to find what he was looking for, but finally he spotted a shaft that was just a hole. There were no support beams buttressing the edges, no boards covering the opening, no warning signs nearby, no indication that the mine was even there. It was half-hidden behind some tall dried wheatlike stalks, a black pit around which grew numerous native plants, some of which bent into the cavity. It looked deep. The sun was almost directly overhead, and while the rounded sides of the hole were visible for several yards down, it was impossible to see the bottom. Steve searched the surrounding ground until he found a rock approximately the size of his hand, and, as a test, he threw it in. After several seconds, he heard it hit bottom. The sound was fainter than he would have expected, and though he didn't know how far it was to the floor of the shaft, he knew it was far enough to kill anyone who fell into it.

He looked down into the opening and smiled.

He spent the next few hours covering the hole, gathering light twigs and sticks, using them to gradually form a weak, delicate latticework over which he sprinkled dried weeds, to make the spot blend in with its surroundings. He'd brought no tools and so had to pull the weeds from the ground with his hands. They were tougher than they looked, and by the end, his palms were blistered, cut and chapped.

It was a good job, if he did say so himself, and even he had a tough time pinpointing exactly where the ground left off and the mine shaft began.

Just in case, he placed a series of three rocks at the edge of the hidden opening so he would know where it was and wouldn't fall in himself.

Then he'd hiked back down the trail.

Tomorrow at this time, he told himself, Will would be dead, lying at the bottom of the mine shaft. The thought was exciting. Who knew how long it would take before his body was found? Maybe his body would *never* be found.

No. Will's car would be in the parking lot by the trailhead. After a few days, one of the rangers would call it in. Then there'd probably be a big search-and-rescue effort. They'd bring in dogs, and the dogs would find him.

Steve was about to go take a shower when he stopped.

What if Will told someone tonight where he was going tomorrow morning?

What if he said with *whom* he was going?

Steve kept walking toward the bathroom and the shower. He couldn't think about that now. Everything was already set in motion. Maybe, if it wouldn't arouse too much suspicion and he could find a way to bring it up naturally, he would try to find out whether Will had revealed any of that information to anyone.

But what would he do then? Would he call it off?

Steve thought for a moment.

No. No, he wouldn't.

Come rain or come shine, tomorrow was the day.

The morning dawned clear and warm and beautiful, the type of day on which postcard pictures were taken. What his father used to call a "Rose Parade day." As Steve drove up the Costa Mesa Freeway to Chapman Avenue, he felt happy. He'd wanted to have lunch with Sherry and spend the afternoon together—*not* because he was trying to create an alibi but because he genuinely liked being with her—except that she had a baby shower to attend. So they'd agreed to go out afterward for dinner, and she would spend the night at his place.

Life was good.

He saw Will's Hummer as he pulled into the parking lot. There were two other cars parked nearby, but other than that, the lot was empty.

Good, Steve thought. He didn't want to meet up with anyone who might be able to place the two of them together.

Although he had an alternative plan in case they *did* run into someone else: He would come back down the trail, running for the last quarter mile so he would be all hot and sweaty and could pretend that he'd run all the way, and he'd report Will's fall himself, telling the ranger or whoever he could find that his friend had slipped and fallen down a mine shaft and that he'd left his cell phone at home and so couldn't call.

He didn't like that plan, though. There was a chance that Will could still be alive. Injured but not dead. He would feel much more comfortable if his friend could remain down there for a few days or even a week.

He didn't see Will at first. The Hummer was locked, no one was in it, and there were no people in the parking lot. Through the leaves of bushes and trees that flanked the entrance to the main trail, he caught a flash of blue and red, and when he stepped closer and ducked a little to peer under a branch, he saw Will just past the trailhead doing warm-up exercises.

Perfect.

Now if anyone were around or happened to pull into the parking lot at just that moment, that person would not see the two of them together, would not know that Steve and Will were in any way connected. From all outward appearances, it would seem that they were simply two people independently hiking the canyon.

To further the illusion, he merely nodded at Will as he approached. "Ready?" he asked, not stopping or slowing down, adjusting the canteen strapped over his shoulder as he passed by.

"Let's go," Will replied, breaking into a jog and moving competitively past Steve on the first segment of uphill trail.

Steve couldn't have arranged it better if he tried.

By the time they were over the first hill and above the canyon, the two of them were in sync and walking together—like two men who had met on the trail and become temporary acquaintances. Will, as usual, was bragging about his latest acquisition, some new type of computer phone that he'd gotten access to through his wonderful job but that would not be available to the general public for another six months. Steve smiled, nodded, asked questions that made it appear he was interested, and in general was far less sarcastic and dismissive than he otherwise would have been.

Because he knew what was coming up.

The dynamic was still there, though, and, as always, there was that competitive vibe between them. Even though Steve was not disagreeing with anything Will said, Will acted as though he were and continued a game of belligerent one-upmanship.

They climbed higher and higher, the sun getting progressively hotter.

Soon they could see over the foothills all the way to the ocean. They stopped for a rest and a drink by a tree whose out-of-season fall colors formed the shape of a cross. Steve had no idea whether the tree looked that way naturally or had been trimmed so its branches formed that configuration, but he told Will that if either of them had brought along a camera, they could have sold the photo to a supermarket tabloid for big bucks.

"Get with the times," Will told him. "Tabloids only cover celebrities and weight loss now. Those bigfoot/ alien days are long gone. Although," he mused, "you might be able to pawn off the tree picture on a Christian Web site or something."

"Somehow, I don't think they'd pay as much."

Will gave him a condescending smirk. "That's why you should get a real job. Then you wouldn't have to worry about selling photos of phony miracles."

You'll soon be dead, Steve thought.

It was amazing how that mantra could see him through anything.

They had long since left the main trail, following Steve's secret markers of carefully placed nondescript stones. He'd wondered whether Will would be willing to follow his lead, but each "Hey, let's check out this path" or "Let's go this way" was greeted with an uninterested "Sure" or "Fine."

And then they were at the field.

Steve was sweaty from the climb and the heat of the day, but his palms were sweatier still, and while he was nervous, he was also excited. Casually walking around a spiky plant and quickening his step, he managed to manuever himself into a position on Will's right. He purposely remained half a pace ahead, leading the other man along the makeshift path through the weeds that he had tramped down yesterday. The two of them had stopped talking twenty minutes ago, having run out of things to say, but now Steve reopened the conversation.

"Why are you such an asshole?" he asked.

Will wasn't even fazed. "What's that supposed to mean?"

"You know damn well what it means."

They were approaching the trap. Steve moved a little to the left to make sure Will would hit it head-on.

"You know, I never liked you," Will said. "I was talking to Dennis about that the other day, after you left. Even back in college, I thought you were a weird, squirrelly kind of—"

Steve stopped walking, moved quickly to the left and shoved Will hard in the back. The other man lurched forward, stumbled over the three small rocks marking the edge of the concealed shaft and broke through the thin camouflage cover that hid the hole from view. "Die!" Steve screamed. The scream was loud, and he hadn't known he was going to do it until he did. But it felt good, and he screamed it again: "Die!"

Will couldn't hear it, though. He'd let out a short, sharp cry himself when he'd tumbled into the mine shaft, but that had been cut off almost instantly, and now there was silence. Steve crouched by the edge, peering over, listening, but he could see nothing, hear nothing, and after several moments, he got up, took a drink of water and started back down the trail the way he had come.

He reached the parking lot, got in his car, turned on the air conditioner and drove away.

On the way home, he stopped off at In-N-Out and got himself a burger, fries and a chocolate shake.

That afternoon, he sat down and wrote a new short story.

That night, he had rough sex with Sherry.

And Will lay dead at the bottom of the mine.

Twenty-six

It was weird attending Will's funeral.

He went out of obligation, as did Sherry, but he felt awkward and out of place. Guilty, though he really had no reason to be. Will deserved what had happened to him.

The memorial service was held in a Catholic church. Steve had not even known that Will was Catholic. It was also surprisingly well attended. Will had obviously been a very popular guy, and although Steve should have known that from their college days, he'd sort of let it slip his mind, since, over the past decade, he'd seen the man only once a week at the most, at their happy-hour get-togethers. But there were a ton of people he didn't know at the funeral: men and women their age, older and younger. Most of them seemed to be genuinely upset by Will's passing, and he could only think that they must not have known Will very well.

And people kept asking him questions. Innocuous questions, for the most part, but it was impossible for him to judge their intentions, and he grew so nervous that even though the day was cool, he ended up sweating profusely, so much so that Sherry commented on it, worried that he was getting ill. He lied, telling her he might have a touch of the flu, just to throw her off the track.

They ended up leaving immediately after the grave-side ceremony, and he dropped her off at her apartment before going back to his own place, where he really did end up vomiting in the toilet.

He called in sick the next day in order to keep up the ruse, and allowed Sherry to drop by with a container of chicken soup.

Steve knew now why his father had kept the family moving. It was one of those don't-shit-where-you-eat situations. He understood completely, because he himself had made that mistake and now the stress was becoming almost unbearable. Everywhere he looked were reminders of what he had done: Gina's desk, McColl's office, the streets he had taken while following them, the rental car agency from which he'd gotten his cars, the hardware store where he'd purchased supplies, the bars and restaurants where he'd hung out with Will and his other friends. And his apartment. Always his apartment. Where he had thought up his plans and schemes and decided to carry them out.

How was it possible that he had not gotten caught? Were the police really that incompetent? Or were they working hard behind the scenes to build an airtight case? Was there even now an unseen dragnet closing in around him? He thought not. But while that belief gave him some confidence, it also increased his anxiety. He seemed to be immune from the world of ordinary actions and reactions, from punishment and prosecution. It was as though he had been chosen for this, as though there were some power protecting him from the consequences so that he could go on doing what he was doing.

But he didn't believe in higher powers or unseen forces.

The whole thing made him anxious and distressed, and he understood why his father had wanted to keep moving, to not dwell upon the past but look only toward the future. It was the only way to keep the bad thoughts at bay.

To top it off, he saw his father again. And this time it was not in his bedroom.

He was at Sherry's apartment, spending the night, and he'd gotten out of bed to go to the bathroom. The alarm clock on her dresser said it was five past midnight. Not wanting to wake her, he climbed carefully out of bed and padded across the room. She kept a little night-light on in the bathroom because she did not like to sleep in darkness, a flowery, antiquey thing that plugged into the socket next to the sink counter, and it illuminated the small space, but weakly, faintly, with a soft yellowish glow.

Still, he saw his father instantly.

The old man was standing in the shower stall—
The shower door had not been open earlier
—with his arms hanging limply at his sides and a slack expression on his face. His clothes were different this time—jeans and a T-shirt, the type of clothes his father *never* wore—but they were still soaked with blood, and Steve could see blood on the tile floor of the shower stall, as though it were leaking down from his dad's body. The image was frightening, and indeed he did feel chilled, but his overwhelming response was one of sadness. His father looked so lost, so forlorn, that Steve wished that he could help him. At the same time, he wished the opposite, that his father could help *him*, and he was filled with sorrow that they were now separated by death.

Whether his father's form was a figment of his imagination or not, Steve was unable to urinate in front of him, and he exited the bathroom for a moment, then came back in.

As he'd hoped, as he'd somehow known, his father was gone.

The days passed.

It was the lack of response or reaction, the fact that he was being completely left alone despite the fact that his department secretary, his boss and his friend had all recently died under mysterious circumstances, that made Steve increasingly uneasy. He was nervous at work, though he hid it well, and away from work he was left with far too much time to think. Sherry, the one person who might have been able to understand, was completely in the dark, and so fundamentally trusting that she had no clue what he had done. He wished now that he'd come clean earlier, brought her in at the beginning so they would be in this together, but it was too late now. She might have been okay with what he'd done if she'd learned about each instance individually. The silencing of Lyman Fischer she'd be able to understand, and it was possible that she would have approved of Gina's killing. She may have even countenanced what he'd done to Will—she'd never liked him. But hearing about it all at once, no matter how gently he brought it up, she was bound to think he was out of control. People were not dogs, and, knowing her as he did, he was certain that she would never understand, no matter how many puppies she had strangled.

Did anyone suspect what he had done?

He thought they might. He didn't like the way he was being treated, the friendliness, the niceness, the understanding. It seemed suspicious to him. He went out with Jason and Dennis after work on Friday, and all they did was talk about what a good guy Will had been, how funny he was, and Steve *knew* they didn't really feel that way. He was pretty sure that they were talking up Will for his benefit, but he could not understand what the point of that would be. Were they gauging his reaction? Looking to see if he disagreed or went off on them for their hypocrisy? He didn't know, couldn't tell, so he made sure he had no reaction at all.

His mother, too, might suspect something. Her attitude toward him had not changed—she was still as hostile as ever—but there were subtle differences. He went to her house twice in one week to help her clean out the back room and carry furniture out to the garage for a yard sale she intended to have before she moved, and when they had minor disagreements over where to place a few of the items, she seemed almost afraid of him.

As though she knew what he'd done.

Did she know what her husband had done?

Steve still wasn't sure. It was a question to which his mind kept returning, but it was one that could not be answered unless he talked to his mother about it directly—something he was never going to do.

On the way home from his mother's house, stuck in traffic on the Santa Ana Freeway just past Disneyland, he found himself wondering if his father had had a will.

Will.

His mother had never said anything about it—and even if his father had had one, he'd probably left everything to her—but Steve was still curious. He wouldn't put it past his mother to make a power grab and take everything for herself, whether it was really supposed to be hers or not.

Did his mother have a will?

It didn't really matter. As far as he knew, he was her only living relative. Everything would automatically go to him.

He tried to imagine how she would die. She was

getting on in years, although he was not sure of her exact age. Sixty-five? Sixty-eight? Seventy? Somewhere around there. She was pretty healthy, though. And her own mother had lived to be ninety, although her father had died young. So there was a good chance that she would be around for a while. Probably, he thought, she would die in her sleep at a ripe old age.

But she might have an accident of some kind. She might slip in the bathtub, fall and break her neck. She might trip over a step on the front porch and crack her head open. She might accidentally leave her gas stove on and start a fire. She might die in a car crash. Once she moved to her new place, her apartment or condo or whatever it was, she might choke on a sandwich or experience some type of accident that he could not yet imagine.

Or she could be the victim of a crime. She could be killed in a home-invasion robbery. A gangbanger could shoot her in a drive-by. A lunatic could rape and murder her.

There were a lot of things that could occur.

A lot of ways she could die.

Traffic was finally starting to move. Steve wiped the sweat from his forehead. If his mother *was* killed, murdered in her sleep by some criminal, he would probably be suspect number one. Family members were always under a cloud of suspicion in murder cases. Husbands first, sons next. Even if he didn't do it, the police would probably think he had, and then they would start digging more deeply into his life. Lyman might not turn up, but Gina, McColl and Will certainly would.

That was why it was scary having everyone so close together. Even when his father had killed in the same state, he'd done it in different cities, different regions. The old man hadn't had this geographical proximity to deal with.

Which was why he would probably think Steve was a jack-off and a fuckup once again.

When he got home, he realized that he didn't want to be there. It was a Saturday, and he'd told Sherry he'd be at his mother's until late, so she'd signed up to work at the library in order to build up some comp time. He went over to the library to see her, but she was busy and couldn't talk, so he grabbed a couple of CDs, took them into one of the listening cubicles and sat there with the headphones on until she came and told him the library was closing.

He waited for her outside. They drove both cars back to her place, took a shower together, made love, then took his car to Fashion Island, where they people-watched and window-shopped until the stores were closed. Afterward, in her apartment, Sherry wanted sex again, but he couldn't get hard, and they got in an argument and they both went to sleep angry.

He dreamed about his parents, and they were young and he was a child and it was an entirely different world.

When he awoke, he was crying, and Sherry was holding his head in her lap, wiping the tears from his face. "Shhh," she murmured. "Shhh."

He was embarrassed, but she didn't seem to mind at all. She seemed to enjoy comforting him, and he lay there submitting to it gratefully.

She was a good woman.

Whatever happened in the future, he thought, he could never hurt her.

Never.

Never.

Twenty-seven

Writing Habits

He was what was commonly referred to as a "cult writer," though it was not something to which he had aspired. He wrote of the subjects that concerned him, in the manner in which he felt most comfortable, and unfortunately this appealed not to the general population or to those individuals whose opinions he respected, but to that segment of the reading public that remained perpetually in a state of arrested adolescence. The pseudointellectuals. The phonies. Thin girls who wore white makeup and dressed in black. Boys too cool to comb their hair who bought books not to read but to display in conspicuous locations on their bookshelves. Readers of Kerouac and Ginsberg and Genet, people who continued to think the beats were profound and whose musical taste was always alternative.

It was a depressing situation, but there was little he could do about it. He would be Philip Roth if he could. Hell, he'd be Tom Clancy if he could. But he was who he was, he wrote what he wrote, and he made the rounds of colleges and universities, answering questions on existentialism and deconstruction from intense young men carrying philosophy books under their arms, signing the obligatory copies of his novels with a chic, indecipherable signature.

It would be one thing if he could enjoy his cult status or, better still, use it as a stepping-stone to legitimacy, as so many others had done before him. But he resented his position, and he knew with fatalistic certainty that he was destined to remain forever in this literary ghetto.

Which might have been one reason why the first murder felt so good.

He'd been speaking at UCLA before a fairly large group in a small, crowded theater, and she had come up to him after the lecture, waiting until all of the others had asked their questions and had their books signed before saying what she had come here to say.

"Kill me."

He stared at her. He'd been expecting her to ask about the feminist perspective of his latest work or to inquire about his current reading preferences to see if his tastes were obscure enough to qualify as hip, and this bizarre statement threw him. He didn't know what to say. He clicked his briefcase shut. "Excuse me?"

"Kill me. Take my life."

She was not joking, or, if she was, she was doing an excellent job of hiding it. Both her speech and manner were utterly devoid of levity. He took a closer look at her. She was so completely typical that she was almost stereotypical: black pants, black T-shirt, black plastic-framed glasses, silver earring, short hair. His new book was clutched under her arm. He still was not sure how to respond, so he laughed. "I have to get going," he said. "It's late."

"Kill me," she repeated.

He looked around for help, and one of the professors who had sponsored the lecture walked over. He smiled when he saw the young woman. "Deidre," the man said, nodding to her.

"I was just telling Mr. Childes how much I enjoyed his work," the young woman lied.

"Deidre is one of our brightest students," the professor said.

The young woman beamed.

The professor invited him to the on-campus pub for a drink, and he accepted, grateful that Deidre did not come with them. But she was waiting by his car an hour later, when he returned, slightly drunk, to the visitors' lot in which he had parked.

"Kill me," she said again.

He shook his head and tried to push her aside so he could open his car door.

"Kill me. Take my life."

And he killed her. It required no more provocation than that. It was as if all of the rage that had been building within him for years came rushing through his hands in a surge of power as he grabbed her willing neck and squeezed. His fingers sank deeply into her soft, warm flesh, and beneath the skin he felt tubes and veins, ridges of cartilage. He could not explain why, but at that moment he felt exhilarated, as though he were striking back against fate itself, against all of those intransigent forces and immovable barriers that had been impeding his progress for so long.

The life ebbed and died within her, and Deidre's body suddenly became much heavier. He let it fall to the ground and heard a thump as her head hit the asphalt. There was a smile frozen on her lips.

He left her body there, in the parking lot. There was no worry that he would get caught, and indeed he received no calls from the police or anyone else the next day. Or the day after. Or the day after that. A profound lethargy seemed to have settled over him after the cathartic release of the murder, and he found himself staying inside the house for the rest of the week, wandering listlessly from room to room.

It was after a signing in Brentwood the next Monday that a trendily androgynous young man, carrying a copy of his new book, accosted him on his way to the car. "Kill me," the young man said.

He looked at the youth's carefully plucked eyebrows, at his stylishly cut hair, at the hip clothes hanging from his almost anorexic frame. "You want me to kill you?"

"Yes. Please. Take my life."

He thought for a moment. "Get in the car," he said.

They drove to the mountains, to a deserted area not frequented by either campers or picnickers. Neither of them spoke on the drive up, but when he glanced at the young man out of the corner of his eye, he saw no fear there, no doubt, only an expression of cultivated cool on the feminine face, as though the youth were playing to a nonexistent audience, posing for an unseen camera.

He killed him with a tire iron.

The young man stood on the flat rock, unmoving, as he swung the metal tool like a baseball bat and smashed his head. The impact felt good, and once more he felt a rush of exhilaration as metal crunched against bone, as blood and brains went flying. He could have stopped there—the youth was dead after the first swing—but he continued to beat the body as it lay on the ground, not letting up until what had once been the head was nothing more than a bloody red pulp.

The lethargy that hit him afterward lasted only until a signing at a literary bookstore the next day. This time, he invited the young woman home before killing her with a knife in the kitchen.

She had been holding a copy of his new book.

He made himself a drink and stood there, sipping it. His new book. It was obvious that all of this was connected somehow to his latest work. His other novels had also produced a variety of strange responses in his readers, but he'd always ascribed them to the personalities of those people attracted to his work and not to something within the writing itself. Now, however, he thought back and tried to recall whether there were any patterns to the peculiar requests he'd received, any similarities in the reactions of his readers. Try as he might, though, he could find no common threads in the responses to his previous work.

What was different about this one? Was it possible that his writing had somehow tapped into the collective unconscious of these readers, that the particular sequence of words he had chosen to use in the novel pushed some button within them and caused this reaction?

It sounded like the plot of one of his books.

He stared at the body of the young woman. Even more disturbing was why he went along with their requests, why he felt this compulsion to kill his readers. And why he felt no remorse about it afterward. He had committed murder three times now. But the memory of all three events felt flat, false, like something he had written about rather than done. Even now, looking at the coagulating blood on the body in front of him, he felt no grief, no sadness, no anger, no remorse, no disgust, nothing but a dispassionate intellectual curiosity. Perhaps, he thought, having written words that compelled readers to offer themselves as sacrifices, he had instilled within himself a complementary need to take life.

He finished the drink. Who the hell knew?

Loading the body into the car, he cleaned up the kitchen and drove to a park, burying the dead woman under a pile of leaves and branches before returning home to bed.

He awoke feeling refreshed, and for the first time in over a year, for the first time since he had completed the novel that had just been published, he sat down to write. It was eight o'clock in the morning when he plopped himself down in front of the PC, and it was nine o'clock at night when he finally stood up, his back sore, his eyes tired, his leg muscles cramped. In the output tray of the printer were thirty double-spaced pages. And they were good. He would not cringe in embarrassment tomorrow when he read what he had written. He would not tear up the pages and consign them to the trash, as he so often did. He had written the beginning of what he knew was going to be a great mainstream novel. His familiar themes and writing style were intact, but something had jelled, and he had found a way to express himself in a more universal way.

He hoped.

No. He knew.

He was writing a crossover book.

He felt like celebrating, and he placed the pages in a manila envelope, slipping the envelope in a desk drawer before walking outside. The night was warm. The sky, encased in smog and cloud cover, was an orangish purple, illuminated from underneath by the lights of Los Angeles. He didn't want to get drunk, but he wanted to celebrate somehow, to let off steam and have some fun.

An idea came to him, and he got into his car and drove down the freeway to Westwood, where he walked into the trendiest bookstore he could find. The woman behind the counter was older and fairly average-looking—normal—but there was a young man in a black T-shirt and tight intentionally faded jeans perusing the classics section at the rear of the store. He had a shiny shaved head and was wearing small wire-framed Lennon glasses. Childes smiled to himself as he walked down the narrow aisle and approached the young man. "Excuse me," he said. "My name is Harold Childes, and I'm doing research for a book I'm writing. I wonder if you could help me."

"*The* Harold Childes?"

He smiled. "You've heard of me?"

"I just finished your new book. It was great."

"Thank you."

"Kill me," the young man said.

"Are you sure?"

"Kill me. Take my life."

"I was hoping you'd say that." He smiled. "Let's go out to my car."

*   *   *

He continued killing throughout the year, and the writing went well. Several of his murders made the papers, but none of them were ever linked together, and none of them were ever traced to him. That was odd, given the similarity of the victims' backgrounds and lifestyles, but he supposed part of the cops' confusion had to do with the fact that he never killed the same way twice. He had always been inept at household chores, a failure at cooking, at gardening, at handicrafts, at sports, but in murder he'd finally found a way to express himself with his hands, a relaxing counterpart to the purely mental exercise of writing. In killing he found freedom, and he let his instincts run wild, finding myriad new ways to extinguish human life.

The new book, when it was published, became both a critical and a popular success.

In the months between acceptance and publication, he wrote nothing and killed not at all. In fact, he did not venture outside of the house except to buy groceries and other necessities. His conscience, which had been dormant throughout the past year, suddenly kicked into overdrive, and it was as though all of the guilt, all of the remorse over the murders he had committed descended upon him like a flood. There were days when he did not get out of bed, weeks where he existed only in a drunkenly numbed netherworld. The pain was almost unbearable. At least once a day he started to dial the police and turn himself in, but some kernel of self-preservation always kept him from completing the call. It was as if on some deep, subconscious level, he understood that this torment he was going through, this conscience-inflicted hell, was merely a transitional phase, and that when it finally ended, all of it would remain behind. Emotionally, he did not feel as though he would ever get over the guilt, and intellectually he did not think he should, but some rational writer's core of his being told him that it would be so.

And the guilt did go away, the memory of what he had done fading into flatness, receding in his mind like the plot of a not-very-well-loved novel. And after his book hit number five on the *New York Times* bestseller list, he finally agreed to do some signings.

He let his publisher work out the arrangements.

The signing this time was at neither a college nor a small esoteric bookstore. It was at a Borders in a large shopping center in Orange County. Seated at a table next to a display of his books, he saw a few young hipsters waiting in the long line that wound through the store's aisles—vampiric girls and poseur boys—but for the most part the crowd seemed mainstream and surprisingly, gratifyingly heterogeneous.

The first person in line was a middle-aged man of his own generation, a bearded, bespectacled gentleman wearing a tweed jacket. "I've always been an admirer of yours, Mr. Childes," he said. "But I must tell you, this novel took me completely by surprise. It's absolutely brilliant."

Childes smiled as he signed the copy of the book placed before him. "And what do you do?"

"I teach English at UC Irvine. In fact, I'm thinking of adding your novel to the reading list of my Contemporary Literature course this semester. I was wondering if you would be willing to speak to my class."

He nodded, feeling a familiar rush of exhilaration. "I'd love to," he admitted. He took out a piece of scratch paper and wrote down his cell phone number. "Give me a call."

"I'll do that," the professor said.

He spent the rest of the afternoon autographing books and talking with his fans. His new readers, overall, seemed remarkably intelligent and well-balanced, nowhere near as tunnel-visioned as his cult audience.

After the signing, he wandered through the open-air mall, looking into the small shops between the big anchor stores, before finally heading out to his car.

The young woman stopped him when he was halfway across the parking lot.

"Mr. Childes!" she called. "Mr. Childes!"

He waited as she ran up to him. She was Asian, with long black hair and finely sculpted cheeks, and was wearing a conservative yet classy skirt and blouse. She smiled when she reached him, holding a hand to her chest as she caught her breath. She handed him a copy of the new book, lowering her eyes shyly. "Would you sign this for me?" she asked.

He had a momentary flash of déjà vu, remembrance of another parking lot, nagging persistence and sacrificial blood, but he found himself nodding. "Sure." He took out his pen and opened the book.

Between the cover and the flyleaf were a pair of white silk panties.

"I took them off in the bathroom," the young woman said, looking up at him demurely.

He stared at her, not saying anything.

"Rape me," she said.

"What?"

"Rape me. Use my body."

He thought for a moment.

Then smiled.

"Get in the car," he said.

Twenty-eight

Steve and Sherry both went with his mother to look for a new place to live, spending a Saturday touring senior communities throughout suburban Orange County. The surprising thing was that it had actually been his mother's idea. She had invited them along, and the three of them submitted to well-rehearsed presentations, took golf-cart rides through quiet, kidless streets and asked questions of the low-pressure sales reps. They even had an enjoyable lunch at a Souplantation in Brea, where his mother was uncharacteristically pleasant and actually offered to pay for the meal.

The gated developments they visited were all nice and, despite wide fluctuations in price, appeared to be fairly uniform. Steve honestly couldn't see much difference among them. But his mother seemed to have her heart set on Leisure World, and while she was always polite to the agents, she would get into the car after each visit and declare, "That's not for me."

He'd been right. The Leisure World in south Orange County had incorporated and become a differently named city, but there was still a Leisure World in Seal Beach, and that was their last destination of the day. They encountered no traffic and the trip was quick, but Steve didn't like the drive. It followed the same series of freeways they had used to get to the VA hospital, and all he could think about as they headed west were the many times he had driven this route to see his father. In his mind, he saw his dad doped up and restrained in that psych-ward room. It had been a horrible way to go out, and it made him wonder how he would die. He hoped it would be fast, in his sleep.

Aside from the giant model of the world outside the theme park–like entrance, Leisure World didn't strike Steve as a whole lot different from the other communities they'd visited. But his mother was sold even before they'd made it through the gate, and she grew increasingly enthusiastic as she looked through the brochures in the office, talked to an agent and toured four of the currently available units. There was no pressure, no hard sell, but by the end of the visit his mother was eager to lock up a long-term lease on one of the apartments they'd seen. Steve noticed nothing special about the apartment, and he tried to talk her out of it while they waited at a desk and the agent went in back to get the paperwork. She shouldn't make this decision hastily, he tried to tell her. Her house wasn't sold yet, wasn't even on the market, in fact. There was no hurry.

His mother ignored him, however, and despite his pleas to wait, to take her time and have a lawyer look over the paperwork, she signed every agreement and consent form put in front of her.

He didn't press further. To do so would make her even more stubborn and determined. She'd probably end up *buying* a place rather than leasing. Instead, he waited until they were outside, in the car, before letting her know how he felt. "There was no reason for you to 'lock in' anything back there. Places are always opening up as people die. You should have at least taken the time to make sure this was a good deal and have someone look carefully at the contract to make sure you're not getting cheated. My God, Mom—"

"Do not take the Lord's name in vain!" she ordered him. "How many times do I have to tell you that before it sinks into your thick skull?"

"I was talking about—"

"Do not take the Lord's name in vain!"

"Jesus Christ," Sherry muttered.

He wanted to laugh at that, was glad that she'd taken his side against his mother, but her comment didn't make things any easier, and while his mother did not lecture or yell at Sherry, she remained silent for the rest of the trip home, her mouth pursed disapprovingly, her eyes filled with anger.

The second he pulled into his mother's driveway, the passenger door was open and she was out. She slammed the car door behind her and stalked up the front porch steps.

"Should we get out?" Sherry asked. "Should we apologize?"

"No." He put the car in reverse and backed out of the driveway.

Let the old bitch stew.

At the intersection of Euclid and Crescent streets, just before the entrance to the freeway, they got stuck behind a young woman in a Volkswagen who remained unmoving, talking on her cell phone, as the traffic light turned from red to green. Steve honked at her, and she stuck a hand out of her window to flip him off as she sped forward, changing lanes without signaling and almost getting rear-ended by another driver, who also honked at her.

"Asshole," Steve said.

"I thought it was illegal now to talk on a phone while you're driving," Sherry said.

"It is unless you're using one of those hands-free things."

"She wasn't," Sherry pointed out. She glanced to the left, to the right, then behind them. "Where are the cops when you need them? Someone should give her a ticket."

Steve would have liked to do a lot more than just give her a ticket. He imagined ramming his car into that Volkswagen so hard that it crumpled under the impact, the steering column shoving straight through the woman's chest, killing her in as painful a way as possible. The thought calmed him down, although he got worked up again moments later when he tried to get on the freeway and a jackass in a blue pickup truck sped up to block him as he signaled and tried to pull into the right lane.

"What's the matter with everyone today?" Sherry wondered. "Is there a full moon tonight?"

But the problem went much deeper than that, Steve knew.

Some people needed killing.

That was it exactly. More and more each day, it appeared. He tried to remember when he had not felt this way, for this attitude of his seemed fairly recent. Had he been this annoyed with people in high school? In college? Last year, even? He couldn't remember, but he didn't think so. It was possible that he'd had these feelings and just hadn't been able to express them or had tamped them down, but he was pretty sure that this had all started when he'd learned that his father had killed his first wife—

was a serial killer

—and was not really the ordinary middle-class guy he pretended to be. The knowledge had awakened within him not only an understanding of his father's motives but sympathetic desires of his own, and whether it was nature or nurture, he had quickly come to realize that he was his father's son.

"I'm sorry I antagonized your mom," Sherry said.

"Don't worry," Steve told her. "She deserved it."

"I know, but she's old and she invited us and—"

"It's good for her. She lives in her own little bubble, treating people like dirt, and she needs a dose of reality sometimes."

That was true of most people, he thought. They all lived in their own little bubbles.

Until those bubbles were slashed open.

Traffic was light, and they reached Irvine about fifteen minutes later. It was only five o'clock, but they were both tired. They'd planned on going to a movie tonight but decided instead to just go to Sherry's, stay in and watch one of the many DVDs that she'd bought but had never gotten around to viewing.

There was a Xeroxed sign nailed to a telephone pole in front of Sherry's apartment complex. LOST LABRADOR, it read. Beneath that was a smudged photo of a black dog wearing a Santa hat standing in front of a Christmas tree. ANSWERS TO "SAMANTHA" OR "SAM," the message on the sign continued. MISSING SINCE MONDAY. REWARD OFFERED. CALL JIM AT 555-6543.

Steve smiled. He turned to Sherry. "Did you see that? Someone lost their dog."

"So?" she said.

"Do you know where the dog is? There's a reward if you do."

She took her keys out of her purse. "Come on," she said, annoyed.

He dropped the subject. He wanted to ask her what she'd done with the dog's body, but it was enough just to know that she'd killed the animal. The thought cheered him up for some reason, and as soon as they got into her apartment, he kissed her. She laughed, pulling away. "What are you doing?"

But he grabbed her, kissed her again, kneaded her buttocks. Stepping back, he met her eyes and began unbuckling his belt.

She looked at him, then started unfastening her pants.

They did it on the couch.

In the morning, Sherry went out to breakfast with her sister. She invited Steve to come along, but he bowed out, saying he wanted to sleep in. The truth was, he didn't really like Sherry's sister. Besides, they'd have more fun without him.

He checked through her kitchen after she'd left, found some bread and made toast, poured himself some orange juice. She told him she probably wouldn't be back until after eleven, so he did his usual search of her apartment, then settled down to watch *Meet the Press*. But he soon grew bored. He thought about heading home, leaving Sherry a note or calling her on her cell, but he knew she would take that as an insult. He was also hoping for some sex when she came back.

So he decided to go for a walk. Making sure he had his key so he wouldn't lock himself out, he went out to the sidewalk and, on a whim, turned right.

The streets were completely devoid of pedestrians. There were plenty of cars, and quite a few cyclists speeding down the bike lane, but no one was walking. He was seldom on foot himself, and he hadn't noticed until now how few people walked in Irvine. He felt as though he were in a Ray Bradbury story or a Missing Persons song.

Ahead, in the front yard of a house, two boys were playing on the grass. That at least seemed normal. But as soon as they caught sight of him, they stopped playing and hurried inside. Apparently, it was so unusual to see a man walking down the sidewalk that the children thought anyone who did so was dangerous. Steve felt like the Frankenstein monster as he passed by the suddenly empty yard, and it was all he could do not to lurch about and groan horrifically as he saw the two boys watching him through the front window of the house.

He finally reached a major street that led to a gas station and a shopping center. The morning was not particularly warm but it was humid, and he decided to get something to drink before heading back. Gatorade sounded good, and he walked down the block to the gas station and its minimart. The refrigerator was broken, however, and the only fountain drinks available were various types of soda.

Steve walked over to the shopping center behind the gas station. The smaller stores were all closed, but the anchor supermarket was open, and he strode across the nearly empty parking lot to the entrance. There was a skinny teenage boy with stringy hair and a perpetual smirk on his face standing to the right of the automatic doors, and he fanned out a series of booklets in his hand as Steve approached. "Would you like to support a drug-free nation?" the boy asked.

Steve shook his head and went inside.

The air-conditioning felt good, and he wandered the aisles for several moments until the sweat on his face had dried. Finally, he walked back to the refrigerated beverage case at the rear of the store and grabbed a sixteen-ounce bottle of Gatorade. After paying for it at the checkout stand, he walked back out the front entrance.

The smirking teenager was waiting to pounce. "Would you like to buy a coupon book to keep kids drug free?"

"I already bought one," Steve lied.

"How much did it cost?" the kid asked.

Steve stopped, turned. Was this little punk questioning his truthfulness? Was this smart-ass calling him a liar?

"How much did you pay for it?" the boy wanted to know.

Smiling, Steve hefted the plastic Gatorade bottle in his hand and swung it at the kid's face. The container slammed into the boy's cheek, nearly knocking the bottle from Steve's hand and sending the teenager reeling. The skin on the cheek had been broken, and blood was dripping from the kid's mouth as well.

Steve advanced on him. "You want to know how much I paid for my coupons, huh? You want to know how much I paid?"

The boy's coupon books were scattered on the ground. "Leave me alone!" the kid cried, and ran into the store.

Still smiling, though the smile was starting to feel tight at the edges, Steve turned and walked back across the parking lot toward the sidewalk. He was sure the grocery store had security cameras. And both the teenager and the older woman at the checkout stand could probably identify him. But he wasn't worried. He hadn't been caught yet, and he wouldn't be caught this time. He *couldn't* be caught. He didn't know how or why, but he knew it was true.

Finishing off the Gatorade in several quick chugs, careful not to let any of the blood touch his skin or clothing, he tossed the plastic bottle into a metal trash can located between two of the pumps at the gas station.

He walked easily back to Sherry's apartment, arriving just as she did. He nodded politely to her sister, Denise, still sitting in her car, and gave Sherry a big hug as soon as she stepped onto the sidewalk. Denise said good-bye to her sister, pointedly ignoring Steve, and drove off.

"What did you do while I was gone?" Sherry asked.

"Went out for a walk."

"Was it fun?"

Steve thought for a moment. "Yeah," he said. "It was."

Twenty-nine

At work, one day flowed into the next. As much as he'd disliked Gina and McColl, he missed them. His job had been more interesting when he'd had adversaries to plot against, and without the secretary and the department head around, he realized how boring and useless his job really was.

As much as he hated to admit it, maybe Will had been right.

He started paying more attention to the alumni he was writing about, getting to know them through their backstories and the remembrances of those who had known them when they were young. He tried to guess which ones he would like and which ones he wouldn't, began wondering which ones did not deserve to live.

In one bio Steve transcribed, a graduate of the class of 1999 had been convicted of murdering his wife and was serving a life sentence in a federal penitentiary in Kansas. The man urged his old classmates to write to him in prison.

Steve read that one over several times, even ended up keeping a copy for himself. He thought it very brave of the man to confess what he had done and where he was located, especially when most of his fellow alumni were busy tweaking their bios to make themselves sound as successful and accomplished as possible. On the other hand, what did the man have to lose? He was going to spend the rest of his life in jail, cut off from society. He probably craved contact.

Out of all the people he read about, Steve felt sorriest for the man in prison.

Steve's own ten-year high school reunion was coming up next year, and though he had no plans to go, he did intend to submit a bio to the booklet, if they had one, and he'd been toying with the idea of what to write. He'd been going over his life since high school, remembering his college days, thinking of ways to describe his job. But whenever he thought about listing his accomplishments, his mind kept coming back to his kills. Obviously, that was not something he would ever bring up, but it was interesting that out of everything he had done, he was proudest of the murders he had committed.

Proudest?

Yes. It was wrong, he knew, and not something he would ever admit to another soul. But there it was.

How many kills had he racked up? Four. And over the past few months! It had taken his father years to reach that number. Of course, the old man had been tied down to a family, and society itself had been a lot less violent back then, so his deeds would have been more conspicuous. Still, Steve had accumulated an impressive tally in such a short time, and he had no doubt that his father would be proud of him. Envious, even.

Unless . . .

Unless he would have thought Steve was being foolish and unnecessarily reckless.

That seemed the more likely reaction, and it depressed him to realize that he was a disappointment even to the idealized version of his father that he fantasized about.

They were two of a kind, though. No way to get around that.

The difference between his father and himself was that, aside from Ruth, his first wife, his father had killed people to whom he had no apparent connection, whereas Steve had killed *only* people with whom he had a personal connection. From where he stood now, it seemed that his father had discovered his purpose earlier, had looked beyond the narrow confines of his own life to see what good he could do for the world at large. Yes, the world was better off without Gina, without McColl, without Will. And his killing of Lyman Fischer had been a matter of necessity, required to maintain his father's good name.

But he should be putting his talents to better use, getting rid of those people who really did not deserve to live. Bad drivers. Bullies. Obnoxious teenagers. Ostentatious cell phone users. Women who beat their kids. Men who beat their wives. Thieves. Liars. Religious fanatics.

Of course, he couldn't just go around murdering people right and left, killing everyone who annoyed him. But he could make surgical strikes, taking out those whose existence was a blight upon humanity, removing from society men and women who contributed nothing but problems to the world. He had proved already that he could kill and not get caught, and it was his duty, his purpose, to utilize his talents.

He was special, as his father had been special.

Did it go back farther than that? If he researched his grandfather, would he find that his father's father had had a higher calling as well?

He wouldn't doubt it.

It was in their blood.

But was he always right in his decision on whom to

kill? He was definitely good at killing people, but were his choices correct? Each time he looked back on what he had done—

accomplished

—he could see no other course of action than the one he had taken. He'd needed to get rid of each and every one of the individuals he had dispatched. And yet . . .

And yet his job was not as interesting as it had been. Just as hanging out with Jason and Dennis wasn't as enjoyable as it used to be. Yes, Gina, McColl and Will had been horrible people. But, even though it was negative, they'd brought something to his life, something he now missed.

Maybe he wasn't the one who should be deciding who deserved to live and who did not.

Steve reached for his coffee. He'd bought it at the Starbucks downstairs but had done so purely out of habit. He didn't really need it; in fact, he didn't even want it. The paper cup was still warm to the touch, which meant that the coffee inside was hot, and, on a whim, he tightened the lid of the cup, leaned back in his chair to make sure there was no one walking around who could see him, and threw the cup as hard as he could across the room. It sailed over the nearby cubicles and landed on a workstation somewhere in the middle of the floor. He heard a loud scream as the hot coffee spilled on a woman back there, and he ducked down, closing his eyes tightly and clasping a hand over his mouth, trying his damnedest not to laugh.

"Dennis and I are here, dude. Where are you? I thought you were going to meet us. Give me a call when you get this."

Steve deleted Jason's message.

He called Sherry, grateful when he got her voice

mail. "I'm sick," he lied. "Stomach flu, I think. I'm going to go home and go to bed. I'll call you in the morning."

He was already home, sitting on the floor, his back against the couch, cell phone in his hand. And he sat there until it grew dark, not turning on any lights as the sun went down but remaining in place until his furniture turned into black outlines against the surrounding gloom, and then the gloom turned as black as the furniture, and finally he could see no shapes at all, nothing but blank, endless darkness.

Thirty

Saturday Sherry had to work, and Steve drove to Anaheim to see his mother. She was getting ready for her big move, and the only things in the house that had remained unchanged were her bed and the kitchen table. Elsewhere, there were boxes of dishes on countertops, piles of clothes on the living room couch, sewing materials in bags atop the old console TV set. She'd originally intended to hire a mover instead of allowing him to help—out of spite, he figured, more than anything else—but when Steve had told her that he, Jason and Dennis could do it all for free, her miserly nature had won out and she'd agreed to let them move her.

That date was still a week or two away, but Steve thought it would be a good idea to get a head start and, whenever possible, start taking some of the small stuff over a trip at a time.

He'd been helping his mother pack, hoping to come across forgotten belongings of his father's that might shed some light on the old man's secret life, but so far nothing had turned up. The house was now pretty well cleaned out, but there were still a few loose ends in the garage that needed to be organized, and it was here that he'd been spending most of his time. The frayed piece of rope hanging from the beam still haunted him, and each time he returned, he couldn't help looking up at it and wondering. Today, he found his mother in the garage, sorting through an oil-stained cardboard box he had not seen before.

She looked up as he entered, an accusatory expression on her face. "Did you know about this?"

"About what?" he asked, crouching down next to her.

"This!"

He had to smile as he looked at the skin magazine she held in her hand. It was old and very tame by today's standards, a sub-*Playboy* publication forthrightly called *Naked Ladies*. He took it from her, but the pages were stuck together by the same black oil that had leaked out from somewhere else and soiled the box. Digging through the pile of magazines, he saw that they were all *Naked Ladies* except for one titled *Busty Ladies*.

"It's no big deal, Mom," he said.

"Did you know about this?"

"No," he told her. "Of course I didn't. Do you honestly think Dad would share that with me?"

"I have no idea what that man would do," she said.

Steve reached the bottom of the box, and beneath the magazines, stuck to the cardboard and stained with oil, was a flat cardboard dress-up doll that looked uncomfortably like Shirley Temple. The doll was naked, although the skin was smooth, with neither breasts nor pubic area delineated. Surrounding it and also stuck to the box were colored cardboard pieces in the shapes of girls' underwear, each with folding side tabs that would allow them to be affixed to the doll.

That was a little more disturbing.

He stood up, embarrassed. This was definitely not something he wanted to think about, and not something he wanted to discuss with his mother. "I'm going to get a drink of water," he told her. "I'm thirsty."

He'd passed through the house on his way to the garage, but he'd been looking for his mother and had noticed only the generalities of her packing and cleaning. He saw now, though, that there were items laid out on the floor of the living room, between the couches, that he hadn't seen before.

A sword, a machete, knives.

Steve paused. Instead of continuing on to the kitchen, he walked over and stood looking down at the array of weapons. Had his father gotten these in Vietnam? It seemed the most likely explanation. Steve had seen none of them before, but that was not a surprise. His father had always kept his war years secret, and Steve knew next to nothing about that time in his dad's life.

He reached down and picked up the machete, hefting it in his hands. It was heavier than it looked, and he tried to imagine himself hacking through a jungle, the way he'd seen men do in movies. Unless he did a hell of a lot of exercise to build up his muscles, he'd have to use two hands just to cut through a single vine.

The blade was shiny, and the edge looked sharp. All of the blades looked shiny, and Steve wondered if they had ever been used.

"Those were your *father's*," his mother said behind him.

Startled, he nearly dropped the machete. He hadn't even heard her approach.

"I found them when I was packing. He kept them in our *closet*. In our *bedroom*." Disgust and disapproval dripped from every word, and it was hard to believe now that before his father's stroke, he had never heard his parents argue. They had often been mad at him but never at each other, and he could not have guessed that this sort of resentment had been building beneath the surface.

He could not have guessed a lot of things that had been going on beneath the surface.

Steve put the machete down carefully. "I guess he got these in Vietnam."

"I don't know where he got them. I don't know where he got anything. And I don't care."

"He's dead now, Mom," Steve said gently.

"So? That doesn't excuse who he was. Or what he did."

What he did?

Steve's heart was pounding. He licked his suddenly dry lips. "Mom . . ."

"Don't 'Mom' me."

"But—"

"Why do you keep defending him? Your father was a monster!"

A monster?

She knew.

Steve froze. Slowly, he turned to stare at his mother. She was looking not at him but at the display of weaponry on the floor, and the expression on her face was one of hatred and disdain. It was the expression of a victim viewing the corpse of her tormentor, a look at once deeply wounded and completely pitiless.

This changed everything. He didn't know what his mother had experienced or what she had seen, but she knew what his father had done, and he couldn't trust her to keep quiet. Her anger led her to blurt out accusations without thinking, and she had a temper that, aside from her interactions with his father, she'd never been able to control, along with a religious fanatic's certitude that whatever she did or said was part of God's plan—otherwise why would He allow it?

She had to go.

But he'd known that already, hadn't he? Even if he hadn't been spending his time thinking of specific ways in which to kill his mother, he had been aware of the fact that she would die soon, that she *needed* to die soon, and that he would have to be the facilitator. He didn't want to do this, but as with the people he had dispatched before, this was a necessity. It was not merely his father's good name he was protecting now; it was his own life. If the authorities found out what his dad had done, it was only a short leap to learning about the murders that he himself had committed.

"You don't know what your father was really like," his mother said. "No one does."

Steve nodded in vague agreement, thinking fast. She was old. And she'd had a lot of trauma in her life lately, what with her husband's stroke and his attack upon her, then his death. It would be understandable if the pressure became too much to bear, if she decided that it would be easier to just end it all.

But how?

There were a lot of prescription pills in the house, both his mother's and his father's. There were the ones they'd had already for their various ills and ailments, plus the painkillers and antidepressants his mom had been given after the attack. That was the way most people committed suicide, wasn't it? An overdose of pills? It was clean and relatively painless, and it was much easier to pull off than a hanging or wrist slitting.

Steve took his mother's hand, intending to lead her into the kitchen, where most of the medicines were kept. She yanked her hand away, frowning. "What are you doing?"

"I want to show you something."

"Well, show me, then." She kept her hands to herself but followed him through the dining room and into the kitchen.

As a precaution, he pulled down the shades.

"What is this?" she demanded.

He didn't answer, but opened the far right cupboard above the sink counter. Row after row of white-capped pill bottles filled the bottom shelf.

He was home free.

He started opening pill bottles, using the flat of his palm to turn those annoying childproof caps. He dumped the pills into his hand: small, medium and large; round and oval; white, blue, red and yellow.

"Steven!"

He turned. His right hand was full of pills, and he used his left hand to push down on her shoulder, forcing her to the ground.

"Steven!"

She was flat on her ass now, and in a matter of seconds he'd pushed her onto her back, pinning down her arms with his knees. This was the single worst thing he had ever done. Assaulting his mother like this went against everything he had been taught, everything he was. It was all he could do to soldier on and not run away in shame and humiliation.

But this had to be done.

He held his mother down and pried open her mouth. She tried to scream, and he punched her in the gut. That would leave a bruise, he knew, but old people bruised easily, and for all anyone knew she could have tripped and fell, or bumped into a chair. It would be a stretch to think her son had punched her in the stomach to shut her up so he could shove pills down her throat.

His mother lay gasping beneath him, and he started dropping pills into her mouth. She spit out the first few, but he dropped in some more and then held her mouth closed. She fought against him, still trying to catch her breath, but holding her mouth shut made her swallow, and then he let her open up again and dropped in some more. He didn't know what kind of pills they were or what they were supposed to do, but suddenly, after swallowing the third batch, she began thrashing around beneath him. He wasn't sure whether it was a reaction to the medication or some sort of self-preservation instinct kicking in, but she started bucking like a horse, as though trying to throw him off, and the whites of her eyes grew wide.

He was no longer dropping in pills; he was shoving them in, forcing them past her lips.

"It's your fault!" he started screaming at her, pushing the pills in one after another after another. "It's your fault!" He kept repeating the accusation over and over, but he didn't know why, didn't even know *what* was her fault. For some reason, however, he couldn't stop, and beneath him her body went into convulsions. Spittle flew from her mouth as her head whipped from side to side.

And then it was over.

She stopped thrashing, stopped bucking; her head lolled to the left and thick vomit leaked over her lips, down her cheek and onto the floor. He stood. Her eyes were still open far too wide, and there was a trickle of blood oozing out one of her nostrils. He should have felt something—sadness, guilt, horror—but his mother was nothing to him at that moment, was just an obstacle he had overcome, a problem he had solved. The anger he had felt toward her only moments before, the furious animosity that had come over him and that he still didn't understand, had fled, leaving behind a weary numbness.

He looked around, thinking. His fingerprints were all over the house, but that was okay, because it was his mother's place. It made sense that he'd been here. He needed to take them off the pill bottles, though, and he grabbed a paper towel from the rack, wet it in the sink and used it to wipe off each of the bottles before placing them on the kitchen table to make it look as though his mother had emptied them and left them there.

The room was beginning to smell of the vomit that had continued to leak out of his mother's mouth and was now forming a puddle on the floor. Holding his breath, Steve left the kitchen and made his way toward the back of the house, wondering what was the best way to leave without attracting undue attention. His plan was to come back tomorrow and "discover" her body. He didn't know how accurately science could pinpoint a time of death, but he would swear that she had been fine on Saturday afternoon when he left and that she must have killed herself Saturday night. Science wasn't infallible and wouldn't trump an eyewitness, so they'd probably split the difference and assume she had swallowed the pills immediately after he'd left. Just to be on the safe side, though, he wouldn't "find" her until late tomorrow afternoon.

But right now he had to get out of here. He passed through the dining room, stopped for a moment in the living room, wondering briefly if he should take his father's weapons before deciding it would be safer to leave them as they were, then hurried on.

He stopped almost immediately.

His father was standing in the center of the hall.

Startled, Steve sucked in his breath. He had not expected this. He *never* expected to see his father, but somehow at night, in bed, awakening from a dream state, it seemed more plausible, more understandable. Seeing him in the daytime like this was . . . wrong.

It was midafternoon, but the shades in the rooms were drawn to keep out the sun, and the hallway was dim. His dad was not bloody this time, and he looked much the way he had the last time Steve had seen him before the stroke: casual slacks, short-sleeved shirt, loafers.

There was an expression of sadness on the old man's face, and suddenly Steve felt ashamed. *You tried to kill her, too!* he wanted to shout, but he was too embarrassed and, besides, he was not even sure if his father's ghost was really there.

The figure turned and walked down the hall to the far end. Steve knew he was supposed to follow, but he couldn't. Although this house had been his home, its rooms were alien to him now, and he was afraid of what might be in them. He watched the figure of his father stride through the open doorway of the guest room and disappear into the gloom. Steve turned to go in the opposite direction.

And the doorbell rang.

He nearly panicked and ran through the television room and out the back door, but that would be a suspicious move and a sure indication of guilt.

The doorbell rang again.

Followed by a knock.

What to do? His second impulse, after fleeing, was to lie low, pretend no one was home. That would screw up his story, though. And, besides, his car was in the driveway. Whoever was out there knew that someone was here, especially if the person stopping by was a neighbor.

He had to answer the door.

Steve hurried quickly to the front room, stood there for a moment gathering his wits, then took a deep breath and opened the door. An older woman stood there, a woman he didn't know but who was approximately his mother's age. She smiled. "You must be Steven. I'm June. I'm here to see your mother."

June . . . June . . . He racked his brain trying to remember whether either of his parents had ever mentioned a woman named June, but he and his parents had so seldom spoken that when they did it was always in broad generalities about subjects all three of them had in common. He knew next to nothing about their lives, just as they knew next to nothing about his.

Had known.

They were dead now.

They were both dead.

June was obviously a friend of his mother's, and obviously expected to be invited in. He had to think quickly. "My mom's sleeping now," he said.

June waved a hand at him. "Oh, you can wake her up. She won't mind."

"She doesn't feel well," he said, hoping the anxiousness in his voice was not as apparent to her as it seemed to him. "I think she's sick." From the corner of his eye, he saw his mother's feet on the floor of the kitchen, toes pointed upward like those of the Wicked Witch of the East.

The thought made him want to giggle, and as he looked into June's eyes, he realized with horror that he was smiling. He quickly wiped the expression off his face.

The woman frowned. "I just saw her this morning and she seemed fine. What's wrong with her?"

"I don't know," he said. "I just know she doesn't want to be disturbed. I'll tell her you stopped by, though." He wanted to close the door but realized that would seem too suspicious, so he continued to stand there, waiting. His eyes looked over the woman's head, searching for a car parked next to the curb, but he saw none. She had to be a neighbor. That was good. A casual visitor was much easier to turn away than one who had made a special effort to come here.

"All right," June said uncertainly. "I guess. Will you tell her I'll stop by later?"

"I will," Steve promised. "I will. And it's nice to meet you," he added.

"Nice to finally meet you too," June said.

Right, Steve thought. His mother had obviously been talking to this woman about him. He didn't know what she had been saying, but whatever it was, it couldn't be good.

He watched the woman walk down the porch steps, waved at her when she looked back, then closed the front door. His hands were shaking, and he stood there for a moment, leaning his back against the door, taking deep breaths and trying to calm his nerves. Glancing toward the kitchen, he saw his mother's still body lying unmoving on the floor. He couldn't seem to get away from killing the people around him. As much as he wanted to, as hard as he tried, he could not break the cycle or escape from this loop in which he was trapped.

Maybe he had been fooling himself. Maybe he had no higher purpose. Maybe he was simply the victim of bad genes and bad luck, condemned to murder people because his father had been Joseph Nye, unsung serial killer.

It was a depressing train of thought but one he could not dismiss.

Steve locked the front door, then walked through the house to the back door, locking it as well. He closed up the garage, then walked as casually as he could out to his car. As an added touch, he waved at the front window of the house before driving away. He did not know whether anyone on the street had been outside or had seen him, because he had not looked at them. He never did.

He drove away, feeling better as he left the neighborhood, feeling good as he pulled onto the freeway. He would practice being shocked and grieving tonight. Tomorrow afternoon, he would return and call the police.

Thirty-one

Philip Glass Is the Lord of the Flies

Late spring Sunday. Hot, still air. Down to the library for CDs. Aaron Copland, Philip Glass, Buck Owens: music to borrow, not to buy. Put on the Glass first. One of his oldies, post–*Einstein on the Beach*, pre-*Koyaanisqatsi*. Long, ferociously repetitive, hyperkinetic yet almost stationary. Halfway through

the flies come.

See them on the wall. The music is too loud, can't hear the buzzing, but they're swarming over the white space above the Namingha print. How did they get in? Door closed, windows open, but screens in place, no holes. There are dozens of them, more coming every minute, seeming to materialize from the wall itself. They form a pattern, a shifting amoebalike Rorschach shape, and

it's moving to the music.

See where they're coming in now. A small hole in the juncture of wall and ceiling hidden by brown molding. Dancing, the flies. Fast steps with individuals mirroring the staccato pulse of the music, the changing overall shape echoing broad harmonic shifts.

Running outside through the back door, around the side of the house. The flies are everywhere: on the wall, sneaking in through the hole, coming from the house next door, the alley, the bushes, the trees. Can hear them out here, the buzzing. It's the music they like, the music that's calling to them. The stereo is cranked up, and what's irritating the neighbors with its maddening repetition is talking to the flies, speaking to them.

Running back inside. There's Black Flag under the kitchen sink. Enough to kill them all or just enough to make them mad? Flies covering not just white space but frame now, bigger than half the wall, thousands of them. Does the music sound like the buzzing of flies or has the flies' buzzing grown loud enough to be heard and now become part of the music?

The shape shifting faster, borders and boundaries expanding and contracting. Rounded edges, no corners, almost liquid movement. Sight and sound combining to induce a trance state, a slowing of heart rate and breathing. Blissful. Relaxing. Passive. Accepting.

And

I I I I I

I can have anything I want, they tell me. I can order what I wish. They have powers, the flies, untapped until now, and I who have brought them the music, I who have awakened them, I who have connected them to their lord, I, I, I can make them do whatever my heart desires.

I don't know of how much they are capable; I don't know why they should be capable of anything. It doesn't make any sense, and the rationalist in me wants to turn off the stereo and see what happens. But that same rationalist knows that I could not survive an onslaught from so many.

Must the music go on forever? Must I press the CD player's Repeat button so that Philip Glass never ends? Must I keep them happy and tamed, soothed, lest they attack?

I, I

Still more flies are coming, these from farther off, a swarm of them speeding through the air, dark against the white smog sky, called to my home. See them through the window, almost like a funnel cloud, a tornado of angry insects.

Are flies insects?

Don't care; it doesn't matter. I look again, hear. The movement, the sound. Soothing.

Anything I want.

I want my mother dead.

The Woman

"If you eat my pussy, I'll suck your cock."

Thorton stopped in midstride, looking around to make sure there was no one behind him on the sidewalk, then peered through the open window of the Lexus at the gorgeous blonde who had spoken. She was staring straight ahead, looking as though she hadn't seen him at all, and he wondered whether he'd heard incorrectly. He considered asking her if she was speaking to him, considered asking her to repeat the question, but no, she couldn't have said what he thought she'd said, and he decided to keep walking and continue on.

"Excuse me? I said I'd suck your cock if you'd lick my pussy."

It *was* her, and she *was* talking to him, and now she was looking through the passenger window, smiling. He paused, then opened the car door. He got into the front seat, and saw immediately that her pants were off. Aroused, he slammed the door shut, and it was only then that he noticed her legs were not the same color as her face and hands. It was only then that he noticed the stench.

Her legs were covered with dried smeared excrement.

He put a hand over his nose, trying to breathe through his mouth. "I'm sorry," he said. "Let me out."

The door locks clicked just as he tried to pull up the handle.

"No," she told him, and there seemed to be genuine sadness in her voice. "I can't do that."

Then

We lived for a time in the city of clowns.

Steve couldn't seem to finish a story. He spent as much time writing—or *trying* to write—as he had before, but the ideas he had went nowhere and he was unable to complete more than a page or two before his thoughts derailed completely. This had never happened to him before, and he was at a loss to understand it. What he had was writer's block, he supposed, and the frustration he felt at not being able to produce was as maddening as any rejection letter he had ever received.

The funny thing was that one of his stories, one of his older pieces, had just been accepted last week by the fiction editor of an in-flight magazine. He had no idea what had made him submit to such a market— desperation, probably—but the pay was impressive, and thousands of people flying the friendly skies next October would all have the opportunity to read his work. It was the largest potential audience he'd ever had.

And he might not be able to follow up on it.

He didn't know what was wrong with him. From a writing standpoint, these last few months had been the most productive he'd ever had, and by all rights, that should be continuing, his life experience feeding his fiction and making it stronger. But the creative part of his brain seemed to be shutting down, and whether this was part of a natural up-and-down cycle, a necessary period of recharging or some sort of permanent intellectual realignment, he felt disconcertingly unmoored, deprived of one of the few stable aspects of his life.

Part of the problem was a question of identity. He knew *who* he was but was not exactly sure *what* he was. A corporate researcher and journalist who wrote fiction on the side and happened to kill people? A killer who masqueraded as a newsletter editor and also happened to write fiction? A fiction writer who lived to kill but maintained a regular job to pay the bills and keep up appearances? The lines were blurred, and he didn't know which was his vocation, which was his avocation, which he did out of enjoyment, which he did out of need.

He'd had his mother cremated—against her wishes— and her ashes still sat in a corner of his office in the generic box the mortuary had given him. He had no idea what to do with them. There was no specific spot she really loved, and he wasn't sure he would scatter her ashes there even if there were. He was half tempted to just throw the box away or flush her ashes down the toilet, but there was no way he could explain the reasoning behind that to Sherry, so he did nothing and there the box sat.

He had not gone back to his mother's house since he'd "found" her body and called the police. He'd been there for hours, answering all questions, being the distraught yet dutiful son, but he had not wanted to return. He'd been too afraid. It wasn't logical, but it was real, and a lot of it had to do with that vision of his father disappearing into the gloom of the room at the end of the hall.

That was also about the time that his writer's block had kicked in, and he was sure the two were connected.

He even felt on some irrational superstitious level that if he could go back to the house, he could break the spell and the problem would be over.

But he just couldn't bring himself to do it.

Sitting in front of his PC, he looked at his clown story—or the single sentence of it that he had written—and deleted it. He deleted all of the other fragments as well. If he couldn't write a full short story, he wasn't going to write at all.

He dreamed that night of a clown. It was the same clown he always seemed to dream about, only this time the painted man was running on a treadmill in a zebra-striped room. He was naked, and his entire body was made up like his face, his stomach red, his chest green, his nipples blue, his penis yellow.

The looping treadmill belt on which he ran was made from human skin.

The black-and-white room had two doorways, one at each end, and Steve was standing in the center of one, wondering how he could reach the other without being seen by the clown. He knew he had to make it through that doorway, though he didn't know why, and he also knew that if the clown caught him before he did so, he would be skinned alive, his body parted out and used to make exercise equipment for other circus performers.

The clown looked down at the treadmill controls to see how fast he was running or how far he had gone, and Steve made a dash for it, speeding past the painted man as fast as he could go. He was a step away from the doorway when a big white hand clamped down on his shoulder. He was still trying to run, but he was like a cartoon character, his feet spinning furiously as he remained in place. He looked up, and the clown had grown. The room had grown. The zebra-striped ceiling was a good three stories above his head, and the clown was twice the size of a regular man. His yellow penis, fully erect, hit the side of Steve's shoulder, and Steve's skin burned at the touch.

Through the doorway right in front of him, he could see a land of blue skies and green grass where fathers and sons were fishing and playing Frisbee and having picnic lunches, a land he would never reach.

He awoke when the alarm rang.

And his face was wet with tears.

Thirty-two

Steve knew something was up the second he awoke. He was not psychic—was not sure he even believed in such a thing—but he felt strange, anxious, as though he knew ahead of time that this was going to be an important day.

A bad day.

He took a shower, got dressed, ate a breakfast of cereal and coffee. The feeling of dread did not leave. If anything, it grew stronger, and all the way to the office he was careful to signal when he changed lanes and to slow down as he approached yellow traffic lights, hyperaware that injury and death were but a poor decision away.

He made it safely to work and, once there, decided to take the stairs rather than the elevator, just in case. He knew he was behaving in an extremely foolish and superstitious manner, but he had never experienced anything like this before, and he was filled with the certainty that something major and horrific was about to happen.

What could it be? An earthquake? A disgruntled employee with an AK-47? Was he about to be fired? Was the company bankrupt? What?

He didn't know, but this was one of those walking-on-eggshells situations, and though he dreaded whatever was coming, he wished it would just hurry up and happen, because this waiting and worrying was sheer agony.

Jerry Tortaglia had been named acting department head, and shortly after eight, he called Steve and some of the senior members of each division into the conference room for a meeting. They had a new client, a different kind of client, and Jerry said it was very exciting because it could mark the beginning of AlumniMedia's expansion into other areas of private business. "Schools aren't the only organizations who have alumni," Jerry said. "Employees who retire from a company or who depart on an amicable basis to pursue other interests can also be considered alumni."

"Yeah, yeah," Ron said dismissively. No one had much respect for Jerry Tortaglia, despite—or perhaps because of—the fact that he was lobbying hard to keep the department head position permanently. "Who's the new client?"

Jerry cleared his throat. "Well, in this instance," he said, "the client *does* happen to be a school. But it's a different kind of school," he added quickly, "and, like I said, could lead us to branch out more in the future." He paused dramatically. "We're going to be putting together a booklet and directory for Entertainment Opportunities' Clown College."

There were smirks and chuckles all around.

"I'm not joking," Jerry said. "This is serious business. They are paying us a hefty price to produce a unique product that could be our calling card for the future."

Steve wasn't laughing. In fact, he felt cold.

A clown college.

The very idea of such a place chilled him to the bone, and he could not help thinking that this was a puzzle piece in a larger picture, a picture he was in and that surrounded him on all sides.

"I want two of you to go to the college," Jerry continued. "I want you to talk to Herb Slivitz, our contact there, and try to get a feel for exactly what they want, what they expect, and how we can adapt our resources to meet their needs. I need someone from PR and someone from editorial." He glanced around the table. "Let me see. Bob and, uh . . . Steve. I want you two to head over and learn what you can, put together a presentation of where you think this project should be headed, and then we'll discuss it and take it from there."

Bob Mattacks perked up. "Clown college? Where's it at? Orlando? Do we get a free trip?"

"It's in Los Angeles," Jerry said. "And you get gas mileage."

Steve didn't want to go at all, but he could hardly refuse, and the reason for his apprehension was unclear even to himself. "Okay," he said quietly.

"That's the kind of attitude I like," Jerry announced.

"What an asshole," Bob said as they left the conference room moments later. "If he thinks he's going to get that job, he's crazy. They never promote from within; they always hire from outside. Come next quarter, he's back in the trenches." Bob shook his head. "Really makes you miss McColl, doesn't it?"

Steve smiled tightly, saying nothing.

He wasn't quite sure what he'd expected, but the word "college" implied a campus and buildings with classrooms, so it was with some surprise that they pulled up in front of what appeared to be a large warehouse inappropriately situated on a street of small boutique shops. It was painted a garish pink, and the oversize sign on the roof featured rainbow-colored letters designed to resemble balloons. Two sets of frosted windows were positioned above and to either side of the arched doorway. Steve didn't know whether it was intentional, but from this angle, the windows and door looked like two eyes and a mouth.

A man walked out of the building angrily pulling a green wig off his head. He had the shaved scalp and rough features of an ex-con, and he was carrying in his hand a long-barreled pistol that Steve hoped to hell was a water gun.

Bob got out of the car, slammed his door and took a deep breath. "Just keep repeating to yourself: 'It's a living. It's a living.' "

Steve smiled, but the truth was that he didn't feel very amused. Creeped out was more like it, and he approached the building hesitantly. Another man opened the door and emerged onto the sidewalk, but this one was fully made up and practicing mime moves. He walked past them, waving silently, then pretending to pick a flower and hand it to them. Both Steve and Bob ignored him.

Steve opened the door, and they walked inside.

The ham-fisted attempts at whimsy that characterized the outside of the "college" were nowhere in evidence within the building. Instead, a narrow hallway led to a series of shabby offices, the first three of which were empty. Steve saw kitschy paintings of clowns on the walls of small rooms carpeted with worn shag and furnished with beat-up metal desks, cheap lamps and dented folding tables.

The fourth such room contained an empty desk like the previous offices, but seated on a sagging couch against the opposite wall was an anorexic goth girl who was smoking a cigarette and writing something on a form attached to a clipboard.

Steve knocked on the doorframe. "Hello?" he said.

The girl looked up. "Yeah?" Either she was older than she looked or she had recently dropped out of high school.

"Do you work here?"

"Yeah."

"We're looking for Herb Slivitz," Bob said. "We're from AlumniMedia. He should be expecting us."

There was no change to the girl's bored tone of voice. "I think he's still in the classroom. Come on." She stood, dropping her clipboard on the couch, and led the way out of the office and down the corridor to a much bigger room, this one filled with juggling paraphernalia: balls and bowling pins, boxes and metal rings. A William Frawley lookalike was piling red floor mats against the far wall. "Herb!" the girl called out. "Visitors!"

"Thanks . . ." Steve started to say, but the girl was already gone.

Herb had left the mats and was walking over.

Bob, always the salesman, greeted him, hand extended. "Bob Mattacks," he introduced himself. "AlumniMedia. This is my associate, Steve Nye."

Steve nodded, tried to smile. He thought he detected the residue of greasepaint around the older man's eyes, as though he'd been wearing clown makeup but hadn't been able to completely wash it off.

"Nice place you've got here," Bob lied, looking around the huge room in fake admiration.

"We have eight classrooms, three practice rooms, a staff of twelve and twenty new students admitted each semester from all over the world. Enrollment right now is at a record peak of fifty-eight."

"Impressive," Bob said.

Herb nodded proudly. "We've placed clowns in top circuses all over the world for the past thirty years. This is our thirtieth year in business."

"Which is why you've decided to compile a book of all your graduates," Bob said.

"Exactly."

Steve stepped in. "I'm sure either you or one of your associates has seen examples of our work. I'm a senior editor," he added.

"Yes, we have. In fact, you put together a memory book and directory for our chairman, Ted Thackery's fortieth high school reunion, and that's where we got the idea to hire you for this project. You see, we'd like to put together a listing of all of our graduates and where they worked or are working, with maybe a phone book–type section with their current e-mail addresses and phone numbers."

"That sounds fantastic," Bob said.

"There's a lot of information we'd need to get from you—" Steve began.

"We've been collecting it already. Cat, the young woman who brought you in here, has put together a list of all of our graduates for the entire thirty-year period. We're trying to find photos, addresses, whatever else we can, as well. It won't be complete, of course—our kind of business isn't great about keeping records—but I'm told that investigation is one of the services you offer."

"As long as we have correct names," Steve told him.

"That part's no problem. We'll give you everything we have by the end of the week."

Steve wasn't sure what else they needed to do here; as far as he was concerned, they could leave. But Bob's job was to work on making this an annual project and not just a onetime deal, so he kept talking, emphasizing all of the options AlumniMedia offered: videos, DVDs, CD-ROMs, Web pages. "A booklet or directory is just a starting point," he said. "And, to be honest, those are really geared toward reunions or other events where alumni gather together. Your needs, I feel, may be better served with a more comprehensive package."

Herb looked at him. "A directory," he said. "That's what we want."

"Sure, sure," Bob said, backing down. "Of course." He smiled. "I was wondering if you could take us on a tour of your operation. Neither of us knows anything about clowning, and it would be interesting to see what you teach here. It might also help us to get a handle on the approach we should take for the layout of your book."

"Be glad to," Herb said. "Just let me finish stacking these mats—"

From the doorway right behind them, a clown jumped out, crazily honking a red-bulbed horn.

Steve jumped and let out a startled cry.

Bob and Herb both burst out laughing.

"A little high-strung, are we?" the older man said, saying "high-strung" as though it were a euphemism for "gay."

Steve turned to face the clown, forcing himself to smile to show that he could laugh at himself and had no problem being the butt of a joke.

The man looked like the hitchhiker Steve had seen on Gina's street and then on McColl's. He was wearing bib overalls and a straw hat, and was dancing crazily back down the corridor.

The hairs prickled on the nape of Steve's neck. It was a visceral reaction. But on a more reasoned level, his brain was wondering whether this *was* the same man—and if the man recognized him.

"BoJo," Herb said, chuckling. "One of our soon-to-be graduates. Very talented."

Steve looked back again toward the clown, but he was gone. A frightened, childish part of his brain thought that the man might be hiding in one of the rooms off the hallway, ready to jump out as they passed by. He didn't even want to think about that.

Herb and Bob were still smiling. Bob clapped a hand on the other man's back in an expression of false bonhomie. "Why don't you give us that tour now, Herb. Show us around."

The older man looked at Steve, grinning. "Sure it won't be too much for you?"

Steve laughed it off. "I'm fine."

Asshole, he thought. *I could slit your fucking throat and watch you die like the animal you are.*

The image of that sustained him, and he was still smiling to himself as Herb put away the last of the mats and led the two of them out into the corridor.

Thirty-three

A computer disk and a folder filled with papers arrived from the clown college on the following Wednesday. The disk contained scanned photographs and up-to-date information about current enrollees and those alumni with whom the school was still in contact, while the pages were copies of records and old contact information for those whose whereabouts were unknown. The delivery was a little later than promised, but there was no timetable for completion yet, so Steve wasn't sure whether the delay would even matter.

Jerry had assigned specific tasks to the four of them working on the initial stage of the project, and it was Steve's job to cross-reference the information for the known alumni, make sure it was correct, and then contact each for a preliminary interview. The thought of spending every workday for the next several weeks looking at the faces of clowns on his computer filled him with dread, but he knew that the sooner he did it, the sooner he could get it over with.

He took a sip of coffee, popped in the disk, opened the file, and looked at the photo that appeared on his screen.

It was a clown.

A clown who looked familiar.

Steve's blood ran cold. It wasn't one he had seen at

the college, and it wasn't the one in his dreams, but somehow he recognized it. He *knew* that face.

He stared at the picture on his screen, trying to figure out where and when he had seen it before. For several moments, he didn't know.

Then he did.

Flagstaff.

As a child.

He closed his eyes. He was breathing heavily, as though he'd just finished running several laps—

or been chased by a monster

—and his heart was thumping so powerfully that its rhythm was echoed in that deep inhalation and exhalation of air. His palms and fingers were suddenly sweaty, and he wiped them on his pants.

He remembered clearly now, though seconds before he'd had no recollection of any of it. The memory was fresh and painful, like an untreated wound, unsullied by the years of examination, dissection and deconstruction that would have eroded it and polished it and changed it had he often revisited the remembrance.

He had gone to the circus with his father. Only it hadn't been anywhere near as normal or wholesome as that superficial description made it sound. For this was not Ringling Bros. or Circus Vargas or any of the legitimate shows that traveled around the United States. This was some fly-by-night crew set up in a raggedy moth-eaten tent in a field outside of town.

They'd gone on a weekend afternoon, and his mother had stayed home for some reason, maybe to do some housework, maybe to give them some father-son bonding time. He'd wanted her to come, begged her to come—he'd been closer to her than to his father at that point—but she had refused, and he'd been mad at her for it.

He couldn't recall exactly where the circus had

been, but he knew that it had taken them a while to get there and that they'd parked the car in a big patch of dirt with a lot of other cars. They'd shuffled through the dust to a plywood ticket booth set up in front of the tent, his father had purchased tickets, and they'd gone inside. Within, the big top was as dingy as it had appeared on the outside, and while Steve could tell that an effort had been made to make the performance area festive, that had obviously happened a long time ago, and what had once been bright, vibrant colors had faded into sad, depressing dullness.

They'd found some seats near the middle of the stands, where his father had met up with someone he knew. The two of them had started talking about grown-up stuff, and the other man's son, a boy a few years older than Steve, had asked if the two of them could go explore around the outside of the tent before the performance started. Both dads said it was okay, and the boys had taken off.

Steve didn't remember much about this part, just recalled that the two of them had been searching for the lions' cages or an elephant wagon like the one in *Dumbo*. But he remembered the next part, because they had run into a man putting on his clown makeup in back of a trailer behind the big tent. He was seated on a folding chair and looking into a mirror that had been hung on the trailer's outside metal wall. Before him on the ground was something resembling a giant shoe-shine kit filled with makeup that looked like paint. They could see his face in the mirror, and it appeared magnified, exaggerated, the lines curved and indistinct, like heat waves. He had put on only the white base and some black designs around his eyes, but already he looked more clown than man, as though in a werewolflike transformation he was turning from one into the other.

The two boys stopped to watch.

The clown must have seen them in his mirror because he swiveled around. "What do you two want?" he demanded.

One of them—Steve couldn't remember if it was him or the other boy—answered, "Nothing. We're just looking around."

"Get over here!" the clown ordered. There was something scary about his voice, something mean.

The two boys looked at each other.

"Now!"

The other boy ran away.

Steve started to run too.

"Stop right where you are!" the clown screamed.

And Steve stopped.

The other boy was gone around the edge of the tent, free and safe, and Steve knew that if he could just get around that corner also, he too would be safe. But the clown had caught him, and even if the man wasn't physically restraining him, he was a grown-up and he was ordering him not to go, and Steve did not know how to disobey an adult.

"Come here!" the clown commanded, and Steve turned, walking slowly back toward the trailer. His mouth was dry, and his heart was slamming so hard against his chest it felt as though it would burst. Some sort of briar or sticker stabbed his ankle through his sock, but he did not even dare to stop and check. If he did, he might have been able to escape. Instead, he just kept walking forward.

"You came to see a clown, huh?" the man said. He was grinning, and his teeth were dirty. A few in the back were missing. "You and your friend wanted to know what a clown looks like without makeup? Here's what a clown looks like."

Steve saw with terror that the man's pants were undone, his zipper down. From within that open space protruded a stiff penis. It was long and shiny, oily, and it was the most horrifying thing he had ever seen.

He was close enough now for the clown to grab him, and grab him he did. Rough hands squeezed Steve's upper arm, hurting his muscle. "Touch it!" the clown ordered, nodding toward his lap, and Steve did, because even though he was afraid to do so, he was more afraid not to. He pressed a single finger against the hardened organ. The skin felt sickeningly warm and spongy to his touch.

"Rub it," the clown said.

Steve wasn't sure what the clown meant by that, and for the first time he looked up into the man's face. What he saw beneath the half-applied makeup was a cruel, snarling mouth and eyes that looked deader than a doll's. He still wasn't sure what he was supposed to do, but he was afraid to ask, and, hesitantly, he began moving his finger back and forth, rubbing it as he would a piece of cloth with an interesting texture.

"Grab it, you dummy!"

He was crying, but he didn't want the clown to see, so he kept his eyes downcast and reached out, grabbing the oily penis.

"Not so hard!" The clown let go of his arm to hit him on the side of the head.

This time, Steve ran.

The clown was bellowing for him to come back, but he kept running as fast as he could, knowing that if his friend had escaped, he could too. He was sobbing so hard he could barely see. At the corner of the tent, he ran into the canvas, but he recovered instantly and sped around the side to the front, to the crowds, to safety.

People were looking at him, people he didn't know, and he turned away, hiding by the portable toilets and gathering his wits so he wouldn't have a crying face when he saw his father. He didn't want his dad to ask any questions.

He didn't want to talk about what had happened.

Ever.

He saw the clown in the show, and although he had his full makeup on, Steve recognized him instantly. He twisted a balloon into a dachshund and gave it to another little boy in the front row, smiling at the child. Other kids in the audience rushed forward. Steve felt sick to his stomach watching the act, and when his father leaned over and said to him, "Do you want a balloon too? Go up there. Ask him. He'll give you one," Steve thought he might vomit.

They'd gone home immediately after the show, and he had never seen the clown again. He was not sure he had ever *thought* about the clown again.

Until now.

It was no wonder that he had not been able to remember anything about Flagstaff when he and Sherry were there. His mind had not only blocked out that incident, it had blocked almost everything leading up to it and everything that had come after it. The entire time his family had lived in Flagstaff was little more than a blank spot on his life's résumé.

He wondered if the incident with the clown would even have happened if his mother had come with them to the circus. She'd always been overprotective of him as a child, and he doubted that she would have allowed him and the other little boy to run around outside unattended. Either she would have told him to stay in his seat or she would have gone out with him to supervise. Either way, what had occurred in back of that tent would probably not have taken place.

Maybe *that* was what had been his mother's fault.

It's your fault! It's your fault!

Steve stared at the face on his screen. A ring of curly red hair encircled the back and sides of a bald white head. The face was white too, of course, and the nose red. A soft oval of purple and green surrounded the smiling mouth, and black designs resembling curlicue triangles were painted above, below and to either side of each eye. Even through the filters of time, photograph and computer screen, it seemed to Steve that a malevolent anger shone through those eyes, and he scrolled forward to the page containing the clown's personal information.

Jim Adams was his name, and, surprisingly, he lived in Flagstaff. Steve copied down his address, not wanting to print it out in case the computer kept an e-trail of everything it did. He folded the piece of paper and put it in his pocket, wondering why the man was still in Flagstaff. He knew that circuses traveled all around the country and figured that he'd seen one stop on the show's perpetual tour, had encountered the clown on the one unlucky day when he'd been in northern Arizona. But maybe that wasn't the case. Maybe the circus was a local annual event, put on by the Moose Lodge or the Elks or some other service club. It would explain the shabby tent and faded equipment; they could have been purchased secondhand from a real circus and stored somewhere, to be taken out only for this one event each year. And maybe the circus had been staffed by local businessmen, one of whom had happened to attend clown school in his younger, more idealistic days.

Steve scrolled back up to the photo of the clown.

Or maybe the guy had simply liked Flagstaff and decided to stay.

And prey upon other little kids like himself.

Whatever the reason, his days were at an end.

Steve was going to kill him.

The knowledge gave him not only an emotional charge, the sort of energizing boost that he'd experienced after deciding to take out Gina and Will, his two most premeditated kills, but it filled him with a deeper, more profound realization that this was not a random occurrence. It was part of a pattern, the culmination of a series of escalating interconnected events. He was part of something bigger than himself, and if he had glimpsed hints of that before, its full meaning was apparent to him only now.

Everything had been leading up to this. Everything he'd been thinking, everything he'd been doing, everything he'd been learning. This was what he had been training for; this was why he had been following in his father's footsteps, mastering the skills needed to hunt and slay his prey. His father might have been given a different task—most of his kills had been slutty women or pimps of one sort or another—but Steve had been chosen to take down this clown.

And maybe other clowns.

Maybe priests and rabbis, teachers and scout leaders.

His role was as protector of children, and while he himself had suffered, he would make sure that other kids did not share that fate.

And if they had?

He would kill them, too, in order to put them out of their misery.

He was filled with a glorious sense of purpose and a spirit of determination that carried him through the rest of the day, enabling him to work harder and accomplish more than he otherwise would have, causing him to be friendlier and more sociable with his coworkers than he usually was. Even viewing the clown photos was not that difficult. Indeed, he found that while a vestigial uneasiness remained, he was not really afraid of those painted faces anymore.

After work, he returned to his parents' house to get the machete. Since picking it up and holding it in his hands on his mother's last day, it had never been very far from his mind, and though its weight was significant, he had been unconsciously preparing himself to use it by lifting grocery bags and stacks of books and heavy objects with one hand whenever possible. He'd liked the way it had felt, and whether he wanted to admit it or not, there'd been an itch to use it.

He parked his car in the driveway, got out his keys and walked up to the front door. The grass was overgrown, his mother's flowers were all dead, and someone had graffitied nonsensical letters on the wall. His parents' house was no longer an anomaly. It fit into the decaying neighborhood perfectly, although he would have to fix it up if he ever hoped to sell the place.

And it *was* his parents' house again, not just his mother's. It had reverted back to both of them.

The interior of the house was dark and smelled of death. He stood there for a moment, holding the door open, looking carefully around, afraid he might see his father.

Or his mother.

His fingers reached around the wall to his right, found the light switch and flipped it on. Everything was as it had been: the clothes piled on the couch, the packed boxes, the array of weapons on the floor. He stepped slowly forward, trying to breathe through his mouth. The air was heavy and still. Beneath the chemical scent of disinfectant used by the investigators and paramedics—a scent that reminded him of the morgue in the VA hospital—Steve smelled dried vomit, old blood and excrement.

He walked into the middle of the living room, bent down in front of the machete and picked it up. It wasn't as heavy as he remembered. In fact, it felt pretty good in his hand. It felt right.

This was the perfect weapon for taking care of the clown.

Jim Adams.

Yes, Jim Adams. A mundane name for such a monstrously evil man. Steve preferred to think of him as "the clown." It made it easier to do what he had to do.

No, that wasn't true. It was already easy. He *wanted* to kill the clown.

He was looking forward to it.

Swinging the machete from side to side, listening to the swishing sound it made as it sliced through the air, Steve glanced down at the other weapons on the floor. He decided to take all of them with him, the sword and knives as well as the machete, and he grabbed a couple of his mother's old dresses from the pile on the couch and used them to wrap up the blades. Scouting around, he found a heavy black garbage sack, and he dumped out the knicknacks that his mother had put in there and carefully put the wrapped weapons into the bag.

A strangely loud snap sounded from one of the back rooms of the house, a noise like a dry twig breaking—

His father? His mother?

—and he picked up the garbage sack with both hands and headed out the front door. The weapons were getting very heavy, and he waddled to the car, where he had to place the black bag on the ground before opening the trunk and loading the weapons inside. He returned to lock up, but was afraid to go into the house, and so didn't bother to turn off the light before closing the door and locking it. He hurried back to the car.

He smiled to himself as he pulled out of the driveway and headed home.

Thirty-four

He didn't even think up an excuse this time, didn't bother to tell Sherry he was leaving. He just took off, packing what little he needed and heading east to Arizona. Wanting to leave no paper trail, he drove rather than flew, sleeping only a few hours Friday night before getting up at three o'clock Saturday morning and setting out.

He stopped only for gas, a bathroom break and a quick McMuffin breakfast in the small desert town of Quartzsite, passing through Phoenix shortly before ten and reaching Flagstaff close to noon.

The clown's house was in a poor section of town adjacent to the railroad tracks that ran parallel to old Route 66. Steve passed a series of run-down, once-attractive motels and then turned on a rutted side road that bumped over the tracks and led to a neighborhood of brown-lawned brick houses. Jim Adams's home was identical to those on either side of it except for the fact that the edge of the yard had old pinwheels planted in the ground rather than flowers, and there was a faded rainbow painted on the side of the curbside mailbox.

Steve drove around the block twice, gathering his courage. Finally, he decided to just do it, to not overthink everything but go with his gut. It had served him well so far and would no doubt see him through this as well. He parked on the next street over, rummaging through his belongings until he found the machete. Unwrapping the blade and casting aside his mother's dress—one he recognized as her favorite church outfit—he grasped the smooth handle of the weapon and simply walked down the sidewalk and around the corner, acting as though this were something he did all the time. Two boys were playing basketball in one driveway, and an old man in a wife-beater T-shirt was sitting in a lawn chair drinking beer out of the bottle in another, but none of them noticed anything amiss as he strode by.

His gait slowed as he reached the Adams house, the clown house. His muscles tensed as he realized that he was no longer on the way to his destination; he was *at* his destination. Clutching the heavy machete, he made his way across the nonexistent lawn to the front door, moving slowly, crouching low, trying not to be seen. He felt like Martin Sheen in *Apocalypse Now*, emerging from the steaming water to kill Marlon Brando, and he started humming to himself a vaguely Middle Eastern guitar riff that started out as "The End" but somehow morphed into "Misirlou."

He thought of ringing the bell or knocking on the door, then attacking the clown when he answered. But he didn't want to do anything out in the open, where he could be seen, and he decided to sneak around to the rear of the house. Still humming to himself, he crept up the driveway, went around the edge of the carport and entered the fenceless backyard. On edge, prepared for anything, ready to lash out on a second's notice, he made his way through the dead weeds to the back door. He stopped for a moment to look around, but aside from a leafless tree and a cannibalized motorcycle rotting into the ground, the yard was empty. There was no one there.

If Adams was here, he was inside.

Carefully, Steve reached out and grasped the doorknob. He expected it to be locked, but it turned easily in his hand, and he pulled open the door as quietly as he could. He closed it behind him but not all the way, not wanting the latch to click and alert whomever might be in the house to his presence.

He was in some sort of antechamber filled with old skis, dirty snow boots, and plastic winter toys. A flat shovel leaned against the wall next to him. In the center of the narrow room, an open doorway led into the house proper and slowly, cautiously, he moved forward, creeping on tiptoe so as not to make the floor creak. He poked his head around the corner, saw no one there, and stepped inside.

The interior of the house was decorated like a child's play area. The first room in which he found himself (what was it? a bedroom? a living room? a den?) featured brightly colored trains painted on the walls, and cartoon character mobiles hanging from the ceiling. Instead of ordinary furniture, there were a half dozen or so metal-and-plastic chairs of the type used in school classrooms surrounding a long Formica-topped table with half-finished ship and airplane models atop it. Twin Hot Wheels tracks ran down the center of the room. An open trunk filled with toys sat against one wall.

Steve felt sick to his stomach. It was possible that Jim Adams actually enjoyed looking at childish images and playing with toys. That might very well be his taste. But Steve couldn't help seeing an ulterior motive, and he knew that a lot of young boys would think this place looked cool.

He could not tell yet if the clown was home, but he felt more scared and nervous now than he had at any time he could remember. It was a child's fear he felt,

the same fear he had experienced when he'd first encountered the man—

Touch it!

—and it was all he could do not to turn around,
run out of the house and speed far away from here as
quickly as he could. There was none of the exhilarat-
ing tension he'd experienced while stalking Gina or
lying in wait for McColl, none of the excitement and
anticipation he'd felt setting the trap for Will, none
of the sudden cathartic anger that had propelled him
through his encounters with Lyman Fischer and his
mother. No, this was totally different, and for the first
time, he was afraid to confront his victim and did not
have the confidence that he could pull this off.

He stepped over the Hot Wheels tracks, walked
gingerly around a gumball machine—and promptly
stumbled over an unseen rubber ball. He caught himself quickly, before he fell, but the ball careened off to
the left and hit one of the Hot Wheels cars. The colli-
sion sounded impossibly loud in the otherwise silent
house. Steve waited for a moment, listening, but heard
no noise from elsewhere in the clown's home and assumed he was safe. He continued on, hardly daring to
breathe, keeping both eyes on the floor in front of him.
He was holding up the machete, ready to strike at anything that moved, but the weapon was getting heavy,
and if this went on much longer, his arms would be too
tired to lift the blade when he needed to.

Trying not to make any more noise, he made his
way toward the doorway at the opposite end of the
room. Logic told him that the door should open onto
a hallway, but he could see through the opening that it
led into another room.

Where a man lay prone on a water bed.

Jim Adams.

Steve stopped. Like the room he was in, the one

before him had no traditional counterpart. Yes, there was a water bed in the center of the room, but there was also a refrigerator and a stove. Funhouse mirrors were mounted on the walls, distorting the scene before them. As he moved closer, he saw that a circular mirror was mounted on the ceiling above the bed.

The clown was either dead or deeply asleep, since none of the noise Steve made had awakened him. He was wearing no makeup and was obviously older than when Steve had seen him as a child, but he looked much the same, if slightly heavier. Even in repose, his features were rough and cruel, and Steve wondered how many other children the monster had attacked throughout the years.

He stepped into the room.

He was humming again, though he hadn't noticed that he'd started to do so, and he was moving forward in a defensive crouch, machete raised, like a predator about to attack. Adams heard the noise and awoke, his eyes flickering open, but Steve didn't give him a chance to sit up or say a word. Holding the handle of the machete with both hands, he lifted it high and brought it down hard on the man's neck. The blade sliced easily through skin and muscle, embedding itself deep into bone and cartilage. In the second before contact, Adams's eyes had widened and his mouth opened as if to scream. There was no scream, though. Only the thunk of the blade and a sickening gurgle that issued not from his open mouth but from the gash in his throat.

Suddenly blood was spurting everywhere, along with water from the punctured mattress. With no solid support beneath the body, it was almost impossible to pull the machete out of the neck, but Steve finally managed to do it and brought the weapon down again.

And again.

And again.

Within moments, what had been a man was only disjointed chunks of bleeding flesh floating in a pool of red-tinged water.

Finished with the clown but with his rage not yet satiated, Steve tore through the house on a rampage, upending chairs and tables, stomping on breakable objects, ripping frames and pictures from the walls. If anyone had been in his way, he would have cut the person down, but luckily the house was empty, and he rushed from room to room like a Tasmanian devil, destroying whatever he saw.

He ended up in what was probably supposed to be the kitchen—there was a double sink in the center of a long counter that ran the length of one wall—but instead housed dolls, dummies and stuffed animals of all shapes and sizes. Dropping the machete and bending forward, hands on his knees, he breathed deeply, feeling suddenly exhausted. The muscles in his arms hurt, as did his throat, and he wondered if he had been screaming. He honestly didn't know, and he tried to listen, over the sound of his ragged breathing, for the wail of approaching sirens.

He heard nothing, though, and as his breathing and heart rate returned to normal, he figured that he had gotten away with it once again. All he had to do now was get out of here.

He straightened up, picking the machete off the floor. His hands and clothes were red with splattered blood, and he could feel a tightening wetness on the skin of his cheeks and chin that meant his face was probably covered in blood as well. He thought of making his way back through the strange rooms of the damaged house, but the idea of seeing the clown's dead body—or what was left of it—sent a chill down his spine, and he decided to just exit through the front of the home.

He walked into the daylight, blinking, aware only now of how dark it had been in the clown's house. A woman shaking out a rug next door saw him emerge onto the porch covered with blood, a grossly overweight woman who dropped the rug and ran screaming into her house. Seconds later, a muscular man with a shaved head came barreling out, his features set in an expression of fierce determination. Through the open door behind the man, Steve could see the woman talking frantically on the phone. It was too late to finesse his way out of this one, so Steve ran to meet the would-be hero, machete in hand.

The bald guy could see what he was up against and was looking around for some type of weapon to combat the machete, but he was still moving forward, refusing to back down, and Steve used that to his advantage, lifting his blade high and slashing it sideways across the man's enormous chest. His scream was more like an animal's than a human's, so primal was its agony, but Steve didn't allow it to go on for more than a few seconds. As the man fell to the ground, Steve brought the machete down on the top of his skull, swinging with all his might, and the bald head cracked open, blood spilling out like red yolk from an enormous egg. Two more hacking slices and the man's arms were almost completely severed, attached to the body by nothing more than bone and a few strained strips of tendon.

He could hear the sound of police cars drawing closer, and though he wanted nothing more than to go next door and hack the limbs off the bitch who had called them, Steve knew he was out of time. He had parked around the block, so at least the woman would not be able to identify his car, but no one could miss a bloody man with a machete running down the street, and he wished he had parked closer.

He was about to take off and make a run for it when

it occurred to him that a much faster and safer way to reach the other street would be to cut through Adams's backyard and the yard of the house behind it. That would place him at just about the right spot to reach his car.

With the sirens growing louder, Steve turned and ran around the side of the house to the rear. Speeding through the weeds, past the motorcycle and the dead tree, he saw only a low chain-link fence separating Adams's yard from the one behind him. On the other side of the fence stood a line of scraggly bushes, and Steve hopped the rusted chain link and passed between almost bare shrub branches to enter the other house's backyard.

A young girl was facing him, swinging on a swing.

He was going to ignore her, going to run past, but the girl had to speak.

"I'm telling!" she called to him.

There was no time to reason with her, no time to argue. The sirens were almost here, and that fat bitch was probably still on the phone with the 911 operator, blabbing away.

He turned, sprinted over to the swing set.

The girl must have seen the machete or sensed something in his face, in his action, in his body language, because all of a sudden she grew very afraid. "I won't," she said meekly. "I won't tell."

But he knew that she would. As soon as he was out of here and the threat was gone, she would tell everything to anyone who would listen: her friends, her parents, her teachers, the police.

He dropped the machete and grabbed the girl by the arm, yanking her off the swing. She cried out, a short, sharp yelp of shock and fear.

He twisted her neck.

And she stopped.

Letting her body fall to the ground, he picked up his weapon and hurried on, amazed at how easy it had been. Killing adults was always difficult and messy, involving strength and strategy, requiring his full focus and attention. But dispatching a child was smooth and effortless, scarcely more difficult than throwing away an unwanted toy.

He ran through the side yard of the house out to the street, encountering no one, not the girl's parents or sibling or friend. His car was parked in front of the next house over, and he ran to the car, fishing the keys from his pocket. The two boys had finished playing basketball and were gone, but the old man was still in his lawn chair drinking beer. As luck would have it, his attention was focused on a loud motorcycle racing down the south side of the street, and Steve opened his car door, got in and took off.

He glanced in his rearview mirror at the house of the little girl, wondering how long it would take for her parents to find her, thinking that if they discovered her soon and engaged the cops, it might give him slightly more lead time.

Steve recalled what it had felt like to twist the girl's neck. He'd enjoyed killing her, he realized. He had not expected that, but there it was.

That made him worse than the clown.

No. No, it didn't.

He didn't know why it didn't, but he knew that it was true.

He reached an intersection, saw red and blue police lights speeding down a parallel street to his right, and immediately turned left. Seeing his red hands on the steering wheel, catching a glimpse of his bloody visage in the mirror, he was acutely aware of how conspicuous he was, how eye-catching his appearance would be to other drivers. He needed to clean up. Fast. He'd brought a change of clothes in the car, but didn't know where he could go to get out of these blood-soaked garments. He should have checked into a motel when he'd first arrived in town, before going to the clown's house. He would have been able to go there now, to shower, change, even lie low if need be.

But he hadn't thought this through at all. He'd been so rattled just by the idea of the clown that he figured he'd better act while he was still brave enough to do so. He'd allowed his emotions to hold sway, and it had kept him from coming up with an exit strategy.

He'd done what he came for, though. He'd killed the man and gotten away.

Steve was sticking to the side streets, traveling as quickly as he could through residential areas without attracting attention. He emerged next to the university, NAU, and saw a deserted construction site off to the left, the steel skeleton of a new building arising from what appeared to have been a former parking lot. He didn't know whether the workers were on break or had gone for the day, but he was happy they weren't there, because he saw at the edge of the construction zone a turquoise-colored portable toilet.

Bumping over a break in the sidewalk and skidding to a stop in the dirt, Steve unbuckled his shoulder harness, bent over and rummaged through his suitcase in the backseat. He grabbed two shirts and a pair of jeans. From the front seat, he picked up two bottles of Sparkletts water and, wrapping everything in a bundle made from one of the shirts, he opened the car door and hurried into the Porta Potti.

As he suspected, there was neither mirror nor sink, only a horrible-smelling chemical toilet, but he locked the door, took off his shirt and pants, and dumped them into the metal bowl. Opening up one of the water bottles, he poured it onto the extra shirt and used it to scrub his face. He couldn't see what he looked like, but it had to be better than before, and he took a section of sleeve with no blood on it and wiped his forehead, cheeks and chin. The material came back clean save for a few pinkish smears, so he assumed he looked all right.

Using water from the other bottle, he started to clean his hands. Then stopped. He stared down at his fingers, feeling stupid. He had not worn gloves. His fingerprints were everywhere: all over the clown's house, on the pipe at the top of the chain-link fence, on the door and toilet of this Porta Potti.

Did that matter, though? His prints weren't on file anywhere. So unless he was caught and fingerprinted, there would be no way to identify him.

He finished washing his hands, then threw both bottles and the shirt he'd been using into the toilet, shutting the lid. Putting on the new pants and shirt, he walked out to the car.

Maybe the old fuck on the lawn chair had seen his vehicle. Maybe someone else had. But he was going to assume that no one had turned him in, that the police were bogged down at the clown's house and the little girl's backyard and were combing the streets looking for a bloody lunatic running around with a machete.

He drove past the university entrance and turned left when he reached the highway, staying well within the speed limit as he passed a Hastings bookstore, a Burger King, an Olive Garden.

Outside of town, the highway turned into a freeway and the speed limit went up to seventy, then seventy-five. Within minutes, he was flying south through the pines toward Phoenix, caught in the flow of traffic.

He smiled to himself as he signaled and pulled past a semi truck.

He'd made it.

Thirty-five

Promising to see her tomorrow, Steve said good-bye to Sherry and hung up the phone, breathing a sigh of relief.

She'd bought it. Hook, line and sinker.

He'd arrived home that evening to find not only twenty messages from Sherry on his answering machine but a note from her taped to his door. When he turned on his cell phone, he found that his voice mail was full—with messages from Sherry. She'd obviously been desperate to reach him, and he sat down and tried to come up with the most plausible explanation for his absence, one that would account for his refusal to answer his cell.

After leaving Flagstaff, he'd been too tired to drive all the way through to California, so he'd stopped in the small town of Goodyear, on the western desert edge of the Phoenix metropolitan area, and pulled into the parking lot of a Days Inn. He'd already cleaned up a bit more in a rest area just past Sedona, and while he didn't look like the world's most dapper man, he was presentable. He'd gotten himself a room, taken a real shower and crashed.

He'd slept for fifteen hours.

It was nearly six in the evening when he finally reached Southern California. He'd been more than a little nervous coming back. What if Arizona investigators had pieced things together and figured out it was him? What if he arrived back at his apartment to find a contingent of cops awaiting his return with drawn revolvers?

There'd been nothing like that, though.

Only the messages from Sherry.

He'd ended up telling her that he was up for a promotion and had been whisked away after work on Wednesday and flown on AlumniMedia's private jet to the corporate headquarters in New York, where he'd been given a tour of the offices and interviewed extensively. He hadn't been able to call her, he said, because he'd had no time. And she hadn't been able to call him because his cell phone had not been charged, although he had not realized it at the time.

That was all a lie. There was no AlumniMedia jet. There was no corporate headquarters in New York. They were a small company based here in Irvine with a staff of probably fifty. He was banking that her trust in him would keep her from researching the subject and verifying his story.

Which reminded him: He needed to come up with some sort of explanation for his absence at work as well. He hadn't shown up, yet hadn't called in sick, so they were going to wonder where he'd been.

So . . .

What next?

Where did he go from here?

As hairy as it had gotten in Flagstaff, the experience had left him energized and invigorated. He was anxious to get out there and do it again. *This* was what he had been made for; *this* was what he was meant to do, and it felt wrong to be back in his normal life, cooling his heels, when he should be out there taking care of business.

It seemed to Steve that he should have some type of plan or agenda, a method by which he could determine whom he needed to take care of, and how and where and when.

Some people needed killing.

At work, he had that entire CD filled with photos and information for the clown college alumni, as well as hard-copy listings of other names he could use, as long as he was able to track those men down. That would be a good start.

And there were probably other clown schools out there as well that he could draw from.

He'd read an article in the paper the other day about a priest accused of child molestation whose victims could not sue for damages because the statute of limitations for the crime had expired. That man certainly deserved to die.

Maybe he should just quit his job and roam around the country, killing clowns and priests and . . . whomever. That would be perfect. How would he make a living, though? Doing odd jobs in the various towns in which he found himself? Steve smiled. Who was he kidding? He couldn't do that. He had neither the skills nor the aptitude for manual labor. No, the best thing would be for him to remain where he was and use his vacation time to hunt down those who preyed upon children.

But *he* liked killing children.

He pushed that thought aside. *That* wasn't important right now. He was on a mission. He had been charged with this duty, and it was his responsibility to fulfill it, to rid society of the undesirables that the law and polite society were not willing to remove. He was a dragon slayer, a man uniquely equipped to solve this problem.

Like his father had been.

How had his father gotten started on such a path? Steve wondered. He had no idea. *He'd* gotten started *because* of his father, but what was it that had made his old man embark on this course of action? What had first led him to kill his wife?

And how had he moved on from there?

Steve knew from experience that it got easier each time, but he yearned to understand the emotional and intellectual journey his dad had taken in order to get to the point where he was uprooting his family, taking new jobs, moving to different states, all so he could find the people he needed to kill. Steve wished, not for the first time, that his father had written everything down, had kept some sort of diary and recorded all that had happened.

The clock on the DVD player said that it was nearly eleven. Eleven! He'd just called Sherry only a few moments ago. The clock then had said it was seven fifteen. What had happened to the time? Frowning, he stood and walked into the kitchen to check the clock on the microwave. Its lighted display read: *10:57*.

How was this possible? Had he somehow dozed off and not known it? Had he gone into some sort of trance and zoned out?

Was he crazy?

Feeling unnerved, Steve opened the refrigerator and took out a beer. He downed it quickly, the coolness of the liquid smooth and soothing in his throat. Afterward he felt better. He walked from room to room, restless, unsure of what to do. He couldn't sleep, didn't want to read and wasn't in the mood to write. Sitting down on the couch and turning on the television, he flipped through the channels, stopping finally on TCM . . .

*   *   *

Where a young Robert Wagner is doing research in a university library on toxic substances. He sneaks into a school lab and steals a chemical, but his girlfriend, Joanne Woodward, steadfastly refuses to take any of the "medicine" he provides for her.

So Wagner decides to dispose of her in a different way. He gets an idea after seeing her stand up from a bench and fall. For a brief, hopeful second, he thinks she's been injured or killed, but then she struggles to her feet and he offers her a hand.

Wagner realizes that he would be the primary suspect should anything happen to her, so he has her translate, in writing, a vaguely worded paragraph that could be interpreted as a suicide note. He places the note in an envelope and mails it to her parents.

Then he lures Joanne Woodward up to the roof of the bank building. It is the lunch hour, so the bank and the offices within the building are closed. There are very few people inside, but he cannot afford for the two of them to be seen with each other—one sharp-eyed witness could unravel the entire plan—so he walks ahead of her, pretending they are not together. It is not until they are in the stairwell, walking up the concrete steps, that he slows and takes her hand.

On the roof, they walk about, strolling along the bordered edge, admiring the view of the town from every angle. "I love you," he tells her. "You'll never know how much."

Then he pushes her over the low wall, and she falls off the building, screaming in terror until she hits the sidewalk below.

Steve watched, the blood ice-cold in his veins. It was the same scenario as the one his father had told him about. *Exactly* the same. As though his dad had watched the film and then decided to follow it to the letter when he killed his first wife, Ruth.

That made no sense, though. How could his father have arranged things so perfectly? And why? Had he been that impressed with the movie, or had he merely thought that the filmmakers had come up with a situation that could be easily duplicated? Could it all have been some impossibly bizarre coincidence?

He watched the television, feeling disturbed and uneasy. Nothing seemed right all of a sudden. It was as though he'd been transported into an alternate universe where he was a character in a movie and was only discovering it now. He was in his own apartment, surrounded by furniture he had bought and picked out, but he felt disoriented, as though he were sitting on a stage set designed by others.

He needed to call Jessica Haster, Ruth's aunt, in Copper City. She knew all the details of his father's early years. She would be able to sort things out for him. Maybe there was a logical explanation why the reality of Ruth's death hewed so closely to the plot of an old movie. Steve had no idea how that was possible, but he held on to that hope and went into the other room to find the old lady's phone number.

It was an hour later in New Mexico, which meant that it was already after midnight, and the phone rang for a long time before Jessica Haster picked up. "Hello?" she said. Her voice was groggy, but there was an edge of anxiety to it. No call coming this late could bring good news.

"Hello," he said. "This is Steve Nye."

"Who?" She sounded confused.

"Steve Nye. Joseph Nye's son. I came to Copper City a few months back to talk to you about my dad and Ruth, his first wife?"

"Oh, yes. Now I remember." There was a clicking sound and some static, as though she were adjusting something on her phone. When she spoke again, her voice was clearer. "Do you realize what time it is, young man?"

"I do, and I'm sorry," Steve said. "I just got back from a . . . trip to London, and my body's not yet adjusted to the time difference. I apologize for disturbing you. I just wanted to ask you a few more questions about my dad and Ruth."

There was a long pause. "Why don't you call back tomorrow. It's late."

"This'll only take a minute or two. I swear."

"All right."

"When Ruth fell off the building—"

"Building?" Jessica said, and there was a note of genuine surprise in her voice. "Ruth didn't fall off any building."

"But I thought—"

"Land sakes! You thought she fell off a building? No. She fell off the turtle rock in Collins Park. How could you think . . . ? I thought we told you what happened. She was in the park, on the rock, and she fell and hit her head on the concrete path below."

"But you said it was a suicide."

Jessica was wide-awake now. "That's what some people thought. But only because it didn't make any sense that she was up there in the first place. They thought the only reason she'd be there would be to kill herself. 'They.' " She snorted. "*Me.* I thought that too, for a long time. But then Hazel reminded me that Ruth always used to sit up on the turtle rock to think whenever she was worried or troubled. And, of course, being pregnant, she probably had plenty to concern herself with. Remember, she was only around nineteen or twenty when it happened, practically a child herself. It was only natural that she'd want to be alone to think and sort things out. And, like Hazel said, it would've been real easy for her to slip off."

"This 'turtle rock . . .' "

"It's in the center of Collins Park. They built the park around it. Or at least the picnic and play areas, not the baseball diamond. It's a big boulder that's shaped kind of like a turtle's shell. There's a cluster of four or five boulders, as you probably saw coming into town. Kids like to climb on top of there. The turtle rock is the one on top and it . . . looks like a turtle."

"But why would she be up there?" His voice sounded whiny to himself, and Steve realized that he was grasping at straws, trying to think of some way that his father could still be responsible for his first wife's death, though it was pretty clear by now that that was not the case.

"That's why a lot of people thought it was suicide. They thought she jumped. But, like Hazel said, she'd always gone up there to think, to be by herself, and that's probably what she was doing. She probably just fell trying to get up or trying to get down, and she happened to land the wrong way and . . . died." Ruth sighed. "Everything would have been different if she had lived."

Everything would have been different.

Steve was filled with a feeling of rising panic. "Thank you," he said hastily. "You've been a big help. I'll let you go now. Bye."

He hung up.

His father had not killed his first wife. She had fallen off a boulder in a park. The description his dad had given was from an old movie he had seen.

And the two had nothing to do with each other.

Steve began pacing the room. It was only a surface similarity in the broad contours of the stories that had made him think that one described the other, that the fictional murder applied to the real-life death.

But if his father hadn't killed Ruth . . .

Steve's mind leaped to the next logical question: Had his father killed *anyone*?

He thought back over what he knew, desperately trying to determine what honest-to-God facts he possessed. Almost none, he realized. The evidence he had was all circumstantial. A handful of unsolved deaths that had occurred in the same cities in which his family had lived and that vaguely resembled the murders—no, *movies*—his stroke-victim father had described to him.

For he realized now that the old man had not been talking about people he had killed. He had not even claimed to be doing so. That was an asumption, an intellectual leap that Steve had made himself. His dad had only been describing scenes from old movies. His favorites, perhaps. Ones he'd seen, enjoyed and remembered. His addled mind had latched on to memories of the past, and those memories had not been of actual events but of old films. He had merely related their plots in a manner that made it seem as though the information was highly important, and Steve had automatically assumed that was the case.

But on some subconscious level, Steve must have known the truth, because the killings his father had *not* described, the ones for which he had deduced the details on his own, had all come from movies as well. And aside from that first recounting of the Robert Wagner film, even the ones his father *had* talked about had been only roughly sketched, because he no longer had the capacity for intricate description. It was Steve's own mind that had filled in the blanks, that had made the events conform to preexisting narratives in his head. The Mexican prostitute—who had probably just left town and not died at all—had been poisoned like Ingrid Bergman in Alfred Hitchcock's *Notorious*. The pimp in Tucson had been strangled like the crime-lord Uncle Joe in Orson Welles' *Touch of Evil*. The single mother in San Diego had been stabbed and dumped in the water like Shelley Winters in Charles Laughton's *The Night of the Hunter*.

They were all familiar to him, he realized now. The reason he had understood them so thoroughly and bought into them so quickly was because he already knew those scenes. He had visualized the murders so clearly in his mind because he had seen them on-screen.

They probably hadn't happened that way at all.

He thought of Don Quixote, the old knight-errant seeing the world through the prism of his own melo-dramatic taste in fiction, turning windmills into giants and flocks of sheep into enemy armies. He'd done the same thing, albeit on a much smaller, less grand scale. He'd converted his memories of old movies into accounts of his father's murders.

And that had given him permission to start killing people himself.

But his father had had nothing to do with any of it.

It was him. It was all him.

Steve stopped pacing and stared past the window at the darkened world outside. Now he was trapped in this nightmare of his own making, with no way out.

That wasn't true.

There was a way out.

He could tie up all of the loose ends, get rid of ev-eryone who might know or suspect what he had done, starting with Jessica Haster in Copper City. After he had dispatched them all, he could retire, like his father had, and lead a normal, average life from here on in.

His father *hadn't* retired, though. His father had never done anything like this. His father had not been a serial killer.

It didn't matter. That was what *he* needed to do. Take out, one by one, the peripheral people who might be able to finger him until he was at last totally safe.

No. That was exactly what he *shouldn't* do. He needed to quit cold turkey. To stop now, never kill again and never look back.

But there were people who could trip him up. He needed to silence them.

Only . . .

Only that wasn't the real reason he was thinking along these lines, was it? The truth was that no one was after him, no one was suspicious, no one was on his trail. So he didn't actually have to worry about being caught, did he?

No.

He just wanted to do it again.

He looked down at his hands. They were clenched into fists, and he forced himself to open them. He glanced toward the doorway of the bedroom, as black and forbidding as a tomb. Within the closet there, clean and shiny, was the machete, as well as his father's other weapons. The weapons were the only things that were not explained in this new narrative. Why had his dad bought the blades to begin with, and why had he kept them all those years? It was a question that would never be answered. They could have been nothing more than souvenirs . . . or he could have had them in his possession because he secretly wished to do exactly what his son had done.

Steve closed his eyes so tightly they hurt. He had to stop thinking this way. He needed to put all that behind him. He had gotten offtrack. He had made . . . mistakes. But the past was the past, and while he couldn't change what had already happened, he could change what would happen in the days and months and years to come. The future was open, and it was up to him to make sure that he acted differently from here on in.

The killing was over.

Forever.

It had to be.

It had to be.

Thirty-six

I Am God

I am God. I am sitting here in the back of the classroom, pretending to be a sixth-grade student, pretending to listen to Mrs. Keefe's boring lecture on Christopher Columbus. Every so often, Mrs. Keefe will stare at me because I pretended to miss a question about Columbus when she asked me, and now she thinks I didn't read the chapter in the book.

She doesn't realize that I am God.

No one realizes that I am God. I have been here only a few moments, but I have created memories of Steve Blye, the boy I am pretending to be, in everyone's minds. Jason Bevans, sitting next to me, thinks that I am his best friend. He thinks we grew up together. He thinks that I live three houses away from him and that I have always lived three houses away from him. He thinks my sister is going out with his brother. He thinks our dads carpool to work each morning.

But I have planted all of this in his brain. I have no sister. I have no dad. I do not live three houses down from him and never have.

I like making up these kinds of stories. It gets boring being God. I have to amuse myself somehow. So I create these lives and make everyone believe I am a normal person. When I am through, when I get bored, when I have had my fun, I erase these memories and no one ever knows that I have been there.

Now Mrs. Keefe is calling on me. She is picking on me

because I pretended not to know the last question. She could have called on anyone else in the class, any of the other thirty-one students, but instead she has chosen to call on me.

That is why I am pretending to be dumb. I want to see how people treat those less fortunate than themselves.

She is staring at me, waiting for me to answer. I will pretend that I was not paying attention.

"What?" I ask.

The class laughs.

Mrs. Keefe silences them with a look. "Which was the first of Columbus's ships to return to Spain?" she asks.

I look at her blankly.

"You don't know, do you, Steven?"

I shake my head.

"For that, you will—"

I do not let her finish the sentence. With one quick bolt of my almighty power, I fry her on the spot. Her body is instantly burned to a crisp. Her arm, pointed toward me, is whittled down to a blackened stick and falls onto the floor. Nothing is left of her but a charred skeleton, and as the class watches, I turn the skeleton into a life-sized Gumby doll.

Most of the class is amazed. They stare, not sure how to react. Then they start clapping. I am their hero. No longer will they have to obey her rules. Now I am the boss. My first rule? No math. Math is abolished. And no history. History is boring and stupid.

Now the students are putting me on their shoulders and parading me around the room. They still do not know that I am God, but they know I have powers beyond their wildest imaginings. I can do whatever I want.

But not all of the kids are happy.

Will Nichols is staring at me with jealous hatred. I have planted the memory in his mind that I broke his thermos last year and that he beat me up for it and that I told my dad and my dad called the principal and Will had to stay after school for two weeks. He thinks he has hated me ever since, even though none of those things ever happened. Now he is jealous of what I did to Mrs. Keefe.

I look at him, and I make his clothes disappear. He is standing in the middle of the class naked, and now all the girls are staring at him and laughing. He tries to run away, but I make sure he cannot move his legs. He tries to cover himself with his hands, but his hands will not work. He has to stand there and take it while everyone points and stares and laughs at him.

But not everyone is laughing. Will's friend Lyman McColl is watching me. He wants to help Will, but he is afraid to do so. He is afraid of me. He does not know the extent of my powers, though. He does not know that I can read his mind, that I know exactly what he is thinking.

I turn him into a cherry Popsicle, and he melts into a sticky red puddle on the floor.

I turn his friend Dennis Merrick into a fly that gets caught in the puddle and drowns.

Now they really feel my wrath. The wrath of God! They are running in fear, trying to get out the door, but I am mowing them down. Jessica Harrison's feet get stuck to the floor, and as she sprints toward the door, her legs are jerked from their sockets. Her feet and legs remain cemented to the tile, and her body flies forward, a bloody stump. Gina Suzuki, who thinks I like her and thinks she is too good for me, is stripped naked and starts floating into the air. She is screaming, and I turn her over slowly so that everyone can see her from every angle.

I make the twins strangle each other.

Little Joey Lynne, the crippled feeb who was in an accident when he was a baby and has limped ever since, tries to get everyone to calm down, but I make Don and Geoff and Roland kill him, pounding on him with their fists until his weak little heart stops. Then they pull apart his body and start eating.

But I am beginning to tire of all this. It is becoming too

much. I look up at the clock in the front of the room, above Gumby's unmoving form. Ten minutes have passed since I burned up Mrs. Keefe. That's enough. I've had my fun.

I turn back time. Instantly, everything is back the way it was. No one will ever know what really happened. I time everything so perfectly that Mrs. Keefe finishes her sentence exactly where she left off.

"—answer twelve questions instead of six at the end of the chapter tonight."

I smile at her, nodding, and she does not understand why I am smiling. She thinks I am crazy.

She does not realize that I am a kind God, a benevolent God. I could have allowed her to remember what it felt like to be burned alive. I could have turned her into a slug and dissolved her with salt. I could have made her run down the highway and not stop until the muscles snapped in her legs. I could have gone back and given her an unhappy childhood. I could have made sure she was never born. I could have killed her at age ten.

But I am kind. I have done none of these things.

Life is short. Eternity is long. Maybe I will continue to be Steve Blye for a lifetime. Maybe I will create a mother and father for myself, a family. As I grow older, I can plant memories of myself in all kinds of people. Why not? It will be fun. What is sixty years to me? I will live here on earth as Steve Blye. Perhaps I will change my name. Perhaps I will become a teacher myself. Who knows? There are millions of things I can do.

I am God.

Thirty-seven

Steve finished editing the booklet and directory for Entertainment Opportunities' Clown College, and did so without incident, relieved to discover that he no longer seemed to be scared of clowns.

Jerry Tortaglia was demoted back to his old position after an outside candidate, Milton Hauser, was hired as department head.

Another short story was accepted by another magazine.

All was right with the world.

Deciding that it was finally time to clean out his parents' house, Steve brought Sherry with him on the next Saturday she had off. He had been going there every other week in order to give the lawn a cursory mowing, but had refrained from going inside, afraid to do so, though he was not sure exactly why. Now the two of them went inside.

The smell had lessened. Chemical disinfectant was still noticeable, as was a deeper, darker, more fetid scent—

death

—but the dominant odor was the mustiness of a long-closed house, and once he and Sherry opened the windows, letting in fresh air, a lot of that dissipated.

Steve finished opening the kitchen window and

looked around. In his mind, the official account of his mother's death now seemed like the real one. He knew the truth, of course, but that knowledge seemed old and faded, like an opinion he had heard once and immediately discarded. It was her suicide that seemed more authentic, and he could easily see her standing before the sink, swallowing pill after pill, washing them down with water and finally collapsing on the floor.

He felt a soft hand on his shoulder. Sherry. "Are you okay?" she asked gently.

He patted her hand and smiled. "Yeah," he said. He turned. "Let's start sorting through boxes, see what we can donate."

"Are you sure you don't want to have a garage sale first?" she asked him. "You could probably make a couple hundred dollars."

"I'm sure," he told her.

They went from room to room before finally deciding to start at the back of the house and move forward. Most of the work was done already. His mother had been preparing for her move, and nearly all of her belongings were boxed up. They just needed to sort through the boxes and determine what went where.

Steve opened the flaps of a carton that had been pushed next to the television.

"What's in there?" Sherry asked.

"Some of my old toys, it looks like." He was surprised. "I didn't know she'd kept any of them."

"Maybe she was more sentimental than you thought."

"Maybe," he agreed.

His mother, sentimental? The thought, for some reason, made him sad. He and his mother had never been close, and he wondered now whether that had been his fault rather than hers.

Sherry reached around him into the box and pulled

out a stuffed animal, a yellow Big Bird. "Do you remember this one?"

"Not really," he admitted.

"What about this?" She withdrew a plastic train engine.

"Yeah." He took it from her, smiling wistfully. "That was my favorite toy when I was in kindergarten." He turned the object over in his hands, examining it, then put it back into the box along with the Big Bird. He folded the cardboard flaps beneath one another to seal the carton. He didn't want to take a trip down memory lane right now. It was just too depressing.

"You know, until a few months ago, I still had my favorite stuffed animal, a little puppy I named Boo. I kept him in a box in my closet, but I found that he'd started to get moldy for some reason. I guess moisture had gotten in there somehow."

Steve's antennae went up. He knew where this was going. "So you threw him away," he said, thinking about the puppy in the wastepaper basket and the collar in the suitcase with the tag that said, "Boo."

She nodded. "I had to."

He tried to recall what he'd seen in her bathroom trash can. A small brown animal with an awkwardly cocked head and an upturned ear. He'd just assumed it was real—but he knew now that it hadn't been. Sherry had never killed any dog. How could he possibly have thought she would do such a thing? That, too, had been a misinterpretation, a misreading of the facts based on his own skewed perception.

It was him. It was all him.

"Are you all right?" she asked, putting a hand on his arm.

He nodded. "Let's sort through these boxes."

It was all him.

Yes. It was all him. What did that mean, though?

Was that automatically bad? Did it make his actions
any less valid because he had done something his father had not? He'd been thinking about that quite a
bit lately. He'd originally felt good about what he had
done—

the people he had killed

—because he'd believed he was doing what his father would have wanted. He'd thought that his old
man would probably have been proud of him. But
the truth was that he didn't need anyone's approval.
His father had been a small man, a weak man, and
Steve could not imagine why he had ever cared what
his dad thought, why he had ever let the opinions
and put-downs of that worthless prick get to him.
His father had probably *wished* he were *half* the man
Steve really was, and just because his actions had no
outside support didn't mean they weren't valid. The
people he had killed *deserved* to be killed. He had
done the right thing, whether anyone else realized
it or not.

No.

Murder was never the right thing. It was always
wrong.

His head hurt. He concentrated on the job in front
of him, and he and Sherry finished sorting through the
first pile of boxes. "These are all donation items," he
said.

"Even your toys?"

"Yeah."

"You don't—"

"No."

They started carrying boxes out to the car. A little
Hispanic boy stood on the sidewalk behind the vehicle, staring dumbly at them. "Scoot over, kid," Steve
told him.

The boy spit at him. *"Pendejo!"* he yelled. *"Pendejo!"*

Steve smiled to himself as he unlocked and opened the trunk, pushing his box to the back. The little fucker didn't realize how lucky he was that Sherry was here right now. Because if she hadn't been, he would have grabbed that little shit's neck and snapped it like a twig. He could have dispatched the boy in less time than it took to take Sherry's box from her hands and push it next to his own.

But he wasn't going to do that. He was through; he was done; he was out. And it wasn't going to be hard; it was going to be easy. He didn't even want to kill anyone anymore, so he would have no problem controlling himself. And probably, after a while, he wouldn't even think about it. It would be a faint memory from the dim and distant past, kind of like it had been for his father after—

Steve shook his head to clear it. No. His father had never done anything like this. That was all a . . . a . . . a misunderstanding, a misreading of the situation.

He needed to remember that.

"Let's go get the rest of those," he said. "I think we can probably fit a few more into the backseat, so if you want to start looking through some of those boxes in the bedroom while I carry the other ones out . . ."

"I think that's a good idea," she said. "I probably shouldn't be lifting too much."

Steve looked at her. "Why?"

"Because I'm pregnant," she announced.

She was nervous as she said it, but excited, happy, and he could tell from the expression on her face that she was unsure whether this was the right time or the right way to tell him. Reassuringly, he smiled. "That's great!" he said, though he was not really sure if it was. "I guess we should probably start figuring out a wedding date, huh?"

"Oh, Steve!" She hugged him tightly, leaned up to

kiss him. When she looked at him, there were tears in her eyes.

He put a finger to her lips. "I know this was an accident, but . . . this *is* what you want, right?"

"I didn't know it was, but it is," Sherry said. "In fact, I'd like to have *two* children. A boy and a girl."

"That would be nice," he agreed.

She hugged him again, squeezing hard. "Wouldn't it!"

Steve nodded. For some reason, he could not help thinking of the girl in Flagstaff, the girl on the swing whose neck had snapped so easily. He realized that his hands were clenched into fists, and he opened them.

"I love you so much," Sherry said.

"I love you too," he told her. "I love you too."

ABOUT THE AUTHOR

Born in Arizona shortly after his mother attended the world premiere of *Psycho*, **Bentley Little** is the Bram Stoker Award–winning author of numerous previous novels and *The Collection*, a book of short stories. He has worked as a technical writer, reporter/photographer, library assistant, salesclerk, phone book deliveryman, video arcade attendant, newspaper deliveryman, furniture mover and rodeo gatekeeper. The son of a Russian artist and an American educator, he and his Chinese wife were married by the justice of the peace in Tombstone, Arizona.

BENTLEY LITTLE

The Academy

Something strange is happening at Tyler High. The laid-back principal has become unusually strict. The janitors no longer work nights because of what they hear. The students are frightened by what they see. And things are happening on school grounds that defy rational explanation. But there is an explanation. It's just nothing that anyone can begin to believe—or hope to survive.

The Vanishing

In Beverly Hills a businessman slaughters his entire family and leaves behind a video of the massacre and a cryptic message: "this is where it begins." Sure enough, it is only the beginning. Children everywhere are either being killed or are disappearing. Social worker Carrie Daniels wants to know why. God help her when she finds out.

Death Instinct

Cathy was six when the man next door killed his wife and himself. She heard the screams. She saw the blood and the bodies. Now, 20 years later, the house is no longer vacant. Someone new has moved in. Something terrible is happening to the neighbors. And Cathy has a secret of her own...

"A master of the macabre!" —Stephen King

Bentley Little

"If there's a better horror novelist than Little...I don't know who it is." —*Los Angeles Times*

The Resort

At the exclusive Reata spa and resort, enjoy your stay and relax. Oh, and lock your doors at night.

The Policy

Hunt Jackson has finally found an insurance company to give him a policy. But with minor provisions: No backing out. And no running away.

The Return

There's only one thing that can follow the success of Bentley Little's acclaimed *The Walking* and *The Revelation*. And that's Bentley Little's return...

The Bram Stoker Award-winning novel:

The Revelation

Strange things are happening in the small town of Randall, Arizona. As darkness falls, an itinerant preacher has arrived to spread a gospel of cataclysmic fury... And stranger things are yet to come.

Penguin Group (USA) Online

What will you be reading tomorrow?

Tom Clancy, Patricia Cornwell, W.E.B. Griffin,
Nora Roberts, William Gibson, Robin Cook,
Brian Jacques, Catherine Coulter, Stephen King,
Dean Koontz, Ken Follett, Clive Cussler,
Eric Jerome Dickey, John Sandford,
Terry McMillan, Sue Monk Kidd, Amy Tan,
J. R. Ward, Laurell K. Hamilton...

You'll find them all at
penguin.com

*Read excerpts and newsletters,
find tour schedules and reading group guides,
and enter contests.*

Subscribe to Penguin Group (USA) newsletters
and get an exclusive inside look
at exciting new titles and the authors you love
long before everyone else does.

PENGUIN GROUP (USA)
us.penguingroup.com